Road Dawgz

Road Dawgz

K'wan

www.urbanbooks.net

Urban Books, LLC
97 N18th Street
Wyandanch, NY 11798

Road Dawgz Copyright © 2014 K'wan

Three Legends Press Edition

ISBN 13: 978-1-60162-607-3
ISBN 10: 1-60162-607-X

First Trade Paperback Printing August 2014

10 9 8 7 6 5 4 3 2 1

*This is a work of fiction. Any references or similarities
to actual events, real people, living or dead, or to real
locales are intended to give the novel a sense of reality.
Any similarity in other names, characters, places, and
incidents is entirely coincidental.*

Distributed by Kensington Publishing Corp.
Submit Wholesale Orders to:
Kensington Publishing Corp.
C/O Penguin Group (USA) Inc.
Attention: Order Processing
405 Murray Hill Parkway
East Rutherford, NJ 07073-2316
Phone: 1-800-526-0275
Fax: 1-800-227-9604

ACKNOWLEDGMENTS

First of all, I would like to thank God for allowing me to live long enough to finish this li'l joint here. Tomorrow isn't promised to any of us. Every day that we're allowed to wake up is a blessing.

A very warm thanks from the bottom of my heart goes to my mother, who was gracious enough to share her gift of storytelling with me. Mom, I wish you could've stayed with us long enough to see your granddaughter and behold my accomplishments, but I'm sure you knew what was to be before I did. And more than anyone else, you've been supportive of me and my farfetched goal of becoming a writer.

I'd like to give a special thanks to my daughter, Ni Jaa, who is my constant motivation in this thing that I do. Pampers ain't hardly cheap. I can't forget my sidekicks, Dajanae and Ty Dre Joseph. Good looking on the birthday poem, Dajanae. Ty Dre, stop sucking your fingers.

I must include the mother of my child, Denise. After all these years, you still haven't driven me to the bottle. I guess there's hope after all.

Many thanks to my father, William "Billy" Greene. Told you about those fast-ass girls. Next time listen to your son.

I am so grateful for many people in my life. My grandmother, Ethel M. Foye: in case you were wondering, this is the reason why I have bags under my eyes, not the partying. My other grandmother, Bertha Crocker: I hope you're in a better place now. To Miss Ida Lee Johnson: "Can l get some potato salad?" My immediate family, Tee-Tee, Leslie, Eric. Frankie, and Darrell, aka S.D.W: Divided we all play a significant role in the grand scheme of things. Together we are a force to be reckoned with: just something to think about. My extended family, the Greenes, Crockers, Councils, Gorhams, Johnsons and Wilders. Damn, sure are a lot of y'all.

I definitely can't forget to thank my peoples who helped me get it popping. Michael Phifer of Phifer Media Management. I told you I'm the winning horse; thanks for helping a brother out. Leah Whitney, your editorial skills are superb. I'm glad that you enjoyed the story, and I look forward to working with you again. Nikki Turner, continue to be the diva that you are and my "Bonnie" in this. Do you, sis. My Triple Crown connection: sometimes when I look at the lineup that Vickie Stringer has composed, it seems a little unfair to the rest of the game. Oh well, can't blame us for being talented.

Darren Coleman & B. La'torson Thornton: two stars on the rise. Thanks for showing me hospitality when I was in your part of the world. I look forward to returning the love.

On the ghetto side of things: Ty Weed (sorry I missed you on the first go-round); T.M., Queen, Li'l Willie, Party Tyme, aka the "Jump Off," Highwater, Twan, Boo, Alex ("Commdery" was a hot joint); Coo-Coo Kilz, Champ, Buddha, Thomas Long (another hot author from outta B-more); Rich, from Sand & Sable books; the whole P.C. (y'all know y'all wrong); Rod-o, Smiles, Li'l Sha, Big Shirl (140th mayor); K Ke, Don I. Donovan, Cheryl Grant (a hustler with a badge); the close-minded deputies at Livingston County Jail that got such a kick out of my misfortune (die slow cowards!); Douglass Projects and anyone else that I might have forgotten.

Last but certainly not least, the most special thanks of all goes to my readers. I thank you for showing such strong support for my first novel, *Gangsta,* and for your continued support and belief in me. As long as you love it, I'll keep giving it to you.

100,
K'wan Foye

A HAPPY BIRTHDAY POEM FOR K'WAN

What is a birthday? I don't know.
Just a happy day, when I cry, then smile.
What is a birthday?
I don't know. I'm just a kid.

by Dajanae Joseph, 9

CHAPTER 1

It was a sunny morning in March 1995, when K-Dawg stepped off the bus at the Port Authority. It was his birthday, but there wasn't anything happy about it. He was fresh out the joint and broke as hell. The latter was temporary. K-Dawg inhaled the stale New York air and a huge grin spread across his handsome face. It was good to be home.

It had been awhile since K-Dawg had last been to the deuce. It had changed somewhat, but it was still recognizable to any native of the city. Instead of the whore-infested circus it had once been, Times Square had undergone a rebirth of sorts. People made their way back and forth doing whatever unimportant tasks consumed their lives while police patrolled nearly every corner. Whores still frequented the place, but only at night and at their own risk. The sex shops were still there, but they were far and few.

While K-Dawg was away, he had gotten word that some kind of fanatical crusader had control of the city. The former lawyer-turned-government official had supposedly cleaned up the Apple, handing down football numbers to those foolish enough to try to go against him. The word around town was that he had a crew of thousands behind him. The news sometimes referred to them as "The Gang in Blue." In this new metropolis, it was taboo to violate the law.

This new crime stopper, who pulled the strings, had the city in a smash. His new laws and decrees made it hard for a nigga to eat anymore. The money and opportunities were there, but some of the new hustlers as well as some of the old ones lacked the courage to get down for theirs. The new order of things had them spooked.

This new code of ethics made it nearly impossible for the average cat working outside the law to make a buck. But then again, K-Dawg wasn't the average cat. He reasoned that the people who fell victim to these laws were incompetent and had no concept of how to get money. He was either gonna ball or fall.

Either way, K-Dawg had no intentions of going back to the joint. His next stop would be the penthouse or the morgue.

K-Dawg dodged the swarm of business folks and school kids in search of the subway. He found it without too much of a problem. New York had changed a bit, but the subways were still the same.

K-Dawg paid his fare and passed through the digital turnstile. He strolled through the tunnel and hopped on the Harlem-bound 2 train just as the doors were closing. He took a seat and marveled at the different kinds of people and sights on the subway. The first thing he noticed was the fashion transition. Although New York was the same place he remembered, things had changed quite a bit in that area.

When he first went on his little trip, the era of break dancing and tight pants was dying out, giving way to the retro sixties "black love" thing. Now these eras were altogether dead. The females had traded in their doorknocker earrings and shells for imitation diamonds and hair dye. The curls and twists were gone, replaced largely by hair weaves and stylish cuts. There were a few sisters who rocked tight-fitting clothes and braids, but the styles were different.

Things had changed for the fellas as well. There were no more rope chains or African medallions, and the guys were flossing big jewels and bracelets. Everyone was wearing oversized jeans, with T-shirts sporting some kind of logo or statement. Even the color scheme was different. Everything was bright and festive. It seemed that the black love fad had given way to the age of the baller. If this was the case, then K-Dawg wanted in. It was 1995, and he was home.

A group of about five young girls wearing tight-fitting jeans and silver bubble coats got on the train and took up the row of seats across from K-Dawg. They were giving him the eye, so he tried to get his flirt on. He picked one of the girls out of the group and tried to shoot her a sexy-ass smile. The girl tapped her friend and nodded in his direction. The two girls looked him up and down and burst out laughing. Another girl in the group was even so bold as to point out the secondhand boots he was wearing.

K-Dawg looked at the faded black army suit he was wearing and felt a little out of place. He knew his wears were a little dusty, but he didn't realize how badly he looked. In his head, he made himself a promise that this would never happen again. This would be the last time a chick would laugh at him because he was sporting some ol' bullshit gear.

K-Dawg spent a good portion of his train ride with his eyes glued to the newspaper he had with him. In truth, he wasn't that interested in the article. He was just too embarrassed to risk making eye contact with the girls again. When the train stopped at 116th Street, the girls filed out one behind the other. As they were getting off, one of them stopped and looked at K-Dawg, sitting there embarrassed. Instead of playing him further, she just shook her head and kept it moving.

Once the train was in motion again, K-Dawg breathed a sigh of relief. It was his first day home from the joint, and he had already gotten dissed. It wasn't quite the way he had planned on starting his new life, but what was success without its hardships?

K-Dawg got off the train at 135th Street and headed toward the exit. He looked up and down Lenox Avenue and picked up two distinct odors. The first one was Pan-Pan's Chicken on the corner of 135th Street. The second aroma was unmistakable; there was no trash in the world that smelled like Harlem's. Finally, K-Dawg started to feel like he was home. He made his way east at a slow pace and studied his surroundings. He didn't have anything to rush home to, and he wanted to take in all of the sights that made up his soon-to-be kingdom.

Most of the old stores were there in addition to a few new ones. As K-Dawg crossed Fifth Avenue, he looked over at the school that he had attended for a short time: PS 197. Even as he stepped into his project he was assaulted with old memories, painful memories, which molded him into the young man he had become.

K-Dawg shook off the feeling and kept stepping. As he entered the mouth of the beast, he glanced over at the pool in the playground. It was caked with dirt and dry leaves because housing didn't tend to it during colder weather. K-Dawg stared quizzically at the chipped numbers that revealed its depth and tried to remember what it was like to play in the pool with other kids on hot summer days or dunk a girl who didn't want to kiss you. These memories were few, if hardly existent at all to K-Dawg. He didn't grow up like other children; at a young age, he became a product of the state. Even for those brief periods when he did manage to be reunited with his family, there was always the conflict.

K-Dawg was snapped out of his flashback by the sound of someone calling his name. His instincts automatically put him on guard. When he saw the young man who was approaching him, he relaxed a little bit.

The young man greeted K-Dawg with a shit-eating grin on his face. The sun reflecting off his rows of gold teeth caused K-Dawg to squint a bit. K-Dawg recalled a time when only kids from Brooklyn rocked fronts like that. Now here was his man, Jus, grilled up.

Jus wasn't what you would call a pretty boy, yet he wasn't tom up either. He was just handsome. His mother was of Native American descent, and he had most of her features, along with smooth, dark skin that he inherited from his father, who was a native of Zambia. He had that long Indian hair, which he now sported in two long pigtails. With his long, slim frame, he kind of looked like one of those dolls from Botanica. Back in the day, Jus looked like an escaped fugitive from the fashion prison. He always wore hand-me-down clothes, and the color scheme never quite matched. But in this new era, things had changed.

Jus was sporting a butter-soft black leather jacket with a pair of crisp blue jeans. On each of his delicate hands he sported diamond pinky rings. His Timberlands were crisp as well. The tan suede didn't have so much as a smudge on it. Jus had come a long way from the fashion misfit he used to be.

K-Dawg was a little tight to see his man have it together while he looked a wreck. He wasn't mad at him, though. K-Dawg was never one to hate on the next man. This was just another motivational kick in the ass so he could get his shit together. "Peace, young'un," Jus said extending his hand.

"My nigga!" K-Dawg responded, putting Jus in a bear hug.

"What it be like, god?"

"Ain't nothing," Jus said returning the hug, "just waiting on your return, kid."

"I know that's right. A nigga been down long enough. Them crackers be wanting chunks out a nigga's life. Shit, they act like five years ain't a lot of time."

"Well," Jus said punching K-Dawg in the arm, "you know how to get around that, right?"

"Come on, B," K-Dawg said waving Jus off. "I ain't even on my native soil for ten hours, and you all up in my shit wit' that 'Blacks watch' garbage?"

"You is mad foolish, son," Jus said with a grin. "That ain't what's up, clown."

"Oh, yeah? So why don't you tell me what's up?"

"Well, my blind, deaf, and dumb brother, since you don't know, it's the age of the civilized man: God, cipher, divine."

"Jesus, circle, what?" K-Dawg asked sarcastically.

"See," Jus said with a sigh, "it always gotta be a nigga like you."

"What kinda nigga am I, Jus?"

"See, you one of them ten percent niggaz. You know, but you don't acknowledge."

"I'm fucking wit' you, money," K-Dawg said slapping Jus on the back. "I dig where you coming from. I did a lot of building with the gods while I was away. They make a lot of sense, but at the same time they don't make any. You know what I mean?"

"Yeah, nigga. Like I said, ten percent."

"Whatever, punk. What's up with the crew?"

"Man, let me tell you," Jus said motioning for K-Dawg to walk with him. "The team is still the team. It's just that, well, niggaz need guidance in they lives."

"Fuck you mean?" K-Dawg asked, lighting a GPC. "Guidance? They grown-ass men. Guidance like how?"

"Well," Jus began, while splitting open a White Owl, "it's like this: you know that I would never knock another man's hustle, especially nobody out the crew. But damn, niggaz is wrapped up into all kinds of shit."

"Like what?"

"Okay, there's Pooh. He getting his grind on, and he's getting a few dollars fucking wit' them niggaz on Broadway, but he ain't got no sense of self-worth. I mean, them Spanish niggaz is hitting him, but they ain't trying to give him his own. Pooh only half Dominican, so you know they don't really give him his propers like they should. To them, all he'll ever be is a money-getting mongrel. Just off what I'm hearing, Pooh check at least fifty Gs a week for these niggaz. They threw him a corner for hisself and shit, but what the fuck? Why not give a nigga a block? Them boat-hopping-ass niggaz is straight fucking our peoples."

"That's some deep shit," K Dawg said puffing on his generic cigarette. "So what he doing about it?"

"Not a motherfucking thing. That's the problem. Pooh making enough money to pay his bills and trick off when he wants. He got a nice car and a crib; I'll give him that. But my point is, why settle for an apartment when you're worth a house?"

"True," K-Dawg said waving off the blunt when Jus tried to pass it to him. "You know I'm on paper. What's up with the rest of the team?"

"Okay, then there's Sleepy," Jus continued. "That nigga fli'ting with death."

"What's up with that cat?" K-Dawg asked.

"He on some other shit," Jus said taking a pull off the bomber. "That nigga selling dick. He only got one, maybe two girls, but the boy on a come up."

"So, what's wrong with that?" K-Dawg asked.

"What's wrong with it?" Jus responded. "Man, you got to be crazy. With all this new shit they got floating around, he taking his life in his own hands putting his dick in them nasty heifers."

"Man, fuck that," K-Dawg started. "If them bitches is checking that bread for my nigga, then ain't nothing wrong wit' him laying his cock game down."

"Yeah, but he ain't only doing it wit' his bitches; he plays the game wit' other niggaz' hoes too. And to make matters worse, he ain't even trying to bring them home to his stable. He just does it to rub other niggaz' noses in it. He even fucked a few niggaz' wives from over this side."

"Hmm," K-Dawg said scratching his chin. "I see where that could be a problem. Boy thinking with the wrong head. So what's up wit' my man Demon?"

"Demon," Jus said shrugging his shoulders, "that boy is creepy. I see him floating around here on the late night like a gotdamn phantom and shit."

"I know my boy ain't out here smoking or no shit like that?"

"Nah, you know that ain't his MO."

"So what the fuck he be out here doing? I know he ain't selling stones; Demon hate drugs. But if he ain't using, and he ain't selling, what the fuck is he doing?"

"Hunting," Jus whispered.

"Hunting?" K-Dawg asked confusedly. "Hunting what, pigeons and squirrels?"

"Nah," Jus said, his face becoming very serious. "I guess you ain't heard about that nigga while you was in da joint."

"I heard a few things, mostly rumors and speculation, though. Why don't you run it down to me, Jus?"

"Well," Jus began, "you know Demon has always been an oddball. Even when we were all in the boys home nobody really fucked wit' him like that. Well, nobody except you. And when he touched down in the hood, he wasn't really feeling none of our respective hustles. We were like fuck it, ya know? Can't knock a man for doing his own thing, so we let him be."

"So, what's the problem?" K-Dawg asked.

"Man," Jus continued, "Demon done went and became a cleaner."

"My nigga scrubbing floors?" K-Dawg asked naively.

"Damn, K-Dawg. You really have been out of the loop for a while. If anything, niggaz is cleaning up behind Demon's mess. The boy is a hit man, and a damn good one, the way I hear it."

"Get the fuck outta here," K-Dawg said, trying to hide the excitement in his voice.

"No shit, kid. The boy is out here laying shit down. People tell they kids about this nigga to get them to come in the house at decent hours. The word is that the night belongs to 'The Demon.' They say if you happen to get a good look at him, nine times outta ten you'll be dead before you get to tell anyone."

"Damn," K-Dawg said, "how my man get on it like that? Demon was always a passive dude."

"Well," Jus said, stopping to sit on a bench, "I guess I gotta start at the beginning to bring some clarity to the here and now. You got a minute, kid?" Jus asked, motioning for K-Dawg to take the seat beside him. K-Dawg sat down and listened intently to the tale that unfolded before him.

"Damien," Jus began, "well, 'Demon,' as we all know him, moved up here from a village on the tip of Brazil when he was about six or so. His mom came up with him after his old man got killed in some kinda accident or some shit, but I don't know for sure. They stayed wit' the grandmother out in Brooklyn. You know how that goes.

"Well anyhow, not long after, the mother hooked up with a new boyfriend. Average Puerto Rican stud, ya know? Guy's got a decent little gig, his own spot, and no

wife to complete him or bring light to his life. All a crock
of shit if you ask me, but the grandmother, being from the
old country and all that, was totally wit' it.

"So after a few months of courting they got hitched.
Demon's mother packed them up and shacked with this
dude at his spot in Manhattan, down by that crack 'tel. At
first the marriage was silky. The kid was in school and the
moms got a little gig busing tables at this dive uptown.
All this lasted maybe six months. That's when everything
turned to shit.

"Come to find out, the boyfriend was an undercover
hype. Homeboy had a habit you wouldn't believe. The
mother, not really knowing any better, started chipping
along with him. The next thing you know, they both had
the monkey clawing at 'em, and the kid was getting the
brunt of it.

"For a good little while, they primarily lived dopefiend
lives. They would get as high as the Almighty would
let 'em and kick the shit out of each other. When they
couldn't get high, they kicked the shit outta Demon."

"That's deep," K-Dawg said thinking out loud.

"It gets deeper," Jus continued. "The habit got to the
point where neither parent could hold a job. The little bit
of check Demon's mom was getting went into stepdaddy's
arm. Man, he once told me about how his moms used to
get sick and be like puking and shit. That's some shit to
see when you a li'l nigga like that.

"Well, being that stepdaddy couldn't seem to hold
down a gig, he took to doing stickups, using mama love as
an accomplice. Well, to make a long story short, one day
they tried to rob the wrong mafucka's store, and Demon
found himself without a mother."

"I know all that shit," K-Dawg cut in. "That's around
the time he came to the boy's home. But what flipped him
out?"

"Nigga," Jus said sucking his teeth, "if you quit cutting my wisdom, then I could tell you. Now like I was saying, after the moms was killed, the stepdaddy went on the lam. The grandmother was sick at the time so she couldn't take the kid, and things were too rough to send him home. Our boy found himself in the penthouse with the rest of us.

"Now, if you remember correctly, Demon was only in there with us for a li'l while. After about a year, his grandma does a 360-degree turn and is in shape enough to take care of the boy. Things get back to normal, and our boy Demon is happy again. But you know how it is for folks like us, kid: if you ain't of the fairer persuasion, something always gotta go wrong.

"Now, the rest of this is only what people say. Demon and me still cool, but it ain't like I ever asked him about it. This is just what I heard. One night when his grandmother was coming home from work, some junkie mafucka decided to stick her right in front of her door, son. This punk robbed her on her doorstep. Well, Demon jumped out of his sleep when he heard the sounds of the struggle outside the front door. When Demon snatched the door open, he saw his grandma on the floor bleeding. When he stepped out into the hallway, he saw a figure heading for the stairway. Something about the way the cat moved rang a bell in Demon's head. The curve of the shoulder, the way he sprinted; Demon was sure he knew who it was.

"In a blind rage, Demon leaped over his grandma's prone figure and went after the attacker. He grabbed the man's jacket and brought him to an abrupt halt. They struggled there in the hall for a while, but the attacker was too slippery. He managed to wiggle free of his jacket and break for the stairs. Demon shot his hand out and ripped the mask from the attacker's face. The person who stared back at him sent both men into shock; it was stepdaddy.

"Before Demon could react, stepdaddy jumped the first flight of stairs and crashed on the next landing. Demon pursued him, but he slipped on a broken bottle. The broken glass sliced Demon's bare foot open and cut the chase short. Through half-open eyelids, he saw his stepfather slink off down the next flight of steps and disappear into the night.

"When the police got there, Demon was leaning over his grandmother, mumbling something in a language the translators couldn't even make out. When they asked him if he knew who killed his grandma, he lied and said he didn't know. The police just chalked it up as another robbery gone sour. It was to be yet another unsolved murder, but Demon wasn't having that. "For the next few weeks, Demon wandered in and out of shooting galleries looking for stepdaddy. About a month after grandma's death, Demon broke luck. He found stepdaddy down in Douglass nodding up in some crackhouse. Demon tied up everyone in the house and went to work on his stepdaddy.

"First, he cut out his tongue, said that was for the lies he told. Then he did some ol' bugged shit. He took the knife and cut out stepdaddy's heart, said that was because stepdaddy took his heart when he killed grandma. Fair exchange. As if that wasn't bad enough, he set the house on fire with everybody still in it, ten dead in all."

"Damn." K-Dawg exhaled, realizing for the first time that he was holding his breath. "That boy has got some issues."

"Damn right he does," Jus cosigned. "Listen, K-Dawg. The reason I know a lot of the shit I do about Demon is that I knew him and his peeps before he came to the home. We used to live in the same projects. You can go out to Marcy to this day and niggaz is still talkin' 'bout how he flipped. Police still looking for him to ask about stepdaddy's murder. Thing is, Demon dropped off the map after the shit went down. Sure, the people on the streets see him from time to time, when he wants it like that. But Johnny Law ain't never gonna nab that nigga. I think they want to keep it that way. The boy is bad news."

"I got to see what's up wit' my nigga D," K-Dawg said with a devilish grin. "How can I contact him?"

"K-Dawg, don't you never learn? I just gave you the lowdown on our friend so you'll stay the fuck away from him. I ain't no dummy. You probably already knew what was up wit' Demon before I told you. Probably just wanted to pick my brain to distinguish fact from fiction."

"It ain't like that, Jus. I just wanna see what's up wit' the old homeboys."

"Bullshit, K-Dawg. I know you. You wanna bring Demon in."

"Jus, why I can't just wanna show love to my old crew?"

"Man, go 'head wit' that. You mean our old crew, and Demon ass wasn't never a part of it."

"Jus, you mean to tell me you ain't fucking wit' a nigga 'cause he went through some shit? We all went through some shit."

"Man, you missing the point. I ain't fucking wit' a nigga 'cause he want it that way. That's just common knowledge. Demon don't fuck wit' nobody unless they fuck wit' him. And if a nigga should happen to be stupid enough to fuck wit' him, then he's about a dumb fuck that shouldn't have dropped out of his mama's ass in the first place.

"Keshawn, listen to ya dawg. Demon is a loose cannon. You can't manipulate him like you do everybody else. If you get that nigga started, you ain't gonna be able to control him. And if he happens to think you trying to mind fuck him, something you're very good at, I might add, he's gonna carve you into little pieces. It's a lose-lose situation."

"Well, let me be the judge of that, Jus."

"Why you gotta be so damn hardheaded?" Jus said slapping himself in the forehead. "K-Dawg, we can go on with our plan without involving that nut."

"You know where he stay?" K-Dawg asked looking Jus dead in the eye.

"Yeah, I got an idea."

"Let me get his address."

"Look, K-Dawg. You so hyped on the idea of getting a hold of Demon, cool. But you ain't gonna get me crossed wit' that dude. I'll tell you what: I'll holla at the kid and tell him you wanna sit down with him. Now, me knowing him the way I do, he ain't gonna be feeling that, but I'll ask anyhow, 'cause you my people."

"Good looking out, Jus."

"Good looking out, my ass, K-Dawg. This shit blow up in ya face, you can't say I didn't tell you."

"Ah, nigga, quit crying," K-Dawg said playfully. "So what else is going on 'round here?"

"Same shit," Jus said with a shrug of his shoulders. "Oh, I had seen China 'bout an hour before I bumped into you."

"China?" K-Dawg said perking up. "What's up wit' my sis?"

"Man, she still fine as hell. Truth be told, she need to stop chasing cat and get some dick in her life. Man, if your sister would just . . ." The cold stare K-Dawg sent his way stopped Jus midsentence. "My bad, kid. You know a nigga ain't mean it like it sounded. Your sister out here doing her. She's become quite notorious for her ass-kicking abilities. That girl is bad."

"Yeah, China was always on that kung fu shit. I don't really agree wit' her life choices, but that's still my heart."

"I feel you, kid. That girl is just so damn fine, you gotta understand why a nigga can get salty behind her choices, as you put it."

"True. So what's up wit' my other siblings: C.J., Pearl?" K-Dawg asked changing the subject.

"Well," Jus said a little hesitantly, "I hate to kick dirt on another man's peoples. You want it straight or the sugarcoated version?"

"Jus, you know me better than that. Give it to me real."

"Well, ya brother, C.J., he on some new shit. He runnin' 'round wit' them white boys he go to school wit' and acting like his shit don't stink. He used to do the same shit we runnin' 'round trying to do, but he look down his nose at us for trying to eat."

"Charlie always was a frontin' mafucka."

"The worst part is, he done let them white boys help his ass right into a habit."

"No shit?" K-Dawg asked nonchalantly.

"Yep," Jus continued. "He think the shit is on the low, but you know I hear and see all in the streets."

"Fo' sho.'"

"I'm telling you, K-Dawg, he just chippin', now, but at the rate he going, he'll have a full-blown habit soon, if he ain't got one now."

"Fuck that nigga. What up wit' Pearl?"

"Pearl? Shit, she damn near as fine as China, but Pearl on some bullshit too. She done dropped out of school, and now she hangin' round wit' them li'l chili pimp-ass niggaz downtown. I can't say for sure, but I heard this nigga named Trick turned her out."

"Is that right?" K-Dawg tried to hide his anger, but it showed all over his face.

"One time," Jus continued, "I seen her up in the spot. You know, the strip joint over the bridge? Well, anyhow I steps to her like, 'Yo, Pearl, fuck you doing in here?' Ol' girl flips out on me and causes a scene. I tried to take her up out the spot, then this li'l nigga, Trick, start talking all crazy. To make a long story short, I fucked him up, the bouncers fucked me up, and now I'm banned from the spot. The crazy shit is, she was back wit' the nigga the next day."

"So what you do then?" K-Dawg asked.

"What the fuck you think?" Jus snapped. "I kicked his ass again." The two friends enjoyed a brief laugh. "But on some real shit, though," Jus said soberly, "the boy is a known pimp. Sleepy even had words wit' him over Pearl, but she flipped on him, too. She tried to say that he was just tight because she didn't choose him."

"That's some cold shit."

"Ain't it, though? There's a lot wrong out here, K-Dawg. You can't play Superman and save everybody. You just gotta do what you can, when you can."

"I feel you, Jus. Tell me something, though: you've given me the lowdown on everybody else but yourself. What the fuck is your hustle?"

"Me?" Jus said flashing his gold fronts. "I deal in retail supply and demand."

"And that means what exactly?"

"Well, you know I've always been light fingered by nature, right? I just stepped my game up. Now, instead of boosting from bullshit stores, I take on bigger stings. I do a lit' of everything: jewelry, guns, whatever is in demand."

"You stepped it up, all right, Jus. But I thought you was caking off the boosting thing."

"I was, and I am. See, now I got bitches to handle that shit for me. I get a few hoes to go take off a department store and I hit 'em off. I mostly use young girls, 'cause they don't really know shit about shit. Let's say they bring me racks of shit outta somewhere like Macy's, right? I give 'em maybe a few pieces of bullshit jewelry, a few dollars, and they straight. As long as they can go to school and floss for their friends, they good. Besides, if they get busted, all they get is a slap on the wrist. I pay whatever fine or restitution, and they happy. Everybody wins."

"So you're telling me you out the stickup game?"

"K-Dawg, I don't think you're following what I'm saying to you. A nigga gotta eat. I still bang me a mafucka or so when it's worth it. Now I'm more selective wit' who I get. It's big money now. See, what I do is take it to them. Instead of waiting for cats to fall through the hood before I rob 'em, I go where it's at: stash houses, clubs, sporting events, whatever. As long as there's paper involved, a nigga can get it.

"Like that kid. You know the young boy who play for the Nets? He came across the water to get his party on. All he ended up getting was jacked. I got that bighead nigga fo' everything: jewelry, money, credit cards, shoes—"

"Hold up," K-Dawg cut in. "You took the nigga shoes?"

"Damn straight," Jus said sticking his chest out. "There's profit in shoes. If they my size, I might keep 'em. If I wanna get rid of 'em, I got these two crackheads who got a hookup wit' a shoe store. What they do in the store, if the shoes ain't twisted, is fix them mafuckas up like new and resell 'em. They don't pay a whole lot for 'em, but fuck it. Everything is profit."

"That's some slick shit," K-Dawg said with a grin. "You always did know how to turn a buck. So what's up wit' that pistol action, Jus? Can you front a nigga something?"

"Right back in it, huh?" Jus asked with a smile.

"You know how it is, Jus. A nigga just came home and is trying to get some get right."

"Fo' sho, K-Dawg. I can feel where you're coming from, but dig this: you been my ace since back when we were both just two messed-up kids nobody wanted. Don't even play me like that, B. I could never front you nothing, but check this out," Jus said pulling out a low-caliber pistol.

K-Dawg's eyes lit up like Rockefeller Center at the sight of the gun. The chrome shined like a diamond in his eyes. The fact that he might be about to get a pistol, and the numerous things he could get accomplished, almost made him foam at the mouth.

"That's a nice .380," K-Dawg said trying to sound cool.

"Check it out, kid," Jus said handing him the gun.

The steel touching K-Dawg's fingertips sent a chill through his body. It had been a long time since he had held a hammer, especially a cold one.

"That's for you," Jus said gesturing toward the gun, "if you want it."

"Hell yeah," K-Dawg said putting the gun in his jacket pocket. "Good looking out, god."

"You know you my peeps, K-Dawg. Besides, how can I have the future corner emperor struttin' 'round wit' no jammy?" Jus said sarcastically. "Niggaz would think our team was soft. We can't have that."

"I hear that," K-Dawg said slyly. "Niggaz keep right on sleeping on this one. It's all or nothing wit' me," K-Dawg said patting his pocket.

"True, indeed," Jus said under his breath. "You know I got faith in you, kid. If I didn't, I wouldn't fuck wit' you. You know how I do."

"You my nigga, Jus. And that's why I'm gonna make sure you eat right alongside of me. You different than a lot of these niggaz out here, Jus. You got good sense and a level head. Then on top of that. you grind for your meat. You don't see all them qualities in no one nigga, man. I'm always gonna fuck wit' you, money, 'cause I know you'll voice your opinion when something's wrong. You ain't one of them ol' kiss-ass niggaz who'll just stroke my ego and tell me what the fuck they think I wanna hear. You're my voice of reason."

"K-Dawg, boy, you know I'm all for it. We got plenty of time to set things in motion. Right now, let's focus on you. You've been down for awhile, so I know you probably forgot how to have a good time. I'm gonna take you down to this li'l freak spot and let you drop that five-year load, nigga. What's up?"

"Man, I can't do it," K-Dawg said with a shrug of his shoulders.

"What you mean?" Jus asked in disbelief.

"All I got to rock is this bullshit from out the joint," K-Dawg said hoisting his duffel bag.

"That's all?" Jus asked. "Man, don't even worry about it." Before K-Dawg could react, Jus snatched the duffel bag and threw it into a trashcan. "Come on, K-Dawg. I'm 'bout to take you on Twenty-fifth and get you a few 'fits."

"Man, you ain't gotta be doing all that," K-Dawg protested.

"I know I don't, nigga," Jus said soberly, "but you my homeboy and I'd never see you go without."

"That's love," K-Dawg said slapping Jus five. "Okay, we can do it, but I wanna go over and see my peoples first."

"A'ight then, K-Dawg. When you get finished wit' ya peoples come ring my bell."

"Cool," K-Dawg said, preparing to get on his way.

"One more thing," Jus said putting a hand on his shoulder. "Happy b-day, nigga!"

K-Dawg was wrapped in his own thoughts as he approached the projects. So far he was sure Jus was going to get down with him. That was never really a question, though. Even though they met in the home, Jus had always been a loyal friend. The fact that Jus had stepped up to the status of jewel thief didn't hurt nothing, either. The white boys K-Dawg had hooked up with were always talkin' 'bout how much money there was in hot jewels. Jus's ol' ghetto ass probably didn't even realize the type of money he could get for his services. Oh well, K-Dawg was just the one to show him the light . . . for a cut, of course. Like Jus had said, "Everything is profit."

K-Dawg looked around purposefully at the changes in his little slum village, just as a tourist would've looked at the Great Wall of China. For the most part the construction was the same, but the people were different. There were a lot of new faces staring back at K-Dawg as he crossed the playground. Some faces were pleasant, while others were not. K-Dawg didn't care; to him, they had no significance. They were just pawns, put on the face of the earth to aid in carrying out whatever plan or scheme he could come up with.

As he got closer to his building, his heart began to race. This was the place he grew up in, yet he felt like a stranger. The sight of the dirty lobby brought back memories, horrible memories of days gone by.

FAMILY

History is no mystery. It's only what we've taken from the past and changed over and over again. History is something we know nothing about, because it's been turned inside out. If we were serious about history, our lives and our family's lives, we'd keep alive. No one can ever take your family tree from you, 'cause remember, you grew from it. Looking back to the past, history is still a mystery. But my family tree belongs only to me.

—Brenda M. Foye, 1955–2002

CHAPTER 2

K-Dawg was born to a fairly large family. Unlike most kids in the hood, he was blessed to have had both parents in the home, even if only for a short time. He was the youngest of five children. His brother, Charles Jr., was the oldest. Then came his sisters: Pearl, China, and Kiesha.

Kiesha was his twin. Even though they were born on the same day, she was a whole five minutes older than he was. That's why people always referred to him as the youngest in the family.

K-Dawg and Kiesha were identical in every way, except gender. They both had their mother's beautiful jet-black complexion, a gift that wasn't passed on to any of their siblings, who were very fair skinned like their father. The twins got their curly hair from their Creole grandmother, who some said was a voodoo woman back home. When the twins were young, their sister, Pearl, would braid their hair alike, making it nearly impossible to tell them apart.

Overall, the children were well taken care of. They weren't rich, but both their parents worked to make sure they had the things they needed as well as a few extras. K-Dawg's father owned an auto repair shop in the Bronx where they used to live. His mother worked part time at a hair salon and played hostess at a nightclub on weekends. They loved their children dearly, and they busted their assess night and day to make sure they didn't go without. K-Dawg's mother was a beautiful woman. She was as black as a moonless sky, and she had pearl white teeth. She had long, wavy hair that she mostly wore in a single plait, which hung down to her shapely backside. Rose wasn't a small woman, either; she stood almost six feet tall in flat shoes.

When she moved to New York from Louisiana, all the players uptown wanted to get with her. Black Rose, as they called her, was the baddest chick in Harlem. She was showered with jewels and expensive gifts, but no one was able to capture her heart. Instead of hooking up with a big money cat, she chose a poor working stiff named Charlie. Whenever someone asked her why she chose him instead of a baller, she would simply say, "He has a good heart."

Rose loved all of her children completely, but the twins were different. She called them her miracle babies, and she always seemed to be overly affectionate toward them. No one thought anything of it; to onlookers, she was just a woman who loved her special little ones. No one really had any idea of the dark secret she harbored.

Their father was a different story altogether. When they were babies, Charlie showed the twins as much love as he did the other children. As the twins got older and their features began to define themselves, Charlie changed. He still treated Kiesha fairly well, but for some reason he seemed to dislike K-Dawg. It wasn't like he hated him; it was more like he just couldn't stand to be around him. His temper with the toddler was short, and he was quick to spank him for the littlest things. He claimed he was trying to teach him discipline, but it was borderline abuse. The other children thought Charlie's mishandling of the boy was funny as hell.

That is, until the day the laughter stopped.

Charlie was a good man by most standards. He always divided his time equally between his business and his family. He loved his home life, but an incident from the past had haunted him and changed his life forever. Many years earlier, before the birth of the twins, Rose had suffered an indignity that would alter the future of her family as well as the streets of New York.

It was about three in the morning when Rose left her job at a club she worked at every weekend. Usually Charlie would come to pick her up, but that evening he had business—in the form of a tender, young blues singer—that kept him away. Before Rose had left the house for work, he gave her cab fare to get home, so he wasn't worried. However, his decision to let his little head lead him instead of showing more concern for his wife's safety caused him tremendous regret.

Rose stopped a gypsy cab and instructed the driver to take her home. The long hours she worked caught up with her, and she fell asleep in the taxi. When the car came to a sudden halt, Rose awoke from her nap. Slightly disoriented, she looked around and realized that she was not in front of her house. Instead, she was in an isolated section of the Bronx, where the prostitutes turned their tricks. When she asked the driver what he was doing, she was ignored.

A chilling fear took hold of Rose's entire body, and a voice inside her head yelled, *girl, get the fuck out of this cab and run!* Rose tried the door and learned that there was no way to open it from the inside. She was trapped. The driver turned around wearing a wicked grin. For the first time, Rose got a good look at him, and she knew that she was in trouble.

He was white and in his early thirties. His hair was a tangled red mess, with clumps of it sticking up here and there. His eyes were a wicked green that seemed to glow in the dim light. His teeth were yellow and rotted, like something seen in a "before" picture at the dentist.

"Well, well," he said in a heavy Southern accent, "ain't you a fine li'l black bitch. Umm hmm. I knew'd it when I seen you outside that whore shack where you work. I said to myself, 'Self, that is one fine piece of black pussy.' I sho'nuff did. So tell me, darkie, you ever been wit' a white man?"

Rose shook her head from side to side. "N . . . no. Only man I ever been with is my husband."

"Oh, so you's married?" he asked as he climbed over the front seat and into the back of the car with Rose. "Probably got you one o' them big-dick buck niggers, huh, honey? Well, today is your lucky day. Out of the goodness of my heart, I'm gonna give you a taste of this ol' pink swipe," he said grabbing his crotch.

"Now," he continued, "before you get all nervous and start screaming, you ain't got to worry about me raping you. I don't plan on doing you no harm. What I'm going to do is let you suck on this ol' pecker of mine. Probably a li'l smaller than what you're used to," he said while pulling his penis out of his pants, "but it ain't about the size. It's all about technique. Yep, I'm gonna let you suck on this here, and give you a taste of this joy juice."

Rose thought about pleading for her life, but the maddened look in his eyes told her that he was beyond reason. She was in a serious dilemma, and she had to think fast. With all the strength she could muster, Rose socked the taxi driver square in the jaw. He fell back against the dashboard, and his head bounced off the driver's side window.

Rose had managed to daze the madman, but she was still trapped in the car. She took off her shoe and began to bang away at the glass. Before she could even crack the glass, a powerful hand gripped a big chunk of her hair, restricting her movement.

"Oh, a tough li'l bitch, huh?" he snarled with spit clinging to his lips. "Well, I like it when they fight," he said just before slamming his fist hard into Rose's face, knocking her flat across the back seat of the car.

For a moment she thought she would black out, but miraculously, she didn't lose consciousness. As Rose desperately thought about what to do next, the driver ripped off her skirt and panties in one motion and began to straddle her.

"Look a' here, look a' here," he said while pawing at Rose's vagina. "Such a tender young thang." He lowered his head and lapped at Rose's vagina.

Rose just closed her eyes and tried to drown out the slurping sounds coming from the vile man.

"I'm gonna make you enjoy this, bitch," the driver said fumbling with his pants. When he entered Rose she hardly felt it, but she knew a man other than her husband was inside of her. She tried to squirm, but that only made him more excited, and he thrust himself into her harder.

Within two minutes, the driver had reached his climax. The sweat and funk from his body filled Rose's nostrils and almost caused her to gag more than once. He sat upright and smiled down at Rose, still flat on her back, as if he had done her a favor.

"That wasn't so bad, now, was it, sweetie?"

Rose didn't answer. She just turned and lay sobbing with her face pressed in the seat. The driver, hearing her sobs, suddenly became furious. He snatched Rose's hair and pulled her upper body toward him, so that he could look her straight in the face, eye to eye.

"You laughing at me, whore?" he said with madness dancing in his eyes.

Rose tried to shake her head no, but the pain from his strong hold on her tresses was too much to bear. Rose, being a religious woman, called on God. "Lord, why you do this to me?" She sobbed. "I ain't done nothing to deserve this."

"Shut up!" the driver screamed, punching Rose in the mouth. "You were laughing at me. They're always laughing at me," he said with tears rolling down his cheeks. "They say I'm not a man. Well, li'l bitch, I'm gonna show you what a man is all about."

Instead of letting Rose go, the driver beat her. He beat her and raped her over and over until the sun was peeking over the skyscrapers. When he was done with her, he dumped her body down near the highway on 125th Street. He didn't expect her to make it through the morning, but thanks to a young prostitute, she did. The girl took Rose to the hospital and left as soon as the doctor said she would live. Rose never even got the girl's name so she could thank her.

The police questioned Rose about the rape and the girl who brought her to the hospital. Rose couldn't give a good description of the girl, but she did remember that her attacker was a redheaded, green-eyed monster with the Confederate flag tattooed on his neck.

The rape counselor said that in time the mental scars would heal. Rose had actually started to believe her, until eight weeks later when she found out that she was pregnant. That's when everything turned to shit.

Charlie hadn't been intimate with Rose since several weeks before the rape, so he knew that he wasn't the father. He wanted Rose to terminate the pregnancy or arrange for adoption after the birth, but she wasn't trying to hear it. Even though Charlie didn't plant the unborn seed, Rose insisted on keeping it alive. It was hers, and she would love it regardless.

Six and a half months later, Rose gave birth to twins: Kiesha and Keshawn. At first it was hard for Rose to look at the children; every time she looked down at the two new additions to her family, she saw the green eyes of the rapist staring back at her.

K-Dawg knew his mother's story well, even if he did keep it to himself. He knew it so well because on a few occasions when Rose wasn't around and Charlie was drinking, he would tell it to him. Charlie would describe in detail the tragedy that befell Rose, and K-Dawg would listen intently.

K-Dawg was brought out of the past by the sound of a female voice calling his name. He turned around and saw Nikki grinning from ear to ear. Back in the days, she would always punch K-Dawg in the arm and run away. He never really dug her, though.

Back then, she was skinny as hell and wore glasses. When K-Dawg took a good look at her, he realized that things had definitely changed.

Nikki had come the fuck up. The black spandex pants she wore advertised her new and improved large and shapely booty. She didn't wear glasses anymore. Now she opted for green contacts. Her caramel skin had long since won its battle with acne and was as smooth as K-Dawg's ass. All he could say when she hugged him was, "Damn!"

"Well, hello to you too," Nikki said seductively. "When you touch down?"

"Oh," K-Dawg said, reluctantly breaking her grip "a nigga just touched down."

"Word?" Nikki asked unwrapping her lollipop. She slowly put the cherry red pop into her mouth and began working it in and out. "So what you got planned now that you're in the world?"

"Who knows?" K-Dawg said with a shrug.

"You gonna finish school?"

"Please, been there done that. I'm shooting for bigger game."

"Yeah, I know what that mean. You ain't even been a free man for twenty-four hours, and you already trying to be a hustler."

"Nah, you got it fucked up, Nikki. I'm not trying to be a hustler. I'm gonna be the king."

"I hear that," she said licking her lips. "You always were the dreamer, Keshawn."

"Well, Nikki, you know what they say about dreams: sometimes they become a reality."

"So you tryin' to be that nigga, huh? Excuse me, I meant, you gonna be that nigga."

"Call it what you want, Nikki. I'm 'bout my paper. Point blank."

"So, I better snatch you up from the jump, huh?"

"Do you, girl. You know where to find me." K-Dawg continued on his way home while Nikki kept her eyes glued to him.

"I sure do," she said. "You go right ahead and blow up, but every good king needs a queen. One thing you gonna learn about Nikki is that I'm 'bout my paper too."

CHAPTER 3

K-Dawg made it to his building without bumping into anyone else he knew. He couldn't believe how Nikki had come up.

She had always been a down-ass chick, but she was never much to look at. Now Nikki was all that. However, K-Dawg had never been stupid. He had been down for a while, and Nikki was transparent to him. She was a street bitch. Be that as it may, she might still prove useful; she was sure to have the scoop on the who's who in the hood. Even if the information he was sure to pump from her bore no fruit, he could still tap that ass. It was a win-win situation in his favor, as it should be.

As the rusty elevator door inched open, K-Dawg's nostrils were assaulted with the rancid smell of human urine. Yep, he was home all right. The elevator moved along at a snail's pace. K-Dawg was a little annoyed, but he didn't stress it too much. It was better than riding in an elevator shackled to twenty other men.

On the fifth floor, a scruffy-looking character got on the elevator and took a spot in the corner. He wore a pair of beat-up Reeboks that looked like they had seen far better days. His Columbia was torn, and it was patched together in certain places with duct tape. His stench was enough to make K-Dawg cover his nose.

K-Dawg couldn't believe how this dude could run around smelling like that, but there was something about the filthy cat that rang a chord in his head, something he couldn't quite put his finger on. The character must've felt eyes on him, because he turned around and stared at the young man just inches away from him.

That's when it finally hit K-Dawg. The character in the elevator was his childhood friend, Flip.

Flip was a young man from K-Dawg's building he used to shoot around with as a kid. He was maybe four to five years K-Dawg's senior, but they treated each other as equals during their Saturday morning basketball games. Flip had cut his teeth in the game early. While everyone else was playing Seven Eleven, Flip was learning how to cut drugs. The older fellas used to let Flip sling and hold drugs for them. They knew that because he was so young, the police couldn't really do shit if they caught him. Flip was one of the freshest kids in the hood back in the day. Now he was running around looking like a stone hype.

"Flip," K-Dawg said a little skeptically, "what up, my nigga?"

Flip looked at K-Dawg trying to figure out where he knew him from. One could tell from the look in his eyes that he was fucking around. Every trace of the young boy K-Dawg remembered from the days on the court was gone. Now he stood face to face with a full-fledged crackhead.

Slowly the fog lifted from Flip's brain. As he looked at the handsome young man addressing him, things began to become clearer. At first Flip thought it was someone he might've ripped off, so his hand immediately dipped into his pocket and fingered his switchblade. As he looked closer, he realized it was his chum, Keshawn.

"What it is?" Flip asked in a scratchy voice. "Keshawn, I ain't seen you in a minute. Where the hell you been, man?"

"Been awhile," K-Dawg said extending his hand. "I been down for a minute. Nigga did a bid and shit."

"Straight like that?"

"Straight like that. I just came home this morning. They took five years off my life, Flip. Five fucking joints."

"Damn, that's heavy. So what you gonna do now?"

"I'm gonna do the damn thang, Flip. I gotta ball or fall, man. Them is the rules, kid."

"I know that's right. So who you gonna hook up with?"

"Hook up with? Nigga, my mafuckin' self."

"Man, you just hitting the bricks. You gonna need someone to start you out."

"I'll tell you like this, Flip. This world is mine; I just ain't claimed it yet."

"I hear that hot shit, Keshawn. But what about them cats who done already laid they claim to this shithole?"

"What about 'em? I mean, I ain't setting out to step on nobody's toes, but if I got to, then fuck it. Niggaz is gonna respect my team. There's enough cake out here for us all to get rich, but if mafuckas try to stop my show, then they getting knocked out the box. Straight up."

Flip started to argue his point some more, but seeing the serious look in K-Dawg's eyes he decided to change the subject. "So," he started, "you gonna hook up with the old crew?"

"I thought about it," K-Dawg said. "Me and Jus is supposed to go over a few things. Matter of fact, I might be able to put you down. You still on a paper chase?"

"Man," Flip stated sadly, "I ain't chased nothing but a high in the last few years, but a nigga always down to make a few dollars."

"Say, I been meaning to ask you something, but I didn't wanna come across wrong. What the fuck happened to you, Flip? I don't mean no disrespect, and you know I don't, but you used to be the man. Now . . ."

"Man," Flip said goodheartedly, "that's an easy enough question to answer. A bitch happened to me."

"I don't follow you, Flip."

"Well, let me break it down to you." Flip and K-Dawg weren't that many years apart, but Flip's knowledge of the game was much deeper and he had seen and done a whole lot in his few years. If K-Dawg had things his way, he would pick Flip's brain clean, so he just sat back and listened while this predator-turned-prey ran down the sad tale of his life.

"Now," Flip continued, "we all know I started doing my thing at a very young age. I done a lot and I seen a lot. Them cats I was working for used to bump. Me being the impressionable young ass I was thought that was the thing, ya know? I would bump a little at parties and shit, and here and there at social gatherings. Nothing too heavy.

"At first I was just chipping, then the next thing you know, I had a habit. It was cool, and I thought I had it all under control. As long as I made enough to fuck off and support my habit I was good. That was until I met that bitch, Sherry.

"Man, that bitch gassed me to cook that shit up and freebase it, said the high lasted longer. Well she wasn't lying, 'cause I been high ever since. To make a long story short, I lost my money, my shit, and my dignity. Now here I stand: hustling-ass Flip, a mafucking basehead."

"Man," K-Dawg said under his breath, "them old heads you was pumping for ain't try to pull your coat to the shit? I mean, them being older and all, I'm sure they knew what that rock do to a nigga."

"Shit," Flip said wiping his nose with the back of his sleeve, "if you ask me, they was wit' the shit. Them niggaz seen how I was grinding and knew a nigga was on a come up. I could've had my own shit, Keshawn, my own hood, man. But I had to go and get strung out.

"Worst part was that my fake-ass team ain't do a damn thing to help a nigga when he fell. All them years I hustled for them cats, they couldn't even give a nigga a blast on a day when he was short. You know, just to keep me from getting sick. They'd just post up laughing and shit. The same mafuckas I was lending money to, gigging on me, kid. Can you believe that? I ain't good for nothing, now, except inhaling that mafuckin' exhaust and running errands for niggaz half my age."

"That's some cold shit, Flip."

"That's what I'm trying to tell you, Keshawn. This is the land of the heartless. The rules done changed while you were gone. You gotta know when to use your pistol and when to use your head. Only the coldest mafuckas come up out this wit' they skin on. You gotta be ready to play God: give life and take it. You think you got that shit up in you?"

K-Dawg looked Flip dead in the eye. His green orbs seemed to glisten in the dim elevator light. K-Dawg's eyes danced on the fine line between insanity and genius. With one word, the wheels of fate were set in motion. "Yes."

Flip gazed into K-Dawg's jade green eyes, searching for signs of weakness or insecurity, but there were none. K-Dawg was the real deal. This young kid who Flip used to teach how to shoot free throws was now a man possessed by the lure of the dollar.

Flip knew the look well because he had held the same stare in his prime.

"I'm gonna win, Flip," K-Dawg said emotionally. "This world has cast me aside only to have me reborn as a better man. Instead of prison fucking me up, it made me more focused. Picture me busting my ass for thirty or forty years to put some snot-nosed cracker through college. For what, a pension and a half-fare train pass? I don't think so.

"My ribs is touching, Flip. I got nothing to lose and everything to gain. I'm getting in this game head first, and best believe, my side gonna be the winning side. Now my question to you is, you gonna be content being a fucking store boy, or you ready to step up and reclaim your respect?"

As K-Dawg spoke, Flip hung on to his every word. This was probably his only chance to get back a little bit of what he had lost.

There was no doubt that K-Dawg was gonna put his best foot forward, but could he pull it off? Either way, Flip couldn't lose. If K-Dawg failed, Flip could go back to his life and still probably make off with a few dollars. On the other hand, if he succeeded, Flip would be getting in on the ground floor.

"Keshawn," Flip said grinning, "I got yo' back on this one. We can take this joint, man. I mean we—"

"Hold on, player, 'we' is French," K-Dawg said cutting him off. "I ain't said shit 'bout putting you on, yet. I don't even know how far I can trust you."

"Hey, this is Flip, baby. You know you can trust me."

"Flip, no disrespect to you, man, but I don't know shit, and ain't nothing free. You got to earn my trust."

"Keshawn, man, just tell me what you need from me. What, I gotta kill somebody or some shit?"

"Easy, Flip. I don't even know what you talkin' 'bout on that murder shit. Truthfully, I'm a little offended that you would even ask me some shit like that. Just be cool for now. We'll talk soon." K-Dawg was being careful with his words in case Flip proved to be a snitch.

"A'ight, man. Just give yo' nigga the word and I'm wit' you. These niggaz is gonna shit they pants when they find out we hooked up."

"See, Flip, you speeding again, dog. I don't want nobody to know what's up with us, not even my niggaz.

You gonna be my trump card. Through you, I'll know what's up in the streets at all times. Just keep ya mouth shut and let me work."

"Okay, man. If you need me, you know where to find me."

Flip got off the elevator leaving K-Dawg to his thoughts. So far everything was going smoothly. The knowledge that Flip had bouncing around in his smoked-out brain would be beneficial to K-Dawg in his conquest, but he sure as hell wasn't gonna tell Flip that. Flip was going to be a big help, but K-Dawg knew that his services would only be needed for a short term.

He and Flip had been friends once, but that was a long time ago. Flip was a hype and could only be trusted to a certain extent. As the shit got deeper, he would have to keep Flip close to him. He couldn't be trusted to run around with the kind of information K-Dawg would have to confide in him. As sure as K-Dawg's ass was black, Flip would fuck up if given an opportunity.

The only thing a basehead nigga could ever truly be loyal to was a pipe. When Flip had outlived his usefulness, he was going to die.

Fuck it. He was just another pawn in K-Dawg's game.

K-Dawg approached the door to the project apartment and stared at it as if he was seeing it for the first time. He reached for the knocker but withdrew his hand. He knew that beyond that door was what was left of his family, but it brought him no comfort. He would still be a stranger to them, as he had always been.

K-Dawg had lain awake in the filthy six-by-nine many a night and imagined this moment. He had rehearsed in his head what he would say over and over, but now his mind drew a blank. After debating over it for about ten minutes, he thought, *to hell with it.* It was too late to turn back. Whatever happened once he knocked on that door would just have to be.

K-Dawg tapped lightly on the door. After a few seconds there was no response, so he knocked a little harder. He could hear someone shouting and then footsteps approaching the door.

"Who the hell is it?" someone asked from behind the door.

"Housing," K-Dawg answered playfully. The door swung open and a woman in a bathrobe confronted K-Dawg.

"What the fuck?" The woman started to curse. Once she saw who it was, all the hostility left her voice and a smile spread across her round face.

"Keshawn, is it really you?" she asked in disbelief. "Oh shit, my baby brother." Pearl grabbed K-Dawg and gave him a big bear hug. "Boy, why you ain't tell nobody you was coming home today?"

Without waiting for an answer, Pearl grabbed him by the arm and dragged him into the apartment. "Come on in here, li'l nigga."

K-Dawg looked around the tiny living room and was a little disappointed. Even though it was fairly clean, the furniture was old and coming apart. The only bright spot was the mantle, which was lined with martial arts trophies from various tournaments. China was on her job.

It had been awhile since K-Dawg had seen his sister. She had put on a little weight, but other than that, Pearl was still the spitting image of their mother, only lighter. She had chopped her hair into a Halle Berry-type cut, and her eyes showed early signs of crow's feet, but she was still pretty.

"China!" Pearl shouted. "Girl, bring yo' ass out here and see who's dropped in on us."

China came out of the bedroom sucking her teeth. The gray cutoff shorts she wore showed off her shapely legs and plump rear. Her stomach was flat as a board, so K-Dawg knew that she was still on her workout shit. China's skin was a smooth butterscotch color, making her look anything but black. She got that from their grandmother.

Unlike Pearl, China had let her hair grow down her back and wore it in one plait. It did justice to her already breathtaking china doll features. Now, Pearl was pretty, but when men saw China all they could say was, "Damn!"

China was giving off much attitude, but when she saw who it was, her cinnamon brown eyes grew wide with shock. "Keshawn!" she squealed. China ran across the living room and gave her brother a warm hug.

K-Dawg embraced China and hugged her as tightly as he could without hurting her. He fought back the tears that filled his eyes. He was cool with all of his siblings, but he and China were especially close. They had always shared a special bond that no one ever really understood. It was as if China filled Kiesha's spot when she had died.

"Baby bro," she said crying, "I've missed you so much."

"Not as much as I've missed you," he said, getting all choked up. "I'm home now, sis. Everything's gonna be okay."

Pearl started to say something but held her tongue. There was something about seeing the two of them together that irked her. She had always been jealous of K-Dawg and China's relationship. It didn't really make sense, because they all came out of the same womb and she loved them both. She just wished that she could've been closer to them.

"So," Pearl said interrupting, "how does it feel to be a free man again?"

"It feels great," K-Dawg said smiling. "That place ain't nothing nice. I wouldn't wish prison on anybody."

"I hear that," said Pearl. "Now we just gotta keep you out."

"Sis," he said flopping down on the dusty old sofa, "I ain't never going back to the joint. You can bank on that."

"Never say never, li'l bro."

"Pearl, trust me when I say I'm never going back! I'll hold court in the streets before I see the inside of a penitentiary again. I'm home for good, or at least until the devil calls me to hell. Straight like that."

"Keshawn," China cut in, "why you always gotta talk all crazy?"

"China, I'm dead-ass serious. Me and jail don't mix. That shit just ain't the move."

"So, what you plan on doing with yourself now?" Pearl asked.

"Hmmph," he began with a shrug of his shoulders. "I got a few things lined up, a li'l of this, a li'l of that."

"Well," Pearl said, "you better get yourself a li'l of a job. That's the rule 'round here, Keshawn. We all gotta pitch in and keep things going. Since Granny passed, things have been tight."

At the mention of Granny's name, Keshawn got silent. After their father was killed, Granny held their family down. She wasn't their real grandmother, but she still stepped up to the plate for them.

"Sorry about that, Keshawn," Pearl said. "I know how you felt about her."

"Nah." He waved her off. "I'm over it."

"That was some dirty shit them pigs did," China added.

"It's cool, China. She wasn't my real grandmother. That's why they didn't let me go to the funeral."

"So what? It was still dirty."

Granny was Keshawn's heart. When their mother was sent away, she helped Charlie take care of the family. When she passed, the people who ran the jail wouldn't let

Keshawn attend the funeral. They said that because she wasn't a blood relative, their relationship didn't hold any weight. It was just one more thing Keshawn had to pay the system back for.

"Listen." K-Dawg sighed. "About what happened between me and Charlie—"

"The past is the past," China cut in. "You acted out of emotion and you paid for it. They took five years of your life. I'd say the score is settled."

China might have been right, but K-Dawg didn't think so. When the hour of judgment came, he'd have a lot to answer for. For the crime of killing his mother's husband, the state took five years out of his life. To him, it was worth it. A life for a life. When he killed Charlie, he was only thinking of himself. He didn't think of what it would do to his family. K-Dawg was sorry that Charlie was gone, but he wasn't sorry for killing him. In his mind, it was justice.

K-Dawg was brought back to reality by the sound of a little voice. "Mommy," a boy called as he came out of the bedroom, "who's that man you're talking to?"

Pearl scooped the boy up and kissed his forehead. "That's your Uncle Keshawn," she said hugging him.

Keshawn took a close look at the boy and couldn't believe his eyes. They were almost identical. The boy's nose was a little wider than his, but other than that, it looked like Keshawn could've been his father.

"What up, li'l man?" Keshawn said smiling. "I'm your Uncle K-Dawg. What's your name?"

"Justin," the boy said sizing up K-Dawg.

"Well, Justin. It's nice to meet you."

"How come I never met you, Uncle, K?"

"Well, that's 'cause I been away."

"Are you going away again?"

"Nah, I plan on being around for a while."

"Cool," Justin said leaping from his mother's arms to the couch. "You like video games, Uncle K?"

"Sure do."

"I got *Mortal Kombat*. You wanna play me?"

"I never played that one, but we can get it on."

K-Dawg took Justin by the hand, and they went skipping off into the bedroom. China was happy that her little brother was home. He was the bright spot in her life. Pearl, on the other hand, was leery. She saw the look in his eyes when he said that he was never going back to the joint. It wasn't the look of a changed man but of a hardened criminal. As he went off to play video games with her son, she couldn't help but wonder what kind of evil she had let into her home.

CHAPTER 4

After about an hour of playing with Justin and getting mercilessly beaten, K-Dawg probably broke a record for consecutive ass whippings. Justin was a well-behaved kid. He kept his side of the room clean and spoke to adults with respect. Unlike K-Dawg, Justin was oblivious to how poor he was. From the moment K-Dawg laid eyes on his nephew, he fell in love with him.

He made a promise to himself that Justin would have a better life than the one he had, and he would never know what it was like to do without.

K-Dawg's grumbling stomach reminded him that he hadn't eaten all day. Justin wanted to keep playing, but K-Dawg needed to get something in his belly and handle business. When Justin asked him why he was quitting, K-Dawg responded, "A man never made a million dollars sitting in front of a video game."

K-Dawg went to the kitchen and proceeded to ransack the refrigerator. The contents of the icebox were pitiful. There was little to no food in it. The only things even worth taking a second look at were a few dead roaches and a half-empty six pack of beer. K-Dawg opted for the beer.

K-Dawg grabbed a beer and flopped down in front of the floor-model television that took up the majority of one of the living room walls. As he looked at the rickety old living room set, all he could do was shake his head. Everything was secondhand. His peoples were hurting and he had to do something about it.

Before K-Dawg could get a good sip of the beer, China came out and sat down on the couch beside him. "And what are you doing?" she asked in a motherly tone.

"What?" he asked confused.

"Nigga, don't what me. The beer?"

"Oh, this ain't about nothing."

"What you mean 'ain't about nothing,' Keshawn? Ain't you on parole?"

"Yeah, but they don't test you for this shit. They looking for shit like weed or coke. Them people ain't stressing no beer."

"You still shouldn't be drinking it. Now give me a sip."

The two fell on each other laughing. It had been quite awhile since K-Dawg was really able to let his guard down, and it felt good to laugh. In the joint, you had to always wear your game face. If you smiled too much, a nigga would think you were soft and try you.

K-Dawg had encountered quite a bit of that when he first went upstate. He was the youngest and one of the smallest in his house. After he'd been there about a week, a group of young Puerto Ricans decided to try him.

K-Dawg was minding his business watching Sports Center *and eating a pack of cookies. A man walked up and asked for a cookie, so K-Dawg gave it to him. Then two more men approached and demanded the rest of the pack. When K-Dawg refused, all three men jumped him.*

The first boy folded when K-Dawg hit him, leaving the other two. They were kicking and punching him, but K-Dawg kept fighting, more out of fear than anger. He knew that once he stopped it would be over for him. K-Dawg started to get the best of the two boys so the first one put a knife into his back.

He spent two weeks in the infirmary because of the injury, and on his first day back in population he caught one of the men who had jumped him. Being alone, his earlier courage had left him.

He pleaded with K-Dawg, but it was useless. K-Dawg strangled the man and left him stinking in the day room. The guards came and snatched K-Dawg later on, but they couldn't prove he did it. No one claimed to have seen anything. All they could do was throw K-Dawg in the hole and ship the other two members of the Puerto Rican gang to another prison. This was the first of several incidents that K-Dawg would encounter during his stay in the joint.

"What you thinkin' 'bout?" China asked bringing him back to reality.

"That place," he responded.

"Was it that bad, Keshawn?"

"China, you can't imagine. The things that go on behind those walls are horrific. I done seen some foul shit and I did some foul shit—not 'cause I'm a bad person or 'cause I wanted to; I did the things I did because I had no choice. You either fight for your respect or you get chumped. If you're lucky, you get ya ass kicked and ya goods taken. If you ain't so lucky, you get ya asshole busted and ya manhood taken."

"Damn," China said cringing, "how can they let shit like that go down? That's fucked up."

"Big sis, that's the system. They don't give a fuck about us poor li'l niggaz. You know how many niggaz I done seen get clipped, and the state is still getting a check for 'em? They say that prison is supposed to reform us, but they got it all fucked up. Niggaz in the pen come home as one of two things: punks or mafuckin' soldiers. Yo' baby brother, I'm a fuckin' soldier to my heart.

"China, I'm 'bout to put you up on something, but keep it to yaself. A nigga like me, I got a plan. This nigga I hooked up wit' in the joint is gonna provide me with a means to get us outta here. By this time next year, I'm gonna be at the top of the food chain."

"Keshawn," she pleaded, "don't do nothing stupid. I don't wanna lose you to the system again."

"China, China, China," he sang. "Ain't you heard anything I said to you? Going back to jail is not an option. If they manage to pin another charge on me, they gonna toss the book at a nigga or try to get me to snitch. You know damn well that ain't my MO. Death before dishonor, straight like that. China, I'm 'bout to get paid in a major way, then we getting the fuck away from here."

China just stared at her brother, dumbfounded. She knew from the look in his eyes that he was dead serious. Keshawn had a long road ahead of him on his rise to the top. China loved her brother as much as she loved herself. If he were to travel that road, then she would ride with him.

"Keshawn," she said, "I want in."

"Girl, you crazy," he said flatly. "This ain't no game. I'm about to make a power move that could cause a whole lot of bloodshed. This is serious."

"So you think 'cause I'm a female I can't hold mine? Who the fuck you think put all them trophies on the shelf? I'm a second-degree black belt. I done whipped many a nigga and my gun go off. You better ask these mafuckas 'bout ya big sis."

"China, I don't doubt that you can hold yours with the best. I just ain't trying to have you out there slinging that shit."

"So, let me help you in another way."

"China, how could you help me?"

"Let me watch yo' back. You know you can't trust these niggaz you running with, except maybe Justice. Let me be the eyes behind your head."

Keshawn looked at the seriousness in his sister's eyes and knew she was ready to get busy. It had never even occurred to him that China and her martial arts skills might prove to be an asset.

Besides that, she was lethal with hers. Who better to hold him down than his sister?

"Okay, China," he started. "You'll be my personal bodyguard. I'll let you take care of certain situations, but I wanna make something crystal clear to you: if and when shit hits the fan, you break the fuck out."

"Come on, Keshawn," she protested.

"Come on my ass. That's the deal. You want in, that's what's up. I'm probably playing myself for even putting you on, but I don't ever want you to feel like you gotta depend on no nigga or bitch for nothing. Shit, I already lost one twin and it would fuck me up inside to lose another. These are the rules, China. You can take it or leave it."

"Nigga," she said giggling, "I'm supposed to be the big sister and you telling me what's up. Ain't that some shit."

"China, baby," K-Dawg said lighting a cigarette, "these things I'm telling you are for your own good. You a bad bitch and I'm a cold-ass nigga. Together, there's no limit to what we can accomplish. You just gotta do what ya baby brother tells you. You know I wouldn't steer you wrong."

"A'ight, Keshawn. I'll play it your way, but only 'cause I don't wanna have to fuck you up."

"China, please. I ain't even scared of you," he said holding up his fist. "I'll kick yo' pretty ass for you."

The two siblings clowned around wrestling on the couch. As the sound of someone putting a key into the front door was heard, K-Dawg's jail instincts immediately kicked in and he was on his feet. China, on the other hand, just stretched out on the couch and sucked her teeth. K-Dawg couldn't understand her sudden change in attitude, but as soon as the key holder stepped into view, everything became clear.

"Well, well," Charlie said grinning, "look what the state bus dropped off. What up, baby bro?"

"What's up, Junior?" As K-Dawg stood there and looked at his half brother, all of the old hate started to return. It wasn't really directed at Charlie. It was just that he looked so much like his late father; he had that same yellow skin and wavy hair. The only difference between the two men was that Charlie Sr. was of average height with a wide build, while Charlie Jr. was tall and thin.

"So," Charlie continued, "what's the word, jailbird?"

"Don't play wit' me, nigga," K-Dawg said soberly. "The mafuckin' penitentiary ain't nothing to joke about."

"Go ahead wit' that shit, Keshawn. You niggaz kill me. Y'all come home talkin' 'bout how rough it is in the joint, yet ya assess always wind up going back. All that shit is game."

"See," K-Dawg said trying to stay calm, "I would expect a nigga who ain't never been no farther than a holding cell to say some shit like that. Fuck you know 'bout twenty-three and one, mafucka? Them faggot-ass white boys I hear you run with damn sure ain't telling you what's up. Mafucka, you couldn't come through the yard in Sing-Sing without getting tried. Nigga, you wanna impress me, do a six-five split in county."

"Oh," Charlie said getting in K-Dawg's face, "listen to Mr. Bad-ass Convict. You think you hard, nigga? That li'l bit of time you did don't hold no fucking weight. You still my little brother, and I'll still knock you on your ass."

"Junior," K-Dawg said through clenched teeth, "get up out my face."

Charlie, mistaking his little brother's passiveness for weakness, pressed his luck. "What, nigga?" he said putting his finger in K-Dawg's face. "Fuck, you got frog in you, jump."

K-Dawg grabbed his older brother by the throat and pushed him hard against the wall. For the first time, Charlie realized that this wasn't the same eighty-pound, skinny kid he used to slap up. This was a 210-pound gorilla.

"Nigga," K-Dawg snarled, "I'll twist ya fuckin' head off yo' skinny-ass neck. Let me put you up on something, big brother. I ain't the same li'l ass kid who begged for y'all to accept me. I'm a grown-ass man. You come in here talking slick, but I know what's up. Our family in here starving and you ain't doing shit about it. You ain't no fucking man; you a hype. The more I think about it, the more I wanna end yo' sorry life."

K-Dawg looked at Charlie and didn't see his older brother; he saw his mother's husband. "You took her from me," he said with tears welling in his eyes. "She never did nothing to you. Why you take her?"

The more K-Dawg talked, the angrier he became. He squeezed Charlie's neck until he began to slobber on himself. Had it not been for China, K-Dawg would've probably snapped Charlie's neck.

"Keshawn, don't," China said touching his shoulder. "You home, li'l bro. Don't throw away your life like this. They took five years from you already; don't give 'em any more. Let him go."

The sound of China's voice brought K-Dawg back from whatever far-off place that his sanity was visiting. He looked at his brother's red face and felt ashamed for losing control. Charlie Jr. didn't kill Kiesha, but he needed to be put in his place.

"Charlie," K-Dawg said releasing his grip, "I'm sorry for whatever I did to make you hate me so much. I didn't ask to be born but I was, so deal with it. I'm a man, Charlie, same as you. You either show me the proper respect or I'll give you a proper burial."

"Please," China pleaded, "just come in the back with me, Keshawn."

"Nah," K-Dawg said heading for the door, "I got some shit I need to do." As Keshawn opened the front door, he had a few more words for Charlie. "Listen, big bro, I'm sorry for what I done to your father, I truly am. But hell, if I had it to do all over again, I couldn't honestly say that I'd have let him live. Anyway, man, check this fly shit here: if you think that yo' daddy is the only nigga I've put out of his misery, then you are surely mistaken. Stay out my way, and we won't have no problems." With that, Keshawn was gone.

CHAPTER 5

Keshawn was hot enough to explode when he stepped out of his building. Once again he had let anger override his better judgment. He had mixed feelings about the exchange between him and Charlie. On the one hand, he really felt badly about it. He shouldn't have expected Charlie to understand the situation; Charlie had never done anything worth being locked up for, so he didn't know what it was like for a man to have his freedom snatched.

On the other hand, fuck it. Charlie had always been a funny-acting nigga just like his father. He was always doing mean shit to him when they were growing up. At least Pearl had made an effort to accept K-Dawg and treat him like a brother. Charlie took great pleasure in reminding K-Dawg that he was an outcast. The more he thought about it, the more he wanted to run back upstairs and finish what he started.

There were two reasons why K-Dawg didn't kill his brother. The first was that he knew he would get caught if he wasn't real careful in how he went about doing it, and the last thing he wanted was to end up on the lam for killing that piece of shit. The other reason was Justin; if he killed Charlie in the house, BCW was sure to run up in there and take the boy from Pearl, and there was no way in hell that he was going to let his nephew end up in the system. K-Dawg knew all too well what that kind of life was like. Some of the youth homes were worse than prison.

K-Dawg tried to push that negative shit out of his mind and focus on the business at hand. He had to organize his team for the events that were to come. This thing he was attempting to do was going to be major. If they were going to succeed, he needed every member of his team to be loyal and reading from the same page. Jus wasn't going to be a problem. K-Dawg knew that Justice was a down-ass nigga and would ride with him. His other boy, Sleepy, wouldn't be too hard to convince; once K-Dawg sold him on the idea of stepping up his pimp game, he'd be all too happy to join. Pooh, on the other hand, might be a tougher nut to crack.

Pooh was already getting money uptown. Even though they had all agreed to form a team when they got back in the world, Pooh was already doing him. What if he was content to let them Spanish niggaz fuck him in the ass? K-Dawg hadn't really given that possibility much thought.

Every member of the crew had a part to play. Being that Pooh had a drug connection, his role in K-Dawg's game would be all the more important. If he didn't wanna play, it could complicate things. But K-Dawg was a master schemer. Even as he contemplated the problem, a plan started to unfold in his brain. Pooh would play, all right. After K-Dawg got finished, he wouldn't have a choice.

K-Dawg dug into the pocket of his army jacket and fished out a folded piece of paper. Pearl had given it to him while he and Justin were playing video games. He had read it already, but he had to read it again. He couldn't believe that his former cellmate had kept his word.

What up, Keshawn,
If you're reading this letter, then the pigs must've
finally set you free. I'm happy for you, my friend.
Now that you're free, are you ready to live like a

king? I remember the nights when you used to talk
my head off about all the plans you had. They were
only dreams then, but I'm ready to help you make
them a reality. I told my father what you did for me
and he sends his thanks. The money that he used to
put on your book in the joint was just the tip of the
iceberg. He would very much like to meet you, and
he has asked me to invite you to come out this way
so that we may speak in person. I have forwarded
you my cell phone number. Call me as soon as you
are able so we can arrange a meeting.
Manny
201-555-2969

Just like he said, Manny had come through for a nigga.
K-Dawg hadn't really believed him when he said his
father was a drug lord from the old country. He thought
that Manny was just another loud, frontin'-ass Spanish
nigga. To his surprise, he was keeping it funky.

K-Dawg could remember the incident Manny spoke
of like it was yesterday. He was in the second year of his
bid. He had a few fights, but for the most part, the other
inmates left him alone.

He proved himself whenever a new jack came through
and wanted to test the quiet kid on the second tier. Be it
with blades or fists, K-Dawg never backed down.

It was during the summer, if he remembered correctly.
There was a lot of tension between the Black Gorilla
Family and the Latinos. It had something to do with an
incident on the streets between the two groups. K-Dawg
never found out exactly what that incident was about.

Manny was doing time on a drug charge. He was
Colombian by birth, but he wasn't a part of anyone's
gang. The BGF wasn't trying to hear it, though. It was
open season on Latinos.

One day right before rec, the BGF approached K-Dawg in his cell. They asked him to join their cause and kill Manny. K-Dawg politely told them that he had no beef with the Latinos and didn't want any part of their organization. Needless to say, they weren't happy about his answer. They called K-Dawg a race traitor and said that he was going to suffer the same fate as his cellmate.

K-Dawg didn't want any problems with the BGF, but he wasn't going to get punked either. Ever since he had gotten stabbed, K-Dawg always kept an ox on hand. If the BGF wanted a problem, they sure as hell were gonna have one. He knew that to go at it with the organization would probably mean his death, but he had to get down for his.

A few nights later, after chow, they made their move. The BGF sent four of their soldiers to kill the two cellmates. They ran up in the cell with their blades and set it. Manny was caught off-guard, and he took a shiv in the gut. K-Dawg, on the other hand, was ready.

The attackers dropped Manny without too much trouble and came for K-Dawg. With a homemade knife in each hand and murder in his heart, K-Dawg laid his gangsta down. The first soldier never even knew what hit him, as K-Dawg cut him from his right eye to his left cheek. The second soldier tried to grab K-Dawg from behind and was rewarded with a life-threatening wound to his gut. When K-Dawg couldn't force the blade any farther, he broke the tip off in his attacker's stomach.

The third and fourth attackers began to back away, but it was too late. K-Dawg saw blood and went for his. He grabbed the third attacker and slammed his head into the cell door. Before he could recover, K-Dawg plunged his remaining blade into his attacker's back.

The fourth attacker tried to run, but K-Dawg pulled him back into the cell. He threw him to the floor and proceeded to bash in his face. He was still pounding on him when the COs came in to break up the commotion.

They managed to pull K-Dawg off of his victim, but the damage was already done. One man lay dead, while the other three were on their way to the infirmary.

The stunt that K-Dawg pulled was the talk of the prison for quite some time. At first they were going to throw the book at him for the murder, but a dopefiend named Whistle had seen what went down and testified that the BGF soldiers rolled on K-Dawg and Manny. It was decided that the murder was committed in self-defense, and K-Dawg didn't catch the "L." Sadly enough, though, the BGF killed Whistle a year after the trial for snitching.

The BGF tried K-Dawg a time or two after the incident, but each time their soldiers ended up in the same condition: disfigured or shitting out of a bag. After a while, the BGF took the hint and left the young man alone. They weren't happy about what he had done, but he had earned their respect. K-Dawg had proved that he wouldn't be a lamb in a den of lions. Reluctantly, they gave him a pass for killing one of theirs. From that day forward, he was labeled the Dawg, because he left no room for question that his bite was serious.

K-Dawg walked across the project grounds, once again, to meet up with Justice. For the most part, his hood had stayed the same; the elevators were still pissy and the people were still nosy. He spoke to a few of the older folks, but the majority of the people in his age group didn't know who the hell he was.

K-Dawg had spent the majority of his life in one type of state institution or another. As a child, he endured lonely nights at the Slater Village Boys Home in Upstate New York. In those days, Jus, Sleepy, and Pooh were his family. His mother hadn't been right since Kiesha's death, and other than China, nobody else really dealt with him.

Rose's family members were scattered throughout various parts of the South and had little to no contact with her. Charlie had a few people in the city, but them yellow niggaz acted just like him. They didn't think very highly of Charlie's dark-skinned wife, either. They may have very well been descendants of house niggaz.

K-Dawg's first few weeks in Slater Village were rough for him. He was only about six or seven, so it was hard for him to really understand what was going on. After the investigation, the courts had declared Kiesha's death an accident, and everyone was returned home under the custody of Charlie—everyone except K-Dawg.

The death of his twin hit him harder than anyone could've expected. K-Dawg went into a near catatonic state after Kiesha's death. He would go for days without eating, and he was mentally unresponsive. Pearl and a young China tried to bring the toddler back to his normal self, but it was all in vain. The social worker recommended that K-Dawg be sent to Slater Village where he could be cared for properly.

It was the first time K-Dawg had been away from home for more than a few days, and he didn't adjust well. For the first few nights, he would cry himself to sleep. The other kids would laugh and call him crybaby, but none of them knew what it was like to lose a twin.

After being there for a few months, K-Dawg finally decided to accept his situation for what it was. He would have to be there until he could show the people at Slater Village that he was ready to rejoin society. In all honesty, it would be a long time, if not forever, before he was truly ready.

The way K-Dawg first hooked up with his crew was funny. There was this fat-ass bully at Slater who used to fuck with all the kids. He would take their goods or force them to have perverted sex, depending on his mood. The kinds of things this boy must've seen or been exposed to, to have his mind as warped as it was at such a young age, was something that K-Dawg never once thought about until he got older.

One day, the bully decided to fuck with K-Dawg. He tried to wrestle his chocolate milk away from him at lunch. Little did he know, K-Dawg wasn't having it. They had a good brawl. The bully outweighed him, but K-Dawg wouldn't surrender. When K-Dawg started getting the best of him, the bully pulled a knife. That's when Jus stepped onto the scene.

"Fuck is up with you, nigga?" Jus barked. "You getting yo' ass kicked, so you gotta pull a shank?"

"Mind your business!" the bully snapped. "This li'l nigga here 'bout to get cut."

"Oh, yeah?" Jus asked while pulling his blade. "What if I say different?"

"Man, this ain't got shit to do with you, Justice."

"Well, it does now. You can fight the li'l nigga wit' yo' hands, or you can fight me and go cut for cut."

The bully weighed his options, and they weren't looking good. Keshawn had already shown that he would fight, and he really didn't want any part of the bad ass from Brooklyn, so he did the smart thing and walked away.

"You ain't have to do that," Keshawn told Justice. "I would've fought him again. I ain't scared of no knife."

"Man, don't worry," Jus said to the younger K-Dawg. "I don't like that nigga anyway. I was looking for an excuse to whip his ass for a minute. That mafucka always picking on people smaller than him, fat-ass pervert. What's ya name, shorty?"

"Keshawn."

"Well, Keshawn, I'm Justice," he said extending his hand.

K-Dawg was leery at first, but seeing that Justice didn't pose a threat, he shook his hand. "Your moms named you that, or is it a nickname?"

"Nah, that's my government name. My peoples are Black Foot Indian. It was either that or Kicking Bird." Both of the boys laughed at the joke. "So what brings you to this fine establishment?"

K-Dawg hesitated for a moment before speaking. This was the first time someone other than a fucking social worker or shrink had inquired about his reason for being in Slater Village. It was usually hard for him to discuss what had happened, but for some reason he felt comfortable talking to the tall Indian boy.

"My sister . . ." he began. "My sister died. She drunk some car stuff and it killed her."

"Damn," Jus said sorrowfully, "that's some deep shit. How she get hold of it?"

"My father, he left the stuff sitting out and she drunk it. The lady in the courtroom said it was by accident, but it didn't feel right to me."

"Fuck is you, psychic?"

"She was my twin."

"Oh, my bad."

"It's crazy, the way it happened. My daddy was in the garage fixing up a car while me and Kiesha was playing in the driveway. He went in the house for something, so we snuck into the car to play spaceship. I saw a cup wit' some blue stuff in it. It looked like Kool-Aid, so I wanted it. My mommy always said that I had a bad habit of drinking out of other people's cups. I didn't understand why she always spanked me for it, but I do now.

"I picked up the cup and got ready to drink the blue stuff, but Kiesha took it. She was older, so she always bullied me. Kiesha drunk most of the stuff, then something bad happened. She dropped the cup and started choking.

Her nose started bleeding and she was throwing up on everything. I didn't know what to do, so I ran and got my big sister, China.

"When China saw Kiesha on the ground, shaking and throwing up, she started screaming for my daddy. He came running out into the garage to see what was going on, and he started screaming too. When he came into the garage he was smiling, but when he saw Kiesha on the ground he had this funny look on his face. Guess he was scared.

"We took Kiesha to the hospital, but the doctors couldn't do nothing. They said we were too late. Kiesha died an hour after we brought her in. My mommy had a . . . nervous breakdown, I think they called it. She had to go away, so the people came and took us away. After the lady in the black robe said it was an accident, they let us go home. My brother and sisters got over it after a while, but I didn't. They said my brain was sick 'cause of what happened. That's when they sent me here."

By the time Keshawn had finished with his story, Justice was in tears. He admired Keshawn for being so young and able to deal with the tragedy and still maintain his sanity. He knew that had he been in a similar situation, he'd be in the nuthouse for the rest of his life. *"Damn, kid,"* Justice said, *"I'm sorry to hear about that. I thought I had issues, but my problems ain't shit compared to yours."*

"What did you do to get in here?" Keshawn asked.

"Oh, me? They say that I have violent tendencies, but that's bullshit. One night I woke up and found my uncle playing with my dick, so I stabbed him, plain and simple."

"That's messed up."

"Oh, well. Listen, Keshawn, I dig you, man. You's a cool li'l nigga, unlike some of these other mafuckas. Me

and you, we gonna be friends. Ain't nobody in this nut factory gonna fuck with us." On that day, Justice and Keshawn had become best friends.

CHAPTER 6

K-Dawg rang Jus's bell and was instructed to enter. Justice had an apartment on the top floor of the building. From the outside, it was just like any other project apartment; the door was riddled with dents and the paint was chipping. When Jus opened the door, K-Dawg was totally unprepared for what he saw. The apartment floor, for as far as K-Dawg could see, was covered with a plush, money green carpet. The sofa was designed in a green and gold blend and was as soft as a cloud. A large oak entertainment system, by itself, took up one whole wall. Inside of it sat a forty-four-inch television playing the latest rap video by this skinny kid from Long Beach. K-Dawg was struck by how much he resembled a Doberman.

The most impressive thing in the apartment was the far wall. It was decorated with mug shots of some of America's most notorious criminals. It had everybody, from Al Capone to Larry Davis. Jus was doing big things.

"I see you dig the wall of fame," Jus said, noticing K-Dawg studying the photos. "That's my inspiration, baby boy. Them cats up there was doing it in a major way. Some of them niggas was stone millionaires. And to think, people say that crime doesn't pay. Tell that shit to Capone."

"Yeah," K-Dawg agreed, "I'm feeling that. So, what up, playboy, you ready?"

"Yeah, but first things first, nigga, you ain't going nowhere with me dressed like that. Come on in the back,

K. I should have some shit to fit you." Jus led K-Dawg down the hall to one of the bedrooms. The door had a large padlock on it, which Jus undid with a key he kept around his neck. For a brief moment, when Jus swung the door open, K-Dawg thought he was looking at a small clothing outlet.

There were clothes and boxes of shoes stacked from the floor to the ceiling. In the corner behind some clothes, K-Dawg noticed a small safe.

"Welcome to the vault," Jus said smiling. "You the only mafucka, other than myself, who's ever been in here. The only reason you seeing it, is 'cause you my man. This where I keep most of my shit. I don't never keep no electronics or jewels in here, though. If the police should ever happen to run up in here, it's a lot easier to explain fifty pairs of shoes as opposed to fifty VCRs. Go on and pick out whatever you want, my nigga."

When K-Dawg walked out of the bedroom, he looked like a totally different person. He was sporting a pair of tan three-quarter boots with a matching hoodie. Jus had also set him out with a crispy pair of blue carpenter jeans. To cap it off, Jus dug in his personal stash and set his man out with a link chain, which had a circular medallion swinging from it.

K-Dawg looked at himself in the hallway mirror and couldn't believe his eyes. Just an hour before, he looked every bit of a nigga who had just come home from the joint. Now, thanks to his man, Jus, he looked halfway decent. Jus was a good nigga, and K-Dawg was going to make sure he ate right along with him when they started caking.

"Now," Jus said grinning, "you ready to ball?"

"Damn," K-Dawg started, "thanks a lot, Jus."

"Fuck outta here wit' that lame shit. You my road dawg. If I'm walking up out this mafucka fresh, then you gonna be fresh."

"Fo' sho, my nigga. While I'm thinkin' 'bout it, I need to use ya jack."

"Go 'head. You can use the one in the kitchen."

K-Dawg walked into the kitchen and picked up the white wall phone. After he fished the letter out of his pocket, he punched in Manny's number. After about three rings, someone picked up the phone.

"What up, K-Dawg?" Manny said pleasantly.

K-Dawg looked at the phone suspiciously before replying. "Man, how the hell you knew it was me?"

"For two reasons. Number one: nobody else in Manhattan would have this number. Number two: you just got out of jail about two and a half hours ago."

"What up wit' that shit, Manny? You spying on me?"

"K-Dawg, you know how the game goes. I got eyes and ears everywhere. Keeps me on top, ya heard?"

"I got your kite, Manny. What's good?"

"K-Dawg, you know I don't talk on phones. Just tell me what time I should send the car for you."

"You can send it about eight o'clock, is that good?"

"Yeah, yeah. That's cool."

"Uh, Manny, I was wondering if I could bring my man Jus wit' me?"

"Oh, the Indian kid who was always writing you up north? Sure, bring him. But don't bring nobody else. My pops is funny about that kinda shit."

"A'ight, Manny. So I'll see you later on."

"Yeah, yeah. Make sure y'all bring your appetites with you; my father's gonna have a dinner cooked in your honor. We gonna show you ol' colored boys what good food is."

"Nigga, fuck you," K-Dawg said playfully. "I'm outta here, player."

After K-Dawg hung up with Manny, his face broke into a shit-eating grin. He had a good feeling about this meeting. If Manny's pops had the kind of connections K-Dawg thought he had, he was set. His team would be on top of the game. Everybody would be a'ight and all would pay homage to the king.

When K-Dawg came out of the kitchen, he was smiling from ear to ear. Jus looked at him and wondered what he was thinking. He had known K-Dawg for a long time, so he knew it was probably a scheme. They were peoples, but something about the young man gave Jus the chills. K-Dawg had always been a nigga in search of a come up, but since going to prison his aura had shifted. He now seemed more determined, even sinister.

"What you smilin' 'bout, dawg?" Jus asked.

"Jus," K-Dawg started, "I think things are starting to look up for us. Think you can make a run with me tonight?"

"No doubt, dawg. Where we going?"

"To see my man Manny. He stays out in Jersey."

"Oh, you mean that li'l Puerto Rican kid you was locked up wit'?"

"Colombian, but yeah, that's him. If this shit works out, it's gonna be a white Christmas. Big brah, you gonna have so much fucking cake, you might steal from yo'self. This could be what's up."

"I hear that hot shit, dawg. So what he rappin' 'bout?"

"I don't wanna say too much right now, 'cause ain't nothing definite. I will say this to you, though, my friend: We gonna take it back to '85 uptown. It's about to be popping again in Harlem."

As K-Dawg moved toward Jus, his facial expression appeared to be somewhere on the borderline between madness and brilliance. He extended his hand and looked Jus dead in the eye when he spoke. "We about to go straight to the top, my nigga. We gon' have a long run and paper out the ass, but I need everybody with me.

Jus, in this game, we probably gonna have to shed a lot of blood and pull a lot of bullshit. I wanna know that the niggaz I'm rolling with, especially you, are ready to go there with me."

Jus's face was a mask of complete stone. He looked at his friend, glassy-eyed for a moment, before he answered. He knew that whatever came out of his mouth would dictate his future. Jus had decided a long time ago that he was gonna back his man's play. He knew if it was out there to be had, K-Dawg was gonna get it.

"My nigga," Jus started, "I'm in this to win, same as you. I'm ready to do this, same as you. I'd follow you through the gates of hell if there was a million cash in that mafucka."

K-Dawg pulled Jus to his chest and hugged him. He leaned in so close that Jus could feel his breath on his ear as he whispered, "Loyalty, my friend. Untied by tragedy, and bound by loyalty. A long time ago, no one loved us so the world threw us away. Soon, they will either respect us or fear us. I promise you this, my friend: as long as you are loyal, I will always love you. No one will ever throw us away again. No one."

Jus returned his friend's hug and nodded in agreement. *So be it.* If he was gonna walk the high road to hell, what better nigga to stroll with than his man, K-Dawg? They would either get rich together or lie in the streets cold, side by side.

CHAPTER 7

K-Dawg felt like an outsider as Jus took him on a tour of Uptown. He sat on the passenger side of Jus's '91 Maxima and stared at 125th Street like a kid at the Grand Canyon. The popular strip was changing just like the times. There were still people bumping and pushing up and down the avenue, but not like it used to be. The police were even cracking down on the street vendors, and they were part of the reason two-fifth was hot.

K-Dawg remembered most of the stores, but there were some that were unfamiliar to him. He noticed that black folks were taking control in the fashion game, putting out all kinds of colorful clothing and new designs. The old designers were still getting play, but they had to switch their shit up, so they wouldn't fall behind the times.

After it was all said and done, Jus had spent about $1,000 on K-Dawg. He bought him everything from suits to drawers. And when they were done, he put another $300 in his pocket. K-Dawg knew all that had put a lean on Jus's bankroll, but every time he protested about the cost of something, Jus waved him off and bought it anyhow.

"This shit should hold you over for a li'l while," Jus said as he tossed the last of K-Dawg's bags in the car. "You gonna be so fresh, niggaz gonna think you was lyin' 'bout being locked up."

"Jus," K-Dawg started, "I really appreciate this shit."

"Don't worry about it," Jus assured him. "You can pay me back once you king."

"A thousand times over."

As they approached Jus's car, a voice stopped them short. "Get the fuck outta here. My nigga, K-Dawg, what's good?"

K-Dawg turned around and saw a familiar face coming his way. The young man who approached him was a slim, brown-skinned cat. His hair glistened in the sunlight and gave off an oily appearance. He wore a three-quarter cashmere coat that looked like it was made to fit just him. His cream snakeskin shoes click-clacked on the concrete as he made his way over to K-Dawg with his hand extended. It was his man, Sleepy.

"Sleepy-Sleep!" K-Dawg shouted giving him a bear hug. "What the fuck is up?"

"Nigga," Sleepy said playfully, "don't wrinkle my 'fit."

"Oh, oh," K-Dawg said releasing him. "Damn, nigga, I hear you fly guy. You out here sharper than a mafucka. Can I hang wit' you?"

"Shit," Sleepy shot back, "I'm trying to get up with you."

"Fuck is you talkin' 'bout? You that nigga, pimp daddy."

"Pimp daddy, my ass. Man, one of my hoes ran up on me the other day, talkin' 'bout, 'Daddy, the streets of Harlem got a new king. This pretty black nigga named K-Dawg done came and claimed the hood.' So, I say to the bitch, 'In the time you spent gathering the info on this stud, did he spend any money with you?' So she says, 'No, daddy. He was too pretty to look at and his money was too long to cross.' So I kicks her in the ass and tell her, 'Bitch, you better get yo' ass back out there and lay yo' FSO down.' For you square-ass niggaz who don't know, FSO stands for fuck 'em, slob 'em, and overcharge 'em."

All three of the men fell out laughing. Passersby thought they were high or drunk. They were all quite sober, just happy to see each other, and Sleepy, like Jus, looked like he was slowly on a come up.

"So," K-Dawg said straightening up, "what you been up to?"

"Man," Sleepy started, "I'm just trying to make my way in the world. These mafuckas don't want a nigga to eat."

"You don't look like you starving, Sleep."

"K-Dawg, I'm doing okay, but I should be on top of my game. It's hard, man. These johns are getting tighter and tighter with them purse strings. Then these hoes wanna act all kinds of crazy. Bitches jumping ship when things get a li'l tight. I done ran through about six of 'em in as many months. I got two li'l bitches holding me down for now, but shit, I still gotta take care of me plus keep them looking right. It almost ain't worth it."

K-Dawg grinned devilishly. "Sleep," he said, "what if I were to tell you that I could get you where you need to be?"

"Shit, I'd say, where do I sign? What you got on the ball, kid?"

"Well, you know how we used to always talk about what we were gonna do when we got out of Slater Village?"

"Yeah, but we was just kids with big ideas. We adults now, and survival is rule number one."

"True enough, Sleep. But if we do shit right, we can get where we need to be. I got something cooking right now that may allow us to do just that."

"Well, don't keep a nigga guessing. What's good?"

"I ain't gonna speak on it right now. I'll tell you what: I wanna call a meeting for tonight. I need the whole team together so we can connect thoughts."

"I can dig it, K-Dawg. They got this li'l joint downtown where one of my girls dances. I'm cool with the owner, so I know he'll let us use the back room for a few. We can do it there."

"Cool, but it won't be until late. I got something to do at eight o'clock."

"So, let's say we meet there at about two a.m.?"

"That's fine, Sleepy. I ain't gonna hold you up; I know you got shit to do, plus a nigga hungrier than a mafucka. I ain't ate all day."

"A'ight. So I'll see y'all later at the spot. Jus already know where it's at, and I know you gonna be with this thieving mafucka all day."

"Fuck you," Jus said playfully.

"Nah, but on the real, though," Sleep continued, "you niggaz come on through the spot, tonight." He pulled out his bankroll, peeled off some bills, and placed them in K-Dawg's hand. "It ain't much, but it should get ya hungry ass something to put in ya gut."

"Good looking, Sleepy," K-Dawg said shaking his hand. "I'll see you later on."

"A'ight, Dawg. Oh yeah, happy b-day, my nigga."

Jus took K-Dawg to a soul food restaurant on 135th so he could fill his gut. It had been so long since K-Dawg had anything that even resembled a home-cooked meal. It was a buffet type joint, so he made sure to get as much as he could. He piled his plate with fried chicken, greens, and macaroni and cheese. After swallowing that down, he went back to the buffet and loaded up on ribs, potato salad, and yams. By the time he left the restaurant, he felt like he was going to pop.

"Damn." K-Dawg belched. "I ain't had no shit like that in a minute."

"A welcome change from Jack-Mack & Crackers, huh?" Jus asked playfully.

"Fuck you, brother minister."

"Nah, but on the real, what was it like? I mean, I've been to the Island and Brooklyn House, but that ain't shit compared to a state pen."

"Truthfully, it was hell. When I first got there, I was scared to death. Ain't no shame in my game, Jus. I was a li'l shook-ass nigga locked up with grown-ass men. It wasn't shit like Slater Village. There was so much fighting, murdering, and raping. That shit will fuck wit ya head, dog."

"How did you cope with it?"

"Man, after I got stabbed the first time, I was like, fuck it. I accepted the fact that the pen was going to be my home for the next five years. Even though I was scared, I wasn't going home, so why cry about it? I wasn't going to protective custody, so I had to adapt. Either I stood up for mine or joined a gang for protection. You know I wasn't wit' that shit, so I played the hand that God had dealt me."

"That's some deep shit, Dawg. I'd hate to have to do time, but I guess if I had to . . ."

"Well, just hope you never do. A nigga like me, I've already decided I ain't never going back. They'll be carting my ass outta here on a fucking gurney before I let them put me in irons again."

Their conversation was interrupted by an exchange going on between two young men. They were doing some kind of handshake that looked more like they were swatting insects. Both of the men seemed to be in their late teens and they sported red bandanas on their wrists.

"What's that all about?" K-Dawg asked Jus.

"Man, that ain't 'bout shit. You ain't been around in a while, so you really ain't up on it. This is mostly 'Blood hood' now."

"Get the fuck outta here. That ain't New York."

"I know it, kid. But over the last few years, li'l gang sets been popping up all over. It's getting big out this way."

"There was a few cats that was Blood and Crip up north. I didn't know that shit was going on like that. This kid I was locked up with was telling me something about it, but I didn't take him seriously."

"That shit is getting serious. I heard that big head mafucka in the mayor's office is putting together a task force to try and control that shit."

"Fuck is wrong with him? That shit ain't work in Cali, and it ain't gonna work out here. That's just another waste of money. Instead of building jails and fucking task forces, they need to fix up some of these fucking schools. I walked past the old playground and that shit look like it's coming the fuck apart."

"So, what the fuck else is new? They don't give a fuck 'bout what goes on up here, and wit' us runnin' 'round killing and acting all crazy, that just adds fuel to the fire. To them people downtown, we ain't no better than savage animals. The fucked-up part is, I look at these niggaz nowadays and wonder if they're right."

"We gonna do things different, Jus. When we get this paper, we gonna do something for the people in our hood."

"That's what I'm talkin' 'bout. When you do good, good comes to you."

"We gonna do better than good, my nigga. You watch, Jus. One day, I'm gonna ride through this mafucka wearing a crown and waving like the president."

"You a sick kid, dawg."

"I ain't sick, Jus, just more motivated than a mafucka. Oh, while I'm thinkin' 'bout it, you holla at Demon for me."

"Here we go. I knew you wouldn't let it rest."

"Jus, I just wanna talk to the nigga."

"Yeah, okay. Well, I ain't spoke to him. I heard it through the grapevine he got a spot up on 145th. If you wanna go up there looking for him, that's on you. If he send yo' ass back in a bag, I'll make sure the hood remembers you as a stand-up nigga who didn't know how to leave well enough alone."

"Nah, me and Demon cooler than that, Jus. Look, do me a favor? Take them bags back to your spot for me. It'll be getting dark soon, so I wanna go see what's up with the nigga before we gotta take our li'l trip tonight."

"A'ight." Jus shrugged. "Have it yo' way, but if I don't hear from you by six-thirty, I'm coming through there strapped."

"Good looking, but I don't think that'll be necessary."

"Yeah, a'ight. You got that gun on you?"

"You know I do, dog."

"A'ight, my nigga. Remember what I told you, K-Dawg. That ain't the same nigga from Slater Village. You walking into a snake pit, dawg."

"I'll be a'ight, Jus. And you always remember: niggaz is snakes, but I'm a king cobra."

CHAPTER 8

When K-Dawg stepped out of the cab on 145th and Saint Nicholas, the sun was setting and the streetlights were starting to come to life. He studied the brownstones as he passed several bodegas and chicken spots. Some were nice while others were just fucked up.

K-Dawg wandered up one side of 145th and down the other like a lost tourist. He was looking for signs; Demon shouldn't be too hard to find for someone who knew what to look for. If he was as efficient a hit man as Jus had led him to believe, then he should have some paper. There were a few brownstones where the hunter could be camped out, but it wasn't like Demon to splurge on anything plush. He was a man who valued his privacy.

A brownstone in the middle of the block caught K-Dawg's eye. It was torn up like the rest of them, except the steps and the entrance were clear of debris. K-Dawg peered over the rail and noticed a faint light coming from one of the basement windows. Something told him that he would find Demon in this building.

Cautiously, he climbed over the rail and dropped down to the basement. The door was boarded up, but when he pulled at one of the boards, the whole frame almost collapsed. When he stepped through the door, he found himself in a long corridor. It was dark as hell, but there was a faint light at the end of the hall. Feeling along the wall, he made his way down the passage.

As he walked down the hall, he noticed a distant scraping sound. K-Dawg paused and tried to identify it. As he listened closer, the scraping seemed to grow louder. K-Dawg strained his eyes to see what was coming his way and saw four red orbs.

K-Dawg wasn't the smartest man in the world, but he knew from the increasingly loud growling that the red orbs were the eyes of two dogs. He wanted to turn and run, but he knew that before he could reach the door, the dogs would overtake him. Trying to keep his composure, K-Dawg drew his pistol. The dogs were almost on him when he raised the .380. Before he could let off a shot, a voice boomed out in the darkness.

"Stop!"

On command, the dogs froze in place. They turned and went back down the hall as if nothing had ever happened. It was strange, but K-Dawg sure as hell wasn't complaining.

"Follow the hounds, Keshawn," the voice commanded.

Now that the voice was calmer, K-Dawg recognized it. It belonged to Demon.

K-Dawg made his way down the rest of the corridor and found himself standing in the middle of some kind of storage room. There were boxes and debris scattered everywhere. K-Dawg heard movement behind him and turned around to find himself face to face with Demon and his two guardians. For the first time, K-Dawg got a good look at the two dogs. They were hulking gray mastiffs. The dogs easily weighed 150 pounds apiece, and would've torn K-Dawg to shreds without much effort.

Demon looked just as K-Dawg remembered him. He wore a white tank top and a pair of gray sweats. He wore his hair in five cornrows that hung down to his shoulders. His face was very thin, almost giving him a skeletal look. His body was just as thin as K-Dawg had remembered, but it seemed to have more tone. Demon's cold gray eyes stared emotionlessly at K-Dawg. Then a broad smiled spread across his penny-colored face.

"My nigga, K-Dawg," Demon said pleasantly. "What brings you down into the pits of hell?"

"You know," K-Dawg started, "I just touched down, so I had to check my homie."

"Nigga, don't bullshit me. You come all the way up here, search high and low to find me, then risk getting yo' ass chewed up by one of my babies here, all to say hello? I don't think so, K."

"It wasn't hard to find you."

"Bull. I saw you when you got out of the cab. You were walking up and down the ave peeking in windows and shit. You lucky one of these li'l crack-slinging mafuckas ain't kill you. What's up, Keshawn?"

"Demon, how could you say something like that? Me and you, we been cool since back in the day. Why wouldn't I wanna come check you?"

"Keshawn," Demon said, leaning in close so that he and K-Dawg were eye to eye, "you are so full of shit. You've been out of the loop, but not out of touch. I'm sure you know what people say about me. I'm supposed to be some otherworldly monster that stalks the night, drinking blood and snatching children from open bedroom windows. Some people, boy."

"Yeah, I heard a few things, but I know they ain't true."

"Oh, yeah? How the fuck do you know? Nigga, you ain't seen me in how long? For all you know, I could be some psychotic ass nut who let you in here to kill you."

"Okay, Demon, you caught me. I did come up here to see what's good with you, but there's another reason, too."

"What a surprise," Demon said sarcastically.

"Nah, yo," K-Dawg said. "I'm dead ass, but can you tie them crazy-ass dogs up so we can talk?"

"Nope. I don't believe in caging or tying up animals. The shit is cruel. Besides, they are the guardians of the gate. You invaded their space, that's why they got pissed. Follow me upstairs; we can talk there."

K-Dawg followed Demon through a little side door. He noticed that it was made from a sheet of plywood that had seen better days. "Say," K-Dawg began, "I don't mean to get all up in ya mix, but you might wanna get a lock for your door. I don't doubt that your hounds will chew a nigga, but what if someone were to get past them? This ol' plywood shit you got over here ain't gonna keep much of nobody from coming to the upper part of the building."

Demon looked at K-Dawg and smiled. "I got this, dog."

Then he slapped a red button that was mounted on the wall, and a steel-plated door slid out over the plywood one. "That's three inches of solid steel. Don't underestimate anything you see in here. I got all kinda shit."

"Damn," K-Dawg said, "you got everything covered, huh?"

"You don't know the half. That reminds me. The level of the house we're going to is where I actually live. When we come up from the basement, we'll be going up the main stairs. Use only every other step."

"What happens if I fuck up?"

"First, you'll fall through the steps. Then you'll get yo' ass ripped up by the barbed wire that I got crisscrossing under the stairs. And last but not least, if you're lucky enough to hit the floor, you'll get swarmed by the five hundred or so rats that dwell under this place."

"Shit, remind me never to break into your house again."

"I wouldn't worry about it. The only reason you even made it as far as you did is because I wanted you to. You're just lucky I remembered the dogs when I did. They're so quiet I often forget that they're here."

"I see you still got that fucked-up sense of humor."

"Always. Even the most vicious demons need to laugh every now and again."

On the way up, Demon led K-Dawg on a semi-tour of his fort. The first-floor windows were boarded up and painted black in order to maintain total anonymity. This was the area of the house where he trained. He had all kinds of weights and exercise machines scattered where the living room was supposed to be.

The second floor was completely sectioned off, and an iron door similar to the one in the basement closed that floor off from the stairway. Demon informed K-Dawg that the second floor was where he had built a makeshift firing range. The whole floor was soundproof. When K-Dawg asked to see it, Demon declined to show it to him.

The third floor was different from the rest of the house. There was a homey feel about it, and this was where Demon lived. The floor was lined with a simple gray carpet that wasn't much thicker than a blanket. Demon led K-Dawg to what he referred to as his living quarters. There was a bed, a loveseat, and a writing table with a lamp.

"Have a seat," Demon said motioning toward the love seat as he sat on the circular bed. "Now, what is it you wanna talk about?"

"Well," K-Dawg began, "you remember how me and the fellas used to always talk about the plans we had, right?"

"Yeah, I remember. Dreams of young, impressionable children. What's your point?"

"Well, I got a plan that will put our team on top of the game. We got a chance to get paper in a major way."

"Fuck has that got to do with me? Keshawn, you know I don't fuck with drugs, so why you even stepping to me with this shit?"

"Opportunity, my man. I know you don't sell drugs and I'm cool with that. In the next few months, there's gonna be a lot of shit going down. Some niggaz won't mind what we doing, while other niggaz will be trying to shut us down. I need someone with your talents on my team, someone who can make certain problems disappear."

"I'm afraid I don't follow you, Keshawn."

"Come on, Demon. You're one of the best in the killing game."

"Killing game? You bugging. Where you getting your info, dog?"

"Demon, how you gonna play me like that? We both street niggaz, dog. I know what's up."

"Man, I told you, I ain't killed nobody."

"Damien, we go way back, my nigga. When other mafuckas made fun of you at Slater, who stepped up? Me, that's who, and I even used to share my snacks with you when you were uptight. We was friends back then, and I thought we still were."

"Oh, so now you wanna go there. Yeah, K-Dawg, you befriended a nigga when no one else would. That's why I didn't let Adam and Eve rip you a new asshole, but don't come up in this mafucka acting like a nigga owe you."

"Demon, we bigger than that. I wouldn't never come at you sideways, but I need you with me on this."

"Keshawn, what could you possibly offer me to make me change my mind?"

"Paper, nigga. I can make you a rich man."

"Fuck outta here. Just 'cause I live up in this mafucka with my rats and my dogs, don't assume I'm broke. A nigga got some change. I got a good thing going, Keshawn. I'm freelance and I like it like that."

"Yo, Demon, I'm 'bout to be the next fucking king of Harlem. I'm trying to give you an opportunity to triple your worth."

Demon threw his head back and burst out laughing. "You don't understand, do you?" he asked. "I don't kill for the money. I kill because it needs to be done. The mafuckas I lay down deserve to die. When I kill, I perform a service for God. These people are vile and undesirable. I know it's a sin to kill, but didn't the archangel serve as God's hand of justice? You see? It evens out that way."

Jus had mentioned the fact that Demon was out there, but it was beginning to sound like a bit of an understatement. K-Dawg knew he had to try a different approach. "Oh," K-Dawg continued, "now I understand. What if I were to tell you that I could keep you knee deep in scum bags?"

"Unh, uh."

"Demon, I'm not trying to do this just to get rich. I'm doing it to try to help my family and my community. These mafuckas, they don't care about shit. They sell that poison to kids, pregnant people, whoever. Under me, the rules of the game will change. The people I'll be setting you out on are scum, pieces of shit that have desecrated God's green earth with their presence. I hate to say it like this, but people like your stepfather."

Demon's eyes flashed with rage. For a minute, K-Dawg thought he had gone too far. Demon was his boy, but if the nigga got crazy, K-Dawg intended on popping him. The only problem with that was how was he going to get past Adam and Eve to get out of the building?

After an uncomfortable pause, Demon's eyes softened again. "Keshawn," he said, "your offer is tempting. I'll admit that business has gotten slow because people are becoming increasingly afraid to deal with me. But how do I know I can trust you?"

"Damien," K-Dawg said, relaxing a little, "how far we go back? You can trust me."

"So you say. If that's the case, prove it to me."

"No problem, dog. What you want a nigga to do?"

"Meet me on 112th and Lenox, tomorrow night at midnight."

"What you want me down there for?"

"If you want to gain my trust, then you'll stop asking me questions and agree to meet me."

"A'ight, Demon. You my nigga, so you got that."

"Good, good. I'm still a li'l leery to make this move with you, Keshawn. But if you got as much love for me as you come up in here claiming to have, you will stay true to your word."

"Demon, these people are scum. With your help, we can make a new Harlem, one that's safe for our kids and loved ones. Blood will be spilled, but for a purpose."

"A'ight, Keshawn. You can leave through the side door on the first floor; the dogs won't bother you that way. I got a few things I gotta handle, so I'll holla at you."

"I'll see you tomorrow night, Demon. Oh, you got a phone I can use? I forgot to call Jus."

"Don't worry about it," Demon grinned, resembling his namesake. "When I saw you get out the cab, I hit him up."

"You got everything covered, huh?"

As K-Dawg got ready to leave, Demon stopped him short. "Yo, K-Dawg, no disrespect to you, but I think it's only right that I tell you this: betray my faith and I claim ya life."

The two men stood there for a moment staring at each other. The seriousness in Demon's voice didn't go unnoticed by K-Dawg.

There was no doubt in his mind that if Demon wised up, he'd try to make good on his threat. K-Dawg just had to make sure he kept his hounds happy or tamed with whatever method he decided to use. Demon and his dogs weren't the only ones that knew the thrill of the kill.

CHAPTER 9

In the confines of a modest cottage-style home in New Jersey, Manny lounged in a gold velvet chair, smoking a thin cigar. At first glance, it was hard to tell that he had ever been inside of a prison. Across from Manny in a similar green chair sat a white-haired old man with his legs crossed, and he bounced a white wing-tipped shoe impatiently. He wore a plain white linen shirt and a pair of gray slacks. He was dressed more like a barber than a crime lord. This was Francisco Vega, the biggest cocaine supplier in the Northeast.

"So," Vega asked his son, "this kid, Keshawn, think we can trust him?"

"You can bet on that, Pop," Manny said, while blowing out a cloud of smoke. "K-Dawg is a stand-up guy. He's his own man, too."

"I hope so, 'cause if he ain't, we're sure as hell going to have a time moving the rest of this month's shipment."

"I know. Who would've thought that our biggest earners would get knocked?"

"Fucking snitches," Vega complained as he spat on his own floor. "How could a person look at himself in the mirror, knowing that he's turned on his people? It's a fucking shame, Manny. You could learn from this. Just think, if that had been you in the car with Pablo instead of Mike, your ass would be up shit's creek, all because some junkie, chipping motherfucker couldn't keep his mouth shut. How much do they know?"

"Pop, Mike and Pablo been with us for a while, but . . ."

"How much, Manny?"

"They know about a few spots here and there. They were doing numbers in Harlem mainly, but they supplied quite a few spots, here and there."

"They gotta go, Manny."

"But Pop, those guys were always loyal. You think they would turn on us?"

"That's your problem," Vega said pointing his finger, "you're too fucking trusting. Never underestimate a caged rat, especially one that's never been out of captivity. Rather than go through the motions, they tend to take the easy way out. Why do you think I invited K-Dawg to my little hideaway? He was practically raised in the penitentiary. People like him have an overwhelming desire to stay out of prison. But the other side to people like K-Dawg is that if they do wind back up behind bars, they won't crack. They've lived behind the wall most their lives, so it's nothing. A man that stays true is a man of honor. Let's hope K-Dawg fits the criteria."

Vega flicked a switch on the little gray intercom beside him. "Rick," he barked, "come in here for a minute."

A few moments later, the door to the study carefully opened, and Rick came strutting into the room. He appeared to be in his early to mid-thirties. He had a thick black moustache and wore his hair slicked back like an old-time gangster. His green jogging suit fit him perfectly, with the exception of the bulge beneath his right rib cage.

"What's up, Mr. Vega?" Rick asked.

"We have a small problem, my friend."

"Just say the word, Mr. Vega, and he's a memory."

"Two of our captains got locked up. The feds caught them with six birds and $152,000 in cash. Needless to say, they're going away for a good while. Probably get a kingpin charge. I spoke to our friend, the lawyer. He says that there isn't much he can do for them 'cause they had a witness."

"So, what do you wanna do about it, Mr. V?"

"I doubt if they'll go to the Island, probably hold them on Pearl Street. Who do we have in there?"

Rick scratched his head for a minute before answering. "There's Hector. Nah, he's no good. Hector's only got eighteen months left on his bid, and I don't really wanna jam him. Wait, I got it. My li'l brother's in there. He's fighting a triple murder as it is, so it really won't make him any difference."

"Okay, okay. Tell your brother I'll pay him ten thousand for each one of their lives. Also, put the word out to whoever we got in all the facilities in the five boroughs that it's five thousand per life."

"I'll make it happen, Mr. Vega." Rick turned on his heels and left the room.

"You see," Vega said to Manny, "money talks and bullshit runs a marathon. I give those pricks forty-eight hours the most. Some young hooligan is gonna stick a shiv up their shitholes."

"Yeah," Manny said, "but what if they were never gonna turn in the first place?"

"Why take a chance? If you are ever going to be successful in this game, my son, you have to learn to leave no stone unturned. Food for thought, Manny."

"I hear you, Pop. Not to change the subject, but our guest should be here soon."

"Yeah, your friends. Did you call the girls?"

"You know I did."

"Good. I want your friend to feel comfortable with us, like family. We have twenty-two kilos of cocaine just sitting. It isn't really hurting us, but when the next shipment comes in, it may become a headache. I don't like having back inventory."

"Don't worry about it too much, Pop. Once you lay the deal out for K-Dawg, I'm sure he'll go along with it. When we we're locked down together, all he used to talk about was getting money. He would spend hours on end talking to old cons, mostly the ones with drug charges. He picked their brains cleaner than a Thanksgiving turkey. The boy is sharp, Dad."

"The way you praise this man, I hope so. You know, if this works out, you'll be the one to credit for it. I'll admit, Manny, you've done some dumb shit over the last few years. I was beginning to think I'd have to find another successor. Who knows, Manny, there may be some hope for you yet."

Gloat on, you old bastard, Manny thought. Little did Vega know, young Manny had plans of his own. He was going to use K-Dawg and his team to edge Vega out of power. Manny had every intention on being the next crime lord of the Northeast.

K-Dawg knocked on Jus's apartment door, and he answered wearing a silk bathrobe. "Damn," he started, "it's almost seven-thirty. I thought that nigga Demon fed you to his dogs."

"Hardly," K-Dawg said sarcastically. "I'm 'bout to get dressed so we can skate."

"I take it Demon told you to go fuck yourself?"

"Nah, he was actually open-minded about what I had to say."

"Nigga, quit lying."

"On the real. Demon's a cool dude, like I told you. I'm eighty percent sure he'll ride with us."

"K-Dawg, you never cease to amaze me. How the hell you swing that?"

"Jus, people are people, no matter what their personalities. Everyone has a price, my man."

"Yeah, okay. Let's just hope Demon's price isn't too high to pay."

By the time K-Dawg finished dressing it was ten minutes to eight. He wore a black velour shirt with a pair of black Boss slacks. For footwear, he selected the black suede shoes Jus had bought for him earlier that day.

"Boy, you stylin'," Jus said, adjusting the collar of his red silk shirt. "Let's hurry up and get this over with so we can get our party on, kid."

"Business first," K-Dawg scolded. "We got all night to party. Let's keep our mind on our money. We gotta go out there and make an impression on these niggaz."

Jus locked the apartment door, and the two men strolled down the street. When they got to the avenue, there was a white limo parked on Fifth Avenue. Most of the hood had gathered around, trying to find out if someone they knew could be rolling this large. K-Dawg and Jus casually stepped forward, making their way through the crowd. There were plenty of oohs and ahs from the onlookers, including Nikki, as the two young men slid into the back of the limo.

Most of the ride out to Jersey was spent in silence. K-Dawg, deep in thought, viewed the scenery; he had gotten to see most of the countryside when he came in on the bus, but it wasn't the same as seeing it from a limo. The back of the ride was big enough to seat a small entourage comfortably, so K-Dawg and Jus had enough space not to crowd each other. The two men poured themselves shots of Hennessy from the bar and relaxed on their respective sides of the limo. K-Dawg went over the plan in his head again and again. He had to make sure everything went just right. If he fucked this up, not only would he be back to square one, but he would also look like a bird in front of his peoples. This had to work.

The ride didn't take them as long as they had thought. After about an hour, they were pulling into the driveway of a cottage-style house. K-Dawg looked at the structure in awe. Other than his trips to Slater and Sing-Sing, he had never been out of the projects.

The beautiful home was made of clay-colored brick. It appeared to be at least three stories high and sat alone in the middle of the block. K-Dawg couldn't see the inside of the house because all of the curtains were drawn. But he didn't have to; he already knew he was in love with it. He could definitely see himself living in a place like this one.

Manny stepped out into the driveway to meet his friend. He was dressed in an electric blue suit and black leather shoes. His hair was cut into a short Caesar, making him look almost like a light-skinned black. K-Dawg saw the big grin on Manny's face and relaxed; a meeting that started with smiles, more often than not, ended with them.

"Keshawn," Manny said hugging his friend, "glad you could make it. You must be Justice," he said, turning his attention to the taller man.

"Peace," Jus said, shaking his hand.

"Come on in, fellas. My father is waiting for us out back."

As K-Dawg followed Manny, he noticed a small minivan parked off to the side. He didn't really pay attention to it, but he made a mental note of it in his head. Manny led the two men around to the back of the main house to a smaller one. When K-Dawg entered the smaller structure, he almost drooled on himself.

Inside of what appeared to be a pool house, there were about half a dozen girls, all wearing thong bikinis. The girls were of all complexions and builds, and they were all bad. Sitting off to the side, sipping champagne from a crystal goblet, was a plump, white-haired old man. This had to be Vega.

"Welcome," Vega said standing. "I'm so pleased you could make it. I am Francisco Vega, master of this house and your honored host."

"Mr. Vega," K-Dawg said shaking his hand, "a pleasure to finally meet you."

"Please, spare me the formalities. Call me Frank."

"Okay, Frank. Thank you for taking the time to meet with us."

"Keshawn, I should be thanking you. You saved the life of my only son. For that, I am grateful. Please be seated," he said motioning to the white loveseat.

K-Dawg sat down on the loveseat and Jus followed suit. A tall, brown-skinned female came in from another room carrying a tray of champagne glasses and a bottle. She was wearing a powder blue thong—period!

The young lady set the bottle and the tray on a small table in front of K-Dawg. He could feel his dick getting hard, as he stared hungrily at her soft brown breasts. It had been over five years since he had even smelled pussy. From another direction came a shorter, light-skinned broad. She was wearing a Sunkist orange thong that was almost lost in the crack of her large ass. Her golden tits swung freely as she set a bottle of Hennessy and several shot glasses next to the champagne. Both hotties, now finished with their tasks, went and sat on Vega's lap.

"You like?" Vega asked slyly.

"You have good taste, Frank," K-Dawg admitted, stroking his chin hairs. "They're gorgeous."

"Maybe," Vega continued, while palming the brown chick's breast, "you want a li'l romp, huh?"

"Thank you, Frank. But if you don't mind, I'd like to take care of business first."

"Oh, I see. I like a man who's focused, Keshawn. Manny told me you were good people, but when I saw you come in here and look me in the eye, I knew you were about something."

"Thank you, Frank," K-Dawg said nodding slightly. "Now if you'll allow me to prove it, then I'd feel like I've earned your praise, sir."

"Keshawn, my young friend, flattery will get you everywhere. Jus, why don't you take one of these bottles and go party with the girls. No disrespect to you, but I don't really know you like that, yet. Keshawn is only here because my son vouches for him, and even that only extends so far. He can fill you in later."

"No disrespect to you, Mr. Vega," Jus started, "but I don't know none of y'all like that, and I'm here on the strength that my man say y'all good people. I don't really feel comfortable with that."

"It's cool," K-Dawg said, squashing the drama before it even went there. "I'm good, my nigga. Good lookin', though."

"Yeah, Jus," Vega said waving the girls off, "we'll be done in a few. We're gonna eat, party, and drink. Big fun, boys."

Jus reluctantly allowed the ladies to lead him away. K-Dawg knew he had everything under control. They weren't dealing with some 140-something and Broadway hoods. Francisco Vega was an old school gangster. He knew opportunity when he smelled it. If Vega wanted them dead, there wasn't a whole lot they could do about it. K-Dawg had noticed all the video cameras in the house.

Nine times outta ten, there was some niggaz staked out in the joint with guns. All K-Dawg had to do was play it cool, and there was a good possibility that he would walk out of there a rich man.

"So," Vega said, lighting a cigar, "I hear you're trying to come up, Keshawn."

"Not exactly," K-Dawg corrected. "Frank, what I'm trying to do goes way beyond just a come up. I'm trying to capitalize on a billion-dollar-a-year industry and get mine. This is something that goes on every day on Wall Street; why not in the hood?

"Frank, drugs, will always be around. You know why? 'Cause them crackers in Washington is getting fat off this shit. As powerful as you are, Frank, you probably, knowingly or unknowingly, put some senator's kid through school. It's all about supply and demand, my friend. The reason this business is so profitable is that there'll always be somebody who wants to buy drugs."

"Yeah," Vega said blowing out a cloud of smoke, "that's all well and good, but how the hell you just gonna pop up outta the woodwork and be the one?"

"Frank, I'm determined to win. Damn near everything I love is dead or gone. Fuck I got to lose? I'm a nigga wit' a plan and a reason, Frank. I got the killas and I got the turf. Betting wit' me, you can't lose, Frank."

"You sound like you know where you're going with this, Keshawn."

"To the top, Frank."

"Tell you what, Keshawn, I'll front you a little taste. The going price for a key of good white on the streets is what, about eighteen, maybe 18.5, right? You bring me back . . . twelve and you keep the six and a half?"

"Frank, your offer is a generous one, but I'm afraid it's unacceptable."

Manny and Vega looked at each other in shock. Anybody else would've jumped on that. Even if K-Dawg broke it down instead of selling it wholesale, he could do him. What kind of game was he playing?

"By the looks on your faces," K-Dawg continued, "you probably think I'm either a clown, or crazy as fuck. Well I'm crazy, that's a sure enough fact, but I ain't no fool. I don't like to owe nobody nothing. If you're willing to take twelve for your trouble, then you're probably getting it for like five, maybe seven. I'm fresh out the joint, so my paper ain't heavy. I wanted to come to the table with something, but don't break a nigga."

For a few moments no one said anything. K-Dawg knew he should've jumped on the offer, but he didn't want Vega to know how thirsty he really was. It was too late to take it back; he just had to play it through.

"I have a thought," Manny spoke up. "If it's okay with you, Pop?"

"I'm listening," Vega said sitting up.

"Well," Manny continued, "what if we gave it to Keshawn at kind of like a discount? He buys from us at a flat rate of nine thousand, with a grand in your pocket for the hookup. The extra thousand will only be on a trial basis, of course. There's money in Harlem, Pop, and I know this kid is gonna go out there and get it."

"Sounds okay," Vega said looking at K-Dawg. "I'll tell you what: you looked out for my son and I owe you for that; plus, I like you. I'll give you the coke at that price, but you can't buy anything less than five at a time for your first few cops. You do good, and we'll work something out later."

"Damn, Frank," K-Dawg complained, "that's like fifty thousand dollars a trip."

"Let me break something down for you, Keshawn. When you really start getting money, like I know you will, you'll see that ain't shit. I could wipe my ass with fifty grand. With a deal like this one, sure, you'll spend the fifty to get what you need, but you could wholesale the bricks for seventeen and eat. You'll be undercutting the competition and still seeing money."

K-Dawg felt the wheels in his head turning. He had been away for a while, so he really wasn't hip to what birds were going for back then. Vega was dangling a lot of money in front of him—a whole lot. Not to mention, they could flip it even harder if they broke some of it down and bottled it.

"I think you got a deal, Frank," K-Dawg said smiling.

"Good, good," Vega said shaking his hand. "Manny, go get Jus. We're going to toast to success." Vega waited until Manny was out of earshot before he started speaking again. "Keshawn, you seem like a good kid. You're a hell of a young man, to go through what you've been through and still be able to walk on your own two; that takes a lot of fucking guts, man."

"Thank you, Frank."

"My son, Manny, he's a good kid, Keshawn, you know that. I always hoped that when my time came, my children would be all right. Manny and Gloria are all I have. But Manny, he has a habit of making poor decisions. Try to look out for him, Keshawn. I always liked you ever since . . . you know. If there's anything you need, call me, Keshawn."

"Thanks, Frank."

"Now, let's party."

CHAPTER 10

Vega and Manny showed their guests a good time. They ate all kinds of exotic dishes and drank cognac like it was going to run away. Jus fucked one of the girls from the pool, but K-Dawg opted for some head. He hadn't busted one in a while, so it didn't take him long. After the girl knocked K-Dawg down a couple of times, they just partied and drank. When K-Dawg informed his hosts that he and Jus were leaving, Jus seemed more disappointed than the pool girls.

The meeting had gone well. K-Dawg informed Vega that he'd contact him through Manny in a week or two about his decision. The gentlemen exchanged hugs and parted ways. Vega went upstairs, while Manny led K-Dawg and Jus to the car. When they were heading out the front door, Manny grabbed a gym bag from a closet and followed them into the driveway.

When they got to the car, Manny tapped K-Dawg's arm. "Here," he said handing him the bag, "that's a li'l something to get you started, Keshawn. There's a little over a half a key in there. Do what you want with it."

"I can't take this from you, Manny," K-Dawg said, trying to hand Manny the bag back.

"Man, I owe you my fucking life. That's a gift, so you don't owe me nothing for it. Welcome to the family," he said hugging him. "Make us proud."

The men said their goodbyes and the car pulled off. The Hennessy and champagne had K-Dawg lightheaded, so he cracked the window and reclined. He felt pretty nice. What had started as a shitty birthday had turned out to be a'ight.

"So," Jus said blowing his zone, "them niggaz know how to live, huh?"

"Yeah, man," K-Dawg said sitting up. "Manny and his pops is good people. We gonna be living like that soon, kid."

"Oh, yeah? So I take it everything in there went well."

"Yep."

"So, what's up? If that old nigga, Vega, hadn't told me to bounce, I wouldn't have to ask you. I'd know."

"Jus, you know how them old school niggaz is. They all leery of everybody and shit. He just felt comfortable talking to me dolo, kid. I think you intimidated him," K-Dawg lied. "He said you look like a mean dude."

"Mafuckin' right, nigga. I would've jumped all in his old-ass chest if they had tried to front. So what did he say?"

"I'll put it to you like this. What's the going rate on a key of good coke?"

"About . . . nineteen, maybe 19.5. Why?"

"Nigga, 'cause we gonna set it out for seventeen. What you think about that?"

Jus looked at K-Dawg like he'd lost his mind. "Nigga, is you high as well as drunk? How we gonna do that?"

"Man, that old dude is setting ya man out for nine thousand a wop, but we gotta snatch a minimum of five at a time."

"Okay, so he front us five birds. What we gotta bring him back, kid?"

"It ain't exactly like that, Jus."

"Ain't exactly like what?"

"Well, he offered the consignment, but I turned him down. No debts. We're gonna buy it at nine a key."

"Nigga, you must've fell and bumped yo' head. That's like forty-five grand."

"Fifty when you count Vega's five thousand."

"Get the fuck outta here, Keshawn. Where we gonna get that type of bread?"

"Nigga, don't worry about it. I got half a bird to start us out and a plan to get us up and running."

"K, you might've slit our throats with this shit."

"Oh, ye of little faith," K-Dawg mumbled shaking his head. "Trust in me, my friend. This deal is too good to pass up. Who the fuck you know get coke at nine a key? Nigga, that's like stealing. I got a plan, Jus. Just have a li'l faith in ya dawg."

"I don't know, K-Dawg. It just seems like there's more to it. What makes you so special to get bricks for nine?"

"Well, for one thing, he probably only pay half that when he get 'em. On top of that, I saved his son's life. Loyalty and honor, my friend. Always remember: loyalty and honor."

Manny walked back into the house to find his father waiting for him. "Think you're quite the little businessman, huh?" Vega asked. "Our two people who took the fall were bringing us back much more than that."

"I know, Pop," Manny said smiling. "But you also gotta remember they were working for us. They never took the initiative to step their game up. This kid, Keshawn, he came at us on some other shit. He doesn't want a handout; he wants an opportunity."

"Whatever, Manny."

"I mean, what could it hurt? We get 'em at four thousand. You're still coming up five thousand the wiser, right? You're profiting twenty-five thousand off of five keys; that ain't too bad. Plus I know this kid is gonna do work. Keshawn is focused as hell."

"K-Dawg is a thinker and a master schemer. He's gonna do big things. I ain't never seen a nigga as determined as him, Pop. He's like a coiled snake, watching, ready to claim his prey. You watch what I say, Pop.

"When we was locked up, he used to pick them old niggaz' brains clean. He ate, slept, and shitted the game. He'll either bring us mass amounts of business or get himself killed. Either way, what we got to lose? We got twenty keys we're trying to get rid of, and that kid is going to do it."

"So you say, Manny." Vega walked off toward the stairs wrapped in his own thoughts. He had a good feeling about Keshawn. The boy seemed like a good earner. Unlike most of the younger guys Manny ran with, Keshawn knew where he was going.

Although Vega didn't say it, he had faith in the young black kid. It was his own that he was worried about.

The limo pulled up to Jus's apartment. Jus took half of the contents from the gym bag upstairs and came back down to the car. When the limo pulled up in front of the club, it looked like a car show was underway. There were automobiles of all makes and models parked at all angles in front of the joint. The willies were out, but K-Dawg and Jus shut it down when they hopped out of the white long boy.

Just about everybody knew Jus. They either gave him dap or got the fuck outta his way. Jus had love in the hood, but he also had enemies. He had robbed quite a few people over the years, and niggaz didn't forget shit like that. Most of them just took it as a loss for their own good. Jus was a stickup kid, but he was also a very dangerous man.

K-Dawg strode up in the joint like he owned it. Many of the patrons looked at him like he was out of his mind. Everyone knew Jus, but they were all curious to know who the tall kid with the low Caesar was. He was an unfamiliar face to the niggaz, but to the ladies he was fresh meat.

As K-Dawg walked up the iron stairs, his nostrils were assaulted by the stench of weed and cigarette smoke. He stepped into the dark hall and studied his surroundings. There was a long bar on one side of the room. Small tables were scattered throughout the place. On the opposite side of the room was a stage where the ladies did their thing, entertaining the crowd.

The first person K-Dawg spotted was China. She was sitting at a corner table, sipping a drink and talking to a slim, light-skinned chick. If China wasn't his sister, he might not have recognized her. She was wearing a dark blue business suit with a matching fedora pulled low over her face. Her long black hair was braided and secured with a bow in the back. China noticed K-Dawg enter the spot and called him over to her table. "What up, baby bro?" she said standing up to hug him. The black stiletto-heeled boots she wore made her almost K-Dawg's height, so she didn't have to stand on her tiptoes when she kissed him on the lips.

"Girl," he started, "what you doing up in here?"

"Shit," she said sitting back down, "same as you, nigga: bird watching."

"China, you need help. Say, have you seen Sleep or Pooh up in here?"

"Sleep, he up in this mafucka somewhere. I ain't seen Pooh, yet. Sit down, li'l bro. Let a bitch buy you a drink."

"A'ight, China. Let me get a Henney and Coke. My man Manny put me up on that shit."

As China busied herself ordering the drinks, the light-skinned girl propositioned K-Dawg. "Lap dance, daddy? It's only ten dollars."

K-Dawg openly admired the young lady. She was tall, and thick in all the right places. She was wearing what appeared to be a fishnet stocking that stretched over her whole body without covering shit. Before he could answer, China interjected.

"Bitch," she said, slapping the girl hard on the ass, "that ain't no mafuckin' trick. That's my brother, K-Dawg."

"Oh," the girl said blushing, "my bad. I ain't know, China."

"Well, now you do. Why don't you go see if Sleepy in the back? Tell him my brother's here to see him."

The young stripper sauntered off in search of Sleepy. When she thought that China wasn't looking, she peeped at K-Dawg and blew him a kiss. This was one female who definitely wanted to holla.

It was a trip for K-Dawg, watching his sister in action. The suit she wore was clearly made for a man, but she made it look sexy and feminine. It was no secret that China wasn't really into dick, but K-Dawg had never actually seen her around other women. In a way it made him uncomfortable, but she was his sister and his heart. Was he supposed to love her any less?

"So," China said sipping her drink, "where you been all day? I ain't seen you since you choked C.J."

"I've been on my job, big sis. That letter that came to the house for me, that was from my peoples. Niggaz just set me out, China. So far, the plan is rolling along."

"I hear that, Keshawn. So now what?"

"Well, I'm gonna sit the fellas down and see what's what. When I lay my G down, niggaz is going to feel me. Big sis, ya bro is about to make his mark."

"I know that's right. Oh, that reminds me." China fished around in her inside pocket until she found what she was looking for. "Happy b-day, Keshawn," she said handing him a small golden locket.

"What's this for?" he asked, confused.

"Just open it."

K-Dawg opened the heart-shaped locket, and he fought to keep the tears from rolling down his face. Inside of the locket were two pictures. One was of his mother, braiding the hair of a young, toothless China. The other was of Kiesha.

It was hard for him to look at a picture of his other half—his female half. In truth, K-Dawg had never come to grips with her death. Even though he had avenged her by murdering Charlie, the pain was still there. It probably always would be.

"Look at you and Mama," he said trying to hide his true thoughts. "China, you sure were a funny-looking kid."

"Fuck you, tar baby," she said giggling.

"How is she?" he whispered.

"Mama, she ain't been doing so good. She's in and out, Keshawn. Her sugar is always way higher than it should be, and all that fucking medication they giving her don't help. You should go see her."

"I guess."

"What you mean, you guess?"

"I don't know, China. It ain't as easy for me to deal with that kinda shit, as it is y'all. That woman they got up there, I don't know her. All my memories of her are from when she was strong and healthy. I have been in and out of the system ever since I can remember. I wasn't there when things went downhill for her. Y'all got a chance to get used to it, but I didn't."

"It ain't as bad as you think, Keshawn. She ain't always . . . you know. Sometimes, it's just like it used to be. Before—"

"I know. Before that piece-of-shit daddy of yours did what he did."

"Here we go again," she said throwing her hands up. "Keshawn, why don't you and C.J. let that shit go? The past is the past."

The past. K-Dawg remembered that shit like it was yesterday.

He was on the ave slinging stones for this big head cat named Flint. It wasn't an everyday thing, but it helped out when his pockets were hit. K-Dawg was coming out of the bodega when he bumped into Dirty Bill. D.B. was a drunk from their old neighborhood. The kids used to catch him, wasted, on the avenue and taunt him.

"Well, well," D.B. said adjusting his paper bag, "if it ain't li'l Keshawn."

"What's up, D.B.?" Keshawn said, keeping his distance from the smelly man.

"Everythang cool, baby boy. Got into it wit' some niggaz 'round the way, so I had to relocate. You know how it is."

"Yeah."

"Say, Keshawn, how's the family?"

"Everybody okay."

"Ya daddy still locked up?"

"Nah, he been got out."

"What?" D.B. asked in disbelief. "You mean to tell me they let that polecat out, after what he did?"

"They said it was an accident," Keshawn said, a little confused.

"Shit," D.B. said rolling his eyes, "that's what they say."

"D.B., what you talkin' 'bout?"

"Oh, man, don't pay me no mind. You know ol' D.B. be drunk. It ain't nothing."

"D.B.," Keshawn said while taking out a switchblade, "I might only be sixteen, but I wasn't born yesterday. What you telling me, D.B.?"

"Ah, Keshawn, it ain't my place to tell you."

"Nigga," Keshawn said putting the blade to D.B.'s neck, "either you tell me something, or I'm gonna poke yo' ass."

"A'ight!" D.B. cried. "Man, that shit that happened wasn't no accident."

"D.B., make me understand you."

"Man, he killed her. One night, that nigga was in the bar talking out his ass. He was saying something about how he couldn't stand you and shit. I'm thinking, he bugging out. How you not gonna like a six-year-old? He started talkin' 'bout how God sacrificed his one begotten son for the sins of man. He was tanked up, so I ain't really pay him no mind. Then the next afternoon I hear what happened and how it was supposed to have went down. That mafucka's a snake. Charlie always used to brag that the easiest way to kill a nigga was to poison him. Keshawn, he set that antifreeze out for you."

By now, D.B. was damned near sober and crying like a baby with colic. Keshawn knew that the old drunk spoke the truth.

Kiesha's death was his fault. If he hadn't let her snatch that cup from him, she'd still be alive.

"I'm sorry, Keshawn," D.B. said sobbing. "I thought the police kept him, so I never said nothing. If I had known they was gonna let him off, I would've killed him myself. Man, I . . ."

D.B. found himself talking to thin air. Keshawn was already halfway across the street and heading for his building. At first he was just walking blindly, letting D.B.'s words play over and over in his head. The more he thought about it, the more his heart ached.

This only fueled his rage. On his way to the building, Keshawn took Flint's .32 from the Dumpster where he kept it hidden. He wasn't quite sure what he was going to do with it, but it felt so right in his hand.

Charlie was out in the parking lot with some of his buddies. They were supposed to be fixing cars, but all they were fixing were drinks. When Keshawn saw Char-

lie, he broke into a full run. He zipped right past Granny and never even noticed her. She saw the disturbed look in his eyes, but old age and poor health kept her from pursuing him.

Charlie noticed Keshawn coming his way and turned to face his wife's son. "What?" he asked annoyed. "It's grown folks out here; what you want?"

"Why?" Keshawn asked with tears streaking his face.

"Why what, nigga?"

"Why you kill Kiesha?"

Charlie felt like all the wind had been knocked out of him. That was a secret that he thought he wouldn't have to atone for until judgment day. Well, the secret was out now.

"I don't know what you talkin' 'bout," Charlie lied. "Furthermore, I don't appreciate you questioning me. Fuck you think you is?"

"Charlie," Keshawn said pointing the gun at the older man's heart, "don't play with me. I know you killed her. You left the antifreeze out for me, but she ended up drinking it."

At the sight of the gun, the rest of the men in the parking lot started backing up. Charlie, on the other hand, let his liquor think for him. He pulled a lead pipe from the trash and started to move toward Keshawn.

"Oh," Charlie said smugly, "so now you know. Yeah, Keshawn, I tried to murder yo' li'l ass, but unfortunately, you still 'round this mafucka. I'm sorry for what happened to Kiesha, I really am. You don't know how many nights I lay awake wishing you had gotten hold of that cup."

"I'm gonna kill you, Charlie," Keshawn said, barely able to steady the gun.

"Oh," Charlie said, twirling the pipe, "you think you a man now, nigga? Well, I been waiting for this. I never

liked you. Did you know that? You's a disgrace. Ya mama should've listened to me and got an abortion, rape baby. Nigga—"

"Nigga" was the last word Charlie ever spoke. Keshawn pulled the trigger on the revolver and let the bullets fly freely. The first one hit Charlie right in the heart. He never even felt the other two. Charlie was dead before he hit the ground.

It seemed that, for a moment, the world stood stalk still. It was the middle of the afternoon, so the whole hood was out there to witness the murder. Keshawn collapsed on the curb and cried his eyes out. He placed the barrel of the revolver in his mouth and began to apply pressure. Before he could get the hammer to slam down, Granny had wrestled the gun from his hand.

When the police arrived on the scene, Granny was sitting on the curb rocking Keshawn back and forth in her arms. The police took the boy from Granny and carted him away. The whole time, C.J. had to restrain a hysterical China. She was just coming from practice as they were putting the cuffs on Keshawn.

Being that Keshawn was sixteen at the time, they tried him as an adult. His family couldn't afford to hire a lawyer, so they had to go with a public defender, and the prosecutor wiped the floor with him. The arresting officer tried to help the youth out as best he could. Officer Jackson testified to the fact that Charlie had a lead pipe in his possession, in an attempt to prove that it was a self-defense killing. The judge wasn't trying to hear it. He handed Keshawn a two-to-five like it was nothing. He said that his age was the only reason he didn't give him more time.

The family took it hard as Keshawn was led away, but he held his game face. The sight of another youth getting caught up in the system almost caused Officer

Jackson to break down. He knew what it was like to have a father kick the shit out of you whenever the mood struck him. He really tried to help Keshawn, but it was in vain. One man couldn't change a system that was already designed to work a certain way. He knew that there would never be any real justice for the poor folks in the world. At that moment, he decided that if he couldn't change the system, he was sure as hell gonna milk it.

K-Dawg was snapped out of his flashback by the sound of a voice behind him. "Yo, my man. You in my seat."

K-Dawg stood up and turned around to see who was trying to play him. He was a short, brown-skinned kid with a curly fro. He was shorter than K-Dawg, but wider. K-Dawg stood eye to eye with the kid, sizing him up. There was something familiar about him that K-Dawg couldn't quite place. When he looked closer, he noticed a faint scar over the kid's eyebrow, and then it hit him.

"Pooh?"

"My nigga," Pooh said, giving K-Dawg a bear hug. "Welcome home, dawg."

"Damn," K-Dawg said poking Pooh in the chest. "You done went and got all big and shit. Fuck you on, kid?"

"You ain't the only one been behind the wall, Keshawn. I caught a one-to-three not long after you went away. Them niggaz shipped me off to Grove Land."

"Hey, you know how the game goes. I heard you out here doing big thangs though, Pooh."

"Yeah, a nigga got a li'l something going on. It ain't much, but it's mine."

"I hear that, but peep this: you about to come fuck wit' us. You my folk, and it's time for you to start making some real bread."

"Yeah, I heard you still runnin' 'round screamin' 'bout ya master plan."

"Damn straight. But instead of just talkin' 'bout it, I'm ready to be about it."

"So, what you got up ya sleeve?"

"Ah ah, my man. All will be revealed in the meeting."

"Well let's go. Sleep asked me to come out here and get you. Him and Jus in the back already."

Pooh led K-Dawg through the crowded club to a small wooden door marked PRIVATE. The office was very plain. There was a couch, file cabinet, and a desk that sat in front of a two-way mirror. K-Dawg's team was assembled and awaiting him.

K-Dawg went around the room and gave everybody a pound. "Gentlemen," he began, "thank you for meeting me tonight. What I have to lay down to y'all is something that will change our own personal futures as well as the drug game in Harlem."

For the next few minutes, K-Dawg explained the details of his deal with Vega as he had done with Jus earlier. He had all bases covered: territory, potential income, and any other detail imaginable. The way the young men were paying attention when he spoke, he knew that he had them.

"It sounds good," Sleepy interrupted, "but where we gonna get the money we need to cop major weight?"

"Sleep," K-Dawg replied, "that's a dumb question, but an honest one. Nigga, we criminals. Each of us has an illegal means of income. Jus with his heisting, Pooh with his dealing, and you with your pimping. If we incorporate our hustles and our money, we could take this borough. Matter of fact, this whole fucking city."

"Man," Jus added, "if we set them birds out for two grand less than what niggaz is already getting 'em for, we can G off."

"Okay," Pooh spoke up, "the plan has potential, but, Keshawn, what do you bring to the table?"

"Well," K-Dawg said grinning, "I bring to the table leadership and a bird to get us started. You forgetting, I'm the nigga wit' the plan and the hookup."

"Shit," Sleepy started, "we could all be the kings of our respective trades. I dig the plan and I think we could pull it off. I'm in."

"With me," Jus, added, "it was never really a question. I'm down."

"Well," K-Dawg said addressing Pooh, "what's good, dawg?"

Pooh sat for a few moments weighing his options. "I ain't sure about all of this. By pulling some shit like this, we gonna make a lot of enemies—"

"Yeah," K-Dawg cut him off, "but for setting the birds out at a discount, we'll also make a lot of friends."

"Listen, Keshawn," Pooh continued, "I got a good thing going for myself. I ain't sure if I wanna risk that on a gamble and a scheme. If y'all need me to front y'all some paper or lend support in any way, I'm here for you, but I don't know about giving up what I got."

"Yo, Pooh, what's up with you?" K-Dawg asked. "In the beginning, we all agreed that we'd do this together. Now, you don't know?"

"Man, it ain't like that, Keshawn. Y'all my niggaz and I would never do y'all dirty, but it's a big risk you're asking me to take. Let me think on it awhile. I'll get back with y'all in a few days. Right now I got some shit to do."

Pooh walked over to K-Dawg and handed him an envelope. "It ain't much, my nigga, but it's something. Happy b-day, dawg." Pooh hugged K-Dawg and left the three men to sit and ponder their plan.

"I don't know," Jus spoke up. "That boy could cause a problem. He has a lot of street connects who could prove invaluable to us."

"I ain't worryin' 'bout that," K-Dawg said with a dismissive wave of his hand. "He'll come around."

"I don't know," Sleepy said. "You know how that nigga is. Them cats he hustling for make him feel important. You and I know he ain't eating like he should be, but he's content."

"Sleep, don't stress it. The important thing is that you and Jus are in. Pooh will change his mind, trust me on that."

"Well," Jus said, "now that that's settled, we got a birthday to celebrate. Sleep, set some of them bitches of yours out and let's party."

MOMMY

The most beautiful flower on God's green earth, yet at the same time the most wretched weed. Nurturing, yet neglecting all at the same time. Trying to do everything right, yet only doing more harm than good. As a child, I never really understood the fact that you were only human, and being human, you were entitled to make mistakes. Some days the hate outweighed the love, but there was always an emotion to thrive on. Strong, for being able to raise a boy to a man all on your own, yet weak for falling victim to temptation.

Children never understand such things right away. And more often than not, when they do acquire the wisdom to figure it all out, it's too late to make peace. I understand now. It was your unconditional love for me that sometimes made you hate yourself for your choices. I understand.

—The Author

CHAPTER 11

K-Dawg awoke the next afternoon with a feeling he had never experienced before: a hangover. He and his team had partied with China and her crew until well into the next morning.

Even though it was against his better judgment, he had smoked a blunt for the first time and realized he liked it. This was something else that he would have to atone for down the road.

K-Dawg looked at the pretty young thang lying next to him and couldn't help but smile. After the strip joint had closed, he and his party had popped in on an afterhours lounge. To his surprise, Nikki worked there as a bartender. He spent the remainder of the night sitting at the bar talking to her. After the spot closed she invited him back to her crib for a nightcap. One thing led to another, and before long, he was getting the drawers. She was real seductive about the whole affair, like she had it all mapped out. She sat the drunken young man on the couch and proceeded to strip for him. She took her clothes off slowly and sensually, making sure she had his undivided attention. The way Nikki moved, she could've easily outshined any of the girls at the club.

Nikki stood in front of a grinning K-Dawg, damned near naked. She wore a violet Victoria's Secret outfit that was off the chain. Her young, firm nipples peeked out ever so slightly through the sheer material. K-Dawg let his eyes roam down to her crotch area. Nikki's shit poked out through her panties like a small fist. K-Dawg thought he was going to nut all over himself.

Nikki licked and sucked on various parts of his body as she stripped him of his clothes. K-Dawg tried to match her passion, but he was a little clumsy due to lack of experience. Nikki peeped his awkwardness but acted as if she didn't notice. She knew he'd been gone for a while, so she tried to steer him along as best she could.

Nikki fumbled with K-Dawg's zipper until she was finally able to free his throbbing penis. She had to admit that she was thoroughly surprised at what he was working with; K-Dawg was hung like a horse. She figured that if he knew how to work that big mafucka, she would be able to do her thing for real.

Nikki took K-Dawg by the hand and led him to the bedroom. As she pulled him along, his hand shook like a schoolboy. It was kind of funny though; Nikki was just as, if not more, nervous than he was. She had taken some dicks in her lifetime, but never any that were quite as large as his.

K-Dawg lay on the bed with his heart beating at a thousand miles a minute. He tried to bring his nerves under control, but it was no easy task; Nikki was a bad bitch. It seemed that the only part of him that was willing to cooperate was his dick. His little man stood straighter than a five-star general.

Nikki climbed on top of K-Dawg and slipped him inside of her. When she got his rod in her, she wanted to scream out. It was a combination of pain and ecstasy. It was a rough ride at first, but once she got wet and into a rhythm, it was a little easier on her. Nikki rode the long-time object of her affection, singing soprano the whole time.

After they had been at it for a while, K-Dawg's nervousness was replaced by animal lust. He grabbed her by her small waist and lifted her off him. With one gesture, K-Dawg threw Nikki down onto her stomach. He mounted her from the back and went to work. He jammed himself into Nikki's secret place and went ape shit on that good-good. When it was all said and done, he felt ten pounds lighter, and Nikki was unconscious. It was 11:30 a.m., and as much as he didn't want to, K-Dawg knew he would have to get going soon. Before he slid with Nikki, China made him promise to accompany her to see their mother. It was a hard promise, but he made it.

K-Dawg slid silently out of the bed and lightly paced to the bathroom. He popped two aspirin and got into the shower. The steaming hot water felt good on his body, and it was the first time that he had really gotten to take a shower without the company of ten to fifteen other men.

Nikki was already up and around when K-Dawg got out of the shower. There was a heavenly smell coming from the kitchen, so K-Dawg decided that that was where he needed to be. When he entered the small cooking area, the sight of Nikki's fine ass in a peach silk robe greeted him. She was just putting the finishing touches on his breakfast.

"What up, lover man?" she asked. "Sleep well?"

"Like a rock," he said kissing her on the cheek.

"Well, Mr. Rock, hurry up and eat this. I ain't trying to rush you out or nothing like that, but China made me promise to have you home by 12:30, and I don't want no kinda drama wit' ya crazy-ass sister. If it was up to me, I'd keep yo' ass occupied for the rest of the day."

"I believe you, girl. Shit, after the way you put it on me, I don't think I wanna go anywhere."

"Oh," she said a little embarrassed, "about what happened . . . Listen, Keshawn, I ain't never been one to sugarcoat shit, so I'm just gonna say it. I ain't gonna lie and say that I've never had a one-night stand, but I haven't done that shit in a while, and I ain't no ho."

"Keshawn, for as long as I've known you, I've wanted you. When we were little, I used to fantasize about you asking me to marry you. I know it sounds silly, but those are just the kinds of things that little girls do. When you got locked up, I took that shit so hard. All I did was cry. It got so bad that my moms took me to counseling. That shit was crazy."

"Damn," he said between bites of the steak she had prepared. "Why you never said nothing?"

"Come on, Keshawn, keep it real. If I had stepped to you, you would've laughed at me. I was skinny, had bad skin, and wore glasses. Nobody wanted to fuck with me."

"True."

"Damn, you sure know how to make a bitch feel better."

"My bad, Nikki. You know I didn't mean it like that, ma."

"Yeah, whatever. Listen, Keshawn. What I'm really trying to say is I'd like this to be more than a one-night stand. I know, I know, you just came home and you wanna do you, but I had to put it out there, Keshawn. I'm real like that."

"Damn, Nikki. You keep it funky. I ain't gonna front, I'm feeling you too. I'd like to get to know you a li'l better, if that's cool."

"It's all good, boo," she said smiling. "No pressure. We can take it one day at a time and see what happens."

"I think that could work," he said returning her smile. "One day at a time."

"A'ight, now get up and head out, Keshawn. It's after twelve o'clock, and China probably waiting on you."

K-Dawg dragged himself from the table, and when he got to the door Nikki kissed him passionately on the lips. He strode off to the elevator, floating on air. He wasn't sure, but it felt like he had found his first girlfriend.

***

The ride wasn't long at all. K-Dawg and China hopped on the 1:30 p.m. Metro train and reached their destination in exactly one hour. On the ride up, K-Dawg squirmed around in his seat. He had gone against the BGF, the Aryans, and the Puerto Ricans in the joint, but here he was, scared to death about seeing his mother.

It had been five years since he had last seen Rose. After Kiesha's death, Rose had made a number of trips back and forth to mental institutions, and she always came home. But the mere fact of having a husband in the ground and her baby boy in state prison was too much. Rose finally went away and never came back.

The siblings took a cab from the station to the institution. China had to almost drag K-Dawg out of the cab when they got to the place. It looked too much like Slater Village for him. The high walls and the manicured lawn only hid the evil that lurked within.

The attendant at the front desk seemed quite pleasant, but K-Dawg wasn't fooled. They were just like that at Slater: smiling at the visitors by day and doing all kinds of fucked-up shit to the kids at night. If he had a quarter for every young person who committed suicide because of what went on inside of state institutions, he'd be a rich man.

The nurse directed them to a little sitting room at the end of the hall, where they were told their mother was waiting. K-Dawg was hesitant about taking those first steps. China squeezed her little brother's hand, letting him know she was there for him. K-Dawg proceeded down the hall one step at a time, until he stood in the doorway of the sitting room. For the first time in five years, he laid eyes upon his mother.

It was strange, standing there looking at Rose. She and Keshawn were almost identical. They had the same Hershey-colored skin covering their round, angelic faces. The only real difference was that Rose had soft brown eyes and Keshawn's were jade green. Despite the similarities and having known her all of his life, he felt like he didn't know her at all.

The woman he looked at was not the same woman he remembered from his childhood. Her once long and beautiful hair was now falling out and graying. Rose was only in her forties, but she appeared to be in her sixties. When she looked up at her visitors, there was no fire in her eyes, only despair.

"Rose," the nurse said, "look who's here to see you. It's your children."

Rose looked at China and then at Keshawn. She paused for a long moment. "My children?" she asked suspiciously. "No, no. My children are babies. Has there been some mistake?"

"Mama," China said stepping forward, "it's me, China."

"China? Girl, you got so big, I almost ain't know you. Who's this handsome young man with you? Is he your boyfriend?"

"No, Mama. Don't you recognize him? It's Keshawn."

A broad smile crossed Rose's dried cracked lips. "Keshawn? Baby, is it really you?"

"Yes, Mama," he said trying to keep his voice from quivering. "How you been, Mama?"

"Boy," she said standing, "come over here and give your mama a hug."

Keshawn approached her timidly and embraced her. Rose was so frail that he was afraid he'd break her. She smelled like a mixture of cheap detergent and the sickness that tainted the hospital's air. None of this mattered to Keshawn. He was hugging one of the only people in the world who truly loved him.

"Mama," he said crying freely, "I've missed you so much."

"And I've missed you, baby," she said. "What took you so long to come and visit me?"

"I just came home, Mama."

"Oh, I forgot. How's school coming?"

"School, Mama?"

"Yeah, silly. You home from college ain't you?"

"College? Mama, I just got outta . . ." The look China shot him cut off his response. "Yeah, Mama," he whispered, "I'm home from school."

"You always was a good boy, Keshawn," she said, her eyes becoming misty. "I used to brag on you all the time. My little miracle baby. You know I love you, right?"

"Yes, Mama," he said wiping his eyes. "Nobody loves me like you and China."

"Oh, hush that talk. You know the whole family loves each other the same."

"If you say so, Mama."

"So how you been, Mama?" China asked changing the subject.

"Ah, can't complain," she said with a shrug. "My health ain't too good, but I got my children and I'm still here. What more could a woman ask for?"

"Trust in the Lord, and all things will work themselves out, Mama."

"Yeah, I like to think so, but we gotta face facts, China. Yo' mama ain't got a lot of time left."

"What you talkin' 'bout, Mama?" Keshawn asked with alarm.

"Well," she said sounding almost like her old self, "ya mama got some health issues. You already know about the sugar. Now there's this whole mess about some kind of growth on my ovaries. Shit, I knew about it for the last twenty-one years. Doctors told me about it when I was pregnant wit' y'all."

"Mama," China pleaded, "why you never told us?"

"Wasn't nothing to say. Doctors told me plain and simple, 'Miss, you gotta get rid of them babies so we can take out this thing that's eating up ya insides.' I pleaded wit' 'em, asked if there was another way. Seemed that there wasn't, but ain't no way I was giving my babies up.

"Needless to say, I kept you. I knew there were risks, but they didn't matter. I sacrificed my life because I felt you at least deserved a chance. You and Kiesha was mine."

Keshawn's body grew limp as he stared at his mother. It seemed like the drama in her life never ceased. How someone could make a sacrifice of that magnitude was beyond him. "Mama, I—"

"Hush," she cut him off. "Wasn't none of y'all choice. I loved y'all, all of y'all, equally. Ya know, in a strange way, I don't hate Charlie no more. The man was hurting. He acted out of rage, not contempt. It's okay though; the Lord deals with all accordingly.

"Keshawn, you, China, C.J., and Pearl is grown. Y'all don't need no more raising. I will walk into the arms of my Lord and Savior proud, and with my chin held high. I can finally be a mother to my daughter."

"Mama," Keshawn begged, "please don't talk like that. You ain't dying."

"Keshawn," she continued, "the Lord gives and He takes away. That's just the grand design of things. You can't change what is to be. Now, y'all don't be fussing over me. I get enough of that from Kiesha. Why she ain't come with y'all?"

"Kiesha?" Keshawn asked, puzzled.

"Yes, boy. You deaf or something? Where's your sister?"

"Mama, Kiesha is . . ." Keshawn couldn't go on. This woman, who had sacrificed so much for him, was mad as a hatter. Seeing Rose like this deeply hurt him, and being so helpless to do anything about it almost destroyed him.

Suddenly, a wave of dizziness overcame Keshawn, and he found himself unable to keep his balance.

As he leaned against the doorframe to keep himself from falling, a sense of panic and dread swept over his body. Keshawn knew that if he didn't leave soon, he would surely drop dead of stroke or bang his head against the wall out of sheer aggravation.

Keshawn kissed his mother's forehead and whispered to her, "Mama, I love you. Now and forever, no matter what happens, I love you."

The tears stung Keshawn's eyes when he tried to look at his mother. All that he had missed out on with his old bird could never be regained. God wasn't gonna turn back the hands of time for a poor street nigga. Fuck suffering, it was time to turn it up.

Keshawn reluctantly broke his mother's embrace and staggered to the elevators. He felt like his insides were filling with cement, organ by organ. Before long, the streets would feel his pain and his pockets would reap the benefits.

China watched her brother leave and shed tears of her own. She made the trip upstate at least once a month, but it was still hard for her to see Rose in this condition. She always told herself she'd be stronger the next time, but little did she or Keshawn know that this would be one of the last visits they'd have with their mother. A few months later, Rose would pass from ovarian cancer.

CHAPTER 12

For the rest of the day, K-Dawg found himself in a foul mood. Even on the ride back home, he hardly said two words to China. He was hurt and frustrated, but that didn't deter him from doing what he had to do. When he hit the block, he stepped to his business.

During the course of the day, Jus had mixed and cooked half of the work. He bagged the coke and bottled the crack to prepare it for distribution. The crackhead he used to test it caught a nosebleed when he sniffed it. They definitely had some good shit.

Jus wasn't trying to pitch the product, so he found two neighborhood cats to sling it for him. By the time he bumped into K-Dawg on the avenue, the block was jumping off the new shit.

Keshawn should've been proud of what he had accomplished, but he had other things on his mind.

"What up, dawg?" Jus asked giving his friend a pound.

"Nigga, that shit Manny hit us with is the bomb. These baseheads is going crazy. I got Pete on Park slinging stones and Miles selling ten-dollar bags of coke on Lenox. We got it sewed, kid."

"That's beautiful, my nigga," K-Dawg said halfheartedly.

"What's up with you, dawg?"

"Ain't shit, Jus. I just came back from seeing Moms."

"How she doing?"

"Not good, Jus. She got the big C."

"Ah, dawg. Tell me you wrong."

"Nah, Jus. Shit, I wish I was. She 'bout to leave us, son. The worst part of it is, because of this fucked-up system, I never really got a chance to know her."

"Nigga," Jus said putting his arm around K-Dawg, "I ain't never had a lot of love for my scandalous-ass mother, and I ain't even gonna front like I know what you're going through. But I do know you, my nigga, and you hurting. The only advice I can really give you is this: appreciate Mama Love while she's still with us. As far as the system that put you in this situation, stick it to them in the worst way. Get money. Ball long and ball hard, my nigga."

Jus's words were helpful as always. Sulking wasn't gonna do K-Dawg or his pockets a damned bit of good. For some reason, God decided to make his life as fucked up as possible. It seemed like every time he turned around, something bad was happening. If that's how He wanted to play it, then so be it. K-Dawg, in turn, would create hell on earth, all in the name of paper.

"Listen," Jus said, "I know this probably ain't the right time to bring this up, but I figured you might be interested. These bighead cats from the Bronx got this spot up the way where they doing numbers."

"What they moving?" K-Dawg asked greedily.

"A li'l bit of everything: weed, hash, acid. No powder, though."

"Let's hit 'em."

"That's the nigga I know. I already got a plan, too. I'm fucking this bitch who work up in the spot. Them niggaz stiffed her on some bread, so shorty got a personal grudge. She set a nigga out with the whole setup. All we gotta do is run up in there and tax that shit."

"You think the two of us can pull it off?"

"Probably, but I'm gonna bring my man Creeps in, just to be safe."

"I don't know that nigga, Jus."

"He's cool, dawg. I know him from Crown Heights. All that nigga do is rob and steal."

"A'ight, Jus. But if you bring this nigga in, he's your responsibility."

"Cool. So where you headed now?"

"I gotta go meet Demon."

"You still on that shit, huh?"

"He's the best at what he does, Jus. Demon is gonna play a big part in what we're doing. Shit, I got bodies, but I wouldn't say I'm a killer. How 'bout you ?"

"Nah, that ain't my thing."

"A'ight then. Let me go see what this nigga rappin' 'bout. See if you can set that sting up for tomorrow night, Jus."

"Damn, you don't waste no time, do you?"

"Can't afford to, Jus. We gotta be one step ahead of everybody else if we plan to come out on top. I plan on stepping to Vega for them keys within the next few days. I'll hit you when I get done with our boy, Demon."

"Be careful fucking wit' that nigga, K-Dawg."

"Shit, you better tell him the same about me."

K-Dawg hopped out of the cab on 112th Street at exactly noon. There were a few heads scattered here and there, but no Demon. K-Dawg was beginning to think Demon had stood him up, but all of his suspicions were erased when he felt a ghostly wind on his neck.

"What up, Demon?" he said without turning around.

"Well, well," Demon said stepping into view. "I see you made it, crack lord." Demon was dressed in black jeans and boots. He also sported a black sweatshirt underneath his three-quarters length leather jacket. "I hear y'all got it popping uptown."

"Something like that. Fuck you work for, CNN?"

"Nah, I just like to stay informed. Keeps my ass free of bullets."

"I feel you, D. So what's up, why you got a nigga out here?"

"It's like I told you," Demon said while heading north, "if we're going to work together, I have to know I can trust you."

"Demon," K-Dawg said catching up with the assassin, "I really ain't got time for all this shit. What's really good?"

"Shhh. From this point on, don't say shit; just watch."

Demon led K-Dawg into a small tenement building between Seventh and Lenox. The two eased their way up the broken-down stairs until they reached an apartment on the third floor. Demon looked at K-Dawg and smiled devilishly. Before K-Dawg had a chance to ask what was so funny, Demon kicked in the door.

The occupants of the house scattered like roaches. Demon pulled a sawed-off shotgun from beneath his jacket. His first victim was a young lady who tried to sprint down the hallway. Demon gave her no mercy; he cut loose with the shotgun and sent her flying into the living room.

Keshawn was shocked by the unexpected chaos that erupted around him. Demon was putting holes into whoever stepped into his line of fire. A little boy darted out from one of the bedrooms behind them. Demon spun on his heels and pointed his weapon. Seeing that it was only a child, he continued his hunt.

Maybe even demons have a conscience?

A man came bursting from a bathroom located directly to the left of where Demon and Keshawn were positioned. In his hand he held an eight-inch butcher knife. Keshawn sidestepped the man's awkward lunge and landed a rabbit punch to his gut. The man tried to right himself, but it was too late; Demon stepped around Keshawn and leveled the shotgun at his belly. With a jerk of the trigger, Demon sent him skidding down the hall—minus his stomach.

When they walked into the living room, there was a man in the corner pulling frantically at a window guard. Demon took his time and walked toward him slowly. When the man saw Demon coming, his eyes searched frantically for another escape. There was none.

Demon pulled a Glock from his waistband and shot the man in the leg. He dropped to the floor, howling in pain. Blood squirted from his knee, staining the peach carpet. Demon stood over the man and smiled.

"What up, Gino?" Demon said as if they were old friends. "I've been looking for you."

"Jesus Christ, don't do this," Gino pleaded. "Look, I got some money in the bedroom, and there's an ounce of white in the freezer. Take it all, man. Just, please, don't kill me."

"Maggot," Demon said kicking Gino in the face. "I don't want ya fucking money, you piece of shit. How dare you speak the Lord's name?"

"Come on, money," Gino whined through a now-busted lip. "I don't even know you, B. Fuck you want with me?"

"Yo' life, Gino. You play you pay. That was wrong the way you did Sol. He didn't like it, and neither did I, to tell you the truth. Hence, your predicament. The Reaper has come to call on you, my man."

"Tell Sol I'm sorry."

"Too late to apologize," Demon said shooting him in the shoulder. "You should've thought about that when you took Sol's money. Time to die, bitch."

K-Dawg looked on in horror as this grown-ass man cried like a little girl. Then the unexpected occurred. Demon turned to K-Dawg and handed him the Glock. "Finish him," he barked.

K-Dawg looked at the gun as if it was a viper. When he agreed to meet Demon, he had no idea of what plan was in store. Murder wasn't on his things-to-do list—at least not right away.

"Yo, kid," Keshawn started, "what's this shit all about?"

"Trust," Demon said flatly. "You wanted my trust, I'm giving you an opportunity to prove yourself. If I'm gonna fuck wit' you, you gotta prove ya worth. Seal the pact in blood."

K-Dawg stood motionless, looking at the gun. He had killed before, but only in self-defense. Now, his childhood friend was asking him to kill a man who had done nothing to him. At first he was going to say no. He really didn't need that kind of negative karma, but, he began think, what could it hurt? God had already turned His back on him. If he took this one little life, he would have one of the best hired killers on the East Coast indebted to him.

"Let me see that hammer," he said coldly. K-Dawg pointed the gun at Gino, who was still pleading for his life. *Fuck this nigga,* K-Dawg thought. He didn't know Gino and he didn't owe him shit. His life was just another stepping stone to the top.

"K," Demon said tapping him, "I'm gonna gather the money and work. Finish him and let's get the fuck outta here." Without waiting for an answer, Demon sprinted off.

K-Dawg stood over Gino, pointing the gun at his head. He was hesitant at first. He, unlike Demon, couldn't just kill on a whim; he needed to be motivated. That motivation came when he thought about his mother. Before he could stop himself, Gino's brains were on the windowsill.

K-Dawg stuffed the hot pistol into his jacket pocket and jogged to catch up with Demon in the foyer. The two men exchanged glares, but it was Demon who broke the tension. "Here," he said tossing him a paper bag. "I kept the money, you can have the work."

"That was some bullshit back there, Demon," K-Dawg snapped.

"Don't worry about it," Demon said with a smile. "You'll get used to it after a while."

"Well, I don't plan on making a habit of this shit."

Demon burst out laughing at K-Dawg's remark. "How could someone so ambitious be so naive? You better wake up, my man. This ain't the eighties; these niggaz out here balling; they play for keeps. You bound to get your hands dirty, K-Dawg. One of these niggaz is gonna try you sooner or later. Whatever it is that you got against killing, you better shake that shit off. If you ain't ready to play, get the fuck out the game."

Demon's words stung K-Dawg a little, but he acknowledged that they did make a lot of sense. Niggaz was sure as hell gonna come. It was very likely that K-Dawg would have to take a few lives before it was all said and done. But what did it really matter anymore? He knew he had a front seat waiting on him in hell and he was cool with that. One thing was for sure though: if he was gonna suffer in the afterlife, he was gonna live like a king in this one.

Demon peeked around to see if he had overlooked anything. After making sure that all was in order, he headed for the front door. Keshawn, not being a fool, followed his lead. As Keshawn passed a partially opened closet door, he almost cried out in terror. On the floor of the closet lay the boy who had passed them earlier. He was slumped in a corner, his neck slit from ear to ear. Demon looked back at K-Dawg and shrugged his shoulders.

Keshawn thought back to his earlier theory about demons and realized that he was off—way off.

CHAPTER 13

K-Dawg was back on the block by a quarter past one. For less than an hour of work, he had come off with more than an ounce of snow and a body. The latter was more of an inconvenience than a stripe. The number of atrocities that K-Dawg was involved in was increasing. Fuck a front seat; he was going to end up driving the bus to hell.

When K-Dawg got to the projects, China and Jus were sitting on a bench chilling. K-Dawg tried to pull himself together so they wouldn't suspect anything. He took a few cleansing breaths and approached the duo.

"Peoples," he said hugging them both, "what's the word?"

"The word is paper," Jus said pulling him in close. Jus slid a paper bag full of money under K-Dawg's jacket.

"Y'all trying to do y'all, huh?" China butted in. "That's what the fuck is up."

"Say, dawg," Jus began, "I need to holla at you 'bout something. Can you excuse us, China?"

"Nah," K-Dawg said with a wave of his hand. "You can talk in front of China. She part of the team."

"Straight like that, huh?" Jus asked in a slick tone.

"Straight like that," China said looking Jus dead in the eye.

"So," K-Dawg said, "what's good?"

"Well," Jus began, "them niggaz from Seventh Avenue came over here today. You know, Sticks and Stone."

"Rock and pebble?" K-Dawg asked, baffled. "Nigga, you talking in riddles. Try to help me understand."

"Nigga, quit being silly. Sticks and Stone, you know, them twins from Thirty-seventh? Well, anyhow, them niggaz rode through here a few times. They ain't stop, but they was looking all suspect and shit. Word is, niggaz been coming from as far as Grant to test this raw. Word is out, dawg. We on our way to the top."

"Shit," Keshawn said rubbing his chin, "that's a good thing. Slowly but surely, we gonna get it popping."

"Yeah, but them niggaz might cause a problem."

"Jus, trust in ya road dawg. All we gotta do is keep our heads until we go re-up. I got an O-Z and some change in my jacket. Hopefully, after we take care of that thing tomorrow night, we'll be ready to see Vega. As far as them niggaz, Cement and Brick, or whatever they names is, don't worry about 'em. I'm baking a cake for them niggaz, Jus."

"That's my man," Jus said enthusiastically, "always thinking ahead."

"Fo' sho," Keshawn said yawning. "What up wit' Sleep?"

"Oh, he came through and laid $4,200 on me for the re-up."

"That's my nigga. What about Pooh?"

"That nigga came through. We kicked it for a minute and put a few in the air."

"He say anything 'bout the plan?"

"Yeah, he seen how a nigga had it jumping. Nigga slid me five hundred to give you. I started to tell him to wipe his ass with it, but I figured every li'l bit helps."

"Hmm," K-Dawg said scratching his chin, "don't stress yaself 'bout that, kid. Even the best trained horse will eventually toss its rider. Mr. Kingpin will come around in due time. Right now, I'm gonna go on in with China. If you decide to turn it in, get one of them niggaz you got out there to oversee this shit."

"I got you, dawg," Jus said giving him a pound. "I'll probably have Pete do it."

"To be on the safe side, make sure the li'l nigga got a hammer within arm's reach."

"No doubt, my nigga. We on the grind twenty-four-seven."

"Now you smell me, Jus. The money don't sleep, so why the fuck should we?"

K-Dawg walked silently alongside China, lost in his own thoughts, when a flicker of motion caught his attention. He was so startled that he instinctively drew his gun. K-Dawg focused on the movement and saw that it was someone familiar to him. The figure motioned for K-Dawg to come over.

"China," K-Dawg said tapping his sister, "hold on a second. I gotta go talk to this cat." K-Dawg looked around and slid over to the figure. Flip stood huddled in the shadows, trying to light half a Newport.

"Damn," K-Dawg said, flicking his lighter until it produced a steady flame, "you 'bout scared the shit outta me, Flip."

"Sorry, man," Flip said lighting his cigarette with K-Dawg's lighter. "I know you ain't really trying to be seen with a nigga, so I'm keeping it on the low."

"So what you got for me, Flip?"

"Well, let me start off by saying that the work y'all got out here is the bomb. Y'all got baseheads coming from as far as the Bronx to get at that shit."

"I know that's right, Flip. So, what else is cracking?"

"Well, you probably already know, Sticks and Stone came sniffin' 'round here."

"Yeah, something like that."

"They was checking yo' setup pretty hard, ya know? If I was you, I'd watch them niggaz."

"Good looking on the heads up, Flip. But I wouldn't too much worry about them niggaz. Listen, kid, I got a job for you; two, actually."

"Man," Flip said rubbing his hands together greedily, "I'm always down, as long as the paper's right."

"I figured as much," K-Dawg said. "Look, the first thing I want you to do is go across the way and see Jus. He need a pitcher, so I recommend you."

"Cool, man. I don't mind knocking out a few packs. I could sure use the bread."

"A'ight. Now listen, Flip, you got two choices. You can get paid in cash or work. I'm telling you this because you're a good dude, plus the penalty for theft is quite severe."

"Keshawn, you know I would never try to put shit on you by stealing."

"Flip, all that shit sounds good, but you and I both know when that monkey start scratching, ain't no telling what you might be capable of."

"A'ight, man. What's the second thing you need done?"

"You know them Spanish kids from across town, the ones Pooh fuck with?"

"Yeah, yeah. That's Dino and them niggaz. What about them?"

"Tomorrow morning I want you to go cop from them," he said handing Flip a fifty dollar bill. "While you over there, spread the word. I want them to know that we the cats cutting their flow."

"Keshawn," Flip asked confusedly, "why would you wanna do something like that? Them niggaz is gonna be mad as hell."

"Shit," K-Dawg said with a smile, "I hope so. Tell them there's a team of young niggaz over this way getting paper. We caking off and it's Pooh who running it. Say he been mouthing off 'bout how he tired of not getting his worth, so he branching out. You do this right, Flip, and there's another fifty in it for you."

"Shit, a hundred cash? You ain't said shit but a word. But I gotta ask, why you wanna go and cross ya boy like that?"

"Check this fly shit, Flip. I respect your curiosity, but I ain't paying you to question me. If you can't do like I ask, I'll find someone else."

The thought of losing out on the money Keshawn offered changed Flip's tune. "Nah, I can do it. Ain't no need to be recruiting nobody else. Me and you got an arrangement. I'm on it, Keshawn."

"My nigga," K-Dawg said giving him a pound. "That's why I fucks wit' you, yo. Come check me tomorrow afternoon and let me know how it went."

"Fo' sho, Keshawn. Your boy Flip got ya back."

"A'ight, Flip. Just be on point. And remember, we never had this conversation, ya heard?" Without waiting for a response, K-Dawg walked back to his building to join a very curious China.

"What was that all about?" she asked holding the lobby door for her brother.

"Ain't nothing," he said with a smirk. "Just a li'l insurance."

"Boy, you always scheming." China watched her brother strut through the lobby like he owned it. All the crackheads and dopefiends made way upon seeing him. Whatever K-Dawg was scheming up, China was sure it would put them a step closer to their ultimate goal: paper.

Jus was so tired he could hardly keep his eyes open. He had been running the show all day and a good portion of the night.

He had given Flip a pack and Pete his instructions. Now he could rest his head. He would sleep good after a hard day's work.

Jus dragged his tired limbs across the courtyard to his building. He was so beat that he didn't even see the young cat peeping in the cut. In the game, one had to constantly be on point.

There was always someone out to knock a brotha off his high horse. Jus would have to learn this lesson the hard way.

CHAPTER 14

Pooh hit the block sometime around midmorning. He had pondered K-Dawg's offer but was still leery about the whole thing.

He made good money working for Dino. Sure, he wasn't the HNIC, but he had his own block with his own workers. Why risk that on some childhood dream? Pooh coasted through the block checking on his workers, making sure everything was running smoothly. All of his stash houses were supplied with product and all of his workers were where they needed to be. Pooh figured that since it was a nice day, he might as well do a little shopping.

He double-parked his candy red Civic to a halt in front of the sneaker store on 145th and Broadway. He hopped out, nodding to the niggaz he knew and brushing past the ones he didn't. When Pooh got inside the store he didn't have to shop around; he already knew what he wanted. He picked up a pair of white-on-white Air Force 1s and a lime green Nike sweat suit. The boy loved those loud-ass colors.

When Pooh got outside, he noticed two men sitting on the hood of his car. The first man he recognized as Flaco. Flaco served as Dino's personal assistant. He didn't know the other man.

"What up, Flaco?" Pooh asked extending his hand.

"Sup?" Flaco responded, not bothering to accept the extended hand. "Dino wanna see you, P."

"What he wanna see me for?" Pooh asked suspiciously. "All the spots got what they need and we'll probably be straight until later on tonight. Tell Dino I'll see him this evening."

"That wasn't a request," said the stranger, exposing the butt of the 9 mm that protruded from his waistband.

"Yo, what's going on, Flaco?" Pooh asked nervously. "Why you need a gun to come see me? We peeps."

"It's like I said," Flaco responded avoiding eye contact, "Dino wants to see you, P. Please, just get in the car."

"A'ight," Pooh said walking around to the driver's side.

"Nah," the stranger said placing his hand on Pooh's chest, "you ride shotgun. Flaco gonna drive."

Reluctantly, Pooh did as he was told. Flaco slid into the driver's seat while the stranger sat directly behind him. On the drive to the Bronx Pooh tried to make small talk, but neither man was receptive. It definitely wasn't looking good for him. He had seen things like this in plenty of movies—boss sends for the capo, the goons take him on a ride and bang, another dead capo—only this was real and not some mob flick.

The whole ride was spent in silence. The only sounds Pooh heard were his heart beating way too fast and his bowels shifting inside his gut. He hoped to God he wouldn't shit on himself. Pooh racked his brain trying to figure out what he did, but he kept coming up blank. His best bet was to bide his time and see if he could settle this little misunderstanding with Dino. He had worked for his sister's husband for many years, so he knew he would be given a fair shake—he hoped.

The car screeched to a halt in front of a red brick house on Pauldon Avenue. Flaco got out of the car and motioned for the two men to follow him up the stone steps. On the outside, it looked like a regular ol' middle-class home. But on the inside, it looked like a gorilla camp. There were men moving about the modest house, all armed with submachine guns and automatic weapons. Pooh had been inside Dino's headquarters many times, so he didn't need direction. Still, Flaco and the stranger felt he did, and they pushed him roughly in the direction of Dino's office. Inside the office, two men stood guard behind the door. Both of them were armed with AR-15s. Dino sat behind his cast iron desk, staring malevolently at Pooh.

"Bring that mafucka over here," Dino ordered. Dino was a thin Dominican cat. His skin was almost as dark as K-Dawg's, and he wore his hair in a conk. Physically, he didn't appear to be very powerful, but his connections made him seem damned near omnipotent.

"Dino," Pooh pleaded, "what's this shit all about?"

"Oh," Dino said standing up, "now you wanna play stupid? Listen, Pooh, I'm only gonna ask you one time, so you better play it straight. Why you cross me?"

"Cross you?" Pooh asked, obviously puzzled. "Man, that's bullshit. We family; why would I cross you?"

"Oh, so you deny it?"

"Not only do I deny it, I'm offended by the accusation."

"Okay, Pooh, so tell me then, who's K-Dawg?"

At the mention of his friend's name, Pooh turned white as a ghost. Could Keshawn somehow have something to do with this? *Impossible.* K-Dawg and his crew were getting a little paper, but not enough to irk Dino. Besides, he and K-Dawg went way back. He wouldn't have crossed him, would he?

"Do you know him or not?" Dino barked.

"Yeah," Pooh said, "I know him."

Bam! Someone clocked Pooh in the back of the head with what felt like a gun. Pooh staggered a bit, but he managed to stay on his feet. He almost panicked when he felt the warm blood trickle down the back of his head.

"Dino," he pleaded, "just calm down and tell me what this is all about."

"Nigga," Dino said approaching him, "you know what the fuck this is about." Bam! Dino punched Pooh square in the mouth. "How the fuck you gonna side with them fucking monkeys and think I wouldn't know?"

Whack! Another gun butt to the head sent Pooh spinning. If it wasn't for the desk crashing into his ribs, Pooh would've hit the ground.

"Hold on, Dino," Pooh begged. "Just because I know these cats, I'm going against the grain? Think for a minute, Dino. Why would I—"

Bam! Another punch cut off his response. "Pooh," Dino said pulling him by the collar to his feet, "I made you what you are. I even gave you your own slice of heaven, but I guess that wasn't enough." Bam! Another punch. "The streets are talking, Pooh, and I always got my ear to the ground. You using my money to finance your own thing." Bam! "You ungrateful, half-breed piece of shit. I should kill you."

"Dino, wait," Pooh said inching his hand toward the .25 he kept in his boot. "I'm sure we can talk about this." Just before Pooh reached his weapon, the stranger caught his wrist and removed the gun.

"Can't have you getting all crazy on us, now can we?" the stranger said with a smirk.

"Word, Pooh?" Dino asked getting angrier. "You keep screaming how you're innocent and all, yet you try to draw iron on me?" Bam! "I am so disappointed in you, youngster. Flaco, y'all take this piece of shit somewhere and do what y'all do."

Flaco was hesitant at first. He and Pooh were friends. They came up together, ever since they were both lookouts. The look Dino gave Flaco put some pep in his step, though. Pooh was his friend, but Dino was his boss.

***

K-Dawg leaned against the door of the 2 train reading a hip-hop magazine. He hated using public transportation, but being that he didn't have a ride he had to deal with it. Besides, taking a cab to 346 Broadway would cost him too damned much. K-Dawg hopped off the train on Fourteenth Street and caught the 1 local to Franklin. From there, it was just a few short blocks to his destination.

K-Dawg entered the office building and eyed the plaque on the wall. It read: NEW YORK CITY DEPARTMENT OF PROBATION. He shook off the cold chill that assaulted him.

Anything that had to do with jail or the law made him feel uneasy. Even though K-Dawg had done his whole bid and then some, he still had to see a probation officer. It was one of the conditions of his release that he report to the officer until he completed an anger management course. He thought it was stupid, but he wanted to get out of prison so badly that he agreed to it. *Well, might as well go see the old broad and get it over with.*

The elevator doors slid open on the ninth floor, giving way to two metal detectors and a large waiting room. K-Dawg went through the usual process of emptying his pockets and proceeded to the sign-in window. A skinny Puerto Rican girl was sitting inside the plastic booth, clicking her gum. "Name?" she asked with much attitude.

"Uh, um, Keshawn . . . Wilson," he stammered.

There was a long pause, and the gum clicker just stared at him. "Well," she asked in that same rude-ass tone, "who you here for?"

"Oh," he replied, sounding slightly irritated, "my bad, miss. I'm here to see PO Green. She here?"

"Have a seat," she instructed, blowing a small bubble and popping it. "I'll let her know you're here."

K-Dawg shook his head and took a seat in one of the hard plastic chairs. He looked around at the various individuals scattered around the waiting area. There were mostly black and Hispanic people in the room, but there were a few whites here and there—very few.

One girl sat behind K-Dawg. She had a small child running around climbing on shit, another infant in the stroller, and was about six months pregnant. K-Dawg could tell that she was young, but the bags under her eyes and her sallow complexion revealed that she had lived a hard life. Shit like this was common among the youth, so it didn't really shake K-Dawg.

There were two skinny kids sitting near the bathrooms. The black one was trying his best to mean-mug everybody who stepped off the elevator, while the Puerto Rican kid just looked nervous. K-Dawg and the brother made eye contact, but the boy turned away. The kids were both dressed in baggy jeans and Timbs. They were trying to look thuggish, but to a hardened dog like him, they smelled like meat.

"Wilson?"

K-Dawg turned to see who was calling his name.

A tender light-skinned thang stood in the center of the room holding a clipboard. She looked so good that K-Dawg almost shouted. Shorty was maybe five feet five inches, but the Donna Karan riding boots made her a couple of inches taller. Her smooth skin was the color of sunset against the ocean. Her auburn box-braids were partially pinned up, but the loose ones swept her shoulders.

"Wilson?" she called again, mouthing the words with her pretty pink lips.

"Ah, ah, that's me," he managed to blurt out.

"This way, please," light-skin said strolling down the hall.

K-Dawg followed her and let his eyes roam her body. The blue Guess jeans she wore hugged her ghetto ass.

They got some fine-ass secretaries down here, he thought. When he got done with his PO, he intended to holla at her.

Light-skin led him through two glass doors that required a card to gain entrance. She steered K-Dawg into a tiny cubicle and instructed him to have a seat. He was wondering where his PO was, because there was nobody in the cube. What fucked him up was when light-skin took the seat opposite him.

"How you doing, Keshawn?" she asked, extending a manicured hand. "My name is Melissa Green, and I'll be supervising your case."

K-Dawg shook her hand and was a little surprised at how strong her grip was. Miss Green was thick, but she was still petite.

"Nice to meet you, Miss Green," K-Dawg said, showing off his even, white teeth. When he was sure he had her attention, he made his green eyes become dreamy and seductive.

"Call me Melissa," she said returning his smile and revealing equally white teeth. "I don't really do the last name thing. It makes me feel old. Save that for one of them other POs."

"Okay, Melissa."

"So," she said opening up his folder, "I understand you just got out of prison?"

"Yeah."

"You wanna tell me a little bit about that?"

"Well," he said sitting up straight, "as you already know, I went to jail for killing my pops. When I was little, he used to kick the sh . . . sorry, I mean, abuse me. Me and my sis were from another cat, and pops didn't really dig it. Long story short, he killed my twin, and I killed him."

"I see," she said a little shocked at his bluntness. "I'm a little confused, though. It says you could've gotten out in two, but you did five and a half."

"You see, Melissa, people who have never been to prison will never understand how it is in there. It's supposed to reform you, but that's a crock if you ask me. That place does something to you, rots you on the inside. It's hell for an adult, so imagine how it is for a fifteen- or sixteen-year-old, locked in there with grown-ass niggaz, rapists, murderers, and thieves. I did what I had to do to preserve my life and a portion of my dignity."

"That's deep, Keshawn."

"Tell me about it. Melissa, when you in a pit of savage dogs, you gotta be the hungriest."

"Well," she said trying to lighten the mood, "I know you gonna do the right thing now that you're home."

"Oh, please believe it. I ain't built for another bid, Melissa. I'm keeping my nose clean."

"I'm sure you will, Keshawn. All I ask is that you stay out of trouble and see me when you're supposed to. Here you go," she said, holding a white card between her orange and gold nails. "That's my card. Feel free to call me if the need arises. It was nice to meet you, Keshawn," she said standing.

"Is this for business or pleasure?" he asked playfully.

"Don't get fresh, little boy," she quipped, as they strolled back to the double doors.

"Hey, you only as old as you feel," he said, intentionally brushing against her as he went through the doors.

"Please," she said rolling her eyes, "I'm old enough to have pushed you out. How old do you think I am?"

"I don't know, 'bout. . . twenty-eight, maybe twenty-nine?"

"Thanks for the compliment, boo, but I'm thirty-four. See you next week, Keshawn."

Melissa closed the glass doors right on him and went back to her cube. K-Dawg stood there, dumbfounded, as he watched her thick legs carry her back to her cubicle.

Most people believed that female POs were mediocre or unattractive—not Melissa Green.

Shorty was like that, and K-Dawg was digging her. He believed that he was entitled to anything he wanted. At that moment, he wanted Melissa.

CHAPTER 15

Sleepy relaxed on his sofa, flicking the channel on his forty-two-inch television. A butterscotch sofa and loveseat took up the majority of the living room. On the right wall, there was a wooden bookshelf, cluttered with various books on different topics. He was big on reading. He flexed his pedicured toes on the snow white carpet. His little modern-day, two-bedroom was decked out. For a small-time pimp, he was doing okay.

The lock turning in the door told him that Monnie was home from work. Monnie came slinking into the living room like a jungle cat. The white leather body suit she wore clung to her hourglass figure. Her chocolate-colored face still held its schoolgirl innocence, but her eyes were those of a seasoned bitch. Monnie was Sleepy's bottom bitch, and she was slim in the waist and pretty in the face.

"Hey, baby," she said flopping down next to him. "A bitch is dead tired." Monnie laid her head on Sleepy's lap, and he ran his fingers through her short, bleached blond hair.

"How we looking?" he asked, lighting the blunt that hung between his lips.

Monnie dipped into her bra and pulled out a wad of bills. "Here you go, boo," she said tossing the bills into his lap. "It's only like $560, but I only worked a few hours."

"Monnie," he said counting the trap, "what's up with this few-hour shit? This ain't no nine to five, and paper don't take lunch."

"Come on, Sleepy. You know I was hit for a babysitter last night. Peaches ain't get done at the club 'til like twelve."

"So then you come with this short trap, ma? Monnie, I remember yo' trap game used to always be tight. You was my star, baby. This here," he said holding up the money, "I don't understand this new shit here."

"Daddy," she whined, throwing her arms around him, "stall your li'l freak bitch out. You know I won't bring lame money in no mo'."

Monnie tried to sit up and kiss Sleepy. He dodged and held her at arm's length. "Hold on, Monnie. How you gonna come in here after a long night of doing you and try to kiss me on the mouth? You know you ain't right."

"Oh, I'm tripping, ain't I?" she said embarrassed.

"It ain't nothing, ma. Just go freshen up. I'll get wit' ya." Sleepy helped her to her feet and slapped her on the ass. "Go on and get fresh fo' me, Mo."

Monnie giggled like a schoolgirl and skipped down the hall.

As he watched her depart, he couldn't help but admire how she was put together. Her breasts were full and perky, drawing just a snip of attention away from her apple-shaped ass. Long story short, Monnie was eighteen, mean, and on Sleepy's team.

Sleepy counted the trap again, but the figures still didn't change. This shit wasn't going to do. There were only two girls in his employment, and he was most dependent on Monnie. She was his best earner. The other girl, Patrice, she did okay, but she couldn't get money like Monnie. Patrice was a short chick with a fat ass, but she didn't have Monnie's heart or common sense. There were only two reasons Sleepy even dealt with her like that. Number one: he didn't wanna be labeled a one-whore nigga. It was bad enough that he only had two bitches on the street, but a one-whore nigga was sure to starve. Number two: Patrice had her own ride, which Sleepy was free to use whenever he wanted.

Sleepy's cell phone shook violently in his bathrobe. He set his blunt clip in the ashtray and flipped open the cellular. "Yeah," he said into the phone. "What up, my nigga? Huh? Slow down, kid, you not making any sense. They did what? Oh, hell nah, niggaz violated. I'm 'bout to come get you, man. Where you at? Okay, I'll be there in . . . Say what? Yeah, I got some sweats. Fuck you need with that? What you mean you don't wanna say on the phone? A'ight, man. I'll be to you in like ten minutes." Sleepy snapped his phone shut and dressed quickly. From the tone of his friend's voice, he could tell something wasn't right.

"Monnie!" he yelled, grabbing the car keys. "I'll be back in a few. Hold down the fort for me, girl. If Patrice calls, tell her to come on in." Without waiting to see if Monnie heard him, Sleepy was out the door and on his way to see what kind of trouble his friend had gotten himself into.

K-Dawg strolled casually down 135th Street puffing on a Newport. Going to see a PO wasn't as bad as he had thought. Melissa seemed like a down-to-earth chick. All K-Dawg knew was if he kept his nose clean for thirty days he'd be in the clear. Besides, he could tell Melissa was feeling him, so she wouldn't be too quick to violate him.

K-Dawg passed through the projects and surveyed his kingdom. Pete was still on the bench doing him and things were still clicking. He noticed Flip standing over by 2120 and decided to see how his little plan was going. Flip saw K-Dawg before K-Dawg saw him. He faded into the lobby and waited for the drug lord to approach.

"What da deal, Flip?" K-Dawg said giving him a pound.

"Everything cool, Keshawn," Flip responded.

"Did you take care of that thing for me, yo?"

"Bright and early, kid."

"So what happened?"

"Well, I didn't stick around, so I can only tell you what I heard."

"Well, spit it out, nigga."

"Well," Flip said lighting a cigarette, "the way the streets tell it, Dino sent for ya man this morning. It doesn't take a genius to figure out why he sent for the kid. In the streets, news travels fast. So anyhow, Pooh left for his meeting in one piece. A few hours later, ya man got tossed from a moving car, butt-ass naked."

"Shit." K-Dawg gasped. "Did they kill him?"

"I don't know for sure. I do know they fucked him up. I heard the boy's face looked like a piece of rotten fruit."

"Wow, I didn't intend for him to get murdered. What happened to the body?"

"Hell if I know. By the time I got there, it was gone."

"I got to look into that. Thanks," he said handing Flip a fifty. "Keep ya ear to the streets."

"You know I will," he said stuffing the fifty in his pocket like K-Dawg might change his mind. "Flip got ya back."

"I respect that, Flip. So how my setup looking?"

"I gotta tell ya, youngster, you niggaz is doing the damn thang. It got a li'l slow last night, but things picked up 'round eight-thirty or so."

"That's what's up."

"But . . . Nah, ain't my place to say."

"What, Flip?"

"Ain't my business. I ain't got no say over yo' show."

"Flip, I fuck wit' you 'cause you know these streets better than anyone I know. If something is out of order, put a nigga on."

"A'ight then. Ya boy, Jus."

"What about him?"

"Well, I don't know how to put this without offending anyone."

"Nigga, you'll offend me more by playing guessing games," K-Dawg said, sounding a little irritated.

"A'ight," Flip said, cringing slightly, "I might as well just put it out there. Ya boy, Jus, he know the streets, but he really don't know the game. Don't get it fucked up, Keshawn. Jus is an excellent thief, but he ain't a very good drug dealer."

"What you talkin' 'bout, Flip?"

"He ain't on point, man. Them niggaz from up the way been passing through here a li'l too often. I peeped 'em, but ya boy ain't seem to notice. I tried to bring it to his attention, but the nigga just brushed me off."

"You think they scheming?"

"Without a doubt. Them niggaz is up to something, but I just don't know what."

"A'ight. I'm gonna be on point, Flip. Good looking."

"That's what I'm here for, man."

K-Dawg gave Flip a pound and set out in search for Jus. *So, Sticks and Stone scheming, huh?* he thought. He didn't really know much about the twins, but he did know they were up-and-coming players. Not only that, but their guns rang off. Those two would need some watching. He made a mental note to talk to Demon about it.

Jus was coming out of his building as K-Dawg approached. He wore a pair of gray sweatpants and a black leather jacket. He was strolling like he didn't have a care in the world. Jus was his man, but in order to get things popping, there couldn't be any weak links.

"Peace, god," Jus said extending his hand.

"What up, my nigga," K-Dawg said hugging him. "How we looking, kid?"

"It's beautiful. We almost out of product and got about thirty thousand in the stash."

"That's what's up, Jus."

"Oh, while I'm thinking 'bout it, remember that thing we talked about?"

"What, you mean with the Jamaicans?"

"Yeah, yeah. We can do it as soon as you ready."

"Well, it'll be dark soon. Fuck, let's step to our business."

"You don't waste no time, nigga."

"Fuck, nah. You got them hammers?"

"I already put in the order. I'm gonna take you to see my man, Fat Tone. He got all the latest shit, dawg."

The Harlem cab bounced down Seventh Avenue, hitting every pothole along the way. Fat Tone was this big head nigga from 118th who Jus did business with. He hustled a li'l bit of everything. He provided Jus with certain items that he was unable to get on his own, and Jus provided him with the same service. It was a "one hand washes the other" type of thing.

The building Tone lived in looked like it was about to fall over. It was one of those beat-up tenements that looked like it had been long abandoned. When K-Dawg and Jus entered the building, they were overcome by the stench. It reeked of animals. Before the two climbed the first flight of stairs, a young kid appeared holding a 9 mm.

"What up, Teddy?" Jus called out.

"Well, if it ain't the prince of thieves," Teddy said sarcastically. "What up wit' you, Hudson Hawk?"

"Came to see the fat man. He upstairs?"

"Nah, Tone in the back."

"Why don't you go get him for us?"

"Fuck I look like, Running Ray? Take yo' ass outside."

"Come on, Teddy. Why we always gotta play this game?"

"Listen, Jus, you know I got love for you, nigga, but I'm Tone's doorman, not his personal assistant. Don't be scurred, nigga. Go on out."

"I hear that hot shit," Jus said heading for the rear of the building. It was bad enough coming to see Tone in his raggedy-ass building, but it was worse in his yard.

"Yo," K-Dawg said tapping Jus's arm, "what's that shit all about? Why you acting all funny 'bout going into homeboy yard?"

"You'll see," Jus said shaking his head.

K-Dawg followed Jus down the skinny corridor that led to the backyard. Jus banged twice on the gate and then pushed it open. When K-Dawg stepped into the yard, he saw why Jus didn't wanna come back there. The shit was like something out of Animal Planet.

The grass was out of control; it grew wild and was full of weeds. There were iron poles sticking up from the ground in random areas with dogs attached to them. Fat Tone had hounds in all shapes, sizes, and colors, and they were all pits. Some were on chains, while others were in small cages. If the ASPCA were to run up in the spot, Tone was facing at least $1 million in fines.

"Tone!" Jus called out. "You back here, dawg?"

A figure stepped out from the shadows. Tone was a large man in every sense of the word. He was easily six feet four inches and weighed at least 300 pounds. His skin was the color of a burnt paper bag, making his pink lips seem out of place on his grill. Beads of sweat formed on his large, bald head, as he came closer to see who was calling.

"Jus," he said flashing a rotten-toothed grin, "come on out, nigga."

"I'm cool," Jus said raising his hands in mock surrender. "I'll wait on you right here."

"A'ight," Tone said wiping his hands on his dingy overalls. The big man ambled across the yard with three tiny puppies nipping at his ankles.

"What up, kid?" Tone asked giving Jus his fist.

"Ain't nothing," Jus said returning the fist. "This my man, K-Dawg."

"Yeah, yeah," Tone said giving K-Dawg his fist. "I was on the Island when you came through a few years back. Heard you made quite a name for yaself upstate." It was more of a statement than a question.

"Well," K-Dawg said, "you know how it is: a nigga got to do what a nigga got to do."

"I feel you, money."

One of the puppies Tone had with him took a liking to K-Dawg. It was a female that looked like she was the runt of the litter. She was a little brindle bitch that was no bigger than K-Dawg's hand. He bent down to pet the pup and fell in love with her.

"How old?" K-Dawg asked, scratching behind her ear.

"This bitch here," he said, picking her up so he could get a better look, "she 'bout, three and a half months. Her pops is a grand champion and her moms is a two-time winner."

"Tone is a breeder," Jus cut in.

"Thee breeder," Tone corrected him. "Ain't a nigga in New York got a kennel deep as mine. I deal in the best blood, kid."

"How much ya dogs be going for?" K-Dawg asked.

"I can sell a pup from like a thousand dollars to twenty-five hundred. It depends on the breeding and the attitude. Most of my hounds is top of the line, but I don't know about this ho."

"What's wrong wit' her?"

"First off," Tone said holding her up, "the bitch is way too small. Her littermates knock her around so much I got to feed her separate. It's gonna be hell getting rid of her. She just don't strike me as a game dog. Out of the ten pups in her litter, this dumb bitch is the only one that ain't figured out how to lock yet."

"How much you want for her?"

"You wanna buy this bitch?"

"Sure do."

"A'ight. Since you Jus man, I'll set her out for . . . eight hundred."

"Damn," K-Dawg said frowning, "that's a li'l steep for a bitch you're gonna have trouble getting rid of."

"I said it'd be hard, not impossible."

"Hold on, kid," Jus cut in. "You really want this hound, K-Dawg?"

"Yeah," he said taking her from Tone, "I'm feeling this bitch."

"Say no more, K-Dawg. Tone, I got an idea. You still owe me a thousand for that jewelry I lifted for wifey. Let my man have the dog, plus knock a buck off what I owe you for the shit we came to get and we even. Cool?"

Tone scratched his bald head for a moment. He knew he'd probably end up stuck with the sickly li'l bitch in the long run if he didn't sell her to them. Besides that, Jus came through for him when he'd forgotten his wife's birthday. He could live with the offer.

"A'ight," he said rubbing his belly, "the bitch is yours. I'll get the paperwork to you in a few days. Ya killing me here, kid," he lied, "but since you a friend of a friend, I'll take the loss."

The puppy let out a weak bark, as if she knew she had a new owner. K-Dawg smiled down at his new purchase as he stuffed her inside his jacket. *Fuck what this fat mafucka think. I know you gonna be a thorough bitch,* he thought.

"Now that we got that shit out the way," Tone said, "let me get these hammers for y'all, so you thieving mafuckas can get the fuck from 'round here."

The two men followed Tone up two flights of stairs to a corner apartment. The higher floors didn't stink as bad as the lower ones, but the stench was still present. Tone opened the door for the duo, and they found themselves in a whole new world.

It was a small studio apartment with hardwood floors and black curtains covering every window. The only furniture in the entire apartment was a small wooden chair and a desk. For the most part, it was an average studio. The thing that set it apart from others was the fact that it was lined wall to wall with guns. There were file cabinets on the walls that housed assault rifles. Timberland boxes were stacked neatly in two corners of the apartment. These held handguns of every caliber.

"Damn," K-Dawg exhaled, "you fuckin' plan on going to war?"

"Never know," Tone said closing the door. "I got just what you niggaz need."

Tone pulled a Timberland box from the top of the pile and produced two large handguns. He handed Jus the P89 and tossed K-Dawg the Desert Eagle. The touch of cold steel against K-Dawg's hand brought back memories of the body he caught the night before. The feeling was different this time, though. Instead of feeling unsure and nervous, K-Dawg felt the rush of power that only a new gun could bring.

"This is what's up," K-Dawg said.

"Oh, you ain't know?" Tone asked, getting a little cocky. "I deal in the best dogs and the best guns."

"I can dig it," Jus said tucking his P89 inside his waistband. "I got that paper for you, Tone."

"As always, my man. Look, before you skate off, where could a nigga get some good powder? It ain't for me, 'cause I don't use, but I'm having a li'l thang this weekend."

"I don't know," Jus started. "Let me see what—"

"How much you need?" K-Dawg cut in.

"About an ounce or two,"

"You got that, big man. Me or Jus will get that to you in a day or so."

"I like this kid," Tone said giving K-Dawg a pound. "You got some good peoples here, Jus."

"I be knowing," Jus said grinning.

"Peep this," Tone said opening the door, "take what you owe me off the top of them zones and just bring a nigga the balance with the work."

"Damn," Jus said leading the way out, "you ain't never give a nigga a play like this here before. What the deal?"

"Hey," Tone began, "no disrespect to you, Jus. You my nigga and I got a lot of love for you, but I'm feeling ya man. Something about him reminds me of my li'l brother, Mel, God rest his soul. As long as y'all niggaz come through on y'all end, we straight. Get at me, fellas."

Jus and K-Dawg left Tone with two guns and a puppy. He even threw in a silencer with the pistols. Jus felt a twinge of jealousy toward his friend. In his heart he knew he was wrong, but he had been dealing with Tone for a minute and the fat man had never shown him that much love as far as business was concerned.

K-Dawg just had that type of aura about him that made people like him, something Jus was never much good at. Jus envied him for that.

CHAPTER 16

The last few kisses of the sun's rays were setting over the streets of Harlem, giving way to the cold embrace of the moon. The working-class citizens were settling down for their dinners, while the so-called undesirables were just beginning to stir. For the next few hours, the streets, once again, would belong to the night.

K-Dawg sauntered across the project grounds with his puppy and his gun tucked snugly inside his jacket. He intended to convince Nikki to hold the dog down for him before rejoining Jus so they could pull off their lick. C.J., heading his way from the opposite direction, altered his plan a bit.

"Hey, Keshawn," C.J. said, smiling nervously.

"What up, Charlie?" K-Dawg asked, stone-faced.

"Not much, man," C.J. said sniffling. "You know how it is."

"Um, hmm."

"Listen, Keshawn, about the other day . . . I'm sorry, man."

"Don't worry about it, C.J. It wasn't nothing."

"Nah, man. It might not have been nothing to you," he said sniffling again, "but it was something to me. I ain't have no right coming at you like that."

"Like I said, C.J., don't worry about it."

"We been worried about you, Keshawn. Me and Pearl, ya know? You hardly been by the house since, well, you know."

"I'm good, kid. I see China like every day."

"Yeah, she told us, but you got more than one sister, K."

"I can dig it. I'm gonna swing by and holla at Pearl tonight."

"That'd be nice, man." C.J. hesitated for a while before continuing. "Keshawn, what went down between us, that shit wasn't 'bout nothing."

"I told you," K-Dawg said, while shifting the weight of the package inside his jacket, "I ain't stressing that."

"I know you ain't, kid, but it was bothering me. Regardless of what you might think, you my li'l brother and I love you. Our house is still your house, man. Just because we had a fight don't mean you ain't welcome there. You can come back whenever you're ready."

K-Dawg looked at C.J. like he had lost his mind. "Is that what y'all thought?" he asked grinning. "Man, it ain't even like that. I been out here on one. I'm trying to get myself situated. I just been staying wit' Jus so I don't crowd y'all, Don't worry yaselves over me, C.J. I should have me a crib of my own before long."

"So, you out here hustling?"

"Charlie, just because I spent my adolescent life locked up over some dumb shit doesn't mean I'm a complete fool. Picture me going hand to hand for another mafucka. Man, I'm out here building a foundation."

"Keshawn, these streets ain't nothing nice. Just look at—"

"Save that," K-Dawg cut him off. "I'm a big boy now and I can handle myself."

"Keshawn, I'm just trying to put you on."

"C.J., the difference between me and you is, while you think you know what I'm out here doing, I know what you're out here doing. I don't judge you, so show me the same respect."

"Oh, nah, Keshawn. I ain't trying to judge you. It's just . . . sometimes I forget that you grown. You been out of the loop for a while, so that's just my big brother instinct, telling me to watch over you."

"I appreciate that, C.J. But even the most sheltered flower must eventually grow. I'll catch up with you, big bro."

K-Dawg started to walk off, but C.J. caught up with him. He grabbed K-Dawg and hugged him. "Welcome home, bro. Welcome home."

After an awkward moment, C.J. released him and got on his way. K-Dawg watched his brother from a distance as he greeted Flip and walked to the avenue. *Guess it's about time to get right.* It was amazing to K-Dawg how a nigga who was so smart could be so fucking stupid at the same time. C.J. didn't know it yet, but that monkey that was slowly crawling up his back would lead him on a road to nowhere.

Convincing Nikki to let the dog stay wasn't as hard as he thought it would be. At first she wasn't trying to hear about a dog being up in her crib, but he changed her mind with three words: "Be my girl." Needless to say, Nikki was ecstatic. He gave her a quick nut and dazzled her with ice cream dreams and tales of how they would always be together. As expected, she ate the story up and demanded that he move in with her. At long last, Nikki would be with her childhood sweetheart. Now all she had to do was figure out how to get rid of Moose, her part-time man and current fuck buddy.

After a quick shower, K-Dawg, dressed in his black army suit, kissed Nikki good-bye and was on his way to meet Jus. So far, his plan was going well. He had a small operation set up and was assembling a small crew. Now all he had to do was get the rest of the brick money and get with Vega. In another few days he'd be straight.

Jus answered the door wearing a camouflage fatigue suit, black hoodie, and a black skully. He ushered K-Dawg into the living room where everything they would possibly need was laid out and ready. In the middle of the floor were two rolls of duct tape, a small tube of Vaseline, and several large shopping bags, all sporting different store logos.

"What up, kid?" Jus asked giving him a pound.

"Trying to eat, nigga. You know what time it is."

"Oh," Jus snapped his fingers, "guess who I just got off the phone with?"

"Who?"

"Ya man, Sleep."

"What's up wit' him?"

"He just came from taking Pooh to the hospital."

"Hospital?" K-Dawg said faking shock. "What happened?"

"Dino spazzed on the kid. Him and his peoples gave Pooh a serious whippin' and left him butt-ass naked on 125th."

"Yo, that's fucked up, kid. Them niggaz violated."

"K-Dawg, since before you came home, I been telling Pooh 'bout them cats. The boy's hardheaded. Now look what it got him."

"Pooh a'ight?"

"Yeah. A few cracked ribs and some broken pride, but he'll live. But check it, we can cry over Pooh later. Right now, let's focus on our mission," Jus said pointing at the equipment.

"I see you got it all planned out," K-Dawg said looking over the items.

"You thought I wouldn't?" Jus said while tucking the P89 in his waistband. "This is my thang, here, dawg. Robbing niggaz is how I eat."

"Okay, Justice the Great. What's the plan?"

"It's like this, kid. I just spoke to the bitch and everything is still everything. We gonna go over there and act like we spending long dough. When they open the door, we rush 'em. Straight like that."

"Straight like that, huh? Jus, you making this shit sound too easy."

"This is a cakewalk, baby. Around this time, the flow is slow, so it's only gonna be that bitch and like two other dudes. We got the drop, so they ain't gonna have time to do shit."

"Yeah, a'ight. Let me get that silencer, anyway."

"Man, ain't you heard what I said? We ain't even gonna need these pistols. They just for show. Them fake-ass Rastas ain't gonna flex."

"So you say," K-Dawg said while screwing the silencer onto his Desert Eagle. "I like to be prepared just the same. Let's do this shit."

Jus and K-Dawg moved silently as the night up 124th and Morningside toward their target in Grant projects. Projects were always good to pull heists in, because there were so many different avenues of escape. They slipped silently into 430 and jogged up the seven flights of stairs. Jus found the apartment he was looking for and went to work.

The first thing he did was squeeze some Vaseline from a tube onto the tip of his gloved finger and spread it over the peephole. He made sure to use an amount that would only distort their images. If he used too much, the occupants wouldn't be able to see and might get leery. After checking to make sure K-Dawg was ready, Jus knocked on the door.

"Who that?" the doorman barked with a slight accent.

"It's Smitty," Jus responded.

"Smitty who?"

"Quit playing, man. Open the door."

"Wha' ya wan'?"

"Same damn thang as everybody else who come up this mafucka. Look, nigga, I came to spend some paper so I can get my re-up on. Now if you gonna stay here playing wit' the door all night, fuck it. My money will spend elsewhere. Tell Nester that I came by."

At the mention of his partner's name, Doorman relaxed a little. They claimed they knew Nester, so maybe they were being straight up. He thought about going in the back to ask Nester about this Smitty, but he was in the back room with a bitch; plus, they claimed they were spending. What if it was true and he let a big sale get away? Nester wouldn't like that. Against his better judgment, Doorman started undoing the locks on the door. If the cats tried anything funny, the shotgun he kept by the door would give them a real punch line. He didn't realize the error of his ways until the last lock was undone and the metal door slammed into his face. The force of the fire door broke Doorman's nose and sent a stream of blood flowing down his shirt. He fell to the ground, clutching his nose and forgetting all about his shotgun. When he did clear his focus enough to reach for it, Jus was standing over him with his P89 drawn.

"Reach," Jus whispered, "and I'm busting you."

"Hol' on," Doorman started, "ya no wan—"

"Let's try it this way," K-Dawg said stuffing the Desert Eagle in his mouth. "Shut the fuck up."

Doorman's eyes got wide as saucers at the sight of the cannon. He started to say something, but the silencer was pressed against his wisdom tooth. K-Dawg pulled a roll of duct tape from his pocket and proceeded to wrap it around Doorman's wrists and ankles.

"Where the shit at?" K-Dawg asked pulling the gun out of Doorman's mouth.

"Fuck you," Doorman spat.

"Word?" K-Dawg asked in disbelief, right before he brought his boot down on Doorman's nuts. "You won't be doing no fucking for a while, banana-boat mafucka. Check the back, dawg, while I look around out here."

Jus went off to check the bedrooms while K-Dawg began to ransack the living room. A few minutes later, Jus returned holding a man and a woman at gunpoint. K-Dawg guessed that the woman was Jus's inside connect. She was a short brown-skinned chick who sported a purplish weave. She was butt ass except for the yellow socks that covered her small feet. She didn't have much of a body, so her nudity wasn't really a distraction.

The man had to be the infamous Nester. He was a wire-thin nigga who sported a fade with little twists on top. His too-big medallion sat in the middle of his chest like a small dinner plate.

Nester, too, was damned near naked. The only thing he wore to cover his skinny black ass was a pair of tiger-print bikini underwear.

"Bum-ba-claud," Nester spat trying his best not to sound afraid, "ya know who ya fuck wit', eh?"

"Yeah, we know who you are, li'l fella," K-Dawg said approaching Nester, glancing at his dick. "That's why we here. Where the shit at, money?"

"Fuck off, pussy boy. I no fear you. Me a shotta. Gangsta dem, eh?"

"Why you mafuckas can't never go about shit the easy way?" K-Dawg slapped Nester twice across his face, busting his lip.

"Cough up the bread and we gone. No harm done."

"Ya gwan kill me, eh? Do it. Me no tell you shit."

"Okay, Nester. Have it your—"

A man standing in the doorway holding a McDonald's bag cut K-Dawg off midsentence. "What the fuck!" The man dropped his bag and reached for his gun. Placed in a life-or-death situation, K-Dawg's instincts took over. Without even thinking, he raised his Desert Eagle and squeezed off two shots. The hissing barrel was the only sound heard in the apartment. The first shot hit the man in the stomach, causing him to stagger. The next one hit him in the neck, dropping him.

"What you do that for?" Jus asked in a panic.

"Fuck you think I did it for?" K-Dawg snapped.

"This is bad, dawg. Let's get the money out the bedroom and be ghost."

"A'ight," K-Dawg said grabbing the shopping bags. "Tie this fake-ass Shabba Ranks up while I get the shit." K-Dawg sprinted into the bedroom and returned five minutes later with all of the bags filled. He had managed to scrape up about $12,000 in cash, six pounds of weed, and fourteen sheets of acid. Not bad for a few minutes' work.

"Fuck is all that shit?" Jus asked pacing back and forth.

"Drugs, nigga," K-Dawg snapped.

"Dawg, we were supposed to just take the money and skate. What we need with that other shit?"

"My man, what the fuck you think? We drug dealers, ain't we? We gonna sell the shit."

"Man, whatever. Let's just go."

"Afraid we can't leave yet, kid," K-Dawg said surveying the carnage.

"Why the fuck not?"

"We got loose ends to tie up."

"What the fuck you talkin' 'bou —"

Before Jus could finish his sentence, the Desert Eagle hissed twice more and Nester had two holes in his head. The girl got ready to scream, but the gun pointed at her temple changed her mind. She figured if she kept quiet, she might live. She and Jus were cool, so he wouldn't let this green-eyed lunatic kill her, would he?

"Okay, baby boy," K-Dawg said calmly, "two more and we gone."

"Yo, dawg," Jus said nervously, "this shit is outta hand."

"Man, fuck that shit," K-Dawg said, putting one in Doorman's brain. "Do that bitch and come on."

"I can't, man," Jus said shaking. "I'm a thief, not a killer; plus I know this bitch."

"Justice," K-Dawg said getting serious, "you and me go back to free lunch, man. I love the shit outta you, but don't make me ask again."

Jus looked down at the smoking Desert Eagle in K-Dawg's hand and studied his options. He and K-Dawg were like brothers, but if his hand was forced, would that shit hold any weight? Jus looked at the girl and saw a combination of fear and hate in her eyes. "I'm sorry," he mouthed as the P89 blasted away the majority of the girl's skull.

Jus jumped from the combination of the noise and bits of skull and brain splattering on his jacket. He had shot at people before, but Jus couldn't honestly say that he'd taken a life since killing his uncle. K-Dawg looked at his friend and smirked. The two men disappeared into the night, leaving another unsolved homicide for New York's Finest to ponder.

MY HOOD TO YO HOOD

I can't help being the way I am. Shit, I guess I'm just a product of my environment. In my hood, it ain't nothing nice. You got niggaz throwing sets, niggaz slinging stones, and niggaz clapping guns. And I ain't even talkin' 'bout the grown folks. In my hood, niggaz get murdered and die on a regular basis, sometimes over something as petty as who gets to hustle on what corner. I guess it's like a territorial thang. You know how dogs and other animals mark their territory by pissing on it? Same principle. We piss in the very spots where we lay our heads, but does that make us animals? You be the judge. The way it's set up, we're left to police and govern ourselves, but as soon as we do something to affect the world outside of our li'l hoods, Johnny Law be all in our assess. Where was they when Mel caught it in the back? Where was they when Mizo took them shells going to the store to get a Dutch? Where was they when them clown-ass niggaz tried to blow my head off for a fucking chain? A lot of times we do the things we do because that's what's programmed in us, passed down from parent to child, to child and so on. This kinda shit goes on day in and day out in my hood. What I just ran down to you sounds familiar, don't it? It should, 'cause I'll bet if you look out your window, the same shit is going on. From my hood to yo' hood, it's the same shit. So why don't we act like it and try to do something about it?

—The Author

CHAPTER 17

K-Dawg lay in bed next to Nikki smoking a blunt. As he watched the yellow clouds of smoke drift into the air, he couldn't help but wonder why he hadn't discovered chronic sooner.

Something about smoking weed soothed him.

When he and Jus got back to the hood, they decided to split the shit and go their separate ways. Jus took the money and acid sheets up to his spot, while K-Dawg took the weed to Nikki's crib. They hadn't talked much on the way home. He figured Jus was salty about having to pop that bitch. *Fuck it.* K-Dawg used the same method on Jus that Demon had used on him. This way, they had no choice but to be loyal to each other; can't tell on the next man without incriminating yourself.

"This shit is da bomb," said Nikki, taking the blunt from K-Dawg. "Where y'all get this shit from?"

"Oh," K-Dawg began, "me and Jus helped this couple with their air conditioning, so they set us out with it."

"Um, hmm," she said suspiciously. "Keshawn, you must think I'm new to this."

"What?"

"You helped somebody with their air conditioning, so they gave you six pounds of weed? Don't even try to play me. Look, if me and you gonna be an item, you gotta come correct. I ain't the same li'l chickenhead bitch from '89."

"I dig where you're coming from, Nikki, but peep where I'm coming from. You know I'm in the street doing dirt, so we ain't even gotta touch on that topic. The less you know the better off you are."

"Oh, so it's like that?" she said, turning her back to him. "I'm good enough to fuck and lay up wit', but you can't trust me when it comes to your secrets?"

"Nikki," he said sliding up behind her, "you know I didn't mean it like that. I do what I do for our own good. God forbid if the shit hit the fan and the police decide to question you. This way, you can honestly say you don't know shit. I'm trying to protect you, girl."

"Whatever, Keshawn."

"Come on, Nikki, you know how the game goes. When they build them federal cases, the first person they snatch is the girlfriend. They could lock you up just for knowing what I'm doing. I keep you in the dark because I care about you."

Nikki remained silent, but K-Dawg knew how to get a rise out of her. He slid his hands between her legs and used his middle finger to play with her clit. She started to moan and squirm under his touch. When Nikki became moist, he slid his dick into her. She yelled out and grabbed the sheets as he began to find his rhythm.

K-Dawg grabbed Nikki by the waist and began to grind his wood into her. He did it slowly at first, but the wetter she got, the harder he pumped. After a while, their bodies moved as one. K-Dawg plowed into her, employing several different positions for the better part of an hour. Nikki screamed and moaned as he tried to smash her insides to powder. When he came, it felt like the River Jordan flowing from his dick. The two lovers collapsed in an embrace and drifted off to sleep.

K-Dawg paged Jus for the fifth time with the same result. He had been trying to get at his partner all morning and received no response. At first, K-Dawg thought that

Jus might have taken the money and boated, but that didn't make any sense; they had too much on the ball for him to go out funny style. Still, K-Dawg's instincts told him something was wrong.

K-Dawg dressed quickly, his mind racing the whole time. He threw on his beef and broccoli Timbs and a brown hoodie to go with his black jeans. He stuffed the Desert Eagle into his belt and covered it with his camouflage army jacket.

"Where you headed?" asked Nikki as she came in, carrying the puppy.

"I'll be back," he said kissing her forehead. "Gotta go check on a few thangs, ya know?"

"Well, be careful in them streets, Keshawn."

"Boo-boo, you better tell them streets the same shit about me." K-Dawg shot her a smile and went off to his kingdom: the concrete jungle.

Nikki sat in the window watching K-Dawg stalk his victims. His ambition, after all he had been through, made her wet. He spent his childhood talking with shrinks, and his adolescent and young adult years behind the wall. Nikki could clearly remember everyone saying that Keshawn would always just be a problem kid, but in her eyes, he had beaten the odds.

In a strange sort of way, prison had made him a better man—not better in a reformatory way, but his confidence was up. K-Dawg not only survived one of the illest prisons standing, but unlike most niggaz, he didn't just sit and stew; he benefited. He got his GED, and he was a self-taught student of sociology.

Nikki felt special being with Keshawn. There was so much about the world he didn't know; yet at the same time, it seemed like he knew a little bit about everything. He was her student and her teacher. She didn't feel that kind of connection with Moose.

Moose was Nikki's sometime man, and current under-cover lover. Moose wasn't a local nigga, so he couldn't clock her twenty-four-seven. He and his crew, Game Life, had just gotten a record deal with one of the hottest labels on the scene. The record company was based in Philly where Moose also sold dope, so he eventually secured permanent residence there. He asked her to come, but Nikki was no fool. She had her own crib, a job, and no kids; she was good right there. Besides, Moose had three baby mamas, which added up to three times the drama.

To Moose, he and Nikki were still an item. He did his thing and she did hers, but he could be possessive. The nigga had long paper before the deal, and she could imag-ine how hectic his life was right about now. She knew that shit would end up being more trouble than it was worth. Keshawn was the nigga she always wanted in her life. His wild ass was a gamble, but Nikki decided to roll the dice and play her part however they landed.

Pearl sat in the swivel chair clicking her gum as the little Asian man added the filling to her pinky nail. Trick sat in the chair beside hers, getting a manicure. Trick was prettier than a mafucka, wearing a purple silk suit. Underneath he wore a lime green tie against a black shirt. His lime green gators clicked impatiently against the chairs leg, as he waited for the old Asian lady, who did his nails, to finish.

"Bitch," he said in a high-pitched tone, "you been doing this how long, and ya still can't get it right?"

"Fuck you, Trick," the Asian woman spat. "You so fuck-ing particular about ya shit. Damn, you fucking pimps kill me wit' that shit." The whole shop burst into laughter.

"Don't play wit' me, Miss Yu," he said playfully. "I'll kick yo' li'l ass."

"Trick, you ain't gonna do shit but leave me a bigger tip than you did the last time."

Trick was one of them high yellow niggaz, with hazel eyes and lips like a girl. As he reached up with his free hand to pat his finger waves, the diamonds on his hand and wrist almost blinded everyone in the joint. He was a sportin' nigga, and Pearl was his lady.

Pearl saw China and her friend Shawnna walking by, and when she got China's attention, she motioned for her to come inside the shop. China was sporting a black North Face jacket over a gray Nike sweat suit and a pair of white Airs. Her hair was pinned in a doobie, showing off her round face.

Shawnna wore her brown bomber, as usual. She had on a pair of skintight jeans, covered in denim patches. Her ass was as alluring to men and women alike, as a moth to a flame. On her feet, she wore a pair of tan untied Timberlands, and her blond-streaked hair was styled in fish bones. She wasn't gorgeous, but she was real cute.

"Where y'all off to?" Pearl asked, hugging the pair.

"Nowhere special," said China. "Going to get some boots off 125th."

"You seen ya brother today?"

"Nah, I ain't seen him today."

"China, tell the truth. He ain't been out getting into trouble has he?"

"Nah, Pearl. He's chilling."

"I just be worried about him. Charlie said he seen him the other night and he looked like he was on something."

"Please, Keshawn don't hardly drink, let alone be all up in some heavy shit. Him and his girl stay together now."

"His girl?" Trick butted in. "Them jailhouse niggaz move quick, huh? He ain't been out a week and he shacked up wit' a broad. Shit, he might've could've been a pimp if he wasn't so square."

"Ain't nobody asked you," China snapped.

"Hey," Trick said slithering out of his chair, "it's cool, li'l sis. Ain't no need to be rude 'bout it." Trick tried to brush his fingers against her cheek, but she slapped his hand away. "Damn, China, I guess lack of dick has made you bitter, but I think you need to be taught some respect." Trick advanced toward China, but she anticipated his move. China's hand slid quickly to the inside of her coat pocket, and when it reappeared, it held a glistening straight razor. Trick looked over her shoulder and saw Shawnna pointing a small pistol at him. He knew he had no wins.

"However you want it," China hissed.

"A'ight, China," he said sliding back into his chair, "you got this one."

"And the next one," she said backing out of the shop with Shawnna. "Yo, Pearl," China called out, "you need to find yaself a better class of nigga."

CHAPTER 18

As soon as K-Dawg hit the streets, he flipped open his cell phone. Jus had given it to him a few days prior, but K-Dawg still wasn't used to using the damned thing. Finally, he managed to dial Sleepy's number. From Sleep, K-Dawg learned that no one had spoken to Jus. His girl hadn't even gotten a call. K-Dawg told Sleep to meet him in the projects. Something felt wrong about the whole shit.

K-Dawg stepped off the elevator and proceeded with caution. The first thing he noticed was that Jus's door was open. *A nigga with thousands of dollars worth of stolen shit in his crib ain't just gonna leave his door open.* The whole ride up he had a bad feeling that something had happened to Jus. The partially opened door added to his suspicions.

With his Desert Eagle ready, K-Dawg stepped through the doorway. There in the middle of the living room floor was Jus. He was face down on the carpet, with his hands and feet tied behind him. He lay there motionless, with caked, dried blood in his hair. K-Dawg rushed to his partner's side and checked him for a pulse.

"Jus?" he said turning him over. Jus had a gash in his forehead and his lip was busted, but he was still breathing. "Come on, nigga, wake up," he said trying to slap Jus awake.

"Huh?" Jus groaned. "K . . . K-Dawg? Oh, man. They got me, son."

"Who did this to you, Jus? Who!"

"They had masks on, kid. I couldn't see they faces. Got me for everything."

"Don't worry 'bout that," said K-Dawg using his pocket knife to cut away the tape. "We can get that twelve thousand back."

"Nah, kid, everything—work, jewelry, most of my shit—gone, kid," Jus said shaking his head.

A film of red coated K-Dawg's vision, as he finally made sense of his partner's raving. The work, the money they had saved, all gone, and with it, their dreams. K-Dawg threw his head back and howled in rage. He surveyed the damage to Jus's crib. To say that he was mad was an understatement. Whoever had robbed Jus wanted to hurt him; they busted everything of value in the house and took several leaks on his carpet. Niggaz had violated and would pay.

K-Dawg looked around wild-eyed at the wrecked apartment. The sound of movement behind him caught his attention. He quickly spun simultaneously drawing his Desert Eagle. Just as he was about to squeeze the trigger, he recognized Sleepy and Pooh. Sleep was dressed in blue carpenter jeans and a red leather jacket. Pooh was wearing some black sweats and a sling over his arm. His eye wasn't closed anymore, but it was still bruised. It was obvious that someone had done a number on him.

"Easy," Sleepy said ducking. "What the fuck happened in here?"

"What happened?" K-Dawg barked. "Oh, I'll tell you what happened. Some lowlife mafucka just volunteered to take a ride in the meat wagon!"

"Shit," cursed Sleepy, "what they get him for?"

"You mean us. Them niggaz got us for everything. Yo' money, my money, gone."

Pooh spoke for the first time. "That's fucked up. Who you think pulled this shit?"

"Pooh," K-Dawg exhaled, "I don't even know. But when I find out, it's war! No more playing, kid. Niggaz think they gonna disrespect two of my niggaz and get off? Fuck that shit! We gonna mash whoever the fuck did this, Scarface style. When we get done fucking them niggaz, we gonna pay ya man Dino a visit."

"Word," Pooh cosigned. It made him feel better to see that he was still welcome in the circle. He had brushed K-Dawg off, but the younger cat was still willing to take him back. K-Dawg, though, wasn't quite as forgiving as he had thought. Somewhere down the line, Pooh would be reminded of his slight to the clique. At that time, he would pay accordingly.

After helping Jus clean up a little and change his locks, the quartet went out to the avenue. It was a nice day, and quite a few people were out enjoying the weather. K-Dawg, flanked by his men, stood out in front of the liquor store smoking a blunt. In his heart, he knew who the fuck had robbed Jus. It had to be Sticks and Stone; those were the only niggaz who had been nosing around K-Dawg's setup. He had no way to prove it, but his instincts told him that they were the culprits.

A blue Chevy pulled to the curb in front of K-Dawg, catching him off-guard. The way some of the locals scattered, he knew it was the police. The cop was too close to not have seen the blunt, and K-Dawg was too fucking mad to run. He took his last few pulls and put the blunt out on his shoe. The tall, brown-skinned cop stepped out of the car and came toward the group smiling.

"Shit," Jus mumbled.

"Who that?" K-Dawg asked.

"Action Jackson."

"Fuck y'all call him that?"

"'Cause he want a piece of all the action."

"Fellas," Jackson said stepping up on the curb, "what up?"

"Shit," Pooh responded, "you tell us."

"Be cool, Jose," Jackson said, using Pooh's real name, "you ain't even from around here. Take yo' black ass back up on Broadway and let one of them bean-eating mafuckas stick you in yo' ass."

"Fuck you, Jackson," Pooh said stepping forward.

"Fuck you gonna do?" Jackson asked patting the Glock on his hip. "Make a move, ya fifty-fifty nigga. You don't know whether to steal a car or break dance. I'll slap the shit outta you," he said cocking his hand back, but never swinging.

"We don't want no trouble," Sleep said trying to defuse the situation.

"Fuck you, ya fake Iceberg Slim," Jackson said, turning on Sleepy. "You can't tell me shit, ya lowlife pimp."

K-Dawg watched the exchange and let out a sly giggle.

"Fuck you laughing at?" Jackson asked K-Dawg. "Something funny, nigga?"

"Nah," K-Dawg said still giggling. "I ain't laughing at you, sir."

"You damn right you ain't," Jackson said moving toward him. "Wait a second. Don't I know you?"

"Nah, I don't think we've met."

"Yeah, I know you from somewhere. Which building you from?"

"I ain't lived out here in a while, yo."

"Bullshit. What's ya name, shorty?"

"My name ain't shorty. It's Keshawn."

"Keshawn. Yeah, Keshawn Wilson. I heard of you. They say you was a real bad ass in the joint. Come on the outside to go crazy, have you?"

"Nah, man. I ain't into that kinda shit. I'm trying to keep my nose clean, ya know?"

"Nigga, you full of more shit than a little bit. I bet you all the money in the world if I was to pat you down I'd find a pistol on you."

K-Dawg tensed up as his thoughts raced to the Desert Eagle inside his belt. If this dude was to pat him down, there was no way he wouldn't feel it. He would have to blast it out with the detective. Going back to the pen was not an option.

"Easy there," Jackson said patting K-Dawg on the shoulder. "I'm narcotics. I don't give a fuck about no gun. Let's take a walk, young'un."

K-Dawg was hesitant at first, but what choice did he really have? Jackson had him if he wanted him, but there was an angle somewhere in all this. Reluctantly, K-Dawg walked with Jackson around the corner.

"So, what's up, Keshawn? Or do you prefer K-Dawg?" Jackson asked.

"Keshawn is fine. You sure seem to know a lot about me. What's up wit' that?"

"Man, you sure are forgetful. Take a good look at my face and tell me you don't remember me."

K-Dawg stared hard at Jackson's face, trying to place him. Jackson looked very familiar, but he couldn't figure out how he knew him. Why the fuck did this dude look so familiar?

"Still don't know?" Jackson asked lighting a cigarette. "Keshawn, I was there the day you got arrested."

"Oh," Keshawn said after searching his memory bank, "now I remember. You the mafucka who arrested me. Thanks for fucking nothing."

"Hold on, Keshawn. I arrested you because you committed a fucking crime, for chrissakes. You shot a man in broad daylight. What was I supposed to do? Look,

Keshawn, I fought for leniency at your trial and you know it. Back then I was just a dumbass beat walker who really believed there was justice in the system. What a fucking joke."

"So, who are you now, Jackson?"

"Me, I'm a nigga who knows how to sniff out an opportunity. The system failed both of us back then, Keshawn. I learned how to cash in on my mistakes. How about you?"

"What you trying to say, Jackson?"

"What I'm trying to say is one hand washes the other, dig? I know what the fuck you out here doing, Keshawn. I couldn't place your face right away, but I know your story. I also know that since you got out last week, the murder rate in Harlem has gone up a bit."

"Man, I don't know nothin' 'bout no murders."

"Whatever, Keshawn. Look, you out here slinging shit, and the way I hear it, you're on your way to big things. My question is, can I get mine?"

"Huh?"

"Look, I got it on smash over here, Keshawn. I mean, shit, I'm the law. Who gonna fuck wit' me? I could make things smooth for you out here or fucked up."

"Yeah, what you want, man?"

"Just a li'l something. You give me a li'l taste every month and you'll be the fucking king of these streets. I'll put you up on busts that are coming down, who on the streets is telling, and what kinda cases are being built against you. You and yours are protected from up high."

"You gonna do all that for a little taste? What makes me so special?"

"It's like I said, the system fucked you. I know why you killed ya pops. To tell the truth, I don't blame you. These crackers fucked ya life up, so I'm giving you the chance to be something."

"It sounds good, Jackson. But where's the proof?"

"A'ight, check it. Ya man got jacked last night, right? Of course he did. I can tell you who did it and where to catch 'em."

"I'm listening."

"It was Ray-Ray and Gums. They from Eighth Avenue. Them li'l shit balls work for the twins."

"Sticks and Stone?"

"That's right. A li'l bird told me Sticks will be at the Tunnel tonight."

"Jackson," K-Dawg said extending his fist, "it's going to be a pleasure working with you."

"That's what's up," Jackson said pounding K-Dawg's fist. "Say, Keshawn, maybe you could feed me a bust every now and then, you know, just to—"

"Hold on," Keshawn cut him off, "let's not get beside our fucking selves. Now the money, I'll give you that. But for as long as you fucking know me, don't you never ask me to snitch. I'll kill a mafucka and his whole family if I even thought they was going against the grain."

"Okay, Keshawn. I can dig where you coming from. But listen, when you kill Sticks, and I'm sure you're gonna kill him, can I have his truck? That shit is mean, twenties and all."

"I don't give a fuck. Take it. Niggaz better get ready, Jackson. The Dawgz is on the loose and we coming out hitting."

After his meeting with Jackson, K-Dawg rejoined his crew. He was grinning like a mad scientist when he posted up in front of the liquor store. A connect like Jackson was just what he needed. It would serve to strengthen his hold on Harlem.

"What was that shit all about?" Jus asked.

Keshawn shrugged it off. "It ain't nothing. I'll tell you about it later. Right now, we got some business to handle. Sticks and Stone set jack to move out on you. They sent

some niggaz from Eighth Avenue to do it. Them twin
pussies is out the game."

"So what now?"

"Well, first we divide them six pounds up among our
workers. We whole selling pounds for a thousand and
ounces for seventy-five. Next, we gather all the soldiers
we can between the four of us. It's going down tonight,
kid. Pooh, you got any niggaz who's still loyal to you?"

"Hmm," Pooh said scratching his chin. "Yeah, I got
a few niggaz I can gather up, plus my wild-ass cousin
and his peeps. They just came up from the Dominican
Republic. You know how them niggaz is."

"Holla at them cats," K-Dawg said handing him his cell.
"The Dawgz is loose, and we gonna take our respect."

"Okay, then what?" asked Jus.

"We call Vega and tell him we'll be out for our bricks in
the morning."

"But how? We ain't got the money," Sleep said.

"Don't worry about it," K-Dawg said adjusting his Desert Eagle. "Them faggot-ass niggaz from across town is
gonna pay for 'em. Be prepared, gentlemen. After tonight,
all the drug crews are gonna know who the fuck we are.
It's Black Friday. Let it be forever known that tonight is
the night that all sucker-ass niggaz die."

CHAPTER 19

After placing the necessary phone calls, K-Dawg dressed for his mission. He chose a pair of dark blue slacks and a black silk shirt. He wanted to put on hard-bottom shoes, but they wouldn't be suitable in the event of a quick getaway, so he went with a pair of rubber-soled Hush Puppies. To complete his look, he threw on a pair of wireframe glasses.

China was pressing him all night about the mission. She wanted in on the action. He really didn't want to involve her, but he realized that she might be what he needed, so he put her down.

China got all dolled up in a black Prada dress and a pair of stiletto-heeled shoes. The dress was low at the neck, overexposing her full breasts, while the lower portion accented her ass. She kept her hair wrapped and threw on a short blond wig. She looked so good that K-Dawg, himself, might've tried to holla if she wasn't his sister. The siblings hopped into a cab and headed for Twenty-seventh Street.

The line outside the Tunnel was damned near around the corner. Sunday was the usual hot night at the club, but there was some kind of performance going on that evening. All eyes were on the mock couple as they wove their way through the line like stars.

A few well-placed bribes got them in the club without having to wait on the line or use the small pistol China had in her purse. Once inside, China passed the pistol to her brother and they went their separate ways in search of their prey.

It was K-Dawg's first time in a real club, so it was a little overwhelming to him, and the combination of heat and smoke made it hard to breathe in the spot. The heavy bass from the speakers vibrated deep inside K-Dawg's bones. Under different circumstances, he might've been trying to get his swerve on with one of the many fine ladies shaking their moneymakers on the dance floor. This was business, though. The plan was simple: find Sticks, get him to take them to his brother and the stash, and murder them both.

On the corner of 141st and Seventh, a different scene was unfolding. Pooh sat in the driver's seat of a black Range Rover, relaying instructions to his li'l cousin, Chi-Chi, and his man Hector.

Chi-Chi and Hector had been in the United States for a little over two months. They were on the run from their native Dominican Republic for murdering a government official and his family.

"A'ight, Chi," Pooh started, "we gonna do this shit real smooth. We go up in there, take the shit and leave. Don't kill anyone unless you have to."

"Okay, okay," Chi-Chi said sounding slightly irritated. "How many times you gonna tell me, bro?"

"Nigga, I keep telling you because I know how you are. You and this goofy-ass nigga, Hector, is trigger happy. The last thing I need is to be y'all mafuckas' codefendant on a murder charge."

"Pooh, I don't tell you how to sell drugs, so please don't tell me how to raise hell. I been doing shit like this since I was, like, thirteen."

"Yeah, and you only seventeen now. You a young, hotheaded nigga. That's why I got to damn near hold ya hand on this."

"Whatever," Chi-Chi said getting out of the car. "Come on, Hector."

Chi-Chi was the leader of the duo. He was a tall, lanky nigga, who stood about six feet five inches. He was one of those dark-skinned Dominicans who could pass for black on any given day. He was also a young cat who was desperately trying to make a name for himself. Chi-Chi popped a lot of shit, but could also back it up. And above all else, he'd bust his gun at the drop of a hat.

Hector was the quieter of the two, probably because he didn't speak much English. Hector was a huge kid. He stood at only five feet seven inches tall, but he weighed at least 280 pounds. He was fat, but that didn't make him any less dangerous. Hector used guns when he had to, but they weren't his favorite killing devices; he preferred the little Louisville that he kept tucked in the sleeve of his jacket. The rusty nails that protruded from the tips did the job just fine. The worst thing that customs had ever done was to let those two niggaz into the country.

The young man holding the block down eyed the two as they approached. "What up, fellas?" he asked. "We got that weight, yo. Whatever you need, any flavor or speed, see about us."

"No thanks, man," said Chi-Chi. "But do you have change for a dollar? I gotta use the phone."

As the young man reached in his pocket, Chi-Chi fired one of his twin 9s through his jacket. The bullet hit the young man square in the heart. Between the silencer and the fabric of his coat, not a sound was heard. Before the young man hit the ground, Hector caught him and held him upright. The young man in his arms looked more drunk than dead.

"Fuck you do that for?" Pooh snapped as he approached them.

"Hey, he reached," Chi-Chi said with a shrug of his shoulders. "You saw him, right, Hector?"

The big man grunted and nodded his head.

"Jesus," Pooh said slapping himself in the forehead. "Get that fucking stiff in the building before you get us knocked,"

Hector, carrying the body, flashed a wide grin and led the way into the building as Pooh kept watch on the avenue. The two men hid the body behind the first-floor staircase and rushed to the top floor. Once there, all they had to do was listen. They heard rap music blaring from an apartment and knew that they had found their target. The building predominantly housed Jamaicans and Puerto Ricans, so they figured the assholes blasting Snoop Dogg were the ones they were looking for.

Hector cocked his toy back and swung the Louisville with all his might. The bat took care of the first lock, while his 280 pounds against the door took care of the two additional ones. The occupants of the apartment scattered in all directions, but they never really stood a chance. Hector went to work with his club, bashing in skulls and limbs as he went along. Those who were lucky enough to avoid the club found death in the form of Chi-Chi's twin 9s. When the smoke cleared, the only survivor was a young woman.

She was cowering in the corner, bleeding from where Hector had shredded her arm with the club. Her job was bagging up work for Sticks and Stone to get a little paper. Now she found herself in a whole lot of trouble. There was no doubt as to whether these men were going to kill her. As Hector raised his arm for the final blow, Chi-Chi stopped him.

"Hold on, my man," Chi-Chi said grabbing Hector's arm. "We need someone alive to tell the story. Look, bitch," he said slapping her, "pay close attention, 'cause

I'm only gonna say it once. You tell these slum-ass niggaz in Harlem that the Dawgz are here. The time for playing games is over. You dance to our music or you dance in the dirt. You smell me?"

The girl nodded her head as the man spoke. She breathed a little easier, knowing that she would live. Just as she began to relax, Hector hit her square in the jaw, knocking her unconscious.

China stalked the dance floor like a lioness in search of her prey. She spotted Sticks by the bar, popping bottles of Dom Pérignon and talking shit with some bird bitch wearing a knockoff Gucci 'fit. Swinging her ass seductively, she sauntered past Sticks and shot him a wink. Just as she knew he would, Sticks left the broad he was rapping with to follow her.

China allowed Sticks to accompany her on the dance floor. He swerved with the beat of the music as he pressed himself against her. Overall, Sticks wasn't a bad-looking dude. He was short, with light skin and curly hair. He had pretty teeth, and his Ralph Lauren leisure suit screamed money.

"What's popping, ma?" he asked licking his lips. "My name Sticks. Who you be?"

"My name is Yvette," she said looking him up and down. "I think I might've heard of you, Bricks."

"The name is Sticks, baby. But, uh, bricks are my game. What you drinking, shorty?"

"I don't know, Sticks. A bitch got expensive taste."

"Please," he said pulling out his bankroll, "a nigga caked up. Let's see what we can find for you at the bar." Sticks led China by the hand to the bar area. He proceeded to pop bottles of Dom P like it was going out of style. China had a glass or two, but she let Sticks go ahead and drink one himself. He turned up bottle after bottle, ranting about how he was the biggest player in Harlem. When China had heard enough of his bullshit, she took him by the hand and led him to the bathroom. The restroom at the Tunnel was coed, so men and women were everywhere. There were people peeing, smoking weed, sniffing, and fucking. China led Sticks into one of the stalls after promising him the latter.

When they were both in the stall, China kicked the door closed and locked it behind her. Sticks sat on the toilet, watching the seductress as she slipped out of her lace panties. China slid her hand into Sticks's pants and began to fondle his penis. Sticks's breathing became heavy, as China jerked him off.

"Oh, yeah," he moaned. "Kiss it for me, baby."

China pulled his dick out through his zipper and stroked it faster. She leaned in close and spit on it while still keeping her rhythm. Sticks was so caught up in the hand job that he didn't notice her free hand slide underneath her dress. China pulled a switchblade from her garter belt and placed the blade against Sticks's dick. "What the . . ." Sticks gasped, sounding almost sober. "Bitch, is you crazy?"

"Shut up, nigga," she said squeezing his penis. "Me and you got a little date—elsewhere."

"You must be out ya mind, ho. It's gonna look kinda funny, me walking through the club wit' my dick out. Plus when my peoples see you wit' the blade, they gonna rain on yo' silly ass."

"Yeah, okay," she said removing the .38 he had hidden in his pocket. "You ain't the only mafucka wit' peoples."

China unlocked the stall and Sticks found himself face to face with a familiar-looking cat. He was tall, but not a giant. He was dark skinned with a low Caesar, and his green eyes were constantly scanning for an unseen foe.

"What up, player," said K-Dawg, flashing the butt of his gun. "Why don't you get yaself together so we can go chat?"

Sticks slowly pulled up his pants and inched his way out of the stall. He knew he was in a bad situation, but he couldn't figure out why. The green-eyed kid looked familiar, but Sticks couldn't place him.

"Listen up," K-Dawg whispered. "Me and you gonna walk outta here like everything is everything. You play along, you'll live to kick yaself 'bout this shit. You get funny on me, and I'm gonna vent yo' sorry ass."

China led the way, while K-Dawg brought up the rear. Sticks, the man in the middle, felt like he was going to be sick. He didn't know whether his nausea was from the drinking or the fact that his two abductors were just going to walk him out of there and kill him. His only hope was one of his peoples seeing him and moving to intervene.

K-Dawg and China moved hurriedly through the club. All they had to do was get Sticks outside and they were good. From across the dance floor, Bill, one of Sticks's peoples, saw him making the rushed exit. It was unlike Sticks to just dash off like that without telling anyone. Something was funny. Bill sprinted through the club in pursuit of the trio.

K-Dawg peeped him on their heels and began to sweat. If homeboy ran up, it was on. The last thing K-Dawg wanted was a shootout inside the club. It was too risky. K-Dawg added some pep to his step, as he and his small entourage neared the exit. Bill was almost on K-Dawg when luck swung in his favor; like a shadow, Demon appeared out of the darkness. Bill never even saw the man standing behind him.

Demon snatched an ice pick from his sleeve and jabbed Bill twice: once in the kidney and once at the base of his skull. Bill crumpled to the floor, and Demon disappeared back into the shadows.

***

"Nigga," K-Dawg barked, slamming a punch into Sticks's stomach, "I can do this shit all night, and yo' gut is gonna get tired long before my fist."

Sticks sat semiconsciously in the cast iron chair. K-Dawg and Demon had been beating the shit out of him for the last half hour. His hands and feet were tied to the chair, so all he could do was grunt and take it. When they had first started in on him, he had tried to scream. It was useless; they were deep within the bowels of a long-abandoned building on 106th Street.

"Look, stupid," K-Dawg said wiping his face with his tank top, "all you gotta do is tell us what we want to know."

"Fuck you," Sticks coughed.

"Ya know," K-Dawg said letting loose another blow to Sticks stomach, "I just don't understand what it is with that phrase. Two or three people already told me that this week. And ya know what?" Whump! "Them mafuckas is dead. Look, Sticks, I ain't looking to body you or ya brother, but y'all niggaz done stole from the Dawgz. You either gonna give up my shit or yo' life."

"Suck my dick."

K-Dawg was about to hit him again when Demon stopped him. "Hold on, dawg," he said. "We ain't getting nowhere your way. Let me try something."

"Do you, kid," K-Dawg said stepping back.

Demon walked over to a rusty old table and picked up the pillowcase he had brought with him. K-Dawg was curious about the contents but decided against asking him about it. Demon kicked over the chair Sticks sat in, causing him to bang his head on the ground. He dipped his hand into the pillowcase and pulled out a small rattlesnake.

"You see this?" he asked clutching the serpent by the head. "Pretty, ain't he? Yeah, this one only a baby, but still quite poisonous. Listen, Sticks, my man was trying to be nice, but I ain't got that problem. Since you didn't tell him what he wanted to know, maybe you'll tell my pet here."

"Hold on, man," Sticks said trying to squirm loose. "What you gonna do wit' that?"

"Don't worry," said Demon, dropping the serpent back into the pillowcase. "For the most part, these babies are pretty calm. When you get 'em riled up, though," he said shaking the pillowcase, "they can be downright nasty."

Sticks eyed the pillowcase as Demon leaned in close to his head. The snake thrashed and hissed in the bag as its master looked on in amusement. At first, Sticks didn't believe they'd actually take him out like that. But when Demon began to slip the bag over his head, Sticks lost control of himself—bowels included.

"Okay! Okay!" he said jerking violently. "Just chill, a'ight? I'll tell y'all."

"That's what I'm talkin' 'bout," Demon said backing up.

"A'ight," said K-Dawg as he sat Sticks upright in the chair, "now we're getting somewhere. But this is the thing, Sticks. I ain't so sure ya info is on point, so let's say you take us to the spot."

"Man, come on. I'm already giving you the location of the spot. What more you want?"

"Check this out, man. I don't give a fuck what you talkin' 'bout. You ain't in no position to bargain. I could just kill you and be done with it. Sure, it might take me longer to find ya brother, but that snake would slither out eventually; so when I untie you don't get funny, 'cause my man will put one in you."

Sticks looked nervously at Demon, who was playing with a Glock in the corner. There was no doubt that the spooky man would gladly obey K-Dawg's wishes. Sticks knew his best bet was to play along; maybe he could still come up with a plan to get out of this.

That was a big maybe.

On 149th and St. Nicholas, another phase of the plan was going into effect. Jus stood on the street corner with the youngest recruit, La Miene, or Li'l La, as everyone called him. He was a kid from around the way, and like K-Dawg, he didn't have much family to speak of. Most of the time he slept in the local parks, and when it was cold, he'd stay with different homeboys. La was just another kid nobody wanted, so he turned to the only thing that kept his fifteen-year-old mind occupied: crime. Jus used La to boost for him, but La wanted to step up his game. K-Dawg gave him a one-shot deal on this lick.

"Yo," said La, shifting his weight from one leg to the other, "where this nigga at?"

"Patience," Jus whispered. "You young niggaz is always in a hurry."

"Shit, it's cold out here."

"You got on that big-ass North Face and you still cold?"

"What can I say, Jus? A nigga cold-blooded."

Neither man had a chance to enjoy the joke, because their vic, Go-Go, came out of the building that they had been watching. He was tagged that nickname because his job was to go from spot to spot, picking up money and delivering drugs. It was shift change time on the block, and inside the suitcase Go-Go carried was the money from the previous twelve-hour stint.

"Yo, there he go, son," La whispered.

"A'ight," Jus said spying the bagman, "when he go to get in his Benz, we'll get him."

"Nah, we should get him before, dawg."

"Be easy, La. I'm the pro, li'l nigga."

The two men walked a few paces behind Go-Go as he headed for his car. The short, stout man was so busy yapping on his phone that he didn't even notice La run up on him. Swinging with all his might, La brought the butt of his .45 down on the back of Go-Go's head. Go-Go stumbled twice and hit the ground. When he tried to turn over, La kicked him in the ass.

"Don't move, nigga," La barked. "You know what it is, so come up off that."

"What's this shit about?" Go-Go asked, his eyes darting from La's .45 to Jus's .357.

"Up the case, lard ass," Jus ordered.

"Man, I can't give you this. Y'all know who I work for?"

"Fuck Sticks and Stone, chump," said La, snatching the case. "It's a dawg-eat-dawg world, now. Find a new boss, punk mafucka."

Just as the two robbers were turning to leave, a new player entered the picture. There had been another man in the car that neither Jus nor La had seen. The man was crouched behind the driver's side of the Benz, and began busting a 9, shattering the car's windows. Jus broke left, while La just ducked down.

The gunman thought he had La, so he advanced on him.

Just as he cleared the hood of the car, La let loose with his hammer. The heavy slugs sent the gunman sailing back over the car and into the street. La tucked the case and started to run, only to find a beat walker rushing at him with his gun drawn. La rolled toward the street, letting off two shots. One shot went wild and the other flipped the cop backward.

"Come on, nigga!" La shouted.

Jus looked at Go-Go, who now had beads of sweat rolling off his charcoal face. He didn't share his young

accomplice's thirst for blood, but they had just killed a
cop. No way in the fuck was he was leaving anyone to
tell the tale. He fired two shots into Go-Go's face and
followed La into the night.

Stone sat on his plush sofa getting head from a pretty
young thang. He flicked the cable channels back and forth
with the remote while shorty took him to paradise. Stone
was in heaven, until someone knocked on the door.

Stone sucked his teeth and pulled shorty off of him.
The only person it could be was Sticks. Nobody but he
and his brother stayed at the safe house. He had to have
keys made time and time again for him. It seemed like
every time Sticks got drunk, he'd lose his keys. Stone
looked through the peephole, and, sure enough, it was
Sticks. He was sweating and fighting to keep his balance,
and Stone knew he was drunk. As Stone opened the door,
Sticks tried to shout a warning. But it was too late.

Demon kicked in the door, and Stone, startled, fell clean
off the couch. K-Dawg followed close behind, throwing
Sticks to the floor violently. Stone couldn't believe his eyes
as K-Dawg and his unknown friend stepped into his living
room holding guns. Stone looked at his dumbfounded twin
and vowed to kill him if he was to survive this.

"What up, nigga?" K-Dawg asked, pointing his Desert
Eagle. "Bet I was the last mafucka you expected to have
for dinner."

"Yo," said Stone, "ain't you that li'l nigga from the
projects?"

"Yeah, nigga," K-Dawg barked. "That same nigga you
robbed."

"What you talkin' 'bout?"

"Here we go again. Stone, don't play me, man. Y'all
took my shit, so now I want mine and yours. Ante up,
punk."

"Fuck you. I don't know what you talkin' 'bout."

"You know Demon?"

The name rang a chord in Stone's head. He knew who Demon was, because he had used him for several jobs. If the skinny kid standing in his living room was the Demon, then he knew he was a dead man. He would need to come up with a plan, ASAP.

Demon sighed and screwed the silencer on his .22. Stone backed up because he thought Demon was coming for him. To his surprise, Demon stepped over him and went to the girl on the couch. She tried to run, but he grabbed her by the hair. Demon looked back to make sure he had everyone's attention, then he put two in the back of the girl's head.

"I want my shit, Stone," K-Dawg barked.

"A'ight," Stone said standing up, "just don't kill me or my brother."

"Stone, I don't want ya life. I just want my shit," K-Dawg said reassuringly.

"Okay. It's in the back room."

"A'ight. Demon, watch Sticks. I'll be out with the shit in a few."

K-Dawg escorted Stone to the bedroom, never once taking his gun off him. Stone's brain was spinning, but he couldn't think of a way out of this shit. His brother had told him it was a bad idea to rob the upstart crew, but he had to be greedy. Now he was probably living his last night. It was only Friday, and he hadn't even gotten a chance to enjoy the weekend.

Stone led the way into his carpeted bedroom. K-Dawg looked around at the fancy decor and was very impressed. Stone had a fly-ass bedroom. The walls were painted a blend of smoky gray and white, giving it a misty effect. There was a king-sized circular bed in the center of the floor, and there was a window that took up a whole wall.

The most impressive item was the four-foot safe that sat in the back of a walk-in closet.

Jackpot. "Open it, slowly," said K-Dawg, nudging him with the gun.

Stone's hand shook violently as he tried to punch in the digital combination to the safe. He tried to bring himself under control as best he could. If he played it cool, he might live long enough to get revenge. Then something occurred to him. Neither K-Dawg nor Demon was wearing masks. They had even used Demon's name. If they planned to let him live, why hadn't they taken any precautions?

Stone punched in the last number and the safe beeped open. It was now or never. Stone slipped his hand inside the safe and grabbed his .25. His hand had almost cleared the safe when K-Dawg kicked it closed. The door smashed Stone's wrist, causing him to drop the gun.

K-Dawg picked it up and smiled down at him. "Fuck was you trying to do?" K-Dawg asked, checking the gun. "Niggaz always wanna pull some Rambo shit. What if I had shot you by accident?"

"Damn, man," Stone whined holding his wrist. "Just take the money, man."

"Oh, believe it. And I thank you for it, Stoney boy."

Stone watched helplessly as K-Dawg began to load the money into pillowcases. He prayed that they would just take the money and leave, but that's when he heard it. There was a whistling sound, then a loud thud. Stone knew his brother was gone. He crawled into the corner and began to cry as K-Dawg raised his gun.

"That was stupid," K-Dawg said smirking. "The stupidest thing a man can ever do is to try to take a dog's food while he's trying to eat." K-Dawg squeezed his trigger twice and laid Stone to rest.

***

After it was all said and done, the team regrouped at Jus's crib. All of the strikes had gone off without a hitch. Sure, quite a few people had been killed, but nobody really gave a fuck when a drug dealer was murdered. The final score read something like: seven keys of coke, one bird of dope, and about $265,000 in cash.

"Damn," Sleepy said holding up a small pile of cash, "y'all came the fuck off."

"Fucking right," K-Dawg said separating another small pile.

"I told you niggaz, Black Friday, baby. Anybody fuck wit' the Dawgz, we financing trips to hell. What we've done here is crazy. We started out as four, but now we're nine strong. Only the hungriest dawgz will eat in this game. As long as we stay down for each other, ain't no stopping us. Y'all my Road Dawgz, and I love ya."

"Road Dawgz?" asked Pooh, counting his bread. "I'm feeling that. We the Road Dawgz."

"Hell yeah," cosigned Sleepy. "We sure as hell biting niggaz on the streets. Why not call us Dawgz?"

"Road Dawgz," mumbled K-Dawg, "I can dig it. We close like family and as vicious as any mafuckin' stray. Road Dawgz it is."

"This cat is brilliant," Chi-Chi said counting his money.

"Yo, y'all should've seen how shook Demon had niggaz," K-Dawg said passing him his cut.

"You say Demon?" asked Chi-Chi.

"Yeah, this my man . . ." Before K-Dawg could finish his sentence, Chi-Chi rushed Demon. Demon stepped back to fend off an attack that never came. Chi-Chi got on one knee and offered Demon one of his 9s.

"You're the best in this game," Chi-Chi said looking up at Demon. "It would be an honor to watch you work and maybe learn from you."

"Fuck outta here," Demon said, annoyed. "Murder ain't something you can get lessons in, dumbass li'l nigga. This shit here is supposed to be done with purpose and craftsmanship. Get the fuck away from me."

"I don't know, D," K-Dawg cut in. "I heard Chi-Chi and his man is thorough. How 'bout it, my man? You feel like taking on a student?"

"K-Dawg, you know I gotta do what I do alone. It's my calling, feel me? Besides, this nigga think 'cause he killed a few mafuckas tonight, he qualified."

"Yo," Chi-Chi said standing, "I've killed seven people already and I ain't even eighteen. Give me this man. Show me and Hector how to lay it down."

"Come on, D," said K-Dawg, "if they gonna be working with the team, might as well put the niggaz to some use doing what they're good at. We can't have these wild-ass li'l niggaz runnin' 'round with no guidance. Give 'em a try."

Demon looked into Chi-Chi's pleading eyes and found himself moved. Chi-Chi reminded Demon of himself a few years back. Demon, who was just a small time body catcher, had sought out the seasoned hit man called Charlie "the Chopper" Brown. He had begged the old timer to take him in and teach him the craft of killing. Chopper taught Demon to be clean and swift with his hits, making him all the more dangerous. It was these same teachings that Demon had used on Chopper when he found out he was talking to the police.

"Man, whatever." Demon sighed. "Just don't be all up in my fucking mix."

"Ah, shit," Pooh called out, "you done hooked up three of the wrong niggaz. Looks like you got your own personal angels of death, K-Dawg."

K-Dawg laughed at Pooh's joke and slapped him on the back. It was funny, but true. Demon and the two stooges could sure get their kill on. K-Dawg intended to make them prove their worth.

China came in at the ass end of the joke. She had traded in her dress and heels for black spandex and Timbs. Demon took one look at her and was speechless. China was the most beautiful girl he had ever seen.

"Hi," she said, extending her hand to Demon. "We didn't get a chance to meet earlier. I'm Keshawn's sister, China."

"I'm, uh, Demon," he stuttered.

Demon? The Demon? China thought. China had heard many stories about the man called Demon, but he seemed so different in person. He was supposed to be a savage killer who resembled a walking corpse, but this man didn't appear to be any of these things. To her, he was soft spoken and quite beautiful. China had been attracted to a few men in her life, but none of them moved her like Demon. Could she be thinking about going back to dick?

K-Dawg quickly divided up the money each player would get for his role that night. Demon got the biggest cut, because he did the most work. K-Dawg paid Demon $10,000 for each body he had caught that night, plus an extra $1,000 for his trouble. Chi-Chi and Hector got $4,000 apiece, with the promise of more once they came up. China got $5,000 for her part, and K-Dawg floated La $10,000 with instructions to get low for a while. They had more than enough money, along with the $17,000 that Sticks and Stone donated, to buy the keys from Vega. The remaining money was divided among K-Dawg and the original team. It was time to come up.

CHAPTER 20

Bright and early the next morning, K-Dawg and Jus stepped to their business. Instead of copping five keys, they bought ten. When they hit the block, it was on and popping. Jus had moved into one of his other stash houses on Park Avenue, and that's where they were holding the work. With the help of their soldiers and supporters, the Dawgz locked the avenue down and began to expand.

The months that came after proved to be quite good to the Road Dawgz. The word was out on the streets that there was a team of young cats on the rise who had some bomb-ass work.

The best thing was that these young niggaz was letting it go for a couple grand cheaper than the competition. The up-and-coming hustlers loved K-Dawg for what he was doing. He made it possible for even the niggaz who wasn't holding major paper to eat. While the younger hustlers loved him, the older ones were getting tight.

He was fucking up their flow by whole selling his product and hitting their former clientele on consignment. Dino was one of the people hurt by K-Dawg's actions. People who had been buying keys from Dino were now spending their money with Keshawn and his Road Dawgz. The product was not only cheaper, but it was more potent. One could get more of a cut on the shit K-Dawg was slinging. Therefore, one could profit more from it. While most niggaz' shit couldn't take more than a four or five, a seven could be put on K-Dawg's product and it would still be some bomb shit.

Dino, being the hating-ass nigga he was, grew tired of seeing the young blacks eat. The Dawgz, as they were now called on the street, weren't invading other hustlers' turfs or trying to intentionally cut their flow, but Dino was hating anyway. He sent a group of local cats to rob one of K-Dawg's spots. The robbers made off with two keys and $10,000 in cash.

K-Dawg sat heated on the project bench. He had just received some disturbing news. He had heard the story already, but he still couldn't believe that it had happened or that his nigga was stupid enough to let it go down. It was so unbelievable that K-Dawg kept repeating the question: "You what?" K-Dawg asked looking at Mike. "Make me understand this."

"Yo," Mike said lighting a blunt, "we got robbed. Them niggaz ran up in the spot and jacked us."

"Mike, that's why I make sure all the Dawgz carry hammers. Where the fuck was yours?"

"Man, it happened so quick I couldn't get to it."

"You know why? 'Cause that weed is frying ya fucking brain," he said slapping the blunt from Mike's lips. "How many fucking times I gotta tell y'all dumb mafuckas, when you on shift, be the fuck sober!"

"K-Dawg, it wasn't my fault. I—"

"Fuck you mean it wasn't ya fault? Didn't I put ya chronic-blowing ass in charge of the spot?"

"Yeah, but —"

"But my ass. That means it was your fault. Look, this how we gonna do this: you send Pete to the spot, then you go get yaself a pack and start trying to get my money back."

"K-Dawg, how you gonna do me like that? It's gonna take me months to get ya paper up."

"Like I give a fuck. By right, I should kill you. When you got down wit' us, you knew how we was on it. You fucked up, so accept my judgment."

"That's some cold shit, K-Dawg."

"Mike, miss me wit' that shit. Do like I told you, fo' I let Hector bash ya skull in."

"A'ight, K-Dawg," Mike said walking away. "That's some foul shit, but I'll deal wit' it."

"Stupid mafucka," said K-Dawg as he flipped his phone open. "Chi-Chi," he barked, "I need you down here, dawg. A'ight, see you when you get here."

K-Dawg strolled back to his building in search of his so-called advisor. Flip was standing in front of the project, holding down the block as usual. When he saw K-Dawg, he slid into the building. K-Dawg waited a few minutes and then joined him.

"What up, kingpin?" Flip said giving him a pound.

"Not yet, Flip. I still got clown-ass niggaz fucking up my flow."

"Yeah, I heard one of ya spots got hit."

"Fucking right. Niggaz got us for two keys and some paper. I'm heated, Flip."

"Well, whatever you need, Keshawn, just ask."

"Who pulled the caper?"

"I had a feeling you were gonna ask me that. The way I hear it, Supreme done the job."

"Who the fuck is Supreme?"

"God Supreme Allah. Since Jus started running with you, Supreme is the top stickup kid on the streets. Ask Jus about him. They ran together, so I'm sure he can get a line on him."

"Jus's old partner? A'ight, Flip," K-Dawg said while peeling two one-hundred dollar bills from his bankroll.

"The Dawgz is gonna see ya man. That god is gonna learn what happens to those who steal from us."

"Damn, you niggaz is racking up quite a body count. Maybe y'all should slow down."

"Fuck that shit, Flip. The game is wide open. Examples have to be made so other mafuckas don't try any shit."

"A'ight, Keshawn. But I gotta tell you, Supreme is a mean-ass dude. If you flex on him, you gonna have to kill him."

"Oh, I know. Believe me, I know."

After hooking up with Jus, K-Dawg got the rundown on Supreme. He was a hardheaded nigga from the Bronx, trying to make his bones in Harlem. Since Jus wasn't out robbing and stealing like he used to, Supreme was trying to slide into his spot.

Jus didn't give two shits, though. His activities were now limited to big scores like jewels, eighteen-wheelers and shit like that. The niggaz he placed under him handled the petty crimes.

"That nigga Supreme is so stupid," said Jus taking a pull on his Newport. "Of all the mafuckas to rob, he picks you?"

"Yeah," said K-Dawg. "He fucked up, so we gotta show him the error of his ways."

"Damn, this shit is fucking wit' me. Supreme was my student."

"So you siding with him over us?"

"Hell no! We was peoples long before I joined the five percenters, but do we gotta kill him? I don't think he knew who he was robbing, so let me try talking to him first."

"Sure thing, Jus," said K-Dawg checking his weapon. "Let's go talk to the kid."

Jus knew K-Dawg better than anyone in the crew, with the exception of China. He agreed with the plan a little too easily for Jus. He figured K-Dawg might just kill Supreme anyway. Supreme was his man, but Keshawn was top dawg. Who was he to argue?

They found Supreme sitting inside of McDonald's on 132nd and Lenox. He was hunched over a chicken sandwich talking to two other kids when Jus walked in, followed by K-Dawg. Supreme saw Jus coming and a smile formed on his huge lips.

"Peace, god," said Supreme standing.

"Peace," Jus responded.

K-Dawg and Supreme sized up one another. Supreme was a big man. He was about six feet five inches with broad shoulders. His skin was a pasty yellow, and he had a scar that traveled from the bottom of his right eye to his beard. He wore a thick rope chain, with the number "7" engraved on the crescent moon that hung from it.

"I ain't seen you in a minute," said Supreme sitting back down. "What da deal, god?"

"I need to holla at you about something," said Jus.

"About what, god?"

"My money, kid," K-Dawg cut in. "You hit one of my spots for some bricks and some paper."

"And?" Supreme asked picking his teeth. "I rob a lot of niggaz. That's how I eat."

"I feel you," K-Dawg said calmly, "but I ain't a lot of niggaz. I'm K-Dawg."

"Fuck," Supreme said getting loud, "that's supposed to mean something? Yo, my man, fuck you think this is, Jimmy Jazz? Ain't not fucking refunds or exchanges."

"Supreme, hear me out," said Jus trying to defuse the situation.

"Nah," Supreme barked, "you hear me out. You and me is god. So that's always gonna be peace. But ya man is bugging. I'm Supreme Allah. No one is over me, god. This nigga coming through like he feeling some kinda way. Fuck this clown. I should slap fire out this nigga." Supreme placed his 9 on the table and continued. "Let me tell you something: when you come at me, come correct. I ain't no new jack, and I damn sure ain't Sticks or Stone. Get the fuck up from 'round me wit' that sideways shit. Fuck out my square, kid."

"Yo, Supreme, don't do it like this, god," Jus pleaded. He knew Supreme was signing his own death warrant.

"Jus, take ya man and bounce, word. I'm about to start clapping. Matter of fact, both of you clown-ass niggaz get gone. Peace."

"But, Supreme—"

"Nah," K-Dawg said cutting him off, "it's cool, Jus. Sorry to bother you, God Supreme Allah." K-Dawg lit a cigarette and escorted Jus from the fast food joint.

"Fuck wrong wit' them niggaz?" said Supreme addressing his crew. "Funny-style mafuckas. You heard that shit, god? 'I'm K-Dawg.' Fuck is wrong wit' dat man? Yo, these fake-ass studio gangstas be killing me. Word."

Supreme and his crew kept cracking jokes and ranking on K-Dawg. They were still laughing when Chi-Chi's motorcycle jumped the curb and skidded to a stop in front of the window where they sat. The three men looked up in shock. Before they could figure out what was going on, Chi-Chi let loose with his Uzi. The bullets ripped through the glass as well as Supreme and his crew.

Chi-Chi revved his engine and took off like lightning up Lenox Avenue.

The two friends were just crossing Fifth Avenue when they heard the gunshots. Jus almost jumped out of his shoes, but K-Dawg didn't seem the least bit surprised. Jus looked up just in time to see the wicked grin on K-Dawg's face. He knew Supreme hadn't lived long enough to regret his words.

Bam! Bam! Bam!

K-Dawg rolled out of the bed and grabbed his gun. As his grogginess subsided, he realized that what he heard wasn't gunshots; someone was banging on Nikki's door.

He eased to the door and looked through the peephole. As soon as he saw the two white dudes, he knew that they were cops. K-Dawg stashed his pistol and opened the door for the two men.

"Keshawn Wilson?" asked the first detective, flashing his badge.

"What up?" asked K-Dawg yawning.

"I'm Detective Hargrough, and this is my partner, Detective Mills."

"And what is that supposed to mean to me?"

"We need to ask you some questions."

"About?"

"A couple of homicides," said Mills.

"Look, Officers, Detectives, whatever. I don't know jack shit about no homicides."

"Oh, we doubt that," said Hargrough. "Why don't you put something on and come with us?"

K-Dawg sucked his teeth and went back into the bedroom.

As he was putting his sweats on, Nikki kept asking him what was wrong. K-Dawg gave her the short version of the situation and told her not to worry. She insisted on coming, but he convinced her to hold down the fort. K-Dawg returned to the waiting officers and allowed them to escort him downtown.

"So," said K-Dawg, exhaling his cigarette smoke into Detective Mills's face, "fuck y'all bring me down here for?"

"It's like we told you, Keshawn. We wanna know about the murders," demanded Hargrough.

"And it's like I told you, I don't know shit."

"Come on, Keshawn," Mills chimed in, "we know your story already: poor li'l ghetto kid goes to jail for killing his mother's husband. It was in all the papers, ya know?"

"Thanks for the history lesson, but I was there. I gave up over five years of my life behind that shit. What's your point?"

"Our point is this, shit bird. When you came home, things started getting crazy in Harlem. Some of the biggest drug dealers in Manhattan done gone and got themselves killed. Coincidence? I think not," said Mills.

"Like I give a fuck what you think, cracker. Y'all ain't gonna hang me wit' this shit. You better get back out in the streets and find another herb."

"Listen, Keshawn," Hargrough said, "word on the street is there's a new crew tearing shit up around Harlem, call themselves 'the Road Dawgz.' Sound familiar?"

"Nope."

"Bullshit!" Mills shouted. "Paul, this fucking boot is trying to play us. We know who the fuck you are, K-Dawg. You're trying to get us to believe that it's just dumb luck that a group of punks named a crew after you right around the time you got out of prison?"

"Yep."

"Now you listen to me," said Mills, snatching K-Dawg by the collar. "We're wise to you. We got witnesses who place you at the scene of at least two murders. You feel like talking now?"

"Nope."

"Why, you black son of a bitch. I'm gonna kick your half-breed ass. You fucking—"

"If you lay one hand on him, Officer Mills, I'll have both your badges." Suddenly, a strange voice came from the doorway. The speaker was a short, balding white guy, wearing a brown suit that looked as if it had seen better days. He had a potbelly, and he was holding a manila envelope. His presence seemed to calm the detective.

"Arnold Levitz," he said whipping out a business card, "attorney at law. Now, which one of you can tell me why my client is being held?"

"Your client," Mills started, "is a fucking drug dealer and a murderer."

"Where is your proof?"

"W . . . well, we've got witnesses."

"Then let them come forward in court. Is my client being charged with these alleged murders?"

"Well, uh, no. But—"

"But nothing. If you're not charging my client, we're leaving. Let's go, Keshawn."

On the other side of the two-way mirror, a man sat smoking a cigarette. He watched from his hidden area as the detectives and the lawyer exchanged words. He chuckled silently as the crooked attorney escorted K-Dawg from the interrogation room. He had been watching Keshawn ever since he got out of jail.

When Keshawn was sent away, he thought the judge was entirely too lenient with the sentence. He went along with it just to kiss ass. Now that he was holding a little weight, Assistant District Attorney Michael Greene would make sure the youth got his just due.

After K-Dawg left the building, the detectives joined Greene. "Did you see that shit?" barked Mills. "The nerve of that fucking kike. Who the fuck does he think he is?"

"Easy, Mills," Greene cautioned. "Don't get yourself all worked up. We'll get the fuck sooner or later."

"Any luck with Cromwell?" asked Hargrough.

"I'm afraid not. Mr. District Attorney thinks I'm too emotionally attached to this case, says I'm overreacting," said Greene.

"Bullshit," snarled Mills. "That eggplant is dirty and we all know it."

"True enough, Detective Mills. But without evidence, it'll be hard to build a case against our young up-and-coming friend."

"Well, let's get cracking."

"Indeed we shall, Mills. Be it by hook or crook, Keshawn 'K-Dawg' Wilson, along with his Dawgz, is going down."

Standing outside One Police Plaza, K-Dawg was trying to make sense out of his situation. He had never retained a lawyer of any sort, let alone Levitz. Yet, here he was like a savior, pulling his ass out of the fire. Something was up and he intended to find out what.

"Thanks," K-Dawg said lighting a cigarette. "Them dudes are trying to set me up."

"Please," said Levitz. "You and I both know you're as dirty as yesterday's laundry, but that's beside the point. A mutual friend, Thomas Jackson, sent me here."

"Jackson sent you?"

"Indeed. He caught wind of the detectives' little plan and set me on the case. From now on, I'll be your legal counsel."

"Shit, fine by me. I figured I'd be needing a good lawyer."

"And so you have one. Here," said Levitz, handing him a business card. "We'll discuss my fee later."

"A'ight, Levitz."

"My advice to you, Keshawn, is to stay out of dumb shit. You're on your way to being a big man on the streets. Be smart. The next time someone needs to be . . . removed, hire someone else. You stay out of hood shit. I'll be in touch."

K-Dawg watched the lawyer wobble away and shook his head. That Jackson was on his job. His gut told him to accept the dirty cop's offer and it had paid off. The game was wide open, and K-Dawg intended to take it for all it was worth.

K-Dawg lay in the king-sized bed of the hotel room, smoking a cigarette. He looked at the naked bronze honey in the doorway and felt proud of himself. The girl wasn't gorgeous, but she was cute. She had a nice figure, but was a little on the chubby side. She felt insecure about her weight, but K-Dawg showered her with compliments. He was good at playing on people's weaknesses to get what he wanted, which was the case here.

"Damn, K-Dawg." She sighed. "You know how to lay it down."

"Nah, baby," he said pulling her into the bed. "You threw it and I just went with the flow. I should be thanking you."

"Oh, cut it out."

"It's the truth, Gloria. You need to stop doubting yourself."

"Well, you would to if your father was always putting you down."

"Girl, you don't even know the half. My daddy ain't have a bit of love for me. You got it good. Frank's good people, just a li'l old school."

"Oh, that reminds me." Gloria picked her purse up off the floor and removed an envelope. "Here," she said, handing it to him. "It's only a few thousand."

"Shit," he said, scanning through the bills. "It's better than nothing. Ain't you scared ya daddy gonna find out that you tapping the till?"

"Please. My daddy got millions in his wall safe. Even if he do notice it's missing, he'll just blame it on Manny."

"Fuck it. If you like it, I love it."

"I gotta go do something," said Gloria slipping her jeans on, "but I wanna see you again soon."

"We'll see."

"Don't be like that, Keshawn."

"Gloria, you know I got a wifey and a business to run. My time is limited."

"You always say that, and you make promises that you don't keep."

"Baby, you know I love you, right?"

"Yeah, but you got a funny way of showing it."

"I do what I do for a reason. Trust me, Gloria, when I get my affairs in order, it's gonna be me and you against the world."

"Yeah, well, what about Nikki?"

"Baby, she's the here and now. You're the future. Now go do whatever you gotta do. I'll call you later."

"Okay," she said, kissing him. "I love you, Keshawn."

"And I love you, ma."

K-Dawg waited until he was sure that Gloria had gone before he burst into laughter. It was fucked up, the way he was stringing Frank Vega's daughter along, but fuck it; she was just a pawn like everyone else. Him fucking Gloria Vega kept a few dollars in his pocket and an ear in Frank's house. If that bitch thought they were gonna ride off into the sunset, then let her. Nikki was his boo, and China was his heart. Everyone else just played a part in his grand scheme.

CHAPTER 21

The summer of '95 was a good one for the Dawgz. They were caking off the wholesale bricks as well as the few coke and crack spots they had set up. K-Dawg had even stepped up his game to include dope.

As promised, he made sure that all of his crew prospered at their respective hustles. Sleepy now had six girls in his stable. K-Dawg sent Chi-Chi and Hector to clear out two city blocks in lower Manhattan; only Sleepy's girls were allowed to work the area. Any new girls who came down that way and wanted to eat had to choose Sleepy as their pimp. Sleepy caked off as a result, because a lot of the working class in that area liked his girls and sought them out regularly for recreational purposes. On a good night, Sleep could clock anywhere from $1,500 to $2,000 per girl. Young Sleepy was climbing the underworld ladder and was on his way to becoming a top-notch pimp.

Demon and his Death Angels, as they were now called, enforced the laws of the young drug crew. K-Dawg was fair to the other hustlers, but if they violated they got dealt with. Under Demon's tutelage, Chi-Chi and Hector were perfecting their craft.

As their thirst for blood grew, so did their notoriety on the streets. Among the thieves and hustlers, they were the law. Jus, too, was making a name for himself. Previously, when people called him Prince of Thieves, it was meant as a joke, but the way he was putting it down, it had become more of a description than a nickname. Jus had his little team of boosters hitting everywhere. They were jacking shit from all the major department stores in New York as well as the surrounding areas.

Jus had even broken into a racket that was reserved for mobsters. He was jacking trucks as well as jewels. And he didn't just get jewels from snatching chains or doing stickups; he was down in the diamond district. Jus had become quite the jewel thief. He would bang a spot for rare stones and sell them through Levitz to the highest bidder. In a short time, Jus had quite a bit of paper stacked.

Pooh had become K-Dawg's field general. It was his job to make sure all of their operations were going smoothly. K-Dawg was the brains behind the Road Dawgz, but Pooh was the front man. Some of those not in the know even mistook Pooh as their leader.

That was fine by K-Dawg. His philosophy was simple: let Pooh get all the attention, as long as he got the bread.

K-Dawg was a young nigga on the rise. He had a good chunk of Harlem on smash and his reach was growing. As powerful as he was becoming, there were still challengers to his claim. Those foolish enough to go against the drug lord would learn the hard way—you don't fuck with the Road Dawgz.

China came out of Macy's with an armful of bags. Her role as K-Dawg's unofficial bodyguard had proved to be a sweet job. She'd slapped a few cats up here and there, but for the most part it was sweet. K-Dawg made sure that his sister had as much as the fellas, and her pockets were getting heavy.

China stood with her arm outstretched in an attempt to get a taxi. But for a person of color, it was easier to catch a case than a cab. As she walked toward Eighth Avenue, she spotted Nikki in front of the train station. She was about to call her name, until she noticed that Nikki wasn't alone.

She was talking to a kid who appeared to be very cozy with her. He was a tall, light-skinned dude who wore his hair in cornrows. His baggy blue jeans hung off his ass just enough to show his multicolored boxers. He was sporting a blue silk shirt that he rocked unbuttoned to show off his muscular chest. The kid was a little too close up on Nikki to be just a friend. If Nikki was trying to play K-Dawg, China was going to bust that ass.

China strolled across the street wearing a phony smile. She wanted to flip, but she played it cool. It was best to see what kind of lie the bitch was going to try to come up with before she reacted. If the shit didn't sound kosher, she was going to fuck her ass up.

"Hey, Nikki," said China.

All the color drained from Nikki's face. She thought meeting Moose on Thirty-fourth Street would allow her some privacy. Now this crazy dyke bitch popped up. This was not good.

"What up, China?" said Nikki, hugging her. "What you doing down here?"

"Nothing much, just a li'l shopping. I came down to Macy's to see what kinda sales I could catch, but instead I ended up catching you. Who this?" she asked, looking Moose up and down.

"What's good, baby?" said Moose, trying to look sexy. "My name is Big Moose. You probably heard of me?"

"Can't say that I have."

"Word? Shorty, I'm the front man for Game Life."

"Oh? So, what, you a rapper?"

"Yeah, yeah, something like that."

"So Nikki gonna be in one of your videos or something?"

"Shit, she can be in all of my videos if she want. Nikki my boo."

"Word," said China, setting her bags on the curb. "That's ya boo, Nikki?"

"Hold up, China," Nikki said backing up, "it ain't even like that. Me and Moose is old news. I just—"

Nikki never even got a chance to finish her sentence. China caught her with a jab, sending her flailing to the ground. Moose tried to grab China from behind, and his effort was rewarded with a kick to the chest. Moose was flat on his back in no time.

"You lowlife bitch," said China kicking Nikki in the ribs. "You fucking around on my li'l brother. You gonna learn 'bout fucking wit' the Dawgz, bitch!"

China dipped her hand into her bra and produced a straight-edge razor. She grabbed a handful of Nikki's braids and gripped them tightly, balling her hand into a fist. China raised her blade to cut Nikki's face when someone grabbed her arm. China motioned to swing on the intruder with her free hand, but her momentum was used to bend her arm behind her back.

"Easy, ma," he whispered.

To China's surprise, the voice was familiar to her. When she finally stopped struggling, the stranger released her arm. China spun around to attack again, and she found herself face to face with Demon.

"Be cool, China," said Demon in a soothing voice. "What's this shit all about?"

"Demon," China hissed, "this bitch is trying to play Keshawn. She creeping with this ol' studio gangsta-ass nigga."

"Is this true?" he asked, helping Nikki to her feet.

"Demon," said Nikki holding her lip, "I would never creep on Keshawn. That's my heart. Me and Moose used to be an item, that part is true. But when I hooked up with ya boy I wanted to break it off with him. He wouldn't listen."

"Lying bitch!" China shouted.

"Hold that down, China," said Demon touching her shoulder. Something about the way he touched her calmed China.

She settled down and let Nikki continue. "It's the truth, Demon. If you don't believe me, ask him."

Demon knelt down next to Moose and slapped him awake. "You a'ight, money?" Moose nodded his head and allowed Demon to help him to his feet. "What up wit' you and Nikki?"

"Shit," said Moose shaking off his dizziness, "not a damn thang, now. I got too many hoes to keep chasing her skank ass."

"So you admit to being with her?" asked Demon.

"Yeah, but it ain't that serious. Fuck her; she yesterday's trash."

"No need for name calling, kid."

"Nigga, fuck is you? I used to bone that bitch awhile back, and when she need something, I'll be boning her again."

"Cool out, player. Nikki's wit' my man, K-Dawg, now. I'd like it very much if you left her alone."

"Yo, my man, who the fuck is you? I'll do what the fuck I want. I'm wit' Game Life. Fuck K-Dawg. I'll fuck—"

With speed faster than Moose's eyes could follow, Demon slapped him with an open hand. Moose tried to swing back on the seemingly frail man, but Demon was too quick. He slipped under the wild swing and grabbed Moose by the throat. Moose outweighed Demon by about sixty pounds, but for some reason he couldn't break his grip.

"Look," snarled Demon, "I understand you're a li'l upset right now, but if you ever try that dumb shit again, I'll body ya faggot ass. You stay the fuck away from Nikki, or believe you me, I'll make ya life hell. I'll murder ya mama and ya kids, nigga. Test my gangsta."

Moose wanted to reply with something slick, but the madness flashing in Demon's eyes kept his mouth closed. Nikki was a bad bitch, but she wasn't worth his life. There was no doubt in Moose's mind that his life would be the price for testing the man standing in front of him. He would catch up with Nikki and her new man another time, but he'd be damned if he was going to test the Demon.

K-Dawg sat on the comfy leather couch in his family's home. Once he had gotten on, he made sure he bought Pearl some new furniture. That old shit she had up in the joint was so not the move. He wasn't a millionaire, yet, but it was the least he could've done.

K-Dawg had the movers take all of the family's old stuff out and replace it with new furnishings. The ratty old couch was replaced with a butterscotch leather sectional. The bootleg television was replaced with a modest, forty-one-inch model. Even the beds in the apartment had been replaced. Justin wouldn't have to sleep with his mother or on a pallet anymore. K-Dawg set him out with a nice day bed and about $300 worth of video games. The family was more than grateful for what he had done, but K-Dawg didn't do it for their praises. Even though life had dealt him a bad hand, he didn't feel that his family should suffer.

"Keshawn, I just love the furniture," said Pearl, stroking the back of one of the new chairs.

"Yeah, and the video games are fresh, Uncle Keshawn," added Justin.

"Ain't nothing," said K-Dawg. "I gotta look out for fam."

K-Dawg's cell phone chirped, causing him to flinch. He still hadn't gotten used to the portable phone thing, but he found that it was very necessary; besides, he got it hot without having to have his credit checked. Everyone in his crew used burnouts. For about a buck fifty, anyone could get a jacked-up phone, allowing them to call anywhere for a good few months. The Road Dawgz weren't some corporate America-type cats; they were hustlers, just like everybody else, trying to make a buck.

Noticing that it was Vega's private number, he stepped away to take the call. Over the last few months, K-Dawg and the drug czar had become very close. Vega respected K-Dawg's style.

Here was a kid, he thought, who the world had bent over and taken a shit on, on his way to being a major player. His money always came straight, and he took care of his own headaches. You had to respect a youngster like that.

"What up, Poppy?" said K-Dawg.

"My friend," Vega sobbed into the phone, "I'm not feeling too well, you know?"

"I know, sir. I'm sorry, but—"

"No, no. I gotta make this call. This shit breaks my heart, but . . . what am I gonna do ya know? This shit here, it's a slap in the face to me, as well as both my family names. I'm asking you to do this because I trust you."

K-Dawg thought it was more like, *because I wanna test you.* He knew that Vega had taken a liking to him and wanted to really set him out when the time was right, and he just needed a show of loyalty. Niggaz played so many head games in the street, but wasn't nobody sneakier than K-Dawg. He was the master of his own fate, and it showed more and more with each dirty deed that he committed.

"You're like a father to me since I came back," K-Dawg started. "I do this thing with a heavy heart. But if this is what you ask of me, then I'll do it. My peoples already got it under wraps. I was just waiting on the nod."

"Then you have it," Vega said with conviction. "Find out how much he told them and who put him up to it. Take care of this for me and I'm gonna make you a fucking ghetto star. But clean, understand?"

"Then it's done." K-Dawg flipped his phone closed and immediately began formulating a plan. It was kind of fucked up, but he needed the play. *Fuck it; niggaz is expendable,* he thought.

China came strolling out of the kitchen with an ice pack on her swollen knuckle. K-Dawg looked at her and almost fell out laughing. Demon had already called ahead and told him about what had happened. Even though he was a grown man, China was still very overprotective of him. Just the thought of China and Nikki going at it on Thirty-fourth Street was laughable. He just hoped that China didn't hurt her too much.

"I don't know what the fuck is so funny," said China to a grinning K-Dawg.

"Watch ya mouth in front of Justin," Pearl snapped.

"My fault, Pearl. But ya li'l brother is stupid."

"China," started K-Dawg, "why I gotta be the stupid one and you was the one on Thirty-fourth Street trying to reenact the final scene of *Rocky?*"

"That ho had it coming. How she gonna play herself?"

"Big sis," said K-Dawg, examining her hand, "Nikki ain't hardly slicker than ya li'l bro. I been knew about Moose. I didn't know at first, but you know how mafuckas gossip. I know, but she don't know that I do."

"So, if you know, why you still wit' her?"

"To be honest, 'cause I don't give a fu . . . my bad, Pearl. I mean I don't care. Nikki's my boo, and I got feelings for her. If she say she really through wit' this nigga, then I'd like to believe her. But if she still playing, you already know how I'm getting down."

"A'ight, Keshawn. So what's the order of business?"

"Same as usual, girl: paper chasing. I gotta go check this cat 'bout something."

"Let me roll?"

"I don't know, China. This is one of those situations."

"Come on, Keshawn. You say I'm an equal member, but you don't never want me in on stuff. What up wit' that?"

"China," said K-Dawg, slipping into his three-quarter-length black leather jacket, "I'm just trying to keep you out of harm's way."

"That's wack and you know it. If we gonna be a team, you gotta let me in."

K-Dawg pondered on it for a moment. China had a good point. She had already proven that she was down for the cause, but he still felt funny about exposing her to the violence of the game. But if she was determined to get down, then why not let her? Maybe after she saw what the fuck he was about to pull, she'd get turned off and make a career change. "A'ight, baby girl. You wanna roll, it's on you. But just remember, I told you not to come."

K-Dawg led the way as he and China descended a spiral staircase into the bowels of an unmarked building on Third Avenue. It was one of a few abandoned buildings the Road Dawgz used to conduct some of their more unsavory business. China held her nose as the stench of urine and other kinds of funk assaulted her senses. She had no idea what her brother could be doing in this place, but she figured it was something devilish. Since he got deep in the game, his personality had changed. It was as if his dark side was overshadowing everything else.

They went about three floors down and stopped at a small iron door where Jus stood guard. He changed since K-Dawg had forced him to kill that night in the spot. The remorse he felt had faded, leaving him with another feeling: a craving lust to kill again.

Holding someone's life in his hands made him feel powerful.

"Boss Dawg," said Jus grinning. "We were waiting on you."

"What's good, Jus? How we looking up in there?"

"We crew-thick, as requested, dawg. We've been making some progress, but he's a tough li'l shit."

"Hmm, we'll see."

K-Dawg stepped past Jus, and he led China by the hand through the door and greeted his court. All of the homeboys were sitting around in what looked to be a basement. The walls of the room were covered in shower-like tile, and little waste drains were built into the floor. The Dawgz sat smoking and sipping in the far left corner, and in the center of the room stood the master: Demon.

The young killer's hair was loose and flopping about his back and shoulders. His meat-cutter's smock was soiled with blood around the hem, evidence of the room's purpose. This was Demon's flesh factory. This was where people were brought to when they had to be taught a special lesson, which was now the case.

Demon left his victim and met K-Dawg and China at the door. "Sup?" he said with a nod.

"Nothing good," said K-Dawg. "The word is in. We gotta take out the trash."

Demon noticed China staring at him, and he felt a little embarrassed. He could only imagine how he must have looked, standing there in a bloodied smock holding a stun gun. "Why you bring her down here?" Demon asked.

"Who?" K-Dawg looked around. "China? Nigga, she ain't nobody. Let's go take care of that shit. Y'all dudes pay attention!" he shouted to his crew.

K-Dawg drew everyone's attention to the center of the floor, where Manny sat strapped to a chair. His eye had begun to swell from taking punches and his nose was busted the fuck up, but he was still in pretty good shape. But how long was he going to stay that way? Vega had gotten the word that his own flesh had betrayed him.

Manny had gotten light fingered; he was stealing a pretty good chunk of money and drugs from his old man. Then he was taking it and selling it to Dino and his peoples uptown. That was some rotten shit, but it wasn't what had Manny strapped to a chair; he was snitching, and according to the code, he had to die.

"Manny," K-Dawg said crossing his arms, "*Que pasa?*"

"Yo, K-Dawg," Manny pleaded, "what's this shit all about, bro?"

"You mean to say you've been strapped to this chair for the last hour and a half and ain't nobody tell you?" K-Dawg slapped Manny viciously across the face. "Don't fuck wit' me, Manny. You know why the fuck I'm here, nigga."

"Look, look, look. K-Dawg, man, this is all just a mix-up."

"Manny, don't go there, a'ight? The shit is in black and white, baby. It's real fucked up that you stealing, but snitching? Why, Manny?"

"Man, you don't understand. Them cats had me cold busted. I had four keys in the trunk and a gun under my seat."

"So what! How many times we tell yo' dumb ass not to ride dirty? That's your stupidity. How much you give Hargrough and them niggaz?"

"Man, I only gave them scraps. Nothing serious, bro."

"Like what, Manny?"

"Nothing, man."

"Oh, okay. You wanna play it like that? Hector, let me see ya club." The big man was all too happy to pass his little toy off to his boss. "Let's try this again. What you give 'em?"

"K-Dawg, man, I—"

K-Dawg's arm swung around in an arc, bringing the spiked Louisville down on Manny's knee, crushing it. Manny's body jerked, but the chair held him steady as pain shot all through his throbbing knee.

"Oh, God!" Manny shouted. "My knee. My fucking knee. Chill man, a'ight?"

"Make me a believer, dawg."

"I gave them little people, ya know? Small time niggaz. I never said anything about you."

"So who you give 'em?"

"Nobody, really. Just a few lieutenants, some grunts, shit like that."

"Who?"

Manny cast a wayward glance at Jus. Jus looked around, baffled, and then realized that Manny was looking at him. "You li'l mafucka," Jus said pulling his gun. "I'm gonna dust this pussy."

K-Dawg waved Jus back. "Manny, you mean to say you gave them shit on my dawg?"

"Man." Manny shivered. "It ain't nothing serious. He's a fucking thief. He gets picked up, he'll be out in a year."

K-Dawg's lips parted into a smile. He swung the club again and caved in one of Manny's ribs. Manny struggled to catch his breath as blood gushed out of his throat and spilled from his mouth.

Manny looked into K-Dawg's eyes, searching for signs of mercy. He found none. All he saw in the twin jade mirrors was hatred.

"Snake mafucka," K-Dawg barked. "You could've had it all, Manny. Ya pops would've laid it all out for you."

"Man." Manny sniffled. "I had four bricks, dog. Wit' my record, they would've thrown the fucking book at me."

"Fuck that, Manny. You ridin' 'round wit' all that snow in ya trunk, for what? Where was you going wit' it?"

"Huh?"

"What you mean, huh? Oh, now I see. You was probably taking that shit to Dino's punk ass."

"Man, me and Dino don't pump like that."

"Don't lie, son. You sucking that cat, and you must've thought I ain't know about the paper Dino put on me. You went to your pops to get a referral, and he told me. You gotta go, Manny."

"K-Dawg, you don't understand."

"Nah, B, I don't understand. You squandered a beautiful opportunity. Don't worry, though; I'm gonna step up like you should've and take mine." K-Dawg raised his gun to Manny's eye.

The room suddenly became filled with a horrible stench as Manny shitted his slacks.

"W . . . wait," Manny pleaded. "It was all Dino, man. He made me. But, K-Dawg, I brought you in the game."

"Yeah," K-Dawg sobbed, "and I'm taking you out."

K-Dawg squeezed the trigger twice and Manny's body violently jerked. K-Dawg passed the gun to Demon, and he let off a shot. The process went on repeatedly until it was China's turn. She hesitated momentarily and then grabbed the smoking pistol.

"What you doing, girl?" asked Demon.

"I'm part of this crew," said China, leveling the gun. "I'm going all the way wit' y'all."

The crew turned to K-Dawg to get his reaction. All he did was stare at China. China was an adult who could make her own decisions. K-Dawg tried to steer her away from the game, but she wanted in. She looked at Manny long and hard and put one in his cabbage.

ROSE

Black dressed and Sunday best, are for this event required.

As mourners weep, and winos pour liquor over back alley fires.

Everybody's sad when the dead are laid to rest. I don't know what for, they free from this mess.

Six-foot plots and headstones, are all that's left for the withered and bone.

Tragedy struck, when Rose went home.

CHAPTER 22

The end of summer was a sad time for the Wilson family, as the news of Rose's passing hit them suddenly. K-Dawg sat there in his black suit as the preacher delivered the eulogy. China, along with the rest of the family, was bawling and falling out; but not K-Dawg.

For some reason he couldn't find the tears. He looked at the withered old woman in the casket and saw no trace of his mother. It was odd for him because he knew he was sad, but he didn't feel like everyone else. Instead, he felt a part of himself shrivel up like a dead leaf.

Nikki sat at his side holding his hand. He had confronted her about the thing with Moose and she came clean. She gave him the whole rundown with no funny stuff; at least, that's what it seemed. K-Dawg continued to rock with Nikki, but he knew he had to feed her with a long-handled spoon, just like everyone else.

A lot of people showed up at the house afterward. Trick's ol' phony ass was sulking around like he was all broken up. The boy showed up at the funeral wearing an electric blue sharkskin suit. He looked more like a circus clown than a pimp. K-Dawg wanted to grab him by his skinny neck and snap it. China, seeing her brother's aggravation, patted his arm in an attempt to comfort him. He managed a faint smile but couldn't hide the venom behind it. He needed to get up outta there.

K-Dawg went down the stairs to the eighth floor and tapped on a dented-up apartment door. Flip answered the door and ushered in his young pupil. Flip was still a drug addict, but K-Dawg had helped him clean himself up a bit. He made sure Flip kept a haircut and a clean set of clothes on his ass. The knowledge that Flip had laid on K-Dawg was a big help to him. It was only right that he took care of the older hustler.

"What's happening?" asked Flip, his eyes misty.

"Nothing, man," said K-Dawg pinching the bridge of his nose. "I just needed to get some air, ya know?"

"Well, my home is ya home. Relax, man."

"Thanks a lot, Flip."

"Fo' sho, kid." Flip paused for a moment before speaking again. "Listen, I'm sorry 'bout ya moms, kid."

"Thanks, Flip. I guess that's just the way things go."

"Yeah, we all born to die, Keshawn. Best thing to do is enjoy the precious time we got in this shithole."

"True indeed."

"So, I hear you're moving up in the world, Keshawn."

"Like I said I would, big player. If it wasn't for your guidance, I would've had a tough time doing it."

"It's the least I could do, kid. I fucked up my life, but ain't no reason why I can't help you do something with yours."

"Thanks. I guess you already know about Manny."

"Yeah," said Flip, popping open two bottles of beer and handing one to K-Dawg. "The old man had his own son murdered, huh?"

"Yep."

"That's some cold shit."

"Yeah, but it was necessary. Remember what you told me when I came home? You said, 'you gotta be a cold mafucka to win in this game.'"

"Yeah, I remember. You got ice water running through ya blood, kid. You winning. Now you gotta establish yaself in the game."

"What you mean, Flip? I thought that's what I was doing."

"You doing all right, kid, but there's more to it. You've brought the Dawgz up and made them a powerful factor in the game, but if you wanna really be the king, y'all niggaz gotta be *the* factor."

"I'm listening."

"See, young'un, what y'all gotta do is make a power move. You see, the streets got mixed feelings about what y'all are doing. A lot of folks love you 'cause you providing opportunities for 'em. Then you got some folks who hate you for what you're doing. It's the haters who'll come gunning for you. You know who I'm talkin' 'bout?"

"Dino?"

"Yeah, you follow. Right now, that's the only nigga standing between you and supremacy. He'll keep putting it in people's heads that you just a know-nothing li'l nigga who can get got. As long as there's doubt, people will always try you."

"What you saying, Flip?"

"Dawg, this is me. You know what I'm saying. Dino is the man holding power in Harlem. He's the top dog right now. You murder him and take over his operation. Doing this will remove any doubt from people's minds about whether the Dawgz is real."

"Yeah," K-Dawg said rubbing his chin, "I bet Vega will really respect my gangsta then."

"Boy," Flip said swigging his beer, "you still thinking too damn small. Fuck Vega! That nigga don't really love you, Keshawn. He had you murder his one and only son. Fuck you think is gonna happen when you fuck up?"

"Nah, Flip. It ain't like that wit' me and Frank."

"Fuck you mean it ain't like that? To him you just another tool to use. You're making that old fuck richer than he already was, and you've proven that you would kill for him without question. In his eyes, you ain't no more than a faithful dog. If you really wanna be king, you better start thinking on a grander scale. You got killers and you got money, Keshawn. Step ya game up."

K-Dawg left Flip's house with mixed emotions. He totally understood where Flip was coming from, but he didn't like what he was saying. Killing Dino would be tough, but not impossible. Fuck, he would've gotten murdered eventually, but it was the part about crossing Vega that he really didn't like.

He had only known Vega a short time, but they were close. Vega had always been there when K-Dawg needed him, kind of like a surrogate father. But Flip was right. If something went wrong, would Vega hesitate to send someone for him?

K-Dawg shook those thoughts from his mind. Here he was, the future king, allowing his actions to be manipulated by a crackhead. Flip was knowledgeable, but he didn't know everything. K-Dawg was the master of his own destiny, and he'd be damned if a nigga was going to tell him what to do. Dino would die, but on K-Dawg's terms. All he had to do was bide his time and wait. One thing that being locked up had taught him was patience.

The next morning, K-Dawg hit the block bright and early. Levitz was very adamant about him keeping out of the spotlight, but for a king to rule justly, he had to be among his subjects. The crackheads were roaming about, trying to find that next blast of fool's paradise, and La was holding down the fort.

K-Dawg had taken a liking to the youngster from day one. La was very much like himself: no family and not a whole lot to live for. K-Dawg used to see La sleeping on benches and in stairways, so he decided to give him a job. The crew wasn't real sure about putting La down 'cause he was so young. But the young man had quickly proved his worth. He was down for whatever, wherever. K-Dawg showed him how to focus his negative energy and took him on as a protégé of sorts. Needless to say, La was grateful for the helping hand, and thus loyal to K-Dawg.

"What up, baby bro?" asked K-Dawg, sitting on the bench next to La.

"Ain't nothing, god," responded La. "A nigga out here on one."

"Right. I thought I asked you to get low. That shit you pulled been on the news since it happened."

"I did, man, but it's boring as hell on Staten Island. I had to be among my people."

"You's a hardheaded nigga, La."

"You ain't gotta tell me, K-Dawg, I know. Look, I'm sorry about your moms."

"Don't worry 'bout it, La."

"Nah, man. I would've come to the funeral, but—"

"I know, dawg. It's okay."

"Nah," La said teary-eyed, "it ain't okay. Did you know that back in the days when Moms used to smoke our check up, Rose and Granny fed us? They would always make sure me and my little sisters had something to eat when we needed it. When Rose went away and Granny died, it was like the world forgot about us. My mom is God knows where and my sisters are in the system. Shit, I'll probably never see them again."

"Don't worry 'bout it, La. You'll see them again."

"Nah, maybe it's better this way. I ain't in no position to do shit for 'em right now. Fuck, I'm depending on you to eat. K-Dawg, I don't think you know how much I owe you."

"La, you don't owe me shit. I do what I do because I got love for you."

"And I got love for you, K-Dawg. These niggaz," he said with a sweep of his hand, "they scared of you. Even certain niggaz in our crew. I know it 'cause I can smell it, dawg. But me, I ain't scared; not because you ain't the coldest mafucka on the streets, but because I understand you. We cut from the same stone, man. Look at all this shit you done accomplished in the six months you been home."

K-Dawg had never really thought about it like that. He had been so caught up in scheming that he hadn't really had a chance to step back and appreciate what he'd accomplished. He was barely old enough to drink, but he had laid the groundwork for what could prove to be the biggest drug operation in Harlem since Rich and them niggaz. He wasn't a millionaire, yet, but he was hardly broke. The kid the world had given up on was doing okay.

"You're living proof," said La speaking again, "that there's still some kinda hope for kids like me: the forgotten children. God don't love us no more, but as long as it's niggaz like you around, there will always be hope."

As K-Dawg listened to La's speech, he found himself almost crying. He had no idea that what he was doing could affect someone so much. He had love for La, and if he could, he would make sure the kid lived to be a ripe old age. But if not, fuck it. In the grand scheme of things, self-preservation held the highest importance above all else.

The two hustlers' touching moment was cut short when Hargrough and his partner, Mills, came walking toward them. La gave K-Dawg a pound and walked away. He wasn't afraid of the detectives, but he knew he was dirty. If they decided to pat him down, it'd be kind of hard to hide the 9 in his belt.

"Hey, homeboy," Mills called after La. "Where you off to?" La just stuck his middle finger up and kept stepping.

"What's up with him?" Hargrough asked, resting his foot on the bench next to K-Dawg. "He got something to hide? He might as well have stuck around; we'll catch his li'l ass sooner or later. Right now, we're hunting bigger game."

"Man." K-Dawg sighed. "What you dicks want wit' me now?"

"You know what we want," said Mills.

"If I knew, would I ask?"

"Look, K-Dawg," Hargrough spoke up, "the son of a very respected man was murdered a few days ago; know anything about it?"

"Nope."

"Don't bullshit us, K-Dog," Mills interjected.

"That's, Dawg, not Dog. Get it right, Millie."

"Whatever, eggplant. What do you know about the death of Manuel Vega?"

"Never heard of him."

"I think you're full of shit."

"And I think you're overweight, but that's just my opinion."

"Keshawn," said Hargrough, trying to be the voice of reason, "we already know you knew Manny. You two were cellmates for a time, remember? Or did you forget about that whole situation with the Black Gorilla Family? We also know you and Manny hooked up when you got outta jail. You feeling talkative yet?"

"Nope."

"Jesus," said Mills, pulling at his stained brown tie, "we're trying to help your dumb ass. Do you know who that kid's father is? Frank Vega. What do you think is gonna happen when he finds out that you had a hand in his kid's murder?"

"Look, fellas," said K-Dawg stepping off the bench, "I already told you, I don't know shit! Why y'all keep fucking wit' me when you know you can't touch me? You silly mafuckas is wasting ya time. Now, if you insist upon fucking with me, I'll have you brought up on charges."

"You motherfucker," Mills snarled. "One of these days, someone is gonna put a gun in that big-ass mouth of yours."

"Be cool, Mills," warned Hargrough. "Sorry to bother you, Mr. Wilson. Come on, Mills."

As the two detectives walked back to their car, K-Dawg had a few parting words for them. "That's right, crackers!" he shouted. "You better be fucking sorry. I'm like Midas, baby: everything I touch turn to gold. Why don't y'all go write a parking ticket or some shit?"

Everyone within earshot whooped and cheered at K-Dawg's verbal lashing of the two detectives. Mills wanted to go back, but his partner steered him toward the car. "Let him have his fun," he said smiling. "We'll get him. K-Dawg is a smart kid; I'll give him that. But even the smartest people make mistakes. Just let him keep talking; he'll fuck up. That's when we're gonna nail his black ass. I don't give a shit how long it takes. We're gonna nail that cocksucker.

CHAPTER 23

Perks was jumping that night. All of the ballers as well as the sack chasers were up in there sipping and chasing a dollar. K-Dawg, Sleepy, and Jus were at the bar drinking with two old friends, Party Tyme and Eddy Mush.

These two cats were like the Mutt and Jeff of the underworld. Party Tyme was a tall, high yellow nigga who was somewhat of a pretty boy. He was a former basketball star who got caught up in the street game. He got himself a prison record, and the NBA kind of forgot about him after that. His latest hustle was promoting parties. Party was well on his way to being a big wheel in that game.

Eddy Mush was also tall, and he and Party were at opposite ends of the color spectrum. Eddy was almost jet-black. His soft brown eyes gave off the impression that he was friendly and trusting, but those that knew him knew better. The kid was rotten from day one.

Eddy lived a hard-knock life, and it showed in the way he carried himself. He had a chip on his shoulder the size of a Volvo. Eddy was one of them cats who didn't know which aspect of the game he wanted to be involved in, so he dabbled in lots of different areas: pimping, drugs, robbery, to name just a few.

"So how you like the joint?" asked Party.

"This shit is cool," said K-Dawg, sipping his Henney. "Y'all put this thing together?"

"Yep. Me and my man Mush."

"I told you these kids threw some bomb parties," said Sleepy. "These niggaz been making spots jump for a minute now."

"Yeah, yeah," said Party. "We got like a knack for this kinda thing, ya know?"

"I feel you, kid," said K-Dawg nonchalantly. "So, what's this gotta do wit' me? I know y'all niggaz ain't invite me down here 'cause you enjoy my company."

"Hold on, K-Dawg," Sleepy spoke up. "We was just getting to that. We were talking about something I thought could benefit us all."

"I'm listening."

"Look, dawg, these niggaz is up and coming on the party circuit. They got this as well as a few other spots jumping off. We figured if we had our own spot, we could clean up."

"What, you mean like a club?"

"Not just any club, dawg: the Dawg House. Think about it, kid. It'll be the ultimate gentlemen's club. We could pool our resources like we did wit' that other thang and make some heavy bread. We might even be able to get out of the game in a few years."

"Shit." K-Dawg chuckled. "So far, the game been good to me. Ain't got no intention of getting out."

"At least think about it," said Eddy, speaking up for the first time.

"Hold on, dawg," said K-Dawg downing his drink. "First off, I don't really know either one of you niggaz; miss me wit' ya suggestions. The only reason I came down here was 'cause Sleep asked me to. Why the fuck should I take this li'l leap of faith, 'cause you say it's a good idea? Make me a believer."

"I had a feeling you might say something like that," said Party. "Ladies!" Party snapped his fingers and four fine-ass females came over to the table. "Allow me to introduce Tee, Lace, Kianna, and Li'l Black: Party's Angels."

The crew eyed the luscious young hotties like hungry wolves, but K-Dawg sat unmoved. Tee was a thick chick, not fat, just thick as hell with a big, Southern ass. Her long brown hair fell slightly over her left shoulder as she nodded toward the men.

Li'l Black was the ghetto girl of the crew. She was dark skinned and had a pretty face. She stood quietly puffing her Newport, letting the smoke sift through her full lips as she eyed Jus. She spun around so the crew could get a full view of her ass, and they were quite impressed.

Lace was a cute li'l thing who carried herself like she owned the joint. She had medium-length black hair and a petite body. She didn't have ass like the other girls, but she was sexy in her own little way.

Kianna had the full package. She was light skinned with an innocent smile, and she had the appearance of a well-developed schoolgirl. K-Dawg figured that she was probably just a very good bullshit artist. Kianna was a little bit of all the angels rolled into one. Needless to say, she was a bad bitch.

"You like?" asked Party grinning.

"I'm sold," said Jus, matching Li'l Black's stare.

K-Dawg, however, wasn't so easily impressed. "They a'ight," he said standing up. "I gotta go take a leak."

K-Dawg walked toward the bathroom shaking his head. Some niggaz were so easily sidetracked by a little fluff. In the street game, a mistake like that could prove to be fatal. An overactive dick would be the downfall of a lot of cats, but not K-Dawg.

After relieving his bladder, K-Dawg was ready to rejoin his party. A group of young men toward the back got K-Dawg's attention. They were huddled around a small television, whooping and hollering about something. K-Dawg's curiosity got the best of him, so he took a peek to see what the deal was. When he looked at the nineteen-inch screen, his green eyes flared in anger.

At first he just saw one man hitting this girl from the back, while she gave another man head. The music, along with the cheers from the crowd, muffled the sound, but the way the man was plowing into the girl, she had to be going through it. K-Dawg was about to walk away until the camera angle switched, and he saw that the girl was Pearl.

At the sight of his sister playing herself on camera, K-Dawg's emotions took over. He roared at the top of his lungs, scaring the shit out of everybody in the club. Before the bouncers could reach him, K-Dawg had yanked the television from the wall and smashed it on the ground.

Glass and sparks showered everyone in the back of the club, but K-Dawg didn't give a shit. The bouncers moved to grab him and were met with fists and feet. The first bouncer got hit square in the lip, and blood sprayed on K-Dawg's suede jacket, adding to his rage. The second bouncer managed to grab K-Dawg from behind, but he misjudged his strength and skill; before he could lock his fingers, K-Dawg tossed him over his shoulder, sending him through a glass table.

The heavyweights moving toward K-Dawg caused Jus to show his hand. He licked two shots in the air with his Glock, causing everyone to hit the ground. He and Sleepy grabbed K-Dawg and dragged him out of the club. It took the two of them to keep their enraged boss from going back in and creating even more havoc.

"Be cool!" Jus shouted.

"Fuck that!" K-Dawg barked back breaking his friend's grip. "I don't believe this shit, son. That was Pearl, yo!"

"Fuck is you yellin' 'bout?" asked Sleepy, sounding confused.

"Pearl, nigga. That punk mafucka Trick got my sis on tape, yo."

"What?" shrieked Jus. "Oh, hell nah. Call the Dawgz and let's go swallow this nigga up."

"Nah, Jus. I'm killing Trick myself."

"Look, fellas," Sleep cut in, "I'd love to get in on the li'l debate, but y'all must've forgot we was just up in there shooting. May I suggest we get the fuck off 123rd?"

"Oh, shit," muttered K-Dawg. "You right, my nigga. Peep it, Sleep, see if you can find out where that meatball-ass nigga stay at. I'm going to the house."

"Don't do nothing stupid," Sleepy warned.

"Nah, I'm taking Jus. Everything gonna be cool."

"That's what ya mouth say, but for some reason I'm having a hard time believing you, K-Dawg."

Mike stood in the shadows, slinging his stones and trying not to freeze. It had been a good while since K-Dawg had demoted him to pitcher, and his authority hadn't been restored yet. That was some cold shit, and Mike would carry that grudge for a while.

K-Dawg was on a power trip that Mike, along with a few other cats, wasn't feeling.

"Fuck K-Dawg," he said. No sooner than the words were out of his mouth was he looking around to make sure that no one had heard him. Mike talked a good game, but in all truthfulness, he was a coward. He would never be more than a fucking yes man in the underworld, and he knew it. But still he allowed his mind to daydream about all of the possible outcomes of various situations if he was head dawg.

Mike was so wrapped up in his fantasy that he didn't even see Mills sliding up behind him. Mills landed a solid right to his kidney, causing him to double over in pain. With the help of his partner, Hargrough, they dragged Mike to their car and threw him in the back seat.

"What's up, there, Mikey?" snickered Mills.

"Fuck y'all want with me?" asked Mike, still a little dazed.

"Boy," Hargrough exhaled, "you probably got an asshole full of crack, and you got the gall to ask some dumb shit like that?"

"You know what I mean, pig. Y'all are homocide, not narcotics. What da deal?"

"You know what da deal, Mikey. K-Dawg da deal."

"Never heard of him."

"Don't try to play us, Mikey," said Mills turning to face him. "You ain't hardly smart enough. We know ya story: been down with the Road Dawgz since day one. You made one little mistake and you're in the dawg house. We know, Mikey, and we also feel that it's unfair."

"Fuck outta here."

"No, no, Mikey," Hargrough joined in, "we're on the level here. We don't give a shit about the drugs. It's like you said, we're homicide, remember? As long as you fucks don't come 'round where we live, who gives a shit? What we do care about is the murders."

"Damn right," scoffed Mills. "That nut job is running around shooting up Harlem and making us look bad. We never had a misunderstanding wit' you guys before. As long as you kept the bullshit under the radar, we were cool. Now, this K-Dawg, he's changing things."

"Listen," Hargrough added, "if you keep following this dip shit, you'll catch a nice lengthy bid, or possibly even the death penalty if we can tie him to that cop's murder."

"Or?" Mikey whispered.

"Or, you can help us help you. We don't want you to wear a wire or nothing like that. Well, not yet, anyway. All we want you to do is provide us with information from time to time."

"Well, what if I say I ain't wit' it? Then what, y'all lock me up?"

"Heavens, no. In that case, we'd drop you off on the corner of 140th and Lenox, hand you a hundred bucks, and shake ya hand and say thanks."

"So, I ain't got much of a choice, huh?"

"Mikey, there are always choices, but we know you'll do the right thing."

"Fuck it. What y'all wanna know?"

Between the liquor and his adrenaline, K-Dawg misjudged his strength. When he arrived at his family's home, he had intended to open the door forcibly but not be brutish about it. K-Dawg swung the door open with so much might that he knocked several pictures down and opened a small hole in the wall. Pearl came out to see what all the commotion was about and found herself eye to eye with a rabid dog.

"Keshawn?" she whispered.

"Whore," he hissed. "Did you think I wouldn't find out?"

"Boy, what you talkin' 'bout?"

"Don't play me, Pearl," he said approaching her. "I saw the tape, you fucking bitch." K-Dawg clamped a hand around her neck and squeezed slightly. "Here I am, trying to make things better for y'all, and what do you do? You let some slick talking-ass nigga convince you to blow some cat on tape."

"W . . . wait, Keshawn."

"Wait for what? For you to try to worm ya way outta this shit?"

"Keshawn, ain't no shame in my game. I do what I do to feed my son. Ain't like it was no man 'round here to help out. Yeah, I sell ass from time to time, but fuck it; I'm grown and it pays well. Furthermore—"

That was about as far as Pearl got before K-Dawg slapped hellfire out of her. The blow sent her sailing across the room and bouncing off a wall. K-Dawg's eyes blazed as he advanced on her.

Jus moved to stop him but he waved him off.

"I can't believe this shit," said Pearl.

"Oh, believe it, Pearl. You my fucking sister, and I'll kill you before I let you shame yaself like that again."

"Fuck you, K-Dawg. Who the fuck do you think you are? You're part of the reason why this family is so fucked up, you and your revenge, remember? It was that shit that took both of our parents. You were rotten, then, Keshawn, and you're rotten now."

"You don't know shit about me, Pearl. I do what I do for us."

"That's bullshit, and you know it is. I know just who you are, Mr. Hotshot Drug Dealer. Keshawn, you're a liar and a murderer. I know what you do in the streets. You bring death and destruction. You talk about us this and us that, but the only person who matters is you. It's only a matter of time before Jus and the rest of ya dawgs find out what kinda nigga you are."

"Watch ya mouth, Pearl."

"Fuck you, Keshawn. You can't scare me like you do everyone else. I'm not Pooh or one of them niggaz afraid to speak out against you, or that dumb bitch, Nikki, whose so blinded by love that she can't see you for the monster you really are. They call Damien 'Demon' but that name suits you so much better. There wasn't a lot of love between me and Daddy, but I can agree with him on one thing: Mama should've gotten rid of you."

That last statement hit K-Dawg like a physical blow. He and Pearl had exchanged words before, but never of this magnitude. At that moment, Pearl wasn't speaking out of anger. Her words were from sheer hatred.

K-Dawg stood there dumbfounded. The beast in him wanted to kill Pearl, while the little boy in him wanted to cry. A wave of madness washed over K-Dawg. He started to speak, but his words were mostly gibberish. One word that Pearl did hear as clear as a bell was "death."

"Excuse me?" she asked.

"Death," he repeated. "Death: this is the judgment that I have made. Trick's worthless-ass life belongs to me."

"You leave him out of this, Keshawn."

"You know what, Pearl? You about a dumb bitch. That no-good pimping-ass nigga using you and you too blind to see it. When I catch him, he gonna die. If I catch you with him, he gonna die in front of you."

"You don't own me, Keshawn. I'm your big sister; you don't tell me what to do!"

"I've made my judgment, Pearl. I love you, so I can forgive your words here tonight. But, love you as I do, someone has to suffer. I choose Trick."

"You bastard! I hate you, Keshawn. I wish they'd never let you out of prison."

Pearl continued her verbal assault, but K-Dawg didn't listen. He was too busy trying to head out the door before the tears came. What Pearl said had hurt him, but that wasn't what brought the tears. Seeing Justin's face as his mother aired his dirt was what had really hurt him. In his nephew's eyes, he would forever be a monster.

K-Dawg sat on the leather sofa in Nikki's living room trying to suck the life out of the blunt he held in his hand. He was trying to relax a little after his and Pearl's spat, but it was hard. His blood boiled at the thought of what Trick was forcing his sister to do.

Actually, he wasn't really forcing her to do anything; Pearl was a grown-ass woman. The fact that his sister was a filthy, sack-chasing whore, and Trick was her pimp, was just the grim reality of it all.

Isis walked over and laid her head on K-Dawg's lap. He stroked her head and smiled down at his little pet. She had come a long way from the sickly little thing he purchased from Fat Tone. Isis had put on a little weight and a whole lot of attitude. She had grown to be quite vicious and very protective of her master.

The more Pearl's accusations crept into K-Dawg's thoughts, the more he wondered if it was true. It had sounded absurd at the time, but the more he thought about it, the more sense it made. If he hadn't let his rage overshadow his judgment, Charlie would still be alive and his family would still be whole. But then again, no, it wouldn't. Kiesha would still be gone. *Fuck Charlie.*

"Do you think I'm a monster?" he asked Isis. The hound looked at him quizzically and licked his hand. "You a good bitch, ma. As long as I feed you and show you love, you'll always be down for me. Fuck everybody else."

"Who are you talking to?" asked Nikki, coming into the room.

"Ain't nothing. Just kicking it with Isis."

"Keshawn, I don't know whose crazier: you or that damn dog."

"Nah," he said rubbing the hound's chin, "she a'ight."

"Whatever," said Nikki flopping down on the couch next to him. "That bitch is 730. My friends don't even come by here no more to fuck wit' her."

"Well, that means she's doing her job. Them grimy bitches ain't about shit anyway."

"Nigga, please. Ya friends worse than mine."

"How you figure?"

"Keshawn, I really wish you would stop treating me like I don't know what's up. I know what y'all niggaz in the streets doing, and I don't mean selling drugs."

"Sorry, Nikki, I don't know what you're talkin' 'bout."

"Keshawn, even a blind woman could see. Look how many people have died since you been home. Harlem ain't been this live in years."

"What's that got to do with me?"

"What do you think? Baby, people are talking about you everywhere. Even when I go to the beauty salon, the Road Dawgz is usually the main topic of conversation— the infamous K-Dawg and his crew."

"Nikki," he said pulling her to him, "you know how bitches gossip, so why feed into it?"

"Why? Because this shit has caused all kinds of hell in my life. Some of my girls don't even wanna hang with me anymore. They think somebody's gonna jump out of the shadows and get one of them trying to get at me."

"Them hoes just paranoid. I'm the baddest mafucka to ever shit between a pair of shoes, and you my lady. A nigga gotta have a death wish."

"Oh yeah? Well, tell that to ya crazy-ass sister, China. I mean, damn. The bitch snuffed me and I let it ride, but she still wanna be looking at me all crazy. What up wit' that?"

"Let's keep it real, Nikki. You brought that shit on yaself."

"How?"

"Don't play stupid. If you had just told me what was up wit' Moose, that wouldn't have happened."

"Keshawn, how many times you gonna throw that shit up in my face? I told you I was sorry."

"I know, Nikki. And I believe you. But you can't front; you was trying to be sneaky about it."

"No I wasn't, Keshawn. I was scared to tell you. When you came home, we were just fucking. I ain't know whether we was gonna be together or what. I kept telling Moose over the phone that it was a wrap for him and me, but he wasn't trying to hear it. That's why I went to tell him face to face."

"Nikki, I love you, girl. You don't have anything to fear from me."

"You say that, but . . ."

"But what? Nikki, if you got something you wanna say, then say it."

Nikki cleared her throat. "Well, people, they say things about you."

"Like?"

"Keshawn, they say you're a killer. They tell stories about how you be having Pooh cousin and his man execute people."

"That's bullshit, Nikki. Niggaz just like to talk."

"Keshawn, I see it in you. You're not the same person I used to know. You might not mean to be, but in a sense . . . you're evil."

"Evil? Nikki, you got a wild-ass imagination. Just because I sell drugs don't make me evil."

"Well, what am I supposed to think? Your peoples sell crack, coke and dope like they slinging hot dogs. They do it all out in the open and the police turn the other cheek? Come on, Keshawn."

"It's like I told you before, Nikki: don't worry about things that don't concern you. I'm gonna keep getting money and you gonna keep being the baddest bitch in Harlem. We a team, baby."

"I know, daddy. It's just that with all that's going on in the hood, is it safe for us to keep resting our heads here?"

"You right about that there, girl. But don't worry. As soon as I get my weight up, we gonna move."

"Oh," Nikki said jumping to her feet, "I'm glad you said that. I got a surprise for you." Nikki went into the bedroom and came back holding an envelope. She tossed it into K-Dawg's lap and stood back smiling.

"What's this?" he asked, examining the envelope.

"My Section 8 came through. Now all we gotta do is find a nice apartment. Maybe even a house."

"That's what's up," he said pulling her into his lap. "Have 8 will travel. When you wake up tomorrow, start looking for a place."

Nikki clapped her hands excitedly. "Thank you, daddy."

K-Dawg's cell phone going off cut their moment short. He put the phone to his ear and listened as the caller spoke. After a few minutes, he hung up the phone and smiled.

"What you cheesing about?" Nikki asked with attitude. "What, that was one of ya bitches?"

"Nah," he said as he stood up, "you and Isis are the only bitches in my life. I gotta make a run right quick, but I'll be back."

"Here we go with this shit again. Keshawn, I hardly see you anymore. Why don't you stay with me tonight?"

"I will, I will. I just gotta go see somebody right quick. You want anything while I'm out?"

"Yeah, you can bring me some soul food. A bitch ain't eat since this afternoon."

"Anything you want, ma."

K-Dawg kissed Nikki and headed out the door. Nikki sat stroking Isis's head thinking about her life. She was no dummy to the streets. She knew just what K-Dawg was doing, and it wasn't nothing nice. But what did it really matter? She was being well taken care of, and that was the important thing. K-Dawg was well on his way to being the king of the underworld, and what good was a king without a queen?

"So what you got for me?" Jackson asked, steering the big Yukon down Twelfth Avenue.

"You know I got you," said K-Dawg handing him a thick envelope. "You take care of me and I'll take care of you."

"That's why I fucks wit' you," said Jackson scanning through the bills in the envelope. "You know how to do business. The rest of these cats always got an excuse or some shit. My whole thing is, when I do what I do for yo' ass, I don't make excuses; so don't make none up when I come for my bread."

"I know that's right, Jackson. When it come to money, ain't no time to play. These lobster-ass niggaz just don't understand the game."

"Speaking of the game, I got something you might be interested in."

"Well, what's up?"

"That shit wit' you and Dino is about to take a turn for the worse."

"How you figure?"

"Come on, K-Dawg. Don't play stupid with me. I'm Action Jackson, baby. My ear always to the street."

"Man, fuck Dino and the rest of them bean-eating niggaz. They can't do me none."

"A'ight, tough guy. Just watch yo' ass. A lot of people are saying your crew killed Manny. They stepped to Vega about killing ya li'l ass, but for some reason, he keep saying no."

"Imagine that."

"I should hope you wasn't stupid enough to lie down with that greasy old bastard on this hit."

"Nah, not the kid."

"Keshawn, if Vega had his own son murdered, fuck you think he could do to you?"

"You got it wrong, Jackson. I'm just a cool dude people take a liking to. Maybe Vega just likes my style."

"Yeah, a'ight, Keshawn. I got my own theory about that, but I'm gonna leave it alone. And them li'l care packages you've been sending out ain't helped much."

"Oh," K-Dawg said laughing, "you heard about that, huh?"

"Keshawn, that shit might be funny to you, but all it did was draw a lot of attention to ya crew."

"That's why I did it. These niggaz gotta understand that the Dawgz is hungry. We ain't come in the game coming at these niggaz sideways; they made it like that."

"Whatever. You say tomato, I say tomahto. Either way, it's only a matter of time before Dino try to have ya li'l ass killed. You got two choices, Keshawn: tone it down or kill Dino. If not, somebody gonna front page ya ass."

Before Keshawn could respond, his cell went off. He put his ear to the phone and was greeted by a frantic China. She was talking so fast that he almost couldn't make out what she was saying.

"China, slow down," he said trying to cut her off. "What? Fuck you mean, gone?"

CHAPTER 24

Dino sat at the head of the conference table looking over his esteemed guests. There were twelve men in all: six chiefs escorted by one lieutenant apiece. The chiefs were: Blood, from Brooklyn; Terror, from Queens; Shai, from Staten Island; Boss Hog, from the Bronx; Banks, from Harlem; and Flaco.

The men at the meeting were among some of the most dangerous in New York. They each held sway in their own part of the city, keeping relative peace within the crew. They would often get together to discuss politics or to squash beef among their numbers, but this meeting was different. They were gathered in one of Dino's houses to discuss a common problem: the Road Dawgz.

"I don't know," Terror spoke up. "Maybe we should just hear them out, fellas."

"I agree," said Banks. "The kids are playing fair with the rest of the small timers they hitting. Why not cake off for two thousand cheaper?"

"Gentlemen, gentlemen," Dino cut in, "I respect your opinions, but I think we're all missing the bigger picture. We are the controlling factors in New York's drug trade. We keep the peace 'cause we think with our heads and not our guns. These kids are just new age cowboys."

"Humph," grunted Boss Hog. "I can recall a time when you played by those same set of rules, Dino."

Boss Hog was the elder of the crew. He was a wide, dark-skinned man, with beady little eyes and huge purple lips. His most defining feature, though, was the scar that ran from his right eye down to his upper lip. Boss Hog had run his operation in the White Plains section of the Bronx with only minor skirmishes for some years. The other crews respected him for his fairness as well as his willingness to commit violence.

"All well and good," Dino continued, "but I never took it this far." Dino slid two eight-by-ten photos to the center of the table for all to see. "I'm sure I'm not the only one to have received these."

The photos caused some of those assembled to turn their heads. Those whose stomachs were a little stronger looked on in amazement. The first photo was of a person whose sex was hard to tell, because the body was so badly mangled. The upper torso and face were practically shredded, and there were two large holes in the skull where the eyes once were. The second photo was of two large mastiffs tearing a body to shreds—a grotesque sight indeed.

"Do you see this shit?" Dino asked. "This came to my house by messenger."

"Yeah," said Shai, speaking for the first time. "I got one of them shits too. Came to my baby mama house. Them pricks got some fucking nerve."

"My point exactly," said Dino standing. "Who the fuck do these Road Dawgz think they are? These snot-nosed punks are barely old enough to wipe their assess without getting shit on their thumbs, but they send messages to men of our caliber? I can't speak for y'all, but I ain't going out like that."

"So, let's kill 'em and be done with it," snarled Blood. "I got some people on my team who'll do it."

"Easier said than done, my friend," warned Banks. "Dino, you sent Supreme for K-Dawg, and he came back in a box. That boy's mama had to have a closed-casket funeral."

"Gotdamn," said Terror. "Them niggaz was the ones who killed Supreme? Shit, him and me had a falling out last year over that stickup shit. Nigga sent two of mine on a first-class flight to hell. Supreme was a mean mafucka."

"That there is food for thought," said Boss Hog. "I say we see what kinda shit the youngster is rapping about. If he's setting work out cheaper than what we're already getting it for, why not hear him out?"

"I'm with the fat man," cosigned Banks. "I met K-Dawg a while back. He's a reasonable kid; mean as all hell, but reasonable. Plus his work is butter."

"I can't believe this shit!" Dino said in disbelief. "Y'all is supposed to be gangstas. How you gonna let this li'l know-nothing mafucka put fear in ya hearts?"

"It ain't about fear," said Boss Hog rising to his feet. "Some of us just ain't with no unnecessary violence right now. Things is hot enough with them angels of death, or whatever, killing every fucking thing in sight. If we can squash this and still turn a profit, I say it's worth at least looking into."

"The Hog is right," said Terror. "I'm willing to listen. If we don't like what we hear, then we kill 'em. But let's at least give 'em a play."

"Fuck this!" Dino shouted, slamming his palms against the table. "Y'all niggaz do what y'all will. I know this much, though: New Year's will be here in three weeks, so that's all the time that little shit is gonna get. If he still acting crazy, I'm putting him down myself. Fuck it!"

One by one, the men filed out of Dino's office. They all had mixed feelings about how to deal with the Road Dawgz. Some agreed with Dino, while others sided with Boss Hog. Whatever the outcome, they knew that they'd have one hell of a fight on their hands trying to get at the Road Dawgz.

***

Pooh and Chi-Chi sat in the living room of their duplex apartment playing PlayStation and talking shit, while Hector busied himself with free weights. Chi-Chi loved the apartment that K-Dawg had helped them get. It was quite a few steps up from the overcrowded, rodent-infested hovels he was used to. K-Dawg had made sure the crib was hooked up to their specifications and was equipped with all the modern appliances they would need to live comfortably. Whenever Chi-Chi stepped into the pad, he felt like a king. Pooh, on the other hand, wasn't satisfied.

"I'm still hyped off this shit," said Chi-Chi, tapping away at the controller. "Ya man knows how to take care of his peoples."

"This shit a'ight," said Pooh, taking a long swig of 151. "I seen better."

"Fuck is up wit' you, primo? Why you always complaining and shit?"

"Nigga, 'cause I want more outta life."

"What more you need? We living good and we eating good with K-Dawg."

"Fuck that shit, yo. Y'all niggaz act like he God or something."

"It ain't like that, Pooh. But the nigga put us on. You gotta respect that."

"Respect my ass. I was the one out here on the grind, while that nigga was looking at three hots and a cot. Who the fuck is he to come home and give orders?"

"He's the man who built this, kid."

"Fuck outta here," said Pooh, taking another guzzle. "All he did was capitalize on what I already started. That nigga more of a thief than a savior."

"You got jokes," said Chi-Chi. "Fuck was you building, a corner of your own? This black kid is reaching for the stars, primo."

"You about a dick riding-ass nigga, Chi-Chi. If you wanna give somebody head, it should be me. I brought you in."

"Hold on, hold on," said Chi-Chi, putting down the controller. "First of all, watch how the fuck you talk to me. Second of all, you ain't pull me in until K-Dawg put you down, you fake-ass kingpin. Don't be coming at me like a mafucka gave me shit. I earned my right to be a Dawg. How many mafuckas you killed throughout all this shit?"

"Chi-Chi, all I'm saying is it should've been me. Why the fuck should he be the next king?"

"Because, you drunk mafucka, he actually wants it. Niggaz like you talk about it, while niggaz like him is about it. You better pull yo' ass outta that bottle and get hip to what's going on. If I gotta ride with K-Dawg into the gates of hell so I can live good while I'm here, I'm cool with it."

"Whatever," said Pooh, staggering to his feet. "We'll see. Every dog has his day, and mine is coming. Then we'll see who you follow."

Pooh half stumbled and half walked up the carpeted stairs. Chi-Chi looked over at Hector and shook his head. The two men had been down for so long that neither had to speak to know what the other was thinking. Pooh was Chi-Chi's first cousin and he loved him, but if he tried some dumb shit to fuck up their quality of life, he could get it too. To the two poor kids from the DR, there were some things more important than family.

K-Dawg entered the apartment to find China on the couch crying. When she had called and told him of Pearl's departure, he thought she was exaggerating. Now that he stood in the threshold of their family home, he saw that she wasn't. Most of Pearl and Justin's clothes were gone.

Some of their stuff still remained, but the valuables had been taken. There was no note or sign of where they had gone to, but K-Dawg knew the cause.

He slumped down on the couch next to his sister and tried to comfort her. K-Dawg opened his mouth to say something, but he couldn't find the words. He tried to think positively about the whole situation, but it was damned near impossible. He knew Pearl had left because he had threatened to kill Trick. At the time, he had spoken out of anger. He and Pearl had both said some pretty fucked-up things to each other, but he never imagined that this would be the outcome. His rash temper had delivered yet another crippling blow to the Wilson family.

"We'll find them, China," he whispered. "We're gonna get them back."

"Oh, Keshawn," she sobbed into his chest, "why she do that? Why Pearl had to break our family up?"

"I . . . I don't know," he lied. "But let's not worry ourselves about that. The main thing is getting them back."

"What if we can't find them?"

"Hush with that foolishness, China. This is K-Dawg, baby girl. We'll get 'em back."

K-Dawg wished that he was as confident as he sounded. The truth of the matter was that fucking with a slick-ass nigga like Trick, they could be anywhere. One thing for sure was that when he did find Pearl and Justin, he would apologize to them both. Then he would put a bullet in Trick's head. As reassuring as the thought was, it would be quite some time before K-Dawg would see his nephew again, and it would be under different circumstances.

For the next week or so, K-Dawg walked around in a daze. He couldn't eat, sleep or conduct his business. In the game, those who weren't on point usually wound up on some coroner's table. Jus understood this and stepped to the plate. He had Nikki put his friend on bed rest while he ran the operation.

For days, K-Dawg lay in bed trying to unscramble the mess in his head. He had people searching high and low for his family, with little to no results. Someone had spotted them in Jersey, but they had disappeared before he had a chance to follow up on the lead. Nikki had tried to arouse K-Dawg, but it was useless. Even faithful Isis couldn't bring her master out of his depression. She just lay at his bedside, waiting for him to snap out of it.

The holiday season was coming, so everyone was busy getting their shop on or doing whatever it was they did around that time of year. The Road Dawgz also had their hands full, organizing their first annual Christmas banquet. They rented the Kennedy Center and invited all of the families in the hood to come out for free dinners and toys. It was originally K-Dawg's idea to earn the favor of the people. But him being in a near vegetable-like state, his peoples stepped up and carried out his wishes.

It was Christmas Eve, so Nikki dipped out to do some last-minute shopping. She tried to get K-Dawg to go with her, but he was content with staying in bed and sulking. She felt for her man, but she didn't want to rush his recovery and cause more damage. Nikki kissed him on the forehead and left Isis to watch over him.

K-Dawg lay there in a dreamlike state. He wasn't asleep, yet he wasn't awake, either. He heard the front door open, but something about the way it sounded wasn't right. He heard heavy footsteps on the tile floor, and knew that it wasn't Nikki. Isis stood alert, but she didn't bark. She pulled at the bedspread cover, but K-Dawg couldn't bring himself to move. He wanted to rise, but he lacked the strength. Even if the intruder meant him harm, it didn't matter. In a sense, he welcomed death; it would be a release from all of the pain he was feeling at that moment.

The two masked men scurried to the closed bedroom door with their guns drawn. The first man stepped into the darkened room and all hell broke loose. Isis lunged out of the darkness and clenched her teeth on to his arm. The pressure of the pitbull's locked jaw on his flesh was so severe that he dropped his gun.

The second man tried to focus a bead on the hound, but the darkness worked against him. Even with the infrared beam, he couldn't get a clear shot at the thrashing pit. He quickly tucked his gun and pulled a knife. With a flick of his wrist, he slashed Isis across the back, causing her to howl.

The sound of another loved one being hurt stirred K-Dawg. As the haze lifted from his mind, the scent of blood mixed with adrenaline awoke the killer in him. K-Dawg rolled off of the edge of the bed and crouched down. After retrieving the small box-like machine gun from under his bed, he was ready to bang.

Isis was hurt, so she wouldn't be much of a problem. Unfortunately, for the intruders, they wasted too much time worrying about the wrong dog. They looked toward the bed for their target, but he was no longer there. By the time they spotted his shadow, muzzled flashes blinded them. The bullets screamed across the room, seeking sustenance to feed their hunger, and the intruders did just that.

The bullets invaded the first man's chest and blew the majority of his lower jaw to pieces. He was dead before he hit the ground. The second man took three to the stomach and forearm, but he was still breathing. K-Dawg flicked on the light to examine his handiwork. Blood was splattered all over everything in the room.

The mirror was shattered and the door was perforated with holes. After checking on Isis, K-Dawg turned his attention to the survivor.

"Punk-ass nigga!" he shouted, kicking the man. "Who sent you?" The man groaned in pain but didn't answer. "Oh, so you a bad mafucka, huh? Let's try it like this."

K-Dawg snatched off the man's ski mask and found himself face to face with Dino's yes man, Flaco. Flaco's eyes danced with fear as K-Dawg put the gun's hot barrel to his lips. He thought K-Dawg was going to kill him, but he wouldn't be so lucky. Flaco was going to the flesh factory.

K-Dawg flipped open his cell and punched in a number. "D," he barked into the phone, "I need you to come by my house. Nah, I'm cool. Isis is a li'l banged up, but she'll live. Had a li'l spill, so bring some cleaning supplies, feel me? A'ight, kid. Good looking."

The next call was to Nikki. K-Dawg instructed her not to come back to the house. She asked him if something was wrong, but he just shushed her and continued with his instructions. She was to meet him at his family's home and he would explain there.

"Yeah," said K-Dawg kicking Flaco, again, "y'all niggas thought you could come for me? That's a'ight. I tried to be the good dude, but that wasn't good enough, huh? The gloves are off now, baby. It's a wrap for you and ya mafuckin' man, Dino. But Dino gonna die quick. You, my friend, you violated my home. I got something special planned for you."

Flaco wanted to say something. It didn't matter what, just anything that might save him. Seeing the maddened grin on K-Dawg's face, he knew he didn't have a chance. Flaco closed his eyes and prayed that God would let him die before this madman had his way with him.

CHAPTER 25

K-Dawg sat at the banquet table, greeting guests, as his crew brought him up to speed on what he had missed. All the Dawgz were decked out in Armani suits of various hues for this event, courtesy of K-Dawg. Even China and Nikki managed to play nice for this one. K-Dawg rewarded them both with stunning ball gowns, tailored to fit their respective figures.

Plenty of people turned out for the event. Even the older people, who had once cursed K-Dawg, were praising him for the glorious shindig that he'd arranged. What surprised everyone was when Demon slithered into the banquet hall and took a seat next to China. K-Dawg made a mental note to himself to find out what was up with that.

After the food and the toys were given out, K-Dawg thanked everyone for coming and bid them good night. When the hall had cleared, K-Dawg had La escort Nikki home and began the meeting. The topic was Dino, to no one's surprise.

"Them mafuckas came in ya house?" asked Chi-Chi. "I say we go dump on all them niggaz right now."

"Hold ya head," cautioned Demon. "I'm sure our benefactor has a plan."

"Indeed I do," K-Dawg said smiling. "Yeah, I took a little powder, so mafuckas thought I was going soft. Won't make that mistake again. Niggaz came in my house, kid. That's where me and wifey lay our heads, and they violated. Demon, that bitch-ass nigga Flaco still with us?"

"Yeah," said Demon sipping his drink. "That fuck is still holding on, but barely. We got Hector watching him now."

"Good, good. You see, what's bugging the hell outta me is, how they know where Nikki stay? If they had run up in my people's spot, I would've understood; everybody in the hood knows my family. But they didn't go by there. They went straight to Nikki's. Why is that?"

The crew exchanged suspicious glances, but nobody said anything. They all knew where K-Dawg was going with that, but no one wanted to admit it.

"Nobody got shit to say, huh? Only a few people know that I stay wit' Nikki, and even fewer know that I was up there in a stupor. Somebody talking."

"Yo, you think it's one of us?" asked Jus.

"Jus," said K-Dawg, resting his knuckles on the table, "it ain't what I think, it's what I know. Either one of us, or somebody close to us, is running they yap."

"Fuck a snitch!" yelled Ch-Chi, rasing his gun. "Death to any and all who break the circle."

"Easy," said Demon, patting Chi-Chi's arm.

"Nah," said Sleepy, "I'm with him on this one. We living too large for this shit. My ho game ain't never been tighter than it is now. If a nigga telling, he gotta go."

"And go he shall," said K-Dawg, firmly gripping Sleepy's shoulder. "I got it all worked out."

"Well, put us on," said Pooh.

"Can't. No offense to anyone here, but I ain't too sure who I can trust right now. I got my suspicions about who I can trust and who I can't. But don't worry, my niggaz. All will be revealed in time. Now, y'all niggaz go be with ya families. Merry Christmas, Road Dawgz."

One by one, the crew filed out of the banquet hall. The only ones left were K-Dawg, China, and Demon. He asked them to stay behind, because they would play key roles in his plan.

"So, what's up, K-Dawg?" asked Demon.

"Murder, my man, plain and simple. We've played the background long enough. It's time to play our hand."

"Dino gotta get it, li'l bro," said China.

"I know, sis. You gonna be the one to help me give it to him."

"You mean like with Sticks?"

"Nah, this is a li'l different. I need a bad bitch to pull this off, but not you. This will be Dino's last New Year."

"Keshawn, I ain't scared to body a nigga."

"I know, China. But trust me when I say you don't wanna ride out on this one. I need you to find me the baddest bitch you can to do me a favor. Tell her there's ten grand in it for her."

"I'm on it."

"And what about me?" asked Demon. "What part will I play in all of this?"

"Demon, as always, you'll be the wolf amid the sheep."

Demon slipped out, whichever way he slipped in, while K-Dawg and China walked out the front door. They were laughing, trying to get into the Christmas spirit, when Hargrough and Mills stepped out of the shadows. Any mirth that K-Dawg might've felt vanished at the sight of the detectives.

"Merry Christmas, crack lord." Mills smiled.

"Fuck you," K-Dawg snarled. "Fuck away from me and my sister."

"Oh," Mills started as he rudely gawked at China, "such a pretty young thing."

"Why, thank you." China smiled. "If I had a dick, I'd invite you to suck it."

"Fuck you, cunt!"

"Cool out," Hargrough said to his partner. "It's the holidays, buddy. K-Dawg, we didn't come to exchange insults with you; just wanted to bring you a little gift."

"I don't want shit y'all got to give me."

"Oh, I think you do. We come bearing the gift of knowledge. Your ship has sprung a leak, dawg; only a matter of time now."

"Look," said K-Dawg scratching his head, "didn't we go through this already? You square-ass niggaz couldn't catch a cold. I got an idea, though: why don't you lick out the crack of my ass and tell me if it tastes like chocolate?"

"Okay, smart ass. You think this shit is funny and we're only trying to help you."

"How the fuck could you possibly help me?"

"Work with us. Help us to bring down—"

"Fuck outta here!" barked K-Dawg. "Picture me going out like that. You mafuckas is crazy. I tell you like this, kid: if y'all mafuckas ever come at me on that snitch shit again, I might forget you're cops."

"Is that a threat?" asked Mills stepping forward.

"Take it how you want it, pussy," said K-Dawg, not backing down.

"Come on, Keshawn," said China grabbing his arm.

"A'ight," said K-Dawg allowing her to pull him away. "Last warning, pigs. Stay the fuck away from me."

The two detectives watched them walk away and grinned. They were playing with K-Dawg. They were trying their best to wear on his nerves, and it was working. They knew that in time, they would provoke K-Dawg to lose his cool. When he finally fucked up and did something stupid, they'd be there to pick up the pieces.

The Pink Flamingo was an out-of-the-way bar on 156th Street and Broadway. To the average passerby, it looked like a regular lounge. To those in the know, it was a place where hustlers came to unwind. People could get anything they wanted at the Pink Flamingo: girls, food, booze, or drugs. Whatever the fancy, nine times out of ten, it could be gotten there.

Dino sat in his private booth in the back of the bar, sipping champagne. He had his crew with him, and a big-butt black freak was in his lap. It was New Year's Eve, and he was partying.

Most of the hustlers from Manhattan as well as the Bronx were up in the spot. Everybody was dressed to impress, each crew trying to out-stunt the other. Every kind of material was on display, including fur, leather, silk, and lace. The ballers and the broads were putting it down.

People crowded the dance floor as well as the bar, grooving to the beat and trying to get their stunt on. The party was in full swing, when all of a sudden everything stopped. Eyes bulged and mouths dropped open as K-Dawg stepped into the bar followed by Jus, Sleepy, and La.

K-Dawg was killin' 'em with his 'fit. He wore a charcoal gray suit with a black shirt and black tie. His black gators clicked on the hardwood floor as he strode across the room. To make the 'fit even crazier, he wore a full-length white mink and a matching gangster-style hat.

Jus followed closely behind, looking like a million bucks. He wore a blue silk shirt that was half buttoned, showing off the gold cross swinging on his chest. His black slacks were perfectly creased under his full black mink. In the dim light, he looked more Indian than Black.

La stood to K-Dawg's left, eyeing the crowd for any suspicious movement. He was sporting a powder blue Coogi sweater, a pair of baggy Parasucos, and a heavy black leather coat. His powder blue Timbs treaded gracefully across the dance floor. They had tried to get the youngster to wear something more formal, but he wasn't having it; La was a solider to his heart.

Sleepy came hard for this event. He rocked a black designer suit, and a mink similar to the ones worn by K-Dawg and Jus, but his was dyed canary yellow with black tiger stripes. The shoes and hat he wore matched his coat. He flashed an ear-to-ear grin as he stepped in the joint, flanked by two of his finest girls.

People looked at the crew with mixed emotions. Some felt fear, while others felt envy and admiration. Whatever they felt, they got the fuck out of the way as the Road Dawgz headed toward Dino's booth.

Dino's bodyguards moved to block K-Dawg, but he waved them off. "It's cool," said Dino smiling. "Let them pass."

"Thank you," said K-Dawg, half bowing. "I brought you a gift." When K-Dawg reached into his coat, the guard closest to him grabbed his arm. "Easy," K-Dawg said removing a bottle from his pocket, "it's just champagne. Damn, Dino, ya peoples sure are paranoid."

"Not paranoid," said Dino accepting the bottle, "just cautious. Keeps me healthy, ya know?"

"Fo' sho."

"So, to what do I owe the pleasure?"

"Nothing much, Dino, just came to talk."

"Oh, yeah? So talk."

"Listen," said K-Dawg inviting himself to sit down, "it's no secret that there's bad blood between our crews. You're already an established player in the game, and I'm on a come up."

"Now that you've given us all a lesson on current events, what the fuck is the point?"

K-Dawg suppressed the urge to slash Dino's face and continued speaking. "Look, my man, we can keep going at it back and forth, slinging insults and bullets, or we can try to resolve this like gentlemen."

"Whatever, K-Dawg. You don't know shit about being a gentleman. You're a street punk, and I'm a businessman."

"We all gotta start somewhere, kid. I'm sure you've done quite a bit of dirt trying to come up."

"Yeah, but it was different. Back in the eighties, we had rules. We respected the code. You niggers have no rules."

"You better watch ya fucking mouth, chili boy," snapped La.

"Easy, son," cautioned K-Dawg. "I'm gonna let that one slide, Dino, but please respect me and mine."

"Respect?" Dino laughed. "Fuck outta here. The Road Dawgz is nothing more than a bunch of cowboys. You think that because you murder, we should respect you? Each and every one of you mafuckas is going to end up dead or in jail. When that day comes, I'll still be right here."

"Dino, all I wanna do is move my product and live my life. If you would just—"

"K-Dawg, I'm not trying to hear you, a'ight? Take ya puppies and bounce."

K-Dawg fixed a stone-faced glare on Dino. If looks could kill, Dino would've dropped dead right then and there. K-Dawg tried to be the bigger dude, but Dino had tried to play him. The time for games was over, and Dino was about to be dealt with accordingly.

"A'ight," said K-Dawg standing. "Thank you for your time, Dino. Let's get up outta here, y'all."

Dino watched the crew leave and shook his head. He didn't understand how the other bosses could even entertain the idea of giving the young upstarts a play; they were unorganized and uneducated. Even the mighty K-Dawg had proved that he was a coward without his gun. *Fuck the Road Dawgz.*

***

The New Year had come and gone. Dino staggered from the Pink Flamingo, drunk as a skunk, with the big-butt freak on his arm. He had dismissed the second bodyguard and kept the first one to drive him home. He had planned on going home to bust out the black girl and didn't need an entourage with him.

As soon as Dino's truck encountered traffic, the girl immediately went to work. She pulled Dino's small penis from his pants and began to suck him off. Dino laid his head back and enjoyed the oral pleasure. The girl sucked him so good that he wanted to shout for joy. His trip to ecstasy was interrupted when the driver slammed on the brakes.

"Why the hell did you stop?" asked Dino from the back seat.

"This fucking fool is in the way," said the driver.

Dino looked past his shoulder and saw the human roadblock. There was a thin man standing in the middle of the street. His suit was stained and torn, but otherwise in good condition. Judging by the way he staggered back and forth, he was clearly drunk. Dino's bodyguard beat the horn, but the man didn't move. Dino grew tired of waiting and had his driver get out to move the man.

Dino's driver was a little irritated, but he did as he was told.

He strolled over to the drunken man and put his hand on his shoulder. By the time he saw the blade in the man's hand, it was too late. With speed and skill from years of training, Demon plunged the blade into the driver's throat. The only sound the driver made was a horrible gurgling before falling into Demon's arms.

"What the fuck?" Dino gasped. As he tried to climb into the driver's seat, the girl pulled a blade and pressed it into his throat. At that moment, Dino realized that he had been crossed in a major way.

Dino just sat there in shock as Demon strolled over to the car. He begged and pleaded for his life, but his cries fell on deaf ears. No amount of money that he could've offered would've saved his life; when Demon was sent to kill a man, he did just that. With a flick of his wrist, Demon slashed Dino's throat, sending blood splattering all over the interior of the car.

"Punk-ass nigga," said the girl, spitting on Dino's corpse. "So, when am I gonna get paid? K-Dawg said I would get ten thousand dollars if I—"

Without warning, Demon cut her throat. The girl just stared at him, her eyes wide, as she bled in the back seat of the truck.

Demon wiped the blade on her dress and tucked it back into its secret place. After a quick look around, he slipped into a nearby manhole and disappeared.

The word had spread quickly about what happened to Dino. Most of the big dealers went into hiding, while others just treaded through Harlem with the greatest of care. A wave of fear swept through the five boroughs, and K-Dawg was the reason for it.

K-Dawg and Jus were on the basketball court shooting hoops, when a long white Cadillac pulled up outside the fence. A young girl stepped out of the hog wearing a blue business suit. She scanned the faces in the park until she spotted K-Dawg's and started in his direction.

"K-Dawg?"

"That depends," he said, using his T-shirt to wipe his face. "Who's asking?"

"My name is Joyce Canter. I work for Willie Brown."

"Never heard of him."

"You probably know him by his street name, Boss Hog?"

"Oh," K-Dawg said grinning. "What, the fat man sent you to kill me?"

"Not quite. Mr. Brown would like to speak with you."

"Well, you tell that fat fuck to come on down to the slums and holla at me himself."

"Actually, he's in the car."

Jus and K-Dawg exchanged glances. They knew that they could very well be walking into a trap. Then again, if the fat man did wanna chat, it could be a good thing for the crew. *Fuck it.* They'd come too far to go back now.

"A'ight, Joyce," said K-Dawg. "Tell the fat man we'll talk to him, but I ain't for walking up on no car; he gotta get out of the ride. Ain't no telling what could be up in there."

"As you wish." Joyce walked away swinging her shapely ass.

She was a fine little brown joint. *Another place, another time,* K-Dawg thought. *A bitch will always come sniffing around the biggest dawg.* There would be time for pussy when he was rich. Now, business was the focal point.

Joyce stuck her head into the back of the Caddy. After a few moments, two black suit–wearing individuals emerged from the car. They closely kept watch; one looked east and the other one looked west. Banks, dressed in a blue sweatsuit and a pair of white Air Forces, stepped out and came around to the curb. He stared without speaking. Joyce opened the curbside rear door, and a hulk of a man stepped out of the car. The vehicle's shocks seemed to cry from relief as Boss Hog stepped into full view.

The lord of the Northeast Bronx was a sight to behold. He stood at a towering six feet four inches and weighed over 300 pounds. His salt-and-pepper curls hung from underneath his white brimmed hat and down over the shoulders of his pearl white suit. The diamond stickpin in his tie flashed as the noonday sun hit it.

K-Dawg tried to hide the astonishment he felt upon seeing the fat man, as did everyone else in the park. He had heard stories about Boss Hog, but he never actually laid eyes on him. There was something about this mammoth of a man that spoke volumes of respect, but for some odd reason, K-Dawg did not fear him. When he approached Boss Hog, he wasn't off point but at ease.

"Hog?" K-Dawg said extending his hand.

"Good to meet you, son," said Boss, returning the gesture. "Heard a lot about you."

"Yeah, I'm real popular, lately, huh?"

"That was some bold shit you did to Dino."

"Excuse me? I'm afraid I don't follow, Hog."

"Don't bullshit me, kid. I ain't get this old by being nobody's fool. I'm hip, but I ain't gonna press it."

"What brings you down to the slums, Hog?"

"Look, let's cut the small talk," said Hog removing his sunglasses. His beady eyes seemed to stare into the depths of K-Dawg's soul. "I came to see if we could bring about some understanding of what's going on down here. You niggaz done turned Harlem back into the damn thirties. All this 'bang bang, shoot 'em up' shit ain't what's happening."

"No disrespect, Hog, but how is this any concern of yours?"

"Well, I'll tell you, these niggaz down here is scared of y'all. You laid the pressure on too thick, daddy. Man, if you cats was a little more user friendly, you'd probably be clocking more paper."

"We do what we do, Hog. We don't wanna spill no more blood in the streets, but if stones are cast at us, we throw back boulders, simple as that."

"Like Supreme?"

K-Dawg was caught a little off-guard by that one. How much more did the fat man know? "Yeah." He sighed. "Pretty much. We just trying to eat, Hog."

"And making a damn mess of things in the process."

"So, what's good, Hog?" asked K-Dawg, a little irritated. "What you trying to do?"

"I'll tell you like this, li'l nigga. I got sixty-eight grand in cold cash tucked in the trunk of a Buick on 133rd and Madison. I'm gonna give you the keys and you're gonna put four of them thangs in the trunk. If ya shit is proper, I'll cop heavy. Plus I think I can get a few other niggaz to go along with me." Boss Hog pushed his huge lips into a wide grin. "Let's do some business, baby."

And the king sat on his throne looking out over his kingdom. A mighty empire built with treachery and held together by blood. Long had the king sought to be in a position to decide the fate of others and have legions bow to him, but at what price? The king harvested snakes in his court. And so, the serpents would one day come to claim their due.

CHAPTER 26

The next few years were the best for K-Dawg and his clique. The fiends up in the Bronx flipped over the work. Boss Hog moved the birds by the next morning. Two days later, he came back and purchased twenty more. Boss Hog kept true to his word and set the word out to all the other Willies that the Road Dawgz were good people. In return, K-Dawg flooded the streets with powder. In just a few months' time, the street hustlers were well on their way to baller status.

K-Dawg became the man to see in the streets. He was setting birds out to just about anybody who was somebody in the game. For the most part, the streets loved him and his prices, but there were still the few haters who sought to challenge him. They were dealt with accordingly. If somebody got out of pocket with the Dawgz, they got their wig split. That's just the way it was. One respected the game, or one got taken out of it. The crew decided that it would be best to move out of the hood. It would be safer, and they had the paper. They didn't want to go as far out as the suburbs, but just a good enough distance away from the action.

Jus and his new girl, June, copped a quiet little spot on Central Park West. Sleep moved down to the Village, and only came uptown to check his trap and kick it with the fellas. Demon moved out of that dumpy-ass basement and got himself a spot, God knows where. China got a place in a nice section of the Bronx, but she still kept the project apartment in case Pearl ever decided to come home.

Pooh managed to get caught riding with no license and in possession of a loaded firearm. He was supposed to do a three-to-nine, but he was home in under a year, thanks to a technicality. It seemed that ever since he started getting real money, he was constantly fucking up. He was becoming more of a liability than an asset. Sooner or later, he would have to answer for his stupidity.

K-Dawg bought a little two-bedroom house near Vega. Since he had begun to blow up, Frank started acting differently. It wasn't like he was jealous, but he wasn't as proud of him as he should've been, either. He had even stepped to K-Dawg once about coming to work for him.

K-Dawg respectfully declined. He was caking off getting the keys from Vega and doing his own thing. Vega, in turn, acted as if he had an attitude. Awhile afterward, he raised the price, saying, "It was costing more to bring it in." K-Dawg knew he was full of shit, but he didn't give a fuck. He just met the price. However, he did start forming a contingency plan in case Vega got flaky.

Gloria was becoming more trouble than she was worth. Since Manny's demise, she couldn't rattle ol' daddy's piggy bank as often as before. There was no one else to blame it on, and Nikki was getting suspicious. One evening they had dinner at Frank's, and Nikki almost caught Gloria giving K-Dawg head in the kitchen. Besides that, if Vega found out, it could get ugly. K-Dawg really did want to cut Gloria off, but he still needed her.

Hargrough and Mills popped up every now and again, but they weren't much more than a pain in the ass. They did pull him over with a gun in the car once, but Levitz shredded the case; it was an illegal search. Hargrough and Mills lay low, but K-Dawg had a feeling that they would be showing up real soon. Things were going too well for them not to.

La, Chi-Chi, and Hector played the hood the hardest. They made sure that everything went as well as it should. With those three on watch, the money hardly ever came up short. They were the current rising stars and the future of Road Dawgz.

K-Dawg even bumped pothead-ass Mike back up to spot runner. Mike was the overseer of one of their main locations. He knew how much money came into the spot and the amount of drugs that were distributed in the surrounding areas, but not much else. K-Dawg only told the soldiers what they needed to know.

Nasty information falling into the wrong hands was something he tried hard to avoid.

Around 1999 or so, the word had spread about this kid in Harlem who had that good-good. Niggaz was coming from all over trying to see about K-Dawg. He dealt with most of them through a middleman, but there was one kid that he took a liking to.

Jimmy Black was a skinny kid from out of Philly. He had no family to speak of and ran with a small crew from the south side. When Jimmy would come to the city to buy work, he and K-Dawg would kick it. There was something about the li'l nigga that reminded K-Dawg of himself; he, too, was one of the forgotten children. K-Dawg liked the kid so much that he let him set up shop on a little corner at 131st and Madison. If K-Dawg could have seen the future, he would've had Jimmy Black killed.

The Road Dawgz were balling. K-Dawg couldn't have been prouder of his crew. Everyone was playing their position and doing what they needed to do. K-Dawg had successfully built an empire where he reigned supreme. He was flying high, and no one could bring him down; or so he thought.

***

Chi-Chi pulled his Eddie Bauer up to the curb on 120th Street and Fifth Avenue. He hopped out of the truck with his gun drawn and took a brief look around. After making sure that the coast was clear, he sprinted around to the other side and opened K-Dawg's door.

K-Dawg checked his pistol and hopped out of the truck. Since he was coming up in the world, he rarely carried guns, but this meeting was different. This was the day he was to meet with two up-and-coming players in the game. They were fresh out of Cali and kicking up major dust in New York.

"Yo," Chi-Chi began, "fuck is these niggaz at?"

"Be easy," said K-Dawg checking his watch. "We a little early. They should be here soon."

As if on cue, two young cats jumped out of a gray Tahoe after parking directly in front of Chi-Chi's truck. The first man was a poster boy for trouble. He was dark skinned with an unkempt beard. He wore a thick blue sweatshirt and a blue bandanna around his head. He sized the Road Dawgz up and started in their direction. His whole MO screamed trouble.

The second man was a rather bookish-looking cat. His hair was cornrowed and held in place by blue rubber bands. He had a caramel complexion and soft brown eyes. His demeanor was relaxed, but his eyes were constantly moving. The kid was on point.

"Which one of you niggas is K-Dawg?" asked the bearded man.

"That'd be me," said K-Dawg stepping up.

"A'ight, homie. I'm Gutter. This my man, Lou-Loc." Lou-Loc nodded but didn't speak. "We here, cuz. What you wanna talk about?"

"I wanna talk about what the fuck y'all doing to my city," snapped K-Dawg.

"Man, we just trying to get our piece of the pie."

"Fuck outta here," snapped Chi-Chi. "Any pies out here belong to the master baker."

"Ain't no need to get hostile, cuz," said Lou-Loc.

"I ain't ya fucking cousin, money."

"Easy, that's just the way we speak out West," said Gutter.

"Hold that down, Chi-Chi," said K-Dawg. "Listen, Gutter. We just trying to see what's up wit' y'all niggaz, that's all."

"Well," said Gutter, "we just came out here from the West and we trying to do us. We heard there's money out this piece, and we just trying to cash in. I'm sure you understand."

"Yeah, yeah," said K-Dawg smiling. "We understand totally. It's just the way you're going about it that bothers me. Y'all got these gangbang mafuckas runnin' 'round shooting shit up acting all crazy. What up wit' that?"

"Hey, man, it ain't about nothing. A few niggaz got out of pocket and we had to lay 'em down. I hope them marks we killed wasn't nobody off yo' side."

"Nah, kid. If they were, we wouldn't even be having this conversation. You'd be dead already."

"Is that right?"

"Mafucking right. But I didn't come here to trade threats wit' y'all. I came to do some business."

"Yeah, what kinda business?"

"How much y'all copping ya weight for pharmaceuticals, player?"

"'Bout 18.5 to nineteen. Why?"

"Because, Gutter, from now on, y'all spend ya money wit' me. I'll set you out for 17.5. It'll be cheaper depending on how much you buy."

"17.5?" asked Lou-Loc.

"That's what I said, 17.5. As an added bonus, I'll let y'all pedal ya shit up this way, as long as you kick me something back."

"K-Dawg, ya offer sounds proper, but why should we kick you back anything?"

"Because, Lou-Loc, everyone knows that the penalty for violating our space is death. I just let y'all slide 'cause y'all ain't know no better."

"Man," said Lou-Loc, lifting his shirt to expose the butt of his 9, "you must think we some busters."

"No, no," said K-Dawg holding Chi-Chi back, "I know just who y'all are: St. Louis Alexander and Kenyatta Soladine, a killer and a baller. We know y'all, but y'all don't know us. That's the reason we're even having this conversation. I know ya reputation, but you gotta bend a little on this. It's for the benefit of us all."

Lou-Loc and Gutter conversed between themselves. Gutter wanted to say, "Fuck it," and give it to K-Dawg in gangsta fashion, but Lou-Loc was the voice of reason. He figured that working with this K-Dawg cat could be to their advantage. They were new to New York, and K- Dawg had the best prices. A war with the Road Dawgz wouldn't be in their best interest. They were on their turf and were probably outgunned. It took some doing, but Gutter agreed.

"A'ight," said Gutter, pulling at his beard. "We accept ya terms, but with one stipulation: you give us the birds at seventeen flat."

"Yeah, why would I wanna do that?"

"Because," said Lou-Loc smiling, "y'all ain't the only ones who done ya homework, Keshawn. We know who you are and what kinda heat you got on you. The Harlem Crips might be able to handle some of the beef that come ya way without getting you and yours jammed up. What you think of that?"

K-Dawg couldn't help but be impressed by the two set riders. They had damned sure come correct and raised a valid point. With the Crips putting in work for their side, they could do a lot more dirt. Why not give 'em a play?

"You got a deal," said K-Dawg. "One hand washes the other—"

"And two hands wash the face," said Lou-Loc, finishing his sentence.

"My thoughts exactly," said K-Dawg. "Welcome to Harlem."

K-Dawg and Jus walked into their 138th Street rock house engaged in a slight debate. It seemed that ol' Manny had really gone rat. The police pulled Jus over one day when he had over $15,000 worth of hot goods in the trunk of his car. It wasn't a major charge, but it was still a felony. The judge gave Jus a year, which he was to begin serving the next morning.

"This is some bullshit," Jus barked. "A fucking year? Come on, man, whatever happened to shit like probation or community service?"

"Hey," K-Dawg began, "you know how it is, son. Ain't like you a regular criminal, Jus; you a Road Dawg. That shit means something on the streets. Police hate us, 'cause we winning. And we hate them 'cause they some crooked, dick-riding mafuckas."

"But the shit still stinks, Keshawn. June and me just moved into that spot. I can't leave her or my operation unattended. Fuck am I gonna do, dawg?"

"Relax," said K-Dawg, placing his palms on either side of Jus's neck. "I know it stinks, kid, but that's the game. We got people to do shit like that for us. You should've known better."

"I know, kid. But that was a lot of shit, and ya man was only charging me $6,500. I was coming off."

"Now you pay for ya greed. Look, don't worry about ya shit, kid. I'm gonna make sure June is a'ight and take care of ya business. Just tell ya people that they answer to me while ya gone, cool?"

Something about K-Dawg's offer bothered Jus. He kicked back a portion of his heist money to the organization, but that was his own side hustle, just as Sleepy had his hoes and Chi-Chi had his chop shop. If K-Dawg was left to run his operation, he might realize just how profitable his little hijacking thing was. But what choice did he have? It was either turn it over to K-Dawg, or pray that the thieves in his employ didn't bleed him dry while he was away.

"A'ight," sighed Jus. "I'll get the word out to my peoples. Try not to fuck my shit up while I'm gone."

"Fuck you," said K-Dawg playfully. "If anything, they'll probably make more money under me."

"That's what I'm afraid of," mumbled Jus.

K-Dawg entered the living room where Mike was sitting playing video games with a dude he didn't know. Everyone knew the rules about outsiders in the houses. They could pump the shit on the streets, but they weren't allowed inside any of the locations.

"Fuck is this?" asked K-Dawg pointing at the stranger.

"Huh?" asked Mike, looking real stupid.

"Huh?" K-Dawg shot back. "Who the fuck is this?"

"Oh, him? K-Dawg, this is my man, Jay. Jay, this is the baddest mafucka in the world, K-Dawg. He's the leader of our crew."

"What up, dun?" asked Jay, jumping up to give him a pound. "I be Jay from outta Queensbridge. You probably know my cousin, Terror?"

"Fuck outta here," said K-Dawg slapping his hand away. "I don't know Terror or ya clown ass. Mike, you done lost ya fucking mind?"

"What? What happened?"

"Mafucka, what happened was you violated the rules. You let this clown-ass mafucka up in my spot."

"Nah, I'm cool," Jay cut in.

"Mafucka!" screamed K-Dawg. "Shut the fuck up!" K-Dawg slapped Jay in the face, sending him tumbling to the floor. "I don't know ya punk ass, so don't be trying to tell me shit."

"K-Dawg," said Mike jumping up, "chill, man."

"Mike, you about a dumb mafucka. How long you been bringing this nigga around?"

"Not long. Why you bugging?"

"Why am I bugging? You put me and everyone else in this mafucka at risk. Jus, clear everybody the fuck outta here. We're shutting this bitch down."

Jus ran from room to room, barking instructions and bagging money. Jay looked as if someone had just shredded a winning lottery ticket in front of him as the crackhouse was being shut down. Mike looked around in panic, as K-Dawg pulled a straight razor from his pocket.

"Jay," he said grabbing Mike by the face, "you watch and learn, mafucka."

K-Dawg took the razor and dragged it from one side of Mike's throat to the other. Blood gushed out and coated K-Dawg's sleeve. Jay, still on the floor, scrambled backward, trying to dodge the flow of blood. Then K-Dawg grabbed Jay and put the blade to his face.

"A stupid man is a dead man," he whispered. K-Dawg took the blade and sliced Jay across the face. Jay writhed in pain while Jus just shook his head. Jus stressed to K-Dawg to kill Jay too, but he refused; he wanted Jay to spread the word about what happened to those who fucked over the Road Dawgz. It was a mistake that would cost him.

That night, the crew got together and threw Jus a going-away party at a new club suggested by Sleepy. To everyone's surprise, the neon lights in front of the club read, THE DAWG HOUSE. It seemed that Sleepy had gone along with the business venture without K-Dawg. At first K-Dawg was tight, but after he thought about it, he couldn't be. Sleepy had given him the chance to be down with the club, but he wasn't really interested. Now, Sleepy had a nice li'l thing going on.

The outside of the club didn't have a damned thing on the inside, with its alluring atmosphere. The floor was covered with white linoleum and had black paw prints all over it. A horseshoe-shaped bar dominated the majority of space in the club. The drinking area took up the rear of the bar as well as two adjoining walls. In the center of the horseshoe was a small stage. This was where the feature performers did their thing. The rest of the place was just a wide open dance floor with booths scattered here and there. What really attracted people to the spot were the waitresses; they were some of the finest women Sleepy could find. All of them worked the floor topless. The only thing they were allowed to wear were thongs and the crew's trademark: studded dog collars. Party and Eddy ran the joint, but Sleepy owned it. This was his retirement fund.

Every last one of the Road Dawgz was required to attend the party. Even the street generals were given the night off to bid farewell to their comrade. The talk that night was the closing of the main house and what K-Dawg had done to Mike. There were quite a few people who disagreed with what K-Dawg had done, but they did so in silence. Everyone knew what happened to those who questioned the top dawg.

K-Dawg staggered out of the bar early the next morning. He looked at his phone and it read ten missed calls. He had been so caught up in the party that he hadn't even felt it go off. Well, whoever the hell it was could get called back in the morning.

K-Dawg was too damned drunk to drive, and everyone else had already gone. He decided that the safest way to get home would be by taxi. When he stepped off the curb, he was almost mauled by a blue Plymouth. He was going to bark on the stupid-ass driver, until he saw Hargrough and Mills get out of the car.

"What up, homeboy?" asked Mills smiling.

"Man," slurred K-Dawg, "fuck y'all want wit' me now?"

"Oh," Hargrough spoke up, "we came to take you home, baby."

"Fuck outta here. I can get home just fine on my own. Besides, you don't even know where I moved to."

"You're right about that," said Mills, snapping open his cuffs. "We don't know where you moved to, but we know where you'll be staying: 100 Centre Street, dawg."

K-Dawg's eyes widened with shock. At the mention of jail, he sobered up. "Fuck is y'all talking about?" he asked with a jerk.

"Ya fucked up," said Hargrough, pushing him against the car. "We finally got your ass."

"This is some bullshit. I ain't did nothing."

"You call murder and assaulting a police officer nothing?" said Mills.

"Y'all crazy. I ain't killed nobody, or assaulted nobody for that matter."

"You remember Jay?" asked Hargrough.

At the mention of Jay's name, K-Dawg started to figure out what was going on. Mike was a snitch, and Jay was a cop. He could get locked up for a long time behind this shit. He tried to struggle against the two officers, but the liquor was getting the best of him. After a few moments, they had him cuffed and in the car.

Things did not look good for K-Dawg.

***

China lay in the king-sized bed looking up at the ceiling. Her body tingled from head to toe, and it felt damned good. Never before had a man made her feel like that. The guy who had taken her virginity was hung like a horse and tried to snap her small frame in half. Ever since then, the thought of being with a man turned her off.

China looked over at her sleeping lover and traced the line of his spine with her finger. People said he was cold, but that was because they didn't know him. There was a passionate side to this man that would shock most people. It was this very same passion that had caused her to fall in love with him.

China twirled her finger around one of his long braids and whispered her lover's name: "Demon."

CHAPTER 27

K-Dawg woke up the next morning with a splitting headache. His tongue felt like he'd been licking a carpet, and his eyes felt like he'd been staring at a bright, glaring sun. As drunk as he might've been, he knew the seriousness of his situation. He was in jail for murder, and God only knew what else.

The first call K-Dawg made was to Nikki. She freaked when she heard what had happened, but she was a soldier and followed instructions very well. He had her call Levitz, then China. Each had a part to play.

Levitz got to see his client some time that afternoon. K-Dawg was tired and hungry, but that didn't make much of a difference. The main thing he needed was to be back on the streets. Judging from the look on Levitz's face when he arrived, K-Dawg could tell that he didn't bring good news with him.

"What up?" asked K-Dawg sitting at the small iron table.

"Don't give me that shit," snapped Levitz. "I told you, damn it, I told you."

"I know, man."

"You say you know, but that's what you told me the last time, then you turn around and do some dumb shit like this. What the fuck is wrong with you, Keshawn?"

"Fuck this shit. How am I looking?"

"I gotta be honest. You're looking like shit. These fucks in homicide got you by the balls, son. They got you for trafficking, assault on an officer, and murder."

"Shit! They're gonna try to cook a nigga. Can't you just make this shit go away?"

"Go away? Keshawn, you murdered that boy, and in front of witnesses on top of that. Then you slash a cop's face. This shit is ugly, kid."

"Listen, I'll spare no expense to make this right. Where do we stand?"

"Well," Levitz said opening a folder, "the assault on an officer thing I can get thrown out. Officer Jay Simms never identified himself. The trafficking, that probably won't stick. Simms wasn't undercover long enough to tie anything to you, plus you killed the informant. The murder is your biggest problem. It wouldn't be so bad, but you killed him in front of an officer. You're looking at time, Keshawn."

"Fuck that," said K-Dawg standing up. "I can't do no time, Levitz. That shit ain't an option."

"Boy, are you listening? You've murdered someone in front of witnesses. With your record, there's no way I can get you off clean. The best we can hope for is a plea."

"Fuck a plea. I ain't going to jail, Levitz. That shit's just out. We gonna take it to trial."

"Keshawn, if we go to trial we're gonna lose, and they're gonna give you way more time."

"Levitz, don't worry about that. You just make sure I get bail. Let me worry about the rest of this shit. I got it in the smash, witnesses and all."

"Keshawn, one of the strongest witnesses is a police officer."

"So, fuck him. I got this, Levitz. You just do ya fucking part."

After waiting for God knows how long, they finally called K-Dawg to go up and see the judge. When he entered the courtroom, the first people he saw were Nikki and China. His two down-ass bitches were right up front, holding him down. He spared them a brief smile and ambled over to Levitz.

The prosecutor shot K-Dawg a hateful stare from his end of the courtroom. The blond white boy looked familiar to him, but he couldn't place the face. Fuck it, he'd figure it out later. The important thing was to get out of jail and make preparations to bring his master plan to a close. It had been a good run, but K-Dawg realized that his time was nearing its end.

The entire proceeding sounded like gibberish to K-Dawg. The prosecutor spoke, Levitz spoke, and the judge just nodded at the whole thing. When it was all said and done, K-Dawg's bail was set at $250,000. He could've posted right there, but he had Nikki wait for a week before having her mother put up her house, just to make it look good.

The week of waiting was hell for K-Dawg. The state pen was bad, but the city lockup was worse. It was filthy and damp, and there was hardly enough food to eat. The whole time he was there, K-Dawg had flashbacks of his first bid. There were quite a few nights that he woke up screaming. It irritated the hell out of the other inmates, but who was crazy enough to say anything to him about it?

The following week, K-Dawg made bail with a court appearance for the next month. Nikki picked him up from the tombs with a change of clothes and a winning smile. K-Dawg was so happy that he stripped right in front of the jail and threw his old clothes in the trash. He didn't want anything that reminded him of that place. Regardless of what Levitz or that redneck-ass judge said, he had no intention of going back to prison.

As K-Dawg and Nikki stepped lively to their car, Jackson's truck pulled up to the curb. K-Dawg asked Nikki to excuse him for a few moments so he could go and speak with Jackson. From the look on the dirty cop's face, he knew it was more bad news.

"Got yaself into a li'l jam, huh?" asked Jackson.

"Yeah, something like that," K-Dawg said with a grin.

"I'm glad one of us thinks this shit is funny. Keshawn, you in a lot of trouble."

"It ain't that serious."

"Ain't that serious? Boy, has all that money made you stupid? Murder, trafficking, the list goes on. That fuck Greene has had a hard-on for you for years. All you did was step knee-deep into the shit."

"Don't worry 'bout it, Jackson. This problem will go away just like the rest."

"Afraid not, youngster. Ain't no amount of money gonna get you outta this shit; plus, you'll never get within spitting distance of that fuck Simms. They got that rat fuck under wraps. I can't even get in to talk to him."

"Who said I'm trying to get at Simms?"

"If not Simms, then . . . Oh, no. Keshawn, forget about it. If you even try, they're gonna bring the chair back just for you. Leave it alone."

"Fuck that cracker. His ass is dog food."

"Keshawn, the Mafia ain't even got the balls to do what you're thinking of doing. Get the fuck outta the country and leave this shit alone."

"Don't worry about it, Jackson. I won't get you caught up in this shit. I'll take care of this problem on my own."

"Okay, Mr. Hardhead. I got a surprise for you that might change ya mind."

"Well?"

"I don't wanna say yet, because I ain't sure. I'll bring it by ya house tonight."

"Cool. Thanks, Jackson."

"Take my advice, Keshawn. Tie up all loose ends and get the fuck outta town."

***

As soon as K-Dawg got to his house, he called a meeting. This meeting was for select members only. K-Dawg had spent years constructing this plan, only to have it end like this. But by no means was he going to leave the game empty-handed. Each person on his team had a part to play in his plan. Some were expendable and some weren't.

Assembled at the meeting were Demon, Sleepy, Chi-Chi, and China. They were each instructed not to tell anyone of the meeting; secrecy was vital at this stage of the game. Those who were loyal would prosper, while those who went against the grain would suffer.

"I would like to thank you all for coming," said K-Dawg.

"Baby bro, you know we here for you," said China.

"I know, sis, and I love you all for it. As you all know, them pigs got ya man looped in this murder shit."

"K-Dawg, you one of the smartest niggaz I know. How you let this shit happen to you?" said Demon.

"Stupidity, my nigga, plain and simple. I let my emotions cause me to do some dumb shit, and now they raking my ass over hot coals."

"So, what we gonna do?" asked Chi-Chi.

"This problem ain't all of ours, Chi-Chi. They got me, but they probably ain't got shit on y'all. You can't convict a nigga on hearsay."

"It's still our problem," said China. "We're a team, remember?"

"China," said K-Dawg kissing her cheek, "I admire your loyalty. Big sis, you just as down as any nigga I know. Unfortunately, I gotta walk this mile by myself. Now y'all listen up. I'm taking this shit to trial, but that's just to buy myself some time. I know there ain't a snowball's chance in hell of me winning, but there's a method to my madness."

"Well," said Chi-Chi, "let ya dawgz in."

"Glad you said that, 'cause each and every one of y'all got a part to play in this."

"What up, K-Dawg?"

"I need a few mafuckas dead."

"Just tell me," said Chi-Chi laying his 9 on the table. "Them mafuckas can get it tonight."

"Oh yeah? What if I told you that one of 'em was Assistant District Attorney Greene?"

The whole room fell silent. Demon and Chi-Chi were seasoned killers, but this was some new shit. To murder a man of Greene's standing was risky. K-Dawg wanted a kamikaze pilot, not a hit man.

"Wow," said Demon, "that's some ol' other shit. Taking on this contract is just as good as throwing ya life away. I love you like a brother, K-Dawg, but I ain't about to throw my life away fo' yo' crazy ass. Man, leave that nigga alone and raise up."

"Afraid not, Demon. I'm going out, but I'm going out with a bang. Greene has been a pain in my ass since I was sixteen. That nigga gotta get his shit split."

"K-Dawg," said Chi-Chi, "even if you do have Greene hit, it won't help you. They'll just have someone else prosecute you. Why even bother?"

"To prove a point. We fought long and hard to get here, but it's the final call for the Road Dawgz. But best believe before we close up shop, mafuckas is gonna have something to remember us by. Now, y'all niggaz don't worry 'bout Greene. I got somebody else I'm gonna use for that, but there is another target. Chi-Chi, that's why I asked you to stay behind."

"You know I'm down for a 187, kid, Who is it?"

K-Dawg looked him dead in the eye and hissed, "Pooh."

Chi-Chi just stood there with a blank look on his face. He knew that Pooh would end up getting himself killed sooner or later, but he didn't think he'd be called on to do it. He also knew that K-Dawg wasn't making a request; he was giving an order. Pooh was his first cousin, but K-Dawg was feeding him. If he said Pooh had to go, then it would be done.

"A'ight," sighed Chi-Chi.

"You sure?" asked K-Dawg. "If you want, I can have someone else do it."

K-Dawg's words were full of sincerity, but Chi-Chi knew it was a front. What K-Dawg was really doing was testing his loyalty. If he didn't kill Pooh, there was a good chance that someone would come gunning for him.

"Nah," said Chi-Chi, "I'll do it, but do you mind if I ask why?"

"Your cousin is weak from greed, always has been. You know that, Chi-Chi," said Demon. "Who do you think it was that told Dino where to find K-Dawg? That mafucka been in bed with Dino's people from day one. I don't know for sure, but I think he was snitching, too. We know the penalty for betrayal, don't we, Chi-Chi?"

"Death."

"So he gotta go, son," said K-Dawg. "You feel where I'm coming from?"

"You the boss, yo. If you say he gotta die, then he's dead."

"Glad we understand each other. Now, this is the way it's gonna go down. After you do that, I'm gonna set you out with a million in cash. You do what you want with it, but my advice would be to get the fuck outta town. Shit is gonna hit the fan, soon, so don't get caught up in the backlash."

"I'm on it," said Chi-Chi. "He'll be dead by the end of the week."

Chi-Chi left with his head down. It was fucked up, what K-Dawg was making him do, but fuck it. Chi-Chi was a pawn to be used like everyone else.

"Okay," said Sleepy, "what you want me to do, kill my mama?"

"Ha, ha," said K-Dawg, "you a funny dude, Sleep. Your part in all this is probably the most important. You, Jus, and me are the founders of this clique. Jus is doing a skid bid, and they 'bout to try to throw the book at me. That leaves you as my successor. I know drugs ain't ya thang, but you're the most qualified to carry out my last wishes. I want you to disband the Road Dawgz."

"You can't be serious."

"Indeed I am, Sleepy. I heard through the grapevine that that old fuck, Vega, has been getting at Jimmy Black behind my back. He thinks he can just slide that skinny mafucka in my spot, and Jimmy is all for it. My dumb ass trusted that mafucka, and this is the thanks I get."

"So," said Demon, "why don't I just murder Jimmy Black?"

"I got one of them Cali niggaz on it as we speak. You play a much bigger part in all of this, Demon. I'm trusting you to take care of China."

Everyone looked at K-Dawg in surprise. China turned white as a ghost, while Demon just put his head down. The cat was out of the bag.

"Don't look so surprised," said K-Dawg smiling.

"Listen, it ain't what you think," said Demon. "We—"

"Demon," said K-Dawg cutting him off, "it's cool, man. I knew from the first time y'all laid eyes on each other that this was gonna happen. As long as my sister is happy, I'm a'ight with it. As long as you do the right thing by her, I'm cool."

"K-Dawg, you know I will."

"I'm sure of it. That's why I'm giving you $2.5 million to help you along. Do the right thing," he said holding both their hands. "This game is going sour, so get out while you can. You have my blessing."

China and Demon looked at each other dumbfounded. At first they felt badly about the way they had been sneaking around, but they knew K-Dawg's temper. Demon wasn't afraid of him but they were friends, and he didn't want anything to come between them, even the woman he loved. Now that they knew he was cool with it, they could live the life they had only fantasized about.

Demon hugged China tightly, and he didn't give a shit who saw it. For a long time he had only dreamed about retiring, but it was China who actually made him give it some serious thought. This beautiful woman had unlocked the inner part of him that wasn't ugly or tainted. She made him feel brand new.

"A'ight," said K-Dawg, "don't be groping my sis in front of me, nigga. Save that for the honeymoon. Now, we get to the core of my plan. Sleep, pay the fuck attention, 'cause it involves the Dawg House."

CHAPTER 28

The meeting came to a close around 1:00 a.m. All of the guests had gone, leaving K-Dawg, Nikki, and China alone in the house. In his final days, he needed to be around his loved ones. As soon as Demon and Sleepy pulled off, Jackson drove up the brick driveway. There was someone else in the car with him, but K-Dawg couldn't tell who it was from where he stood. He stepped off the porch and moved to greet Jackson, who was now approaching him.

"What up, Jackson?" asked K-Dawg.

"Trying to get my affairs in order," he replied. "It's getting ugly in the city, kid. Fuckin'-ass mayor is making it hard for an honest nigga to eat."

"Jackson, you 'bout as honest as I am."

"That's beside the point. They coming down hard, man. Ya case is all over the paper. Anyone even affiliated with ya black ass is getting pressured right now. Only a matter of time before they come take this house."

"I ain't worried about it. I don't plan on being here long."

"So, you taking my advice about running?"

"Yep. Right after I tie up some loose ends."

"Keshawn, you still on that shit, huh?"

"It is what it is, Jackson."

"Have it your way. But I got someone in the car that might change your mind."

Jackson went back to his truck and opened the passenger door. He returned leading a small child by the hand.

The child was a little thin and quite dusty. He looked as if he'd been living on the street for quite some time. As the child got closer, his features began to look more and more familiar.

"Justin?"

"Uncle K!" shouted Justin as he ran to K-Dawg.

K-Dawg picked his nephew up and hugged him as tightly as he could without hurting him. Justin was filthy and he stank to high heaven, but none of that mattered. He was back with his family.

China had been watching the whole thing from the window. When she recognized her nephew, she came flying out of the house with tears in her eyes. Upon seeing her, Justin hopped from K-Dawg's arms and ran to China.

"Boy," she said sobbing, "where you been? Where's ya mommy?" At the mention of Pearl, Justin broke into tears.

Whatever had happened to Pearl, it didn't seem at all good.

"China," said K-Dawg rubbing Justin's head, "why don't you take li'l man in the house and fix him something to eat? I'll be in there soon."

China squeezed her nephew to her bosom and started toward the house. After they were out of sight, K-Dawg turned his attention back to Jackson. He needed answers, and he knew that Jackson had them.

"It's fucked up," said Jackson, as if he was reading K-Dawg's thoughts. "Some peoples of mine found the li'l guy living on the streets of Baltimore."

"What happened to my sister, Pearl?"

"The way I heard it, she overdosed a few months back."

"What about that nigga, Trick?"

"Well, that's the only bright spot in all of this. He abandoned the kid after his mom died. Some of my boys managed to track him down last week. Let's just say he won't be troubling anyone anymore. He got killed real nasty-like."

"Jackson," said K-Dawg hugging him, "I owe you, man. I owe you big time."

"Fuck off me," said Jackson, trying to fight back the tears. "You gonna fuck up my suit, li'l nigga. Listen, if you wanna pay me back, take your nephew and leave town. You got money, kid, and I can get you a fake passport."

"A passport? That'd be great, but I'll need three. How soon do you think you can get 'em?"

"Give me a day or two at the most."

"Night. I'll send Nikki to pick 'em up from you."

"I'm glad you finally gave up on this revenge shit, Keshawn. You're doing the right thing."

K-Dawg remained silent and looked at the ground.

"Ah, come on, kid. You still gonna try it, ain't ya?"

"I gotta do what I gotta do, Jackson. I've come too far to turn back."

"Keshawn, all you're gonna do is get yaself killed."

"That's the general idea."

At first the statement had stunned Jackson, but the more he thought about it, the more sense it made. K-Dawg was truly ahead of his time. In another life he would've been a great man. But in this life, he was the undisputed lord of the streets.

Chi-Chi, Hector, and Pooh sat at the bar in Perks, sipping sauce and talking shit. K-Dawg's request had been on Chi-Chi's mind for a few days now. Pooh had a lot of faults, but he was his mother's nephew. Even though Chi-Chi was raised in the DR, they were still close. Pooh had always been his big cousin, and he struggled to come to grips with the idea of killing someone he loved.

"Yeah, nigga," said Pooh, "shit gonna be changing' 'round here real soon. That mafucka K-Dawg is old news. Soon, I'll be the top dawg."

"I don't know," said Chi-Chi, sipping his drink. "Maybe he'll beat the case."

"Shit, that ain't gonna happen. The police got way too much on that kid. Murder is the least of his worries. They got a whole shitload of charges pending against him. That boy gonna fry or spend the rest of his days in jail. Trust me, primo."

By the look Chi-Chi shot him, Pooh knew that he might've overplayed his hand. What would the youngster do if he found out that he was one of the people snitching? Pooh figured he was just being paranoid. Chi-Chi was dangerous, but they were blood. Those country mafuckas in the DR were real big on loyalty. He'd never turn on his family.

"So," said Chi-Chi lighting a cigarette, "what we gonna do if they lock him up?"

"Nigga, we gonna do the smart thing. We gonna link up with Dino's old crew, go to work for Frank, and live like kings."

"You got it all mapped out, huh?"

"Shit," slurred Pooh, "I've been planning it long enough. K-Dawg is finished. It's time for a new king."

Chi-Chi looked at Hector and shook his head. The more Pooh talked, the more Demon's suspicions were confirmed. Cousin and all, Pooh was a greedy rat fuck and he had to be put down.

"Come on, primo," said Chi-Chi taking Pooh by the arm. "You've had enough to drink. We're taking you home."

"Man, I can walk," said Pooh jerking away. Pooh staggered a bit, but he managed to straighten himself out.

Pooh continued to pop shit during the short walk outside the club. Had he not been so drunk, he would've seen the tears running down Chi-Chi's face. Chi-Chi and Hector steered Pooh down 123rd Street toward Morningside Park. After a brief look around, Chi-Chi gave Hector the nod. Hector pulled out his club and bashed Pooh in the back of his knee. Pooh yelled out as he fell to the ground.

"What the fuck is going on?" Pooh asked, looking around wide-eyed.

"Shut the fuck up!" barked Chi-Chi. "You know what this is about, you rat fuck."

"Primo, what you talkin' 'bout? What rat shit?"

"Don't lie, Pooh. Be a man about it. You betrayed the crew."

"Fuck you!" shouted Pooh. "You don't know what the fuck you talking about. You don't understand."

"Well, make me understand," said Chi-Chi pulling his 9. "Come on, Pooh, what up?"

"They made me. Them mafuckas made me do it."

"Lying-ass nigga," said Chi-Chi, slapping Pooh. "You a liar and a rat. You gotta go, Pooh."

"Man, we family. How you gonna—" Pooh never got a chance to finish his plea. Chi-Chi put a bullet in his head and took him out of his misery.

He looked over his handiwork and let the tears flow freely, but he was denied the chance to mourn his cousin. Two unmarked units screeched to a halt right where Chi-Chi and Hector were standing. The officers jumped out and commanded Chi-Chi to drop his weapon. It never occurred to Chi-Chi that his rat bastard of a cousin might be under surveillance. No time to worry about it now.

Chi-Chi pulled his twin 9s and squeezed.

Gloria walked past the kitchen and smiled at her father. He returned the smile, but inside he felt nothing but disgust. The poor, stupid girl thought the fact that she was K-Dawg's whore was a secret. Vega had intended on intervening in the situation, but he decided to let her hang herself. She'd learn on her own what it was like to deal with trash—black trash at that.

Vega looked over the latest news clippings on K-Dawg's arrest and shook his head. The kid had balls the size of boulders, but he was a hothead and his temper had finally jammed his ass. Vega had warned him time and again, but K-Dawg wouldn't listen.

For some time, Vega harbored a certain degree of animosity toward the upstart. He had made it possible for K-Dawg to come up, yet, where was the gratitude? He had even offered K-Dawg a spot in his organization. The way Vega ran it down to Jimmy Black, K-Dawg was getting too big for his britches. That, and the fact that he'd probably be catching football numbers, made him expendable. Vega elected the young Jimmy Black as his successor.

Jimmy Black stepped out of his brand new Lexus and flashed a gold-toothed smile. He was on his way to being a somebody in New York. In Philly, he was a small-time hustler trying to get his like everybody else. Thanks to K-Dawg, he was getting a good amount of paper. The way things were going down was kind of wrong, but a nigga had to do what he had to do to eat. Besides, it was Vega's idea to edge K-Dawg out of the picture.

Jimmy strutted across the street toward Popeye's like he didn't have a care in the world. Vega was making him the new king of Harlem, and he planned on replacing all of the resident hustlers with his Philly niggaz. He passed by a parked Lincoln and never even noticed the two men watching him from the car.

The two men looked at Jimmy, then nodded at each other. The first man slid out of the passenger's side and began to creep behind him. A blue bandanna was tied around his head and the lower half of his face. Dark sunglasses covered his eyes, making it impossible to identify him. When Jimmy got to the door of Popeye's, the masked man made his move.

"Say, cuz, you got a light?" asked the masked man.

Jimmy dug into his pocket and turned to face the man.

When he was fully turned around, he found himself staring down the barrel of a .357. When he opened his mouth to scream, the masked man pulled the trigger. The bullet went in Jimmy's mouth and came out the back of his skull. Before he hit the ground, Lou-Loc was back in the car and speeding west.

K-Dawg was up with the chickens that morning. Even though his life was coming apart, he felt like the richest man in the world. He was sad about what had happened to his sister, but she knew the consequences behind the game she was playing. The important thing, now, was to help Justin readjust and make sure that he never got caught up in the bullshit. If he could avoid it, Justin would never have to hustle or do dirt of any kind. K-Dawg was already condemned, but there was no reason to expose his nephew.

Once everyone else in the house was awake, K-Dawg intended to send the girls and Justin shopping. When he opened the *Daily News,* his heart almost stopped. There, in black and white, was the legacy of Carlo Guzman, aka Chi-Chi:

POLICE ARRIVED ON THE SCENE LAST NIGHT JUST OUTSIDE OF MORNINGSIDE PARK AND FOUND THEMSELVES WITNESSES TO A GANGLAND EXECUTION. RICHARD "POOH" GUZMAN,

TWENTY-SEVEN, REPUTED DRUG DEALER AND LIEUTENANT IN THE ROAD DAWGZ STREET GANG, WAS SHOT AND KILLED AFTER BEING SEEN LEAVING A POPULAR NIGHTCLUB ON THE WEST SIDE.

THE SHOOTER WAS IDENTIFIED AS CARLO "CHI-CHI" GUZMAN, TWENTY, THE VICTIM'S COUSIN. THE POLICE ARRIVED ON THE SCENE JUST AFTER CARLO HAD SHOT RICHARD. WHEN LAW ENFORCEMENT OFFICIALS ATTEMPTED TO APPREHEND GUZMAN, HE OPENED FIRE WITH TWO 9 MM HANDGUNS. GUZMAN KILLED THREE OFFICERS AND WOUNDED TWO MORE, BEFORE HE, HIMSELF, WAS GUNNED DOWN.

ANOTHER MAN, HECTOR BELISE, TWENTY-TWO, WAS WOUNDED IN THE SHOOTING AND IS CURRENTLY LISTED IN STABLE CONDITION. POLICE ARE CHARGING BELISE WITH CONSPIRACY AND HOLDING HIM FOR QUESTIONING ON SEVERAL UNSOLVED HOMICIDES BETWEEN 1995 AND 1999.

THIS IS JUST ONE OF MANY EXECUTIONS CONNECTED TO THE ROAD DAWGZ. THEIR LEADER, KESHAWN "K-DAWG" WILSON, TWENTY-FIVE (SHOWN IN THE PHOTO TO THE RIGHT), WAS ARRESTED LAST WEEK ON CHARGES OF MURDER AND DRUG TRAFFICKING. HIS TRIAL IS SET TO BEGIN AS EARLY AS THE END OF THIS MONTH.

K-Dawg looked at his two photos in the paper. The first one was a mug shot from 1990 and the other was from his recent arrest. The young man in the first picture wore a face that K-Dawg hardly recognized. The boy's face was young and innocent, while the older man's face was hard and cold.

K-Dawg crumbled the paper and threw it in the trash. Everything was turning to shit faster than he had expected. Chi-Chi was one of the few people whom K-Dawg had actually wanted to see make it through all of this. Now, he was just another nigga claimed by the streets. *Fuck it.* At least he took a few people down with him, and that shady mafucka, Pooh, was dead.

Now, the only problem was Hector. He had always seemed loyal enough, but would that hold up when the pressure was on him? No sense in worrying about it, though. Hector was sure to be under twenty-four-hour watch at the hospital, making him untouchable, at least for the moment.

K-Dawg lit a cigarette and scratched his chin. Things were going downhill faster than he had planned. He had to step his game up and do the damned thang. While the girls were out shopping, he had to get on his j-o-b.

CHAPTER 29

K-Dawg strolled through the projects lost in his own thoughts. He had so much to do and so little time to do it in. But that was the life of a hustler, and K-Dawg wouldn't trade it for the world. The first thing he had to do was tie up loose ends. Jackson had called him early that morning and told him the police had gotten to Flip. He wasn't sure whether they had turned him, but why chance it? The knowledge that Flip held could fuck up K-Dawg's whole plan. He had been useful over the years, but it was time to sever all ties.

Flip opened the main door to his apartment building and seemed a little surprised to see K-Dawg. He had heard that K-Dawg was locked up, but here he was, standing outside his door.

Seeing his former pupil made Flip's heart beat a hundred miles a minute. K-Dawg couldn't possibly know what was up, but Flip still felt uneasy.

"What up, baby?" said Flip hugging K-Dawg. "I heard the pigs had you."

"You know how it is," said K-Dawg flopping down on the couch. "You can't stop a stepper."

"I know that's right," said Flip sitting on the opposite sofa.

"They don't make 'em like us no more, kid."

"Fo' sho."

"So, what brings you back down this way? You thinkin' 'bout moving back to the projects?"

"Hell, nah. I just came to see what was up wit' my peoples."

"Man, we still struggling. Ain't no sunshine for us poor niggaz."

"Just look at it like this, Flip: it can't get no worse."

"You sure know how to make a nigga feel better."

"I try, daddy. Say, Flip, I heard you got knocked."

Flip almost lost control of his bowels. K-Dawg didn't seem suspicious, but Flip knew better than anyone else how good he was at hiding what was on his mind. Shit, he taught him how to do it. He had to try to keep his cool. Saying the wrong thing right now would be the end of him.

"Wasn't 'bout nothing," said Flip. "Police always wanna harass an honest nigga, know what I mean?"

"Yeah, I know what you mean. So, what they want with you?"

"Uh, nothing. Caught a nigga wit' some stones and ran me in."

"They ask you 'bout me?"

"N . . . no. I mean, they asked, but I ain't tell them shit."

"You sure?" asked K-Dawg leaning in closer.

"Man, hell nah. Them fools ain't get shit outta ol' Flip. I'm an old school gangsta. Faggot-ass police couldn't get shit outta me."

"That's good to know, Flip. Me and you been down for a long time, man. We seen the good and the bad, baby. You were even there for me when my moms died. I owe you, Flip."

The more K-Dawg talked, the worse Flip felt. They were going to lock him up for a good while. He couldn't bear the thought of not having a fix. Withdrawal was not something he looked forward to, but he felt disgusted with himself after talking to the detectives. He didn't intend to talk, but once that monkey started scratching his back, his mouth had a mind of its own.

"I got ya back, dawg," said Flip.

"That's why you my nigga, Flip. You know, it's easy to see how them pigs could rattle a nigga. With a criminal history like yours, they could try to hang you out to dry."

"Man, I'll turn on my own mama before I turn on you, kid."

"Yeah, man," said K-Dawg standing, "they start dangling numbers in front of a nigga, it's easy to consider a deal."

"Never, baby. I swear on everything I love, K-Dawg. You took care of me when I was down and out. I'll always be faithful to you."

"I'd like to believe you, Flip," said K-Dawg removing his gun, "but a crackhead ain't got no loyalty."

"Hold up, man," said Flip leaping from his chair. "You got it wrong, man. We family, kid."

"I know that, Flip. And that's why I'm here instead of Demon. I'll make it quick, player."

Flip, with terror in his eyes, stared at his friend as he screwed the silencer on his .22. He looked for an escape, but K-Dawg stood between him and the door. He had brought all this shit on himself. If he'd just managed to grow a spine, he might've lived a little longer. The drugs would've killed him sooner or later, but at least he would've had more time.

"This is the way it's going down?" asked Flip with tears in his eyes.

"Afraid so," said K-Dawg.

"I can dig it," said Flip kneeling. "Do what you gotta do, man."

"I trusted you, Flip, and you turned on me. You ain't no better than the rest."

"You might not think so, but you wrong, kid. I might just be a basehead, but I cared. I really cared."

Flip closed his eyes and muttered a prayer. K-Dawg looked at his friend and teacher and steadied his hand. If he could've done it differently, he would've let the old timer live. But it was a dirty game they were playing. Flip had violated the rules and had to pay for his sins. He paid with his life.

Detectives Hargrough and Mills walked down the hallway of St. Luke's intensive care unit. The room they were looking for wasn't hard to find. It was the only one with a uniformed officer guarding the door. The detectives nodded to the officer and walked into the room. Hector was laid up in the cast iron bed with tubes running through his nose and penis. When he saw the two officers, he frowned in disgust.

"Wow," said Mills, pulling up a chair, "you don't look happy to see us."

"What's going on, Hector?" asked Hargrough. "Looks like you done gone and got yourself shot."

"Hector," said Mills, slapping the bed, "you speak English?"

Hector shook his head no.

"Bullshit, I'll bet you understand. Anyway, I'm sure you know you're fucked. Your boy Chi-Chi took the easy way out, went and got himself killed. But you'll have no such luck. We got you on conspiracy for the police murders and we traced that li'l club of yours back to six more unsolved."

"You've been pretty damned busy, huh?" asked Hargrough.

"Don't worry about it. You'll have plenty of time on your hands while you serve out a life sentence eating Jack-Mack."

"You're fucked," said Mills smiling. "You and ya buddy K-Dawg are the last of the Mohicans, pal. We're gonna nail your bean-eating ass, amigo."

"You're up shit's creek," continued Hargrough. "There's only one way you can get outta this, Hector. We don't want you. We want K-Dawg."

"Save yourself," said Mills. "That black bastard ain't got no love for you, chubby. Help us to help you. You know what you gotta do, don't you?"

Hector weighed his options, and they didn't look good. He wasn't a punk, but it was survival of the fittest. Hector looked back and forth between the two waiting detectives. He closed his eyes so the tears wouldn't come and nodded his head yes.

K-Dawg was up and out of the house long before Nikki had arisen. He had to move quickly if he was going to pull this off without a hitch. He drove a rental car into Manhattan and parked behind the Liberty Hotel. He had rented the room the day before, so he didn't have to bother with the front desk. When he got to the room, he stretched out on the bed and waited.

After about a half hour or so, there was a knock at the door. K-Dawg grabbed his gun off the pillow and crept to the door.

He opened it a little and let out a sigh of relief. Gloria came into the room carrying a small duffel bag. She had a worried look on her face.

"Girl," he said pulling her into the room, "what the hell took you so long?"

"I'm sorry," she said, putting her bag down. "Shit is getting crazy out there. Daddy found out about Jimmy Black and went off. He's running around all paranoid and shit. He even moved out of our house and went into hiding."

"Shit, I ain't know it was like that."

"It's worse than you think, K-Dawg. He's telling people that you killed Jimmy."

"Fuck outta here. I ain't have shit to do with that," he lied.

"I believe you, K-Dawg, but Daddy doesn't. I think he even knows about us."

"Girl, you being paranoid. Frank ain't hip to us; at least, I hope not."

"I'm scared, K-Dawg. I overheard him talking to some guys this morning. I think he's gonna have you killed."

"Girl," said K-Dawg, kissing her, "don't you worry about nothing. I ain't that easy to kill, ma. Did you bring it?"

"Yeah. I got as much as I could into the trunk of the car. I waited until the last minute, so it'll probably be awhile before he notices."

"Cool. How much you get?"

"I was only able to snatch about five million. I couldn't carry any more."

K-Dawg almost squealed out loud. He had secretly been stashing most of the money that Gloria had been stealing for him over the last few years and banking it overseas. With the five Gloria had waiting for him, it brought the total to somewhere around $20 million, and that didn't include what he already had.

"You a good bitch," he said, kissing her again. "I told you if you do right by me I'd take care of you. Now, check it. I don't want you going back to Frank's. He's gonna flip when he puts two and two together. You stay in this room and don't move. I've got it paid up for at least another two days. You just lay low while I send my . . . I mean, our money, through the proper channels."

"Daddy, why can't we just go now?"

"Because I got a few loose ends to tie up. Don't you worry, though. By this time next week, you and me are gonna be on an island somewhere sipping some purple shit. Just trust me, Gloria."

"You know I do, baby. Do what you gotta do and come on back to me."

"Don't worry, girl. I'll be back to get you tomorrow night, and then well make our next move. Until then, stay put."

Gloria kissed her man one more time and watched him slide out of the room. She lay on the bed and smiled from ear to ear. People used to tell her that fairy tales didn't come true, but she knew different. All she ever wanted was a man who loved and appreciated her. Now she had him. K-Dawg was her dream come true.

K-Dawg and La sat in the truck parked across the street from the criminal court building. La had been venting about the past month's turn of events. He was working himself into a killing frenzy, and K-Dawg went right along with it.

"These mafuckas gotta pay," said La. "You a street legend, and they ain't giving you ya respect."

"I know it," said K-Dawg passing La a half-empty fifth of vodka. "Mafuckas telling and shit, kid. That ain't hardly gangsta."

"K-Dawg, I'm gonna lay my hammer game down for you, man. These mafuckas is gonna respect the Road Dawgz."

"Just be easy, La. You can't run around wilding. That ain't gonna help."

"Fuck that, yo. My gun goes off, kid."

"La, this shit is outta ya league. Let the big boys handle it."

"What? Yo, you don't think I can get down?"

"I ain't saying that, La, but these are high stakes. This shit needs to get done by professionals."

La kept running his mouth, but K-Dawg only half listened. He was busy watching Greene. The lawyer was standing outside the court building talking to a group of people. He looked as though he thought he was king shit standing out there smiling in his expensive suit. It was okay, though. K-Dawg would be the only one smiling in the next few minutes or so.

"Listen, La," said K-Dawg cutting him off, "I know you can get down, and all that, but I don't think you're ready for this kinda shit."

"K-Dawg," said La, pulling a Mac-10 from under the seat, "all you got to do is give the word. You just say it, and the cause of ya troubles is a fucking ghost."

"Okay, La," said K-Dawg faking despair. "I'm gonna give you a play, but only if you want it."

"Hell yeah. On my life, I ride for you, kid," said La, slurring a bit.

"Okay, shorty. You ready to play in the big league, fuck it. You see that dude over there?" asked K-Dawg, pointing at Greene. "That nigga is the cause of all my troubles."

"That skinny-ass cracker?"

"Yep. He made all this shit happen, kid."

"He's dead," said La opening the car door.

"Hold on," said K-Dawg grabbing La's arm. "You gotta plan this shit out."

"Fuck a plan," said La jerking away. "That cracker is gonna be an example to the rest of these mafuckas." La tucked the Mac under his jacket and got out of the car.

K-Dawg looked at La and smiled like a proud father. He had used La's ignorance to his advantage. Had the li'l nigga managed to pick up a newspaper or turn on the news once in a while, he'd know that the man he was about to kill was a made nigga. La was on a suicide mission and didn't even know it.

Greene still had his back turned when La walked up on him. He was so engulfed in the conversation that he didn't even notice the kid standing behind him. One of the individuals Greene was speaking to saw La, and her eyes nearly popped out of her head when he pulled his hammer. When Greene turned around, La pointed the gun at his face and pulled the trigger.

The bullets tore Greene's face clean off, and blood and skull splattered on everyone within spitting distance. Greene was dead by the time he hit the ground, but La kept shooting. A few court officers moved to stop La, but the Mac knocked them all off their feet.

La turned to run back to the truck, just in time to see K-Dawg pulling off without him. The lump in his throat was big enough to clog a drain. The man he had grown to love as a big brother and a mentor had turned on him. Tears streamed down La's face as he popped another clip in the Mac. By now, police cars were swarming in from everywhere. La was outmanned and outgunned, but it didn't really matter anymore. Any hope he had was lost when K-Dawg left him. La, with the Mac in one hand and his .45 in the other, took his place among the other street legends.

CHAPTER 30

K-Dawg gripped the steering wheel with one hand and dialed his cell with the other. When Nikki picked up, he began relaying instructions. Any other woman would've panicked, but Nikki was a rider. K-Dawg had been training her for this day, so she was ready. She listened carefully as her man spoke, never once questioning him. After she hung up the phone, she set out to fulfill his wishes. It was fucked up, the way he did La, but it was necessary. The weak must die in order for the strong to live.

K-Dawg made it to the highway without incident. He was halfway back to Jersey when his phone went off. "Who this?"

"You stupid li'l mafucka!" barked Jackson. "I told you to leave it alone, but ya just couldn't, could you?"

"That's neither here nor there, Jackson. What's good?"

"Nigga, what's good is I'm locked up."

"Fuck you talkin' 'bout?"

"Ya peoples, man. Not only did they turn the crackhead, but they got fat boy, too. Yo, between the two of them, the ship is sunk."

"Shit, shit, shit!" cursed K-Dawg, punching the dashboard. "Jackson, I'll have someone bail you out."

"Man, worry about that later. Somebody put the finger on you at that thing a li'l while ago. They're coming for you, kid."

"Fuck that," said K-Dawg, taking a long swig from the vodka bottle. "Let 'em come. I got a trick for everybody's ass."

"If you press this shit, you going out the back. Don't even go home, just grab ya peoples and breeze. The shit is thick right now, dawg. Don't try to go Rambo and play yaself. You got Justin and wifey to live for, now. Don't be selfish."

"I feel you, man, but I got some shit I need to handle."

"For once, can you please use ya head?"

"A'ight, old timer,"

"I came by ya crib this morning, but wifey said you was gone. I left them things with her, kid. You owe me fifteen grand: five apiece."

"Don't trip. I'll lay twenty flat on you, now, and another thirty when I get straight. That ain't including the bail."

"Always the stand-up li'l nigga, huh?"

"I'm still the same, man. Only now I play for bigger stakes. Without my strength of character, what am I?"

"Sho, ya right, big dawg. You take care of yaself."

"Shit, if not me, then who?"

K-Dawg parked two blocks away from his house and walked home. He didn't see anything out of place in the quiet, wooded neighborhood, but he was still leery. He knew the people who owned the house next to his were both at work, so he cut through their yard. K-Dawg entered his house through the garage, which was located toward the rear. Once he got inside, he locked the door and exhaled.

After a quick tour, he could see that Nikki had followed his directions well. She had removed from the house all of the things most near and dear to them, but the rest of the items remained.

She had gathered a few pieces of clothing for each of them, along with their personal articles, and left the rest behind. Nikki had done some things that really pissed

K-Dawg off, and at times even hurt him, but she was always down for him and whatever he was doing. She knew her position and played it well. During times like this, he was proud to have a woman like Nikki in his corner.

K-Dawg hurriedly stripped off his dress shirt and rushed to his hallway closet. He stomped down on one end of the floor and the whole side gave. He ripped away the remainder of the floor and was face to face with stacks of money. If there was one thing that K-Dawg learned from his experience in the game, it was saving money.

Back when they first got on, the fellas all wanted to go out and buy shit, but K-Dawg used to sit on his cash. He started out saving it in a coffee can. When the can got too small, he invested in a lock box. After that he got a safe. But having a big safe stashed in the crib could cause trouble if the police shook the place down.

Vega had hipped him to the idea of stashing money in a wall safe. In addition to having two of those, K-Dawg had little false panels built in certain areas of the house. These were the ones that Nikki didn't know about.

K-Dawg sat on the edge of his bed, and using a roll of duct tape, began to tape money to his torso. Before breaking out, Nikki had taped money to her inner thighs and stomach, and even li'l Justin had money taped to his body. K-Dawg figured that if they were going to eat off the money, they might as well pull their weight.

After taping the money, K-Dawg put on a bulletproof vest. It was lightweight, so it didn't really show under his jacket. He would have to ditch it sooner or later, but for the time being it would help to ensure that he got to his destination. K-Dawg didn't believe in taking chances.

K-Dawg stuck two 9s into the custom shoulder holsters. After checking his appearance in the mirror, he was ready to get his carry-on luggage. K-Dawg carefully pulled his black duffel bag from the bottom of his closet and placed it on the bed. He opened the bag and checked the contents. He had four small blocks of C-4 and one hand grenade. He didn't want to go there, but if forced, he was going out with a bang. After placing the triggering devices into the clay, he was ready to go. Just as K-Dawg was heading down the stairs, he heard the beginning of the end. There was loud banging on the door. "Open up! Jersey PD!" This was the last thing K-Dawg needed.

K-Dawg pulled one of the 9s and rushed out the back door. He was halfway across the yard when all hell broke loose. One of the officers spotted him and was charging his way. K-Dawg sucked his teeth in frustration as he raised the pistol. The officer tried to slow up, but his momentum carried him, face first, into a hollow-point bullet. K-Dawg didn't even wait for the body to drop. He just hopped the fence and took off running.

The heavy bag and years of smoking had K-Dawg winded by the time he was halfway to his car. Just as he stepped off the curb, a patrol car clipped his leg. It didn't really do any damage, but it slowed him enough for one of the officers to jump out and grab him.

The cop was a fat white dude, and the chokehold that he put K-Dawg in would rival any pro wrestler's grip. Even though he outweighed K-Dawg by a good many pounds, the youthful hustler was more skilled. K-Dawg grabbed the cop by the top of the head and let his body go limp. The weight caused the cop to fall and bang his chin against K-Dawg's head. That allowed K-Dawg time enough to spin around on one knee and level the gun at the cop's face. The last two things Officer Thomas Seaver saw in his life were a hollow-point bullet and muzzled flashes.

"This son of a bitch has gone too far!" growled Mills. "Cap, we gotta put this dog down."

"I agree with Mills on this one, Cap," said Hargrough. "This kid ordered the assassination of the fucking assistant DA. I mean, I ain't got a whole lot of warm feelings toward the bloodsuckers, but we work for the same boss. Greene was a city official, for chrissakes. If he can convince a little shit to pop a bigwig in broad daylight, what's to stop him from doing it to you, Cap? He's getting too big."

Captain Andrew McCall, or Cap, as they called him, rolled his cigar around between his yellowish teeth. He was a pale-skinned man with thinning gray hair and a gut that hung over his belt. Everyone knew that he was just a yes man and a kiss ass like everybody else, but he played the part of enforcer in his little section of the Apple.

"I agree wit' youse guys," said Cap in a heavy Brooklyn accent. "This J-Dawg, A-Dawg, whatever the fuck his name is, has overstepped his boundaries. I should've listened when youse two jerk-offs told me about him."

"Hey," said Mills, "I didn't wanna be the one to rub it in your face."

"Don't get fucking cute, Mills. I tell you what: I'll bust your ass down to meter maid. You'll be sucking lead dick and swallowing carbon dioxide on the fucking FDR."

"Sorry, sir."

"Now, listen, youse guys. Bring me this shit bird on his knees. I wanna piss in his fucking face when they fry his ass. Toss my name around to get whatever you need. I don't give a fuck if ya gotta call in tanks. You bring that black son of a bitch to me."

Hargrough and Mills looked at each other in anticipation. If they had anything to do with it, K-Dawg was coming back in a box.

This was going to be the sweetest bust in both of their careers.

They would probably get promotions for this. If the high school bullies or girls who never wanted to give them the time of day could see them now, they'd wish they hadn't been so cruel.

K-Dawg let off two more shots at the patrol car and kept it moving. By the time he reached his car, he heard more sirens in the area. They were sure to be hot on his ass, but he had a trick for them. He sped to the highway like a man possessed. There were a few patrol cars on his ass, but he kept them a good ways back with his erratic lane changes.

K-Dawg raced off the highway at 125th Street. He drove the car up Broadway and hopped out across the street from the projects. The NYPD had joined in the chase and were just approaching 125th. They saw K-Dawg sprint across the street and under the train, but he didn't care. In fact, when he reached 3150, he slowed up to make sure that they were still with him. K-Dawg ran in the front of the project building and came out the back. Once in the open, he hopped the short fence and disappeared into the parking lot.

It didn't take K-Dawg long to find his alternate ride. He had about two or three of them planted near various highway exits. This one was an '85 Buick. The car was very average looking. It was two-toned, tan and brown, with factory rims and a light tint. This was done so as not to draw any attention to himself. How often did the police stop hoopties?

K-Dawg pulled the car out of the parking lot, making sure to signal when he advanced toward the street. He spared a brief glance in the rearview mirror and saw the police officers scratching their heads dumbfounded. As he made a left to merge with the southbound traffic, a nosy citizen pointed him out. *Yet again, done in by a snitch.*

K-Dawg floored the accelerator and the car shot forward. Even he was a little surprised by the Buick's horsepower. What the vehicle lacked in looks, it made up for in performance. K-Dawg had the Buick fitted with a BMW engine. He knew the car could get up, but this was an added bonus. K-Dawg led the gang in blue on a video game–like chase throughout the streets of New York.

When he got to Seventy-second Street, he headed for the West Side with screaming sirens blazing in his ears. When he had gotten within a mile or so of his desired exit, he did the unexpected. He jammed both feet on the brakes, causing his car to fishtail. The pursuing officers came to sudden halts and swerved to avoid an accident. The road was a mess of cars, all trying to keep from colliding. K-Dawg used the chaos to his advantage and mashed the gas pedal. By the time the cops were able to continue the pursuit, he had ditched the vehicle and dipped out of sight.

K-Dawg hopped out of the still-moving car on Thirty-fourth Street and Ninth Avenue. He sprinted the rest of the way on foot.

The helicopters had joined the chase and the sirens were getting closer, but so was K-Dawg. As he rounded the corner of Thirty-seventh Street, he saw the Dawg House's awning. He was almost there. Just as K-Dawg stepped out into traffic, a Chevy smacked into him, sending his limp body skidding across the pavement.

K-Dawg had been hit by a car twice in the same day. As he tried to stand, pain shot through his body. He was pretty sure that nothing was broken, but he was hurt to high hell. As the pain eased, he realized that his sight was impaired. When his vision cleared, he wished it hadn't. Mills stood ten feet away from him with his gun drawn.

Nikki sat in her hiding place watching the whole thing on her portable television. Justin was in her lap taking a nap. She was glad that he was asleep, because she had been crying nonstop since the news broadcast had aired. It said that K-Dawg had killed two police officers and caused a traffic accident that injured eight people. If the police caught him, they were sure to kill him.

"Come on, baby," she prayed. "Come on home to us."

CHAPTER 31

"Got your black ass now." Mills snickered. "Thought you were gonna get away, huh? Not in this story, kid."

"Fuck you," spat K-Dawg. "Take me to jail, I don't give a fuck. I'm too tired to run anymore."

"Oh, no," said Mills stepping forward, "you ain't going to jail, boss. You're going to the morgue, nigger. Bringing your stinking ass back in a meat wagon is sure to make me a lieutenant."

"Not today," said a familiar voice.

Mills and K-Dawg both turned their heads in surprise.

China hopped out of a Suzuki Jeep toting a Tech-9. She looked funny holding the machine gun in her tiny hands, but there was nothing funny about the look in her eyes. China didn't come to play.

She came to win.

Jus sat in the day room glued to the television. He had heard that K-Dawg was in the streets wilding, but now he was seeing it firsthand. All hell was breaking loose and his ass was locked up. All of the inmates were rooting for K-Dawg. By him stepping his game up like that, he would forever be a part of ghetto history.

Jus sat on the edge of the plastic chair biting his nails. "Come on, my nigga. You in the final stretch. Bring it on home, dawg."

***

"Are you fucking crazy?" asked Mills. "This place is about to be surrounded by police. That whirlybird up there is videotaping this whole thing. Sweetheart, why throw your life away on this piece of shit?"

"'Cause he's my family." China squeezed the trigger and the Tech rattled off. Mills took it in the chest and slumped against his car. China stood there in shock looking at the bloody mess. She hadn't intended on killing anyone, but seeing her brother at another man's mercy set her off.

"Come on," said K-Dawg taking the Tech. "I didn't want you in this, but ya head is like a fucking rock. Let's get inside."

The club was practically dead, but the few people there all ran for cover. K-Dawg nodded at the bartender, who hightailed it out the back way. He didn't expect for anyone to be in the club this early, but shit could never be that simple. He would pray for them later, but at that moment, they were all faceless corpses. K-Dawg slid the bolt in place over the front door and pulled China toward the stairs that led to the office.

The large window in the office allowed a clear view of the street below. The sidewalks and rooftops were swarming with police. K-Dawg pulled the single file cabinet against the window. It didn't block it completely, but it'd have to do. Now he had to figure out what he was going to do with China.

"China," he began, "what the hell are you doing down here?"

"I . . . I was thinking about, you know, all this. And I wanted to try to talk you out of it. I couldn't get you to stay still at the house, and you don't like talking on the phone."

"Well, you're waist deep in the shit, now, girl. China, you know I didn't want this for you."

"Keshawn, we all we got left. If you face a challenge, then I face it with you. Anyway, it's too late to worry about it now, right?"

"Good point, sis."

"Okay, Keshawn. Now what?"

Detective Hargrough pulled the sheet over his partner's face and allowed the meat wagon to haul him away. He vowed that K-Dawg would pay for this one. If it was the last thing he did, he was going to avenge his partner.

"How we looking?" Hargrough asked a younger officer wearing body armor.

"Well," said the officer, "we've confirmed the fact that there are people inside. How many, we're still unsure."

"Options?"

"We would try to snipe him from the window, but the file cabinet's obstructing the view. We can't tell if they're alone or if there's someone else in there with 'em."

"Any way else to get in there?"

"Small window 'round back. I could probably get in through there."

"I don't think it's wise for you to go in there alone."

"I should be fine, sir. I'll go in through the back window and work on getting the front door open."

"Okay. I don't like it, but we gotta get those people outta there. Take a few men back there with you. They can cover the window."

The officer nodded and ran off to handle his end.

Hargrough glared up at the office window. "Soon enough," he mumbled. "Soon enough."

The young officer managed to snake his way through the bathroom window undetected. He readied his AR-15 and eased out of the bathroom. People were lying on the dance floor with their hands on their heads. He motioned for them to be quiet as he crept forward. He was almost at the front door when he had a thought: What if he turned out to be the one responsible for saving these people and bringing K-Dawg to justice? The sky would be the limit for him.

The officer turned around and walked in the opposite direction toward the stairs leading to the office. His heart was beating hard in his chest as he slid down the narrow hallway. He expected someone to jump out at him at any moment. The office door was open, giving him a clear view. The siblings stood with their backs to him as he leveled his gun from the doorway. Just as he began to apply pressure to the trigger, something cold took hold of his throat. The officer reached to grab it, but it was useless. With a well-placed jerk, his head slid off of his neck.

At the sound of the head hitting the floor, K-Dawg spun around with his gun drawn. He was ready to set his gun game out, but he was shocked when he saw one of his own. Demon stood in the doorway holding a thin wire cord. Blood coated the front of his leather jacket as well as his gloves. K-Dawg wasn't sure where he came from, but he was happy as hell to see him.

"Demon?" said K-Dawg.

"No, the fucking Easter Bunny. It seems like I'm always keeping someone from killing you. Maybe I should've been your bodyguard."

"What you doing here?"

"Following ya silly-ass sister. I missed her right before she came in here."

"Fuck! Now, we all stuck."

"Another fine mess, crack lord."

"Whatever, Demon. I told all of y'all to stay the fuck away from here."

"Like I said, I was following your sister."

"Look," said China, moving to the center of the room, "we ain't got time for this shit. We gotta figure out how we're gonna—"

It all seemed to happen in slow motion. China was standing there being her usual bossy self, and then came the dot. K-Dawg's vision didn't register the red mark at first. By the time he realized what it was, it was too late to warn her. The police sniper placed a bullet through China's heart and laid her down.

"China?" said K-Dawg rushing to her side. "China. China!"

China lay still in a puddle of her own blood. Tears rolled down K-Dawg's face and sprinkled her cheeks. The red spot on her blouse quickly swelled as she bled. China shook once and died in her baby brother's arms. Demon knelt down to touch China's cheek as K-Dawg sobbed. A roar erupted from Demon's chest that sounded more like it came from an animal than a man. Demon leaped to his feet and snatched up the dead officer's head. With one kick, he sent the file cabinet sailing out of the window. While the police were preoccupied dodging the cabinet, Demon tossed them the head of their fallen comrade. The head bounced off a patrol car and rolled until it came to a stop in the street. The police stood around in shock, but Demon was hardly finished. He picked up the AR-15 and sprayed the crowd. Some of the officers were lucky enough to get out of the way, but a good number of them fell under the hail of bullets. The officers recovered quickly and returned fire in unison. The bullets shook Demon from side to side, but somehow he managed to stay on his feet. With his last bit of strength, Demon pulled his blade from its hidden compartment. He looked at K-Dawg and smiled, right before he dove into the crowd of police.

***

Gloria sat crying as she watched the news. She couldn't believe what she was seeing. All that she had gone through to make the relationship work, and K-Dawg was fucking it up. She couldn't marry a dead man.

Before Gloria knew what was happening, the hotel room door caved in, and Frank Vega stepped in flanked by two of his goons. Gloria's heart almost stopped, seeing her father after what she'd done.

"Hello, Gloria," he sang. "I think you need a refresher course in what happens to those who cross me. Daughter or not, you'll learn like everyone else. Gentlemen . . ." The two goons stepped around Frank and made their way over to her. One held a straight razor while the other was pulling out his penis. Gloria kept dreaming that K-Dawg was going to bust in and save her. When the cold steel bit into her cheek, she learned that it wasn't going to happen.

The body crashed to the ground, making a loud noise. Hargrough jumped back as blood squirted on his face and on his off-the-rack suit. He wiped his face as best he could and signaled the troops. "We're going in!" On Hargrough's signal, the officers rushed the door. The battering ram knocked the steel door off the hinges, and the police swarmed the club. Hargrough, who was leading the entourage, charged up the stairs with the force of a bull. He and six other officers surrounded the office door. His moment of victory was at hand, and he intended to enjoy every minute of it. Hargrough kicked in the office door and was greeted by a thunderous explosion. As the fire engulfed him, he had one reassuring thought: at least K-Dawg would be checking into hell with him.

The explosion caused a real mess. The club was ruined, and the body count was rising by the hour. The captain had assembled crews to search for K-Dawg's body, and it was like looking for a needle in a haystack. Some of the bodies were burned beyond recognition, but there was no way that anyone could've survived that blast—not even a snake like K-Dawg.

A YEAR AND A DAY LATER

Jus walked outside and was greeted by the morning sun. Since he had gotten out of jail, he was doing okay for himself. He was one of the few people able to retire from the game and still be in fairly good shape. He had managed to keep his home, he and Sleepy had shared the expenses to restore the Dawg House, and he was still sitting on paper. K-Dawg wasn't the only one who knew how to save. Just thinking about his old friend made him misty eyed.

Niggaz like K-Dawg only came along once in a lifetime.

Jus pulled the mail from his box and began to thumb through it. There were mostly bills in the pile, which he seemed to be getting a lot of lately. At the bottom of the pile was another one of those colorful postcards. Every so often, Jus would get them in the mail. They didn't have a return address, and they were always postmarked from different parts of the world. All they said was, "Having a ball. Wish you were here."

Jus smiled and put the postcard in his pocket. K-Dawg was always the type of nigga to have a plan within a plan. One day he'd have to ask him what really went down in that office. But that could wait until they met again . . . in the next lifetime.

***

The couple stood with their young child looking at the beautiful waters of St. Croix. The setting sun against the shoreline made it look like an ocean of gold. The little boy swayed back and forth, digging his feet into the sand, as he held a white lily. He wiped a tear from his chubby little cheek and tossed his flower into the ocean. The adults followed suit.

There was a feeling of sadness among the trio, but it would soon pass. On the following day, they would be sailing off to another tropical shore. The threesome said their final good-byes to the exotic sands and the spirits of their loved ones. The couple strolled along holding hands, while the boy ran ahead playing with his dog.

"Come on, Isis," he said, kicking sand everywhere. The dog still limped a little, but in time she would be as good as new. Her master would see to that. The vets had said she'd probably always limp, but he wasn't trying to hear that. He was the boss dawg, and his will was greater than fate.